Hope ... "book"! ...
Bob Oliver.
2nd July 2024.

JACK

A Novel By

Robert Dickson-Oliver

Whiteley Publishing

Published by Whiteley Publishing Ltd
First soft cover edition 2013

ISBN 978-1-908586-39-1
Robert Dickson-Oliver has asserted his right under the Copyright,
Designs and Patents Act 1988, to be identified as the author of this work.

For my children, Bonnie-Joy, Bradley, Ross, Brandon and Nathan for their inspiration.
For Brandon in particular who gave his valuable comments.
For my wife Daryl for absolutely everything!

Dedicated to the memory of my mother, Gladys (1929-2012)

Mondays, all things considered, always used to be a good day. But there again, any time spent away from home came under the general heading of "good". His grandmother ("don't call me "grandma", it makes me sound old"), Victorian to the point of being dysfunctional, was light relief from the arguments at home. Of course egg and chips for tea, being able to watch the telly in peace and his weekly couple of pounds pocket money added to the experience considerably.

For all these reasons, and more, William used to like going to see his grandparents... but that was then, not now, not even with the egg and chips. His mother had only dragged him along because she couldn't trust him to be on his own in the house... at least that's what she'd said. But someone must have told her to say that.

The strange thing was that they actually looked like his grandparents, sounded like them, and even did the same things his grandparents had done. But these people were impostors. Jack had told him that and Jack was always right.

The house was the right house, mid terraced with its cream gloss paint and boring but comforting flowery wallpaper with grey/green leafy things and it's even more boring dull red, highly polished lino on the floor. Everything was in the right place, even in the larder.

He knew... he'd checked the cheese.

Whenever something had been wrong with his grandparents, it had always been the cheese that suffered and acted as a sign that all was not well. Like when Auntie Alice had died. Or the year they both got Asian flu. The cheese was the sign that something was not right. Put simply, it had little to do with the cheese itself, but rather more to do with the way it had been stored. When days were as they should be, the cheese resided on the first shelf in the larder in an old green and white cheese dish with its cracked glazing and its wedge shaped lid. When times were more upsetting, such niceties as a cheese dish were thrown to the four winds and the cheese was left to fend for itself in its greaseproof paper and dumped in the fridge. To be fair, even knowing what he now did about his grandparents, someone's attention to detail had been impressive to say the least.

Everything appeared to be done correctly as well, even as far as the ritual with the tray was concerned. "The tray" as it was unsurprisingly called, was one of those things that is barely noticed until it isn't there and, to make it more confusing, nobody else appeared to have the tray ritual in their house. Not even in William's house. But that was OK. This was Nan's house where things were comfortable and safe… even the way the tray was set for "tea". The green tray, handmade by his Grandpa years earlier, was always loaded in the kitchen with a glass sugar bowl, tea pot stand (a wooden creation made of coloured diamond shaped bits of wood, held together with string), the yellow china teapot, chrome tea strainer with pot, white milk jug with yellow cups and saucers and was always put on the table before any food was eaten.

All of this had been normal.

They had cleared away the remnants of tea, tray and all, and his grandfather had done the washing up; which heralded the obligatory low whispered gossip sessions over the now cleared dinner table, now covered in its familiar "everything is back to normal" brown chenille tablecloth. Why couldn't his mother see through them? They were so obviously impostors.

Jack said it was because she had been brainwashed.

William wished he could sit under the table as he had always done when he was younger. He remembered the views of the underside with all its clever bits of wood and doweling that somehow managed to organise themselves into action every Christmas when his grandmother "pulled the table out" to accommodate all of the relatives that descended on them. William used to spend a long time under the table. He had always felt safe under the table.

William so wanted to sit under the table again. Jack wanted William to sit under the table again. But 19 years old is a little too old for such behaviours. William could hear in advance "what are you doing under the table" and "act your age" being hurled at him from the two sages now arranged around the table, preparing to dissect the latest doings of whatever whoever had done to whom, or better still, with whom, in the street. But it would have been so safe under the table.

"Going home soon." Not once, but time and time again, Jack repeated his message, bringing with it the unwelcome but familiar uneasiness.

"Why don't you go and watch television in the front room until we go?" His mother was obviously making what she thought was a helpful suggestion, but the agreement from his Nan for William to go into the hallowed front room (where the smart grey and red three piece suite lived), usually reserved for the same people who had made use of the extended dinner table at Christmas, was totally unexpected.

It was also totally unwanted.

He didn't want to watch the television. It kept sending hidden messages to all the impostors, telling them how to behave so as to prevent them being discovered. Worse still, they talked about him and even though he couldn't hear the words… he knew.

William got up and, with a cursory glance at his Grandpa now firmly ensconced in his silent vigil over the Daily Mail crossword, walked out of the room and into the hall. The remnant of the day's sunshine streamed through the frosted glass above the front door, lighting the hallway with an almost eerie yellow light. Moving into the front room, William became even more aware of Jack. No one else could hear him, no one else seemed to know he existed… but William knew.

Jack told him what to do, what to think, who he could like and, more and more lately, what people were saying about him behind his back. Jack was powerful and knew things. That's why William listened. William's thoughts got muddled. Jack wasn't muddled. Jack was always clear.

When Jack first started talking to him, William had found it disturbing. He knew there was no-one there in the room with him. He could remember, in the early days, lying in his bed sweating with the pure effort of trying to resist Jack's command to get out of bed to move a book 14 inches to the left of where it was. But in the end he gave in… after several hours of futile struggling… it was the only way… Jack would simply not be ignored.

Jack had become more and more persistent as time went by and William became less and less able to resist listening to him, even when other people were trying to talk to him. Mr Robson, his English teacher had given him four detentions for not paying attention in class… Jack didn't like Mr Robson.

William switched on the living room light, even though there was no need to, but made no move to walk across the room to switch on the television, instead choosing to stand by the half open door to listen to the conversation from the next room. He had to find out what they were saying to his mother.

Whispered voices from the next room reached his ears with snippets of conversation that he didn't want to hear, but he just had to listen… "said it was a difficult age"… "couldn't find anything he could put his finger on"… "did the school say anything?"… "bloody doctors… can't they see the boy's not right"… "walks around in a dream"… "always muttering to himself"… "George! Can't you have a word with the boy and tell him to pull himself together"… "if you ask me, he's on one of them funny drugs they're smoking these days".

"You mustn't trust anyone, William. They're all trying to get you, you must understand, William." Jack was becoming more insistent. They were all in on it.

The conversation next door shifted to more mundane matters. William sat down in one of the precious armchairs and almost immediately found himself rocking back and forth. If his mother had been in the room, she would have yelled at him to stop. But she wasn't and he didn't. His mind, even minus Jack, couldn't cope with thinking very well. Nevertheless he tried thinking his suspicions through, tried to rationalise them. But all he was aware of was feelings and bad ones at that. As for his thoughts, well, they were away in the next field somewhere… he could begin a thought, but then it left him to be replaced by a stream of other thoughts, none of which led anywhere.

Everyone was against him… that much he knew and that didn't need thinking about.

William had long since given up trying to concentrate. Thoughts kept coming into his mind that wouldn't form properly and as he tried to chase them, they were replaced by other elusive thoughts and more specifically, bits of thoughts, all at once. It was much easier to listen to Jack, not that he had any choice in the matter.

20:12 hrs

The talking from the next room changed in pitch, becoming more coherent, as if they didn't mind him listening to this bit… so he didn't bother. Within seconds, the sound of chairs being pushed backwards and the increase in noise generally brought with it the instinctual thought that

8

they were about to leave. The last minute bits of conversation, mixed with farewells, continued into the hall and up to the front door, eventually culminating in the almost painfully slow door opening as yet more bits of news were remembered. Promises about phone calls and next visits... William was by now in the front garden, pacing... "if you need anything, let me know" the message being imparted by his grandmother to his mother, but the knowing glare was definitely towards him.

20:27 hrs

It was getting dark as they left his grandparent's mid terraced house. They walked the three or four hundred yards to the end of the road, turned and waved, although by this time his grandmother was heavily involved in the next round of conversations at her front gate with Mrs Holmes from No 23, who happened to be passing.

The results of the family conflab soon became apparent as they turned into Khartoum Road.

"Really don't know what to do next with you,"... "you're not right, haven't been for a long time,"... "you used to work so hard at school." His mother chuntered on and on.

A lot of it just didn't sink in, but it all confirmed Jack's assertions about everyone being against him.

"I'm hungry." William said as his sole contribution to the conversation.

Jack was there and Jack didn't like going home. William was becoming more jittery as Jack was becoming more insistent, his head whirling with the competition between Jack and his mother for his attention, and the feelings of fear welling up inside him.

"You mustn't trust people, you know that."

"You spend half your life staring into space and acting like a complete bloody loony."

"Just hope you get home before they find you."

"Your Dad and I have always been there for you, but look at you now, fine example to your little sister!"

"Even the people in those cars are looking for you, slowing down so they can tell the others where you are, don't you see them?"

"Any other 18 year old would be going out with their mates, but not you."

"Got to get back to your bedroom, you'll be safe there."

20:52 hrs

They reached the bus stop as daylight finally gave up its struggle to hang around any longer. William's mother lit a cigarette and for a few moments, she was silent. He hated standing still near a main road, feeling so vulnerable, particularly under the glare of the yellow street light which was only a matter of feet away from the bus stop itself.

Panic was beginning to take a grip and the shaking started. He began to pace, half answering Jack's insistent and irresistible warnings of danger.

"For Christ's sake calm yourself down!" came the less than sympathetic prompt from his Mother.

She took hold of him and, with both her hands on his shoulders, shook him, presumably in an attempt to rid him of his insanity. But all the while William avoided her gaze and carried on muttering to what looked like thin air.

"William!" Her voice was now showing signs of fear as she continued to shake him, knowing that she was confronted with something that lay miles outside her experience but well within her worst nightmares.

William knew exactly what was happening: he knew that if he didn't get away from the bus stop, they would find him. If he tried to run, they could catch him. Over his mother's shoulder he could see the bus coming and knew the only way to escape was to get on that bus. He pushed her aside and ran into the road to make sure it did stop.

And he did just that.

22:38 hrs

The next thing that William did was probably the least offensive thing he was to do all night... he woke up and vomited large amounts of apple crumble over the surgical houseman who was trying to look into his eyes with a pen torch.

William couldn't remember what had happened.

The bus had stopped as had been William's intention. The chaos that had immediately followed his action was brought about by the fact that it wasn't supposed to stop at all. It wasn't due to pick up passengers from that particular stop and moreover, because it wasn't due to stop, it was still travelling at about 20mph when William dashed out in front of it. In short - it was the wrong bus.

The bus had been skidding to a halt as it collided with William, although he remained unscathed until his head hit the road, rendering him unconscious. The passengers, who between them suffered a variety of fractures and bruises as the bus mounted the pavement and demolished the lamp post next to bus stop, didn't appear to be as grateful for William's deliverance as they might have been.

Once the physically and mentally absorbing task of vomiting was over, William became engulfed in a directionless fear. This had the effect of making him look rapidly around to try to gather some clue as to his predicament and location, a process which wasn't being particularly helped by his memory which had been disabled by a nasty bang on the head and by fragmented thoughts and emotions that elusively refused to fully materialise into a coherent pattern.

The room contained two other people apart from him; the doctor, who was standing with his arms wide apart, looking down at his vomit covered white coat and a nurse, in a dark blue uniform, who was fussing around him.

William was lying on a trolley which was contained in a small, almost claustrophobic, green walled clinic room. Lying on his side, he could feel the cold wall that the trolley had been pushed against, on his back. He was staring at the dark and badly chipped varnished door opposite him, with its round semi-opaque window through which the outline of moving figures on the other side could be seen. Above his head was a large round operating light and next to him, a cream painted trolley with surgical instruments arranged on its stainless steel shelves.

"They've found you."

Jack's voice emerged through the mist, with a certainty and finality that gave William a surge of adrenaline and an overwhelming wish to prove him wrong. Jack repeated his message, increasing William's panic to an unbearable level.

Now, when someone needs a few sutures, or their broken leg examined, a ten foot by ten foot clinical room is probably ideally suited for the purpose. However when the same room contains a seriously paranoid 19 year old male who believes that impostors are everywhere, all intending to do something distinctly inhuman to his brain, it's most definitely not suited to purpose... and so it proved.

Without warning, William leapt from the trolley and attempted to get past the vomit soaked doctor who was making for the door, presumably to seek a change of clothes. He grabbed the doctor's hair with one hand and his arm with the other and hurled him aside, causing him to land astride the instrument trolley, sending forceps and packets of sutures flying in all directions. The nurse was obstructing Williams exit by doing little more than what had occupied her a few seconds earlier, namely fussing around the doctor, who now lay strewn over the upturned trolley. With one swipe of his right arm, he sent the poor girl hurtling into the wall, her face taking the brunt of the impact.

William had made it to the door. How many of "them" were on the other side of the door, he couldn't tell.

Of course if such a thought could have formed properly, it probably would have stopped him going any further. But William's paranoia was not of the logical, everyday sort that prevents us from opening the mail in case it's another bill, or going to the doctor in case he tells us something we don't want to hear.

William's paranoia did not follow logic.

His paranoia was now all engulfing, with fragmented thoughts now coming to him thick and fast, like glimpses of tantalising circus acts entering the ring and then leaving after only the first step had been taken on the tight rope, or whilst the first somersault was still in mid-air... and in the middle of everything...

Jack...

The Ringmaster... always announcing the acts, always saying what they were going to do... so compelling that you became accustomed to not seeing more than a couple of seconds of performance. Who needed to see the act when Jack had told you exactly what they were going to do and exactly what you were going to think of them?

"Get out!"

Was it Jack or his own panic? It didn't matter either way.

He reached the door and yanked it open with considerable force, letting go of the handle as it was in full swing, sending it crashing into the wall. He stood at the doorway, ignoring the carnage behind him. There were people sitting in rows and yet more dressed in what appeared to be nurses' uniforms and others in white coats. All were engaged in the same activity.

They were staring at William.

All of them.

All of the strangers that had been searching for him. The people in the cars that had glared at him on his way to the bus stop. They all knew him. They were all here… and now they had him.

"Get out!"

Jack's voice was now being joined by the sound of running feet, getting louder as they approached. He knew they were coming for him.

William was alone. Surrounded by people, he was alone.

Unaltered… the only one that was unaltered, but they planned to change that.

To say that he decided to run for the door twenty paces ahead would not bear any relationship to what actually happened. Such thought processes were beyond William.

But what he could do was run.

He had barely gone a couple of yards, when the sound of footsteps abruptly ceased and the door to his left was thrown open. Two brown coated porters bustled through, each out of breath and red faced. In a split second they took in the situation… the doctor and nurse in the clinical room amongst the debris… the patients scattering everywhere… and William forcing a path between the rows of rapidly vacating chairs.

Shouting. Shouting and pointing. All with a purpose that was soon apparent. He was surrounded… the two porters, catching their breath… an ambulance crew, now parted from the mugs of tea they had been drinking in reception… a couple of casualty staff… all surrounding him.

Desperately he ran, running headlong into a burly male nurse and was immediately grabbed from all sides. His captors yelled commands at each other about which bits of William to get hold of, until, struggling and cursing amongst a sea of upturned chairs and startled patients, William was wrestled to the floor.

This was it… they had him. He still struggled, but now without any hope of escape.

Slowly William became aware of two voices… one unfamiliar and obviously not in total control of the situation.

"Calm down, William!"

The voice, he could now see staring up from his position on his back, belonged to a breathless doctor who was pinning down his left shoulder.

The other voice was anything but unfamiliar.

"Don't listen to him… don't be fooled by the white coat… he's no doctor!"

Jack's voice was almost mocking.

"Nobody's going to hurt you."

The impostor doctor was talking again.

"Fight, William. Fight."

Jack's commands were becoming more urgent.

"We're only trying to help you."

This time from another impostor who was lying across William's abdomen.

"Fuck off!" Yet another voice… this time it was William's, accompanied by more struggling and a well-aimed spit at the impostor doctor.

Hands gripped him tighter, and more voices joined in, this time giving advice to his assailants as to what to do next.

"Stroppy little shit!" Came one voice.

"Give him something to calm him down" Came another

"10 mgs of Diazepam?"

"Can't… head injury."

The impostor doctor wheezed his diagnosis, obviously out of breath from the unfamiliar exertion of restraining a less than co-operative patient.

"Give him another fucking head injury!" Exclaimed the first voice and, by the nervous laughter that accompanied it, this obviously received the approval of his other captors.

The effort of struggling, combined with his fear, sent feelings of hopelessness through William and he became conscious for the first time of sensations that just made it worse. Sweat was dripping from his face, plastering his unruly mop of black hair to his forehead. His head and shoulder were hurting and he was conscious of every hand and arm pinning him to the floor.

Then the familiar voice returned in his hour of need.

"Play dead!" Jack insisted.

William looked around him. Eyes were staring at him from all directions. His captors and other assorted onlookers just glared at him.

He made an attempt to get free, knowing that he would fail. The restraining increased as did the cursing from those responsible for it.

"Play dead!" The command again. This was not a polite suggestion. It was

clearly a command.

William closed his eyes. He could hear the muttering of the remaining onlookers who had managed to avoid being ushered to a safer (and much less interesting) place by well-meaning staff.

"Play dead!"

He relaxed every muscle in his body (that he had any control over) and held his breath. It had the desired effect.

"Shit!" Came a panicked voice from someone who had been holding his head, which had now become apparently lifeless.

"Give him some air!"

22:45 hrs

Hands that been holding William down began to slacken in response to his apparent collapse, as the sound of a door being flung open and the scream of a familiar voice erupted in his senses.

His mother had been at the reception desk giving William's details, when she heard the sound of raised voices and crashing chairs coming from the waiting room. Distracted, she carried on giving details until one of the staff, in the course of clearing the area of fascinated onlookers from the waiting room to reception, had unwittingly, further ignited a mother's panic by identifying the culprit to the receptionist.

"William!!!!" Screamed his mother as she hurled herself into the collection of bodies that were engaged in dealing with the miscreant on the floor.

William's eyes involuntarily sprang open and his muscles tensed as his body prepared to fight once again.

"Mum!" The words erupted from his lips in a desperate plea and tears stung his eyes before joining the sweat that drenched his face.

Hands from unseen assailants tried to pull her from the tangle of bodies.

"Mrs Phillips!" Came a female voice that appeared to have no other function other than to call her name.

"Mrs Phillips" The nurse continued, this time with an attempted sympathetic tone to the now hysterical woman.

"Come into the office and we'll talk." The comforting voice was not entirely convincing as she helped lead the distraught woman away.

"What have you done to him?… he's only a boy for Christ's sake… he can't help it!"

15

His mother was craning her neck to look behind her in William's direction as she was led away.

"Tell 'em Mum… Tell 'em to get off me."

"You're alone, William…now they've got her as well."

Jack was back.

"Calm yourself down, son," This came through the gritted teeth of one of the brown coated porters this time, as he applied more pressure to William's leg.

Quiet… well sort of.

The chaos had died down as his mother's pleas faded away behind a closing door somewhere behind him.

William was aware of the sound of heavy breathing coming from his restrainers. He felt violated by their close proximity and their solid grip. Violated and helpless.

"Now you've gone and upset your Mum…" A female voice this time and then a whispered question aimed at her companions:

"What was his name?"

"William." Came the reply from the nurse he had thrown aside in the clinical room, now one of the onlookers.

"Hates being called anything else, according to ambulance crew that brought him in."

Armed with this new found knowledge, the voice continued.

"William… you've upset your Mum, William… you don't want to do that, do you?"

"They've got her now, William."

Jack was insistent and urgent.

"If you fight them, they'll hurt her!"

His struggling stopped. He would make it worse for his mother if he carried on making trouble.

"Good lad, William." The nurse seemed satisfied that her strategy had worked, but the hands still gripped him tightly.

"Nice and easy now," She was obviously growing in confidence, "Do you want me to get your Mum to come and sit with you when you've calmed down?"

Obviously a bribe. But he'd take it so he could get away.

William nodded as best he could, given his position. He was staring straight up to the fluorescent light on the ceiling, avoiding eye contact with his captors, knowing that if he was to catch their glare they'd be able to alter him. He felt weakened. His head was still hurting and his breathing was still heavy from the excursion of struggling. He could feel the cold wetness of his clothes from the sweat.

"Shall we get your Mum to sit with you? Do you promise not to fight any more?" Then talking to someone nearby in an almost hushed voice, "Go and get his mother when we've got him up."

"Are you sure, Sister?" A male voice this time.

"Just do it!" Came the answer in an irritated hushed voice that really wanted to be a remonstrating shriek.

"They're trying to trick you, William, you can't trust them."

Jack was once again adding the voice of authority to the debate… *"But don't let them see you panic… don't show you're scared… make 'em think you believe them."*

Voices came from everywhere.

"Good lad, William."

"We're going to stand up now."

"We're just going to help you up"

"Nothing to be scared of."

It seemed that all of his captors had found their voices at the same time. That's because they were linked, joined, their minds were one… all being commanded and all obeying.

Except Jack. He could trust Jack.

"Play along, William, don't make them suspicious."

He could trust Jack. He did trust Jack. Jack was the only thing that was clear and understandable in his life. Except the fear and suspicion. He needed, so much, for someone to make sense of everything for him… and Jack did just that.

22:57 hrs

Strong hands helped him to his feet and he looked around carefully for the first time. In every part of the waiting room people were staring at him. There were upturned chairs, with the odd person trying to pick them up and return some order to the area. William didn't need to look away now as people averted their eyes as he looked at them.

They looked scared.

He was unaltered and that's why they were scared.

"William."

A familiar voice, but shaky, trembling. Call it what you want, but it wasn't right… it wasn't normal. His Mother's voice, but not quite. He turned to look and she looked back with red rimmed, moist eyes.

She had been crying… she was still crying.

What had they done to her after they had taken her away?

"Don't say anything to her… they've altered her."

Jack was there, but this time William's emotions got the better of him.

"What have they done to you? Have they hurt you?" He pleaded as he tried to move towards her… but hands held him back. His mother looked in fear and puzzlement towards the nurse who had brought her back into the waiting room.

"Concussion," came the answer to the unasked question, "quite common. He'll be fine Mrs Phillips."

The nurse's tone of voice and manner was sympathetic, condescending and conspiratorial… all at the same time.

William's mother nodded nervously then looked back at William, her brow knitted in a contortion of concern and her bottom lip quivering.

"Hurt me? Why would they hurt me? You've had a nasty bang on the head, luv… They're only trying to help you."

She held her arm out to touch him in nervous reassurance. "You've got to let the doctor look at you."

Her voice was trembling and so, for that matter, was the rest of her.

William made no move to accept or return her touch. He just stared at her. How could she be telling him to submit to them, knowing what they were going to do to him?

"They've got to her as well."

Jack was there again. He was always there to fill the void, to help William understand the fear and yet his words made the fear even more real.

Again the panic started, but this time as he made an attempt to rush towards the exit, strong arms grabbed him.

"Into Clinic Room 4!"

The command came from the Sister and was immediately accompanied by the restraining arms acting as one to move him against his will to a room to his left. The door was pushed open and he was dragged through.

"Get him onto the trolley. Stan, get his legs."

More garbled commands between them as he was lifted off his feet.

And it was as easy as that. William was on his back, on the trolley, which had now been pulled away from the wall in order that his captors could hold him from both sides. He heard the door being kicked shut and any attempts at niceties evaporated now there was no public, parental or, incidentally, Sister's glare.

"Now calm yourself down, you little shit," Stan's contribution, in addition to holding down William's legs. General approval was echoed by the others with comments similarly aimed at giving unwelcome and threatening advice.

William heard the door open. The grips lightened slightly and the smart comments stopped. He could turn his head slightly to one side and this time could see the small but formidable dark blue uniformed Sister in the doorway.

"Now then, William, that wasn't very clever, was it?"

He could see the bus almost on him, in an unbidden flashback.

Still they held him.

A feeling, a connection, an insight. Call it what you will, the bus and the doctors and nurses were linked, although he couldn't see why, not only because he only had the briefest of flashbacks to go by, but also because he had become incapable of thinking anything through with any degree of clarity.

William let his muscles relax and there was silence in the room for what was, in reality, a couple of minutes, but to William it felt like half a lifetime.

"Have you calmed down yet?"

Sister was taking control again.

William's fragmented thoughts began to rush: his grandmother talking about him in the dining room... the people in the cars going past, staring at him... Mr Palmer his maths teacher who was the first person he knew to be altered... the bus... pain in his head... his grandfather reading the paper... the look on his Mother's face in the waiting room... the bus...

"Did you hear what I said, William?"

Still she persisted.

Dad going to work at night... people looking at him... the bus... Mrs Holmes... got to get home before it gets dark... the bus... pain in his head... waiting room... people talking behind his back...

"William!"

Pain in his head… people being altered… the bus… pain in his head…

William nodded his acknowledgement of his name.

Where was Jack? Feeling scared… the bus… pain in his head… doctors and nurses… pain in his head…

Hands began to loosen their grip.

"If we move away, will you behave yourself?" Sister was talking in more of a disinterested monotone now.

William nervously nodded again.

The pressure on his limbs began to evaporate and the restraint team edged a few feet away from the trolley.

"Now then," The victorious Sister began, "the doctor is going to come in to examine you and I don't want any nonsense this time," obviously now thinking that she could treat him like a three year old, "and when he's finished, I'll let your Mum back in to sit with you."

Her dominance seemed complete and even though he didn't know her, he hated her for it.

23:15 hrs

There were only two men left in the room with him now. One young male student nurse standing by the open door and Stan the porter, leaning with his back to the wall with his arms folded across his generously proportioned stomach.

Both were looking at him.

Neither was speaking.

Through the doorway appeared the re-coated doctor, now apparently recovered from his dose of regurgitated apple crumble and subsequent skirmish. He was short, unshaven and had his head buried in a set of medical notes as he slowly walked into the room.

He stooped just outside of William's striking distance and without looking away from the notes, declared,

"So you've had a bang on the head?"

William took this to be a question and answered as helpfully as he could. "Dunno."

"Can you remember anything about the accident?"

"What accident?" William's memory was still a blur.

"What was the last thing you remember?" The doctor persisted, pen in hand and poised to write in the notes.

William thought... and thought... and, as he was about to answer, *"Don't tell him about trying to escape... don't tell him what you know."*

Jack was insistent and at his most commanding.

Unconsciously William strained to listen to Jack, his head moving almost, but not quite, unperceptively and he appeared to stare right through the doctor as if the doctor didn't exist.

The doctor noticed.

"William... what's wrong?" The doctor was looking at him quizzically.

"Nothing... headache," William lied.

The doctor looked at William, long and hard and then repeated his question.

"What was the last thing you remember?" This time with every word over-articulated and still accompanied by the stare.

"The bus... we were waiting for the bus." William spoke as though he was trying to remember a scene from a long forgotten movie.

"And then?"

"Can't remember." William answered unhelpfully.

"Your mother said that you stepped out in front of the bus. Can you remember that?"

"No." Replied William, only half lying now, being in part possession of a memory in which he could see the bus nearly upon him.

A deep sigh...

"OK then."

The doctor put the notes down and advanced towards him.

"Will you let me examine you this time?"

Both of the watchers in the room made moves to indicate that they were ready for William this time.

"I'm just going to look into your eyes with a light... look straight up."

First one eye, then the other, with what felt like a blinding but brief beam of light.

"Can we slip some of your clothes off so I can have a look at you to make sure you're not injured?"

The doctor was being very cautious in his approach and was now being assisted by an equally cautious male nurse who was helping William into a sitting position in order to remove his shirt and vest. Then William was helped back to a lying position to have a similar operation conducted on his shoes, socks and trousers.

"OK?" The doctor asked and was rewarded with a cursory nod of the head. He prodded and poked various body parts before asking the owner's opinion.

"Any pain here?"

William shook his head.

"Here?"

Another head shake.

"Here?"

Yet another.

"Don't say much, do you?"

More as a statement than a question this time.

"No." Volunteered William

"I'm honoured!" The exaggerated exclamation, complete with raised eyebrows.

Silence… broken by the inevitable.

"So what was all that about, out there?"

The doctor's eyes momentarily shifted to the waiting area before returning to stare expectantly at William.

"Don't tell him."

Jack was back in an instant.

Hesitation that, once again, didn't go unnoticed.

"I was scared."

"What of?"

The doctor leaned forward, obviously expecting to hear something interesting, but was sadly disappointed at the reply,

"Dunno." The response, under strict instructions from Jack.

"You could have hurt a lot of people."

"They're not…" William began to blurt without thinking, but within a fraction of a second responded to a command from Jack to shut up.

"They're not… what?" Prompted the doctor, still leaning forward.

"Can't remember."

Again, the shutters came down, as he corrected himself.

"Are you taking drugs, William? Did you take some tonight, or maybe you smoked something?"

William was shaken out of his cautious defence and replied with a highly indignant and emphatic "No."

The doctor stared, gave a resigned sigh and replied with a mere "OK" before moving on to a less challenging; "Can you tell me where your head hurts?"

"All over." William answered unhelpfully.

The doctor nodded and then pronounced that William was to have an x-ray, at which point the male nurse left the room and reappeared a minute or so later with a wheelchair, clearly intended to convey William to the X-ray department. He then produced a hospital gown to wear in order to "keep yourself decent" as the male nurse put it.

William was helped into the wheelchair and, with Stan the porter pushing and with the male nurse walking by his side, he was taken down several corridors, around unexpected corners and into yet more corridors.

"They're going to get your mind, William."

Jack returned again.

"They're taking you somewhere that you won't be able to find your way back from."

William began to fidget in the chair and looked around nervously.

"Calm down. No-one's going to 'urt yer." Stan's less than comforting voice, accompanied by an even less comforting hand pressing down on his shoulder.

Onwards the wheelchair journey continued, until finally they reached their destination. William felt a little more reassured when he saw that the double door they were approaching had the words "X-Ray Dept." emblazoned on them.

Maybe they were telling the truth. Just maybe.

18th June 1974; 00:37 hrs

William's wheelchair was parked alongside a padded bench whilst it's occupant awaited the summons to have his x-ray taken. This came without much delay, a young female radiographer emerging from behind a large dark-stained polished door. The male nurse handed her a slip of paper which she read silently, looked up and then read William's name aloud.

William knew it wasn't an x-ray machine the minute he was wheeled in. He didn't need Jack to tell him that.

He began to get restless before he even reached the table. William felt a hand on each shoulder, but still he started to struggle. The machine that

23

would alter his mind loomed in front of him. And underneath it... the table, which they expected him to lie on while they worked on his brain.

"If you don't lie down, they won't be able to work on your mind." Jack confirmed and William made another attempt to get out of the wheelchair, this time attempting to dispose of the restraining hands in the process. However their owners quickly changed their position, grabbed him from either side, with an arm either side under his armpit and hands on his shoulders again.

"Is this the one you lot have been sitting on down there?"

The radiographer was keeping her distance and viewing William with extreme suspicion.

"How'd ya guess?" The sarcastic reply from the male nurse.

"Well, I'm not doing an x-ray until he calms down. You can take him back."

By the look the radiographer gave over her glasses, this was obviously not going to be a subject for debate and the wheelchair was turned around, to begin its journey to return from whence it came.

June 18th 1974; 00.15 hrs

"Where's Mrs Phillips?" Dr Moyle enquired of the first nurse to pass the now vacated clinic room. Given the sort of night it was turning out to be, the answer was predictable.

"Mrs... Who?" Came the reply from the nurse, who was clearly preoccupied with something else and rushing to somewhere or other.

The doctor inclined his head to the room behind him.

"The lad's mother!" He retorted, clearly irritated that someone didn't instantly know what he was on about.

"Oh yeah... her... she's in Sister's office with a cup of tea." Came the reply to the prompting, which by the look on the nurse's face, stirred memories of the previous half hour or so that she would rather forget.

With a grunt of acknowledgement, the doctor made his way to the office, keeping his head down to avoid the glare of patients in the waiting area who were becoming distinctly restless at their prolonged wait for treatment.

Upon entering the room, he was confronted with a nervous and clearly shaken woman in her early forties. Jean Phillips was short and slight in build, with black hair (albeit now greying), held up with cheap wire hairclips. Her dark green wool overcoat was quite blatantly too big for her, but somehow its poor fitting shape along with its worn out and tired shabbiness said as much about its wearer and her life as she could have done herself. The cup of tea had been drunk and Jean Phillips was now engaged in the task of vigorously cleaning her glasses with a handkerchief. She looked up like a startled rabbit when the doctor entered the room, which suggested to Dr Moyle that he had found the person he was looking for.

"Mrs Phillips?" The doctor enquired unnecessarily.

"Yes?"

She began to get up but responded to the doctor's gesture to abort the manoeuvre.

"I'm Dr Moyle. I've been asked to look at your son, William."

Mrs Phillips was from a generation that dressed in their Sunday best clothes when visiting a hospital and held doctors in absolute awe, almost to the point of stupidity. Her current demeanour reflected this self-imposed subservience, as she showed just the beginnings of a servile response to the white coated god standing in front of her.

"Yes… thank you, doctor." Her nervous grin and shifting eye contact further betrayed her anxiety.

"I'd like to ask you a couple of questions if I may?" Dr Moyle dived straight into the deep end.

"Can you tell me exactly what happened?"

Hesitation, then… "He was trying to get the bus to stop."

Dr Moyle made a sound, "Uhuh"

A brief silence.

"Pretty bad luck, getting run over when you're waiting at a bus stop."

Dr Moyle's point was obvious and Mrs Phillips shifted a little more uneasily in her seat.

"He… he thought the driver might not see him." She gave a nervous laugh. "You know what these bus drivers are like, the times they go sailing past, leaving you freezing and…"

She was interrupted by Dr Moyle, extending a hand to stop her talking.

"Mrs Phillips I don't want to appear rude, but that isn't quite what I've been told by other people."

"Oh… well you know what people are… "

"Mrs Phillips. Have you noticed anything unusual in William's behaviour... anything that has given you cause for concern, before tonight?"

She shook her head, almost too quickly, with a fake smile that told the world that someone had touched a nerve and a very raw one at that.

Doctor Moyle persisted, "The bus driver told the police... "

"I know... I know... they told me... and I said I didn't know what they were talking about. He's only a boy... I told them... they get up to all sorts at that age..."

Her words were almost tripping over themselves to escape her, but Dr Moyle had heard enough and recognised the verbal outpourings as coming from a woman who was at her wit's end. Again he extended his hand in a gesture to silence her.

"I know what you told the police... but I have to tell you, Mrs Phillips that I believe that you are not telling me the whole story," His words now slower and more deliberate as he leaned forward in an almost conspiratorial way, "and if you don't start telling me what's been happening," Now almost whispering, "I won't be able to help him. Do you understand what I'm saying?"

She stared back him without answering.

"Mrs Phillips?" The doctor persisted.

Tears welled up in her eyes and started to roll down her cheeks, but still she tried to smile, with the result that it ended up as a grimace.

"Mrs Phillips?"

This time he was answered with a nod.

"Good. Now I have to ask this. To your knowledge, does... " But he didn't get the chance to complete his question.

"No. Before you ask, he's not on drugs... never has been." Her answer to the unfinished question was emphatic.

"How are you so sure?"

"Because I know my own son!" She answered almost aggressively. "Can I see him now?"

"He's in x-ray. He'll be back soon. Has this sort of thing ever happened before?"

No answer.

"Mrs Phillips? Has this..."

"Yes!" She blurted out, preventing the doctor from repeating the question.

Her response was quickly followed by the last vestige of emotional restraint disappearing, her shoulder's dropping and any possible conversation being replaced by inconsolable sobbing.

The brief respite from the interrogation that followed only occurred because further conversation would have proved to be impossible whilst she was so upset, but that didn't make either of them any more comfortable. Dr Moyles waited until the sobbing began to subside before continuing his questioning. This time from a less emotive angle.

"Do you want us to contact your husband for you?" He asked, without knowing if such a person existed.

"He's on nights… no… that's not a very good idea." She sobbed.

"Surely you could do with a bit of support?" The statement was more of a probe than anything else.

"David… my husband… finds it very difficult to… to deal with William… they don't get on very well."

This revelation seemed to upset her more again.

"OK. Don't upset yourself. It's OK." The doctor was struggling. "Can we talk a bit about William's past?"

Mrs Phillips nodded her consent.

"Did the pregnancy go well, or did you have any problems?"

Pen in hand, the doctor awaited what he hoped would be a coherent response.

She blew her nose and was obviously glad to be asked about something else.

"William was born a bit early. Only by a week or so. He was gorgeous. Well… your first always is." She was smiling at the memory and had to make a conscious effort to focus on the next question.

"Do you have any other children?"

"Yes. We have a daughter, Julie. She's six."

Mrs Phillips was now beginning to compose herself.

"Has William ever been ill or in hospital before?"

"Only the usual mumps and measles. Oh… and he had his tonsils done when he was five. He was in here for it, under Mr Stevens." She was in full flow and was sat forward in her chair, watching the doctor taking notes.

"Any problems at school?"

Again, the smile in response to happier memories past. "He was always very bright. All his teachers used to say so. We were so proud when he passed his eleven plus."

"So, no problems at all in that direction?" His tone of voice indicated that he was asking rather than summing up.

"Not really… well, not until his O-levels. But that's to be expected, isn't it?" She didn't sound convinced by her own words.

"What's to be expected?" The doctor threw the question back at her.

Mrs Phillips shrugged her shoulders and directed her eyes towards the floor.

"Do you mean that William didn't do very well in his exams? Is that it?" She nodded cautiously.

"They all used to say how good he was… his teachers… he'd come home every night and get his books out… always did his homework… always had his head in a book." She gave a nervous laugh.

"So… what happened?"

"I don't know. It was if… it was like he'd withdrawn… gone away somewhere… I don't know." Her voice was again betraying her inner desperation.

"Did that happen suddenly?" Dr Moyle leaned forward in his chair and took the medical notes from his lap and put them on the floor.

"No. He began to become more moody. We didn't take much notice at first. We thought it was part of being a teenager… growing up… you know?"

The doctor nodded, encouraging her to continue.

"He became distant… spent a lot of time in his room."

"Doing his homework? You said he was always doing his homework?" The doctor searched for an explanation.

"At first," She agreed, "but then he started to get behind with his work and we were asked to go and see his teacher."

"And?"

"He, the teacher, said he was worried about William… said he wasn't paying attention in class… said they kept seeing him staring into space when he should have been paying attention." Having started hesitantly, it now all began to tumble out. "Couldn't even tell the teacher what the lesson had been about. He, the teacher, wanted to know if anything had happened at home!"

"And? Had anything happened?"

"No! Nothing!" She was emphatic.

"Had anything upset him?" The doctor was determined to find a cause, an event… anything. He really didn't like loose ends, particularly when they were as loose as this.

"What about his Dad. Had there been any arguments between them?"

"Not really. They've never had much to do with each other, to tell you the truth."

She noticed the doctor becoming more interested and feeling she may have said too much and been disloyal, she quickly added "David, my husband… he's on nights all the time… he's always left the children to me."

"I see."

The doctor nodded in what appeared to be a knowing way, but there was something about the "I see" that seemed to Jean to be more judgemental than understanding.

"So who is looking after your daughter whilst you're here?"

Almost relieved at the prospect of being able to answer a question with a legitimate and truthful answer, the words rushed out.

"She's staying with my sister for a few days, before they leave for Canada. She lives in the same street as us and Julie gets on really well with her cousin, my niece. They're the same age."

She looked at the doctor as if to gain his approval, but ended up answering an unspoken question.

"You don't understand. David loves the kids. He just doesn't have time to do much with them…"

Dr Moyle looked thoughtful, but not for long, and decided that for now, as far as the subject of "David" was concerned, he'd hit a brick wall.

"You were saying that William was having problems paying attention." He said, changing the subject.

"Yes." Mrs Phillips answered with some gratitude that the subject of her family relationships had been dropped. "He couldn't seem to concentrate on what anyone was saying to him. He seemed to stare right through you and you'd have to say it all over again and, even then, sometimes he didn't seem to be able to understand."

"How do you know he didn't understand you?"

Mrs Phillips thought briefly.

"You can't even trust him to go to the shop." She seemed somehow relieved to be able to give a concrete example and looked towards the ceiling as if was going to help her memory. "Last Friday… or was it Thursday? No, it was Friday… I asked him to go to the shop to get a loaf of bread. It took over twenty minutes of repeating myself to get him to concentrate. He went… but even then he left the money on the sideboard and I had to run after him. He didn't come back for over 2 hours… said he'd been sitting in the park when I asked him. Goes without saying that I had to go and get the bread myself in the end, because he'd come back without it."

"I see," Encouraged, although in reality all he could see at the moment was a semi-hysterical mother, a self-centred father and a teenager who, quite simply, was being a teenager. But still he persisted.

"Anything else you've noticed?"

She thought.

"Only little things like talking to himself." She volunteered, not quite believing that it had any relevance to anything at all.

Dr Moyle was feeling very tired, wanted to go to bed, and felt as though his time would be better spent in just about any other way apart from this. However his attention was grabbed by this last answer.

"Talking to himself?" He repeated the mother's statement, turning it into a question.

"Only when he thinks he's on his own." She replied, clearly thinking that it wasn't that important.

"Has he always done this?"

She thought again.

"No, not really"

"Not really?" A little impatience creeping into his voice this time. "When did you first notice this?"

Again, she looked up at the ceiling, obviously struggling to remember.

"I don't really know… quite a while ago."

"About the same time as he started having problems at school?" Dr Moyles clearly felt that he might just be onto something.

"Yes… I suppose it was… Yes it was about that time." She agreed eventually, mulling the thought over as she spoke.

"And has it got more noticeable lately?"

"Seems to be. Yes… definitely, come to think of it… even worse when he's upset." She was obviously pleased that she could offer something in response to the doctor's questions.

"And what sort of things does he say to himself?" The dog clearly thought the bone was in sight.

"I don't know, really. It's as though he's talking to someone else." Jean Phillips, knitted her eyebrows and was clearly trying to make sense to herself of what she was saying.

"What sort of things does William get upset about?" The doctor tried to find another piece to the jigsaw.

Again, the thinking pose.

"Well, take the other day. We, me and my husband, had to go out for a couple of hours and when we came back… this is silly really… William had been into the airing cupboard, taken out a load of sheets and covered up the television, the radio, the phone, the record player." Again she thought, struggling to remember.

"And there was something else… "

Dr Moyle raised his hand to prevent the inevitable minutiae that he knew would follow.

"Then what happened?"

"David, my husband… he was tired… well… he had a bit of a go at William." She was obviously feeling uncomfortable again.

"You mean an argument?" Dr Moyle offered assistance.

"Sort of… yes." This seemed like an acceptable summary to her. "David had a go at William about the sheets and when he asked him what he was up to, William started pacing up and down, saying "can't tell you, can't tell you" over and over again."

"Is that it? Did anything else happen?" still probing.

"David began shouting and said "I'm getting bloody sick of this, Billy" and that was it."

"So, William…" Moyle hesitated and corrected himself. "Billy then."

She interrupted instantly.

"You don't understand. William hates being called Billy. That's what really annoyed him and set him off."

"Why doesn't he like being called Billy?"

Dr Moyle asked the question even though he felt it was a distraction.

"We've always called him that, until a little while ago. And then he insisted that that we stopped calling him Billy and called him by his full name… and he gets really upset if we forget."

It didn't seem relevant, but there again, there might be something in it. Be that as it may, Dr Moyle left it to one side and continued.

"So what happened when your husband called him Billy?"

"He started grinding his teeth and shouting "I'm not Billy" time and time again, and then he started chucking everything in sight until David finally grabbed him and threw him into his bedroom. But we could still hear him banging and crashing for a while afterwards."

"What did David do then?"

She fell into silence and averted her gaze downwards.

"Mrs Phillips?" Dr Moyle leaded even further forward.

"We... we... had an argument."

"You and you husband?" Dr Moyle volunteered.

"Yes. He stormed out and went to the pub." She began sobbing at the memory, presumably regarding the argument rather than her husband's visit to the pub.

Moyle sat back in his chair.

"Have you seen anyone about William's behaviour?"

She raised her eyes to heaven as a gesture of contempt.

"Oh yeah. I took him to the GP... lot of bloody good that did!"

"Why? What did the GP say?"

"He said it was his exams that was doing it and told me to make sure he got enough rest and a good diet." Her tone was less than complementary.

Moyle decided not to pursue that line of enquiry any further

"Can you tell me if there has been anyone in your family with a history of mental illness?"

A look of surprise and offence came across her face, but she nevertheless gave her answer.

"I don't know, though my grandfather spent a bit of time in hospital, but I don't know why. Everyone said he was nuts... but I can't think of anyone else." Having answered the question, she then asked the inevitable one of her own.

"Are you telling me that William's mad?"

An awkward silence fell before Dr Moyle carefully replied, stating what, by now, was devastatingly obvious to him.

"No. I'm not qualified to say that, but it is a possibility that your son is suffering from a mental illness."

The doctor got up to leave, clearly relieved that the difficult bit, as far as he was concerned, was over but added before he reached the door.

"For now though, I need to keep him in hospital for observation overnight because of the bang on his head."

She didn't argue, or become agitated, because Dr Moyle had only confirmed what she knew already.

"I see… can I see him now?" Her voice appeared devoid of emotion, as if the revelation had drained every ounce of fight from her.

"Of course," he replied, relieved at her inability to argue. "I'll see if he's back from x-ray."

00.52 hrs

Mrs Phillips was escorted by one of the nurses to one of the clinical rooms where William was lying on a trolley, dressed only in the shapeless white hospital gown. Lying quiet and still, his guards now stood a few feet away in the doorway,

William looked at her as she cautiously walked over to him and sat by his side

"Don't worry Mum, I won't let them get you… be careful about what you say, because they've got listening devices hidden all around the room… and I… "

William continued, trapped in his delusional world, explaining what he thought was happening and warning her of the dangers he perceived. But she didn't hear his words as she was trapped in her own world, where William was a baby, a child going to school for the first time, a toddler in wonderment on Christmas morning with all his life and hopes ahead of him. As William rambled on, she gently took his hand in hers and lowered her face to it… and wept as she had never wept before.

June 18th 1974; 02:05 hrs

On the move again, this time with his mother beside the trolley, along cold, semi-lit and deserted corridors. Slowing down now, with instructions being issued to his mother to "take a seat while we get him settled" and swinging left… a rise in temperature as they entered a large open ward. Whispered voices and background snoring as the trolley was manoeuvred next to a bed and the metal trolley sides were lowered.

"Can you move yourself onto the bed, William?"

This time a new voice belonging to the young student nurse standing at the bottom of the trolley.

William looked sideways towards the waiting bed, with its sheets and yellow counterpane folded to one side, waiting for him to enter. Over the head of the bed and fixed to the wall was, what looked like a reading lamp but Jack knew what it really was.

"Don't look at the lamp William, it'll brainwash you... keep your eyes closed... it won't get you if you keep your eyes closed!"

More prompting from the student nurse to move onto the bed and, cautiously, with his eyes shut as tightly as he could get them, he complied.

He laid with his head on the pillow as the bedclothes were swiftly arranged over him and promptly, in an almost military fashion, tucked in.

The male nurse who had accompanied the trolley to the ward was now busy handing over his charge to the female student and, although some distance from the end of the bed and talking in whispers, William, with eyes still shut, could still catch snippets of their conversation.

"Road accident... bus... restrained... Mum's in bits... half-hourly head injury observations... couldn't x-ray... porter to stay on the ward in case..."

"William?" The female nurse was next to his bed now, but he didn't acknowledge her.

"William? Are you going to open your eyes William?" She persisted.

He shook his head and was aware of the ever present Jack, uttering his warnings about the lamp.

"Why won't you open your eyes for me, William?" She sounded kind, but he couldn't trust her.

"The lamp!" He spoke nervously. "Turn out the lamp!"

"Why do you want me to turn..." Her words were quickly cut off.

"Turn it off!" The voice was raised and agitated.

"OK... OK... I'll turn it off." There was the rustling sound of a starched apron near his head and he heard a "click" as the lamp was turned off. The light that had been invading his eyelids disappeared.

"You can open your eyes now. I've turned it off." The explanation was unnecessary as he had already begun to open them.

"I'm Student Nurse Kim Hutchins. You can call me Kim... as long as Sister's not around!"

She smiled, possibly nervously as she added this last bit. William couldn't quite tell, but if she was nervous, she wasn't one of them and Jack wasn't objecting. In fact Jack wasn't saying anything at all.

Kim was just a couple of feet away from his head and he could detect the smell of starch from her uniform and for some reason, he found it reassuring. That or perhaps it had been her willingness for him to share the informality of her first name, clearly in defiance of some higher authority.

"I've got to do some observations on you because of that bang on the head. Is that OK?

William returned her eye contact and cautiously nodded his approval.

Kim reached into her top pocket and produced a small torch. "I've just got to shine this torch in your eyes to… "

Jack was there in an instant.

"Don't let her!" But his intervention wasn't needed, as William was already shouting his own objection.

"No! You can't do that! Leave me alone! You can't force me! I want to go home…"

"OK, OK." She soothed. "Look, I'm putting the torch away… is that what you're afraid of William?"

William looked at her and the expression on her face seemed to tell him that she didn't know why he was afraid.

"I'll tell you what. I'll tell you what I need to do and you can tell me if it's OK?"

William nodded.

"Can I look into your eyes with this torch?" Kim ventured as she showed him the pocket torch.

"Use another one, not that one." Williams tone showed the embryonic beginnings of trust in the temporary absence of Jacks commands.

"I'll go and find another one." Kim's voice was sympathetic, but to William it now sounded a little condescending.

"Don't let her choose it… it'll be another one of their devices!"

Jack returned to deal with the situation.

"No!" William hesitated for a few seconds. "That one… over there."

William pointed to a large black torch on a desk in the middle of the ward.

"Use that one"

Kim looked behind her and returned a quizzical glance to William.

"You want me to use the ward torch. Are you sure?"

William nodded his accent.

"OK… you're the boss." As she walked the few yards to the desk to collect the torch Jack intervened again.

"Don't trust it… don't trust her."

Jack was emphatic but William was in conflict.

William trusted her. He didn't know why… but he trusted her and Jack didn't like it. He didn't want to go against Jack… but he trusted her and the pressure from Jack was becoming unbearable.

"Listen to me, William… listen to me… She's trying to trick you… She's in on it… she's one of them… Listen to me, William!"

"Is this one OK?" Kim seemed to be asking a genuine question.

Jack persisted and his warnings were now almost totally engulfing.

"William… don't let her get near you with a light… they'll have your brain… you know they will… Listen to me, William… you know I'm right… Don't let near you!"

But he so wanted to. He so wanted to trust her … so wanted her not to be one of them. He began to sweat with the pure effort of the conflict. He could only stare back at Kim, unable to respond in any other way.

"Can I use this torch, William?" The request came as she raised the torch to use it, switching it on as she did so.

William was wrenched out of his dilemma… thoughts came quickly, but they were all guided by paranoia, by the blind panic that Jack was so capable of orchestrating.

"Don't let her… don't let her… don't let her!"

Jack was issuing his commands.

Almost instantly, William felt the confusion and fright build inside of him… from his willingness to trust Kim just a few seconds earlier to his utter desperation as he faced the prospect of having his mind altered.

"No… get away… take it away…" he gasped as he struggled to get off the bed; to get away from what he thought was the inevitable.

"It's OK, William; I won't use it if it upsets you. It's OK. We can manage without it." Kim's voice was trembling, but somehow she was still in control as she put a restraining, but somehow re-assuring, hand on William's shoulder.

The male student nurse moved from the other side of the bed where he had been sorting out the notes from casualty and went to grab William's other shoulder.

"Told you what he's like, Kim. Watch yourself! He'll have you… "

"For Christ's sake! Shut it, Paul. Can't you see he's ill? Move away from him!" The turning to William and in a gentler tone "William? William?"

Turning once again to her colleague who had annoyed her so "Paul make yourself useful and go and get his mother!" and then back to William "William... it's OK... nobody's going to hurt you... Your Mum will be here in a second."

Looking up again across the bed "Paul! Go and get Mrs Phillips!" and then in a loud and commanding whisper "Paul... will you go and get his mother... now!"

The male student nurse, after his initial hesitation, showed no willingness to argue and moved swiftly off out of the ward.

William stopped struggling.

"It's OK." Kim kept repeating, now even managing a nervous smile. "Just try to lie flat. You've had a nasty bang on the head. You've got to try and keep still."

Slowly she moved her hand off of his shoulder and William sat up in the bed, bringing his knees up towards him, pulling the neatly arranged sheets off of his legs.

William kept looking at her and whilst at least a part of him felt calm, another part was still as paranoid as hell... and a third part was occupied by Jack.

"All these people in the beds... they're all going to be changed, every one of them... they don't know... they think they're going to get better... they..."

"Shut up, shut up, shut up, shut up, shut up!"

William was rocking backwards and forwards on the bed with his forearms pressing tightly against his ears, his knees drawn up to his chest and his face flushed with the effort of trying to ignore Jack.

"William!" the familiar voice, the worried voice, made worse by the scene that confronted her upon being brought to his bedside. Mrs Phillips laid a hand on his shoulder, but his rocking persisted, and the only words that could be heard were "Shut up, shut up, shut up" time and time again.

She tried again, this time shaking him, gently at first and then with more desperation.

"William... listen to me, William..." his mother persisted and was rewarded with a stare, but not without the rocking, and not without the now almost mechanical "Shut up, shut up, shut up!"

Kim was taking a back seat to someone who, by virtue of being her patient's mother, she perceived as being more of an expert than she was in these matters. She watched as Mrs Phillips grasped William's shoulder and moved her face closer to his.

"Tell Jack to leave me alone, please tell him Mum, tell him to leave me alone."

The words were coming thick and fast now, with barely a space left between them to fit a breath.

"Tell him to go away, Mum, please tell him... the machines are all listening to us, Mum... keep your voice down... they'll hear you... they'll find you... Jack... help me, Jack... take me home... I can't do my homework, mum, the sums... they hurt my head... be careful of the lights... if you look then they've got you... did you know that? They've got you... don't tell Nan you know..."

The words lost more meaning the longer the verbal tirade continued and fairly soon, his mother was left with little alternative but to offer a continuing succession of stroking and "shhhhhh", which to be fair to her, appeared to calm William down as much as anything could, which incidentally, wasn't very much.

"Don't let them get me... Jack says they'll get me... don't let them get me."

"Darling," Mrs Phillips now wore a nervous grin. "Who's Jack?"

William stared back, knowing that he had broken the rule... let the secret out. Told them what they shouldn't know, told them about Jack, and he tried to pre-empt what Jack had told him would be the inevitable response.

"What are you looking at?" Now up on one elbow and backing up the bed. "I'm not mad, there's nothing wrong with my mind" he persisted, to his way of muddled thinking, precisely down the line intended to convince those around about his sanity, and in the process managed to further confirm everyone's thought to the contrary.

Two doses of "it's OK," reached him from two different directions at once... one lot from his mother and the other from student nurse Kim. With the "it's ok's" came reassuring yet at the same time, disconcerting hands of comfort, not surprisingly from the same two people.

He was being humoured and he knew it. Jack was silent... Jack was annoyed with him and William was annoyed with himself, but somewhere deep down, he felt a tiny sense of relief and whether it was the sense of relief, the time of night, the bang on the head or just plain tiredness,

William, for reasons probably not even known to himself, sank back onto the bed and told all around him that he wanted to go to sleep.

Which was a pity because all around him were people, principally Kim, who were going to keep waking him up every fifteen minutes (minus the torch) to see if the head injury was having any effect... which incidentally, was the very least of his problems.

June 18th 1974; 10:25 hrs

His mother had been persuaded to go home an hour or so earlier and William had long since given up the battle to sleep. The unfamiliarity of the ward was deafening, more so than the actual noise that accompanied just about every individual at work with their own particular brand of unique noise. The vacuum cleaners, the bed pans and the trolleys all apparently fine-tuned to give the maximum amount of disturbance with their users determined to let them get away with it.

"William Phillips?" It was more of a statement than a question and came from a man in a badly fitting, ill-kempt dark grey suit who was standing at the bottom of the bed. His uncombed grey haired head was buried in what William assumed to be his notes.

"Had a bit of a bad time last night did we? My name's Dr Trafford... I'm a Psychiatrist... I'd just like to have a little chat with you."

William nodded and felt more than slightly intimidated by the raised eyebrows and the sight of the half mooned spectacles perched on the end of the doctor's nose.

"Who told you to stop the bus, William?"

Silence... just a glare in reply.

"You could have been killed," Dr Trafford continued.

The glare continued and so did the Psychiatrist.

"I think someone told you to jump in front of the bus,"

The glare stopped and William looked away.

"Can you tell me what day it is?"

Jack was there in an instant *"Don't talk to him... he wants your mind!"*

William was distracted by Jack's command and Dr Trafford's knowing expression told William that the psychiatrist had noticed and now appeared to lose his previous interest in naming days.

"Do you have trouble hearing what I'm saying to you William?" Dr

Trafford's words came slower, louder and with clearer pronunciation… William felt as though he was being spoken to like a geriatric aunt and still he only stared back.

"Aren't you going to talk to me today? I'm not going to go away you know," This time accompanied by a glare back at William over his half-moon glasses.

"I think you may be ill, William… Do you think you're ill?"

This time William instinctively shook his head and instantly regretted it. Dr Trafford had found a way in.

"Dr Moyle… you know him, he was the doctor who saw you last night," again he glared over his glasses before Dr Trafford returned his attention to the hospital notes balanced on his knee… "He thinks you can hear voices… Can you hear voices, William?"

"He knows… he knows everything… don't talk to him… he'll fry your brain just by looking at you" Jack was there and his warnings sounded more urgent than ever.

"I think you can probably hear voices now… can't you, William?" Dr Trafford had the bit between his teeth and he wasn't going to let go.

"I think you can hear voices when there isn't anyone else in the room… it must be very frightening for you… your mother's terribly worried about you, you know."

"He's trying to get inside your brain… he's evil… he's one of their leaders… he can hypnotise you with his voice!" Jack wasn't going to be denied… he certainly wasn't going to be ignored.

William quickly and instinctively covered his ears with his hands and screwed his eyes shut.

"You see… you're trying to stop the voices, aren't you?" Dr Trafford sounded condescendingly triumphant.

"Wrong by miles, you smug bastard!" Jack… or was it his own thought… the idea disappeared… in any case it was satisfying to know that Trafford didn't know everything… perhaps if he kept his head covered … the thought broke up again, he had homework; maths, equations… he could smell fish and chips somewhere… at the beach… his football was punctured… Grandpa's car smelt funny…

William's thoughts became more and more fragmented… he wanted his red jumper… cold meat and chips for tea tonight… Ena Sharples was an evil bitch… cutting the grass…

The thoughts and pictures came thick and fast, none lasted before the next one was there... then they began to overlap and merge... William turned onto his side, his hands still covering his ears, his eyes shut tight... knees drawn tightly up to his chest, his hospital gown open at the back exposing his buttocks.

And rocking... backwards and forwards... rocking... backwards and forwards.

"Don't let him in... don't let him in... don't let him in..." Jack sounded like a record with the needle stuck... *"Don't let him in... don't let him in... don't let him in..."*

Still the rocking, backwards and forwards... backwards and forwards.

"Paraldehyde... have you got any intramuscular Paraldehyde?" Trafford was addressing himself to any nurse who was passing, plus probably, a few who weren't.

William was aware of the words being spoken, but they ceased to register, didn't mean anything... but still the words continued.

"We don't keep it, Doctor," A female voice replied.

The metal frame of the bed creaked with the rocking and still the words continued.

"Well, who does keep it?" Came the now agitated Psychiatrist's voice.

William was aware of very little... that wasn't actually touching him... Jack wasn't there... or was he... William couldn't tell where he was, but there again, he wasn't thinking about it... he couldn't string any thoughts together about anything...

Apart from being afraid... being scared... knowing without reason that he was threatened... confused.

"I could ring casualty and see if they have any?" The female voice continued.

"Yes... You had better do that!" Trafford was now being impatient, sarcastic and generally irritable but still with one leg resting on the foot of the bed, as though to underline the fact that he was a consultant Psychiatrist and it was beneath him to participate in any activity that would associate him with other and lesser mortals.

"Yes, Doctor."

Trafford returned his gaze to the figure, still rocking backwards and forwards on the bed and grunted his acknowledgement of the nurse's subservience.

Curtains being pulled around William's bed… muttering from both near the bed and outside the domain of the "curtained off" area… none of it had any content but it was all against him… a tiny part of his mind still knew that.

The chink of a solid object being placed in a metal dish.

The smell of a hospital, ethyl alcohol… somehow was getting closer to the bed, fear building… awareness of people crowding around the bed.

"William…" A female voice aggain, "We are just going to give you an injection to help you to relax."

William curled up into a ball, even more than before and lashed out blindly with one arm before quickly re-covering his ear.

"William… will you let us give the injection now?" The female voice persisted.

William persisted and repeated his action with his right arm before re-covering his ear.

He felt hands lifting up his hospital gown even further and other hands on his shoulder, legs and hips.

"I'm going to give you the injection now… just a scratch and it'll be over." The female voice expressed its owner's intent… then he felt the wet cotton wool at the top of his buttock.

Then the pierce of the hypodermic needle…

Then the Paraldehyde… stinging…

Then the needle being removed and yet more wet cotton wool… hands moving away.

Jacks voice… distant. *"Don't let them"* and again… *"don't let them….you are the only one left, William… you are unique… everyone else is altered… don't let them!"*

And then… Trafford. Trafford the impostor. Trafford the alien. Trafford the mind alterer. Trafford the inquisitor. Trafford the Anti-Christ.

Williams thoughts could not focus or develop any of the "Trafford" concepts… he just knew that Trafford was bad news.

And he knew that he was completely helpless…

"Now then, William, in a few moments you will feel nicely relaxed and very drowsy and you'll probably have a nice sleep." The sound of superiority in Trafford's voice was nauseating.

"Now then, William, I want you to pay attention to what I am going to say to you,"

Trafford had moved to the side of the bed and was now looking down on the still rocking figure of William, who had now opened his eyes and stared back at his tormentor.

"I believe that you are suffering from a psychotic illness that requires treatment as an in-patient in a psychiatric unit and your mental condition renders you unable to make that decision. I am therefore admitting you as an involuntary patient to Greenbeck Hospital under Section 25 of the Mental Health Act 1969 where you will be detained for a period of thirty days while we assess your condition. Do you understand?"

William could only stare. He felt the tears stinging his eyes and he simply couldn't say anything. He'd been caught... he'd fallen into their trap

"Do you understand, William?"

As he tried to think any deeper, so his thoughts, always tinged with paranoia, became more random and muddled, but the result was that he just stared in silence at the Psychiatrist.

Trafford turned to the nurse to his left... "Sister, book an ambulance to take him to Greenbeck, Male 6 Admission Unit at about 4 o'clock... Is his mother around? I'd better tell her what's going on."

"Certainly, Dr Trafford," Came the apparently submissive reply, but then... "I presume that Dr Adams wasn't aware that you were going to inject his patient with Paraldehyde, when he asked you for a second opinion. Would you like me to get him on the phone for you?"

Trafford was not amused at the deliberate and sarcastic reminder from the falsely diminutive figure in the dark blue dress standing next to him.

"Thank you, Sister... but I'm sure I can manage to lift the receiver myself, but perhaps you could occupy your time more constructively by finding out where our second opinion doctor has got to... we need him to interview this lad and sign the Section papers."

"Certainly, Dr... whatever you say." And she turned on her heal and advanced towards William, covered him up and left the curtain enclosed space for the sanctuary of her "psychiatrist free" office.

Trafford finished writing in the medical notes, then, with a grunt and a last glance at his latest patient, threw them on the foot of the bed and left.

William was left alone; the thought of incarceration now overtaken with a thousand other mixed, unrelated and overlapping images and even Jack wasn't making sense anymore.

Which was probably just as well.

43

As sleep began to overtake him, William, just for the briefest of moments, was just a 19 year old teenager, engulfed in a world of his own that he didn't understand, a world that could and would have the label of schizophrenia given to it, but for now, it was a phenomena that was detached from him, but he simply did not have the energy to worry about it... not now. The paraldehyde was having its effects... not curing, not helping, but detaching in such a way that William and his paranoia, hallucinations and delusions were not as one, but rather bedfellows who would continue to consummate their union just as soon as the injection wore off.

June 18th 1974; 08:35 hrs

David Phillips was an objectionable and offensive man who rarely had a good word for anyone, unless of course, there was a faint prospect of them buying him a drink and a remote possibility of them paying attention to his never ending moaning. At least 3 stone overweight, he paid little attention to his physical appearance, or indeed smell. He bathed almost ceremoniously, on a Sunday, which coincidentally was the same day he changed his underwear. This and putting on a tie for his Sunday lunchtime session at the pub were probably the closest he ever got to religious observances.

The best that could be said about today was that he was about to embark on what he was happiest doing... namely being bigoted, self-righteous and odious.

Jean Phillips had returned to the family's second floor council flat and now stood by the kitchen table, still in her shoes and coat, having been confronted by her string vested husband the moment she had let herself through the front door. He had been standing on the other side of the door as she entered and began and his inquisition immediately, not even giving her the time or space to close the door behind her.

"And where the fuck have you been?"

"I've been at the hospital with William... he had an... accident last night."

She had momentarily gazed downwards as she spoke the last part of her sentence and limited in perceptual ability though her husband was, he wasn't beyond spotting a cover-up, particularly if it meant starting an argument.

"You mean he tried to smash something and someone tried to smash 'im back?" The memory of the wrecked stereo was still fresh.

"He was run over if you must know, not that you're particularly interested... not that you've ever bloody cared, you... " But she wasn't allowed to finish her sentence.

"Don't fuckin' start again, you're like a worn out fuckin' record." David Phillips' unshaven face complete with uncombed hair and nicotine stained teeth was now only inches away from his wife's face and she turned her head with a grimace to avoid his bad breath and spittle.

"You've never liked William... nothing he ever did was good enough... you cou... "

Her uncharacteristic stand of defiance was cut short as the back of her husband's hand sent her reeling towards the kitchen sink. She hung on to the edge of the sink for as long as it took to unbuckle her legs and then slowly and very defiantly she cast a cold stare over her shoulder at her assailant who stood in the middle of the kitchen, remorseless and gloating. The left side of her face stung, but her defiance was undiminished.

"That's all you know, isn't it?" She wiped a trickle of blood from the corner of her mouth with the back of her hand and absently examined it. Looking up, she prepared to speak and as she did so, the pressures of the previous night in the hospital, the years of worry and torment, the friends who wouldn't come round anymore and all due to this wanker of a husband... this piece of shit in a string vest who looked after his family nearly as often as he washed... and after years of being a doormat, she finally snapped.

"As long as it's a woman or a kid, you're the big fuckin' man!" her voice was raising in pitch with every word. She was now looking directly at him and grabbed hold of the first thing she could lay her hands on. His gaze moved towards the object she was clasping in her hand and he involuntarily took a step backward.

"What's wrong, dear... won't little wifey lay down and die for you this time?!" She was talking, almost hissing through her teeth in slow, measured words now as she moved slowly towards him with the bread knife in her hand.

As he blindly backed into the kitchen table, she lunged, screaming every obscenity that came into her head and raised her arm to strike.

In the succeeding hours, Jean was unable to pinpoint the exact moment that determined that her husband would survive her frenzied attack. Later that day, as she sat in a police cell awaiting further questioning about the incident, she tried to piece the events together.

Her screams and her husband's shouting had been heard by neighbours through the open front door, but try as she might, she could not recall anything or anyone before realising that someone had tried to get between her and her husband, with the result that her aim with the bread knife went astray resulting in a shoulder wound rather than the fatal blow she had intended.

Her real memory appeared to have started functioning again when she saw her husband slumped over the kitchen table in a pool of blood. Strong arms were holding her back, but she still managed to spit at her husband's torso, but the action was wasted as he had feinted some seconds earlier.

Doris and Sid Brownlow, her neighbours turned restrainers, had led her into the living room, whereupon Sid, looking back over his shoulder, called out to the onlookers now gathered in the front doorway to call the police and an ambulance, which someone must have done because they both arrived in what seemed like a few seconds.

She heard them, long before they entered the flat. The loud echoing voices filled the stairwell accompanied by the gaggle of neighbours convening outside her front door, all thoroughly enjoying the crisis and all wanting to give their account of the events at flat number 41. From that point, events seemed to proceed in spite of her, even though she was the instigator of all the excitement. The policeman, crouching beside her chair (presumably adopting his very best sympathetic mode) asking her for her account of what had happened, the obligatory WPC standing just behind him and the ambulance crew doing their bit in the kitchen.

"I'm afraid we'll have to take you to the station, Mrs Phillips." The WPC spoke at last, but the second part of her message had much more effect than being arrested for GBH.

"Are there any relatives who can pick up your daughter from school and look after her for tonight?"

She stared with wide eyed horror at the police officers.

"Oh my God… my children… What am I going to tell… They need me… You can't take me anywhere… not now… I've got to get dinner… go to the shops." Her speech was speeding up and she was visibly more agitated.

"William!! I can't leave William in there! He needs me to be with him... no one else understands... he's ill... he needs me to be with him!" Arms lifted her from the chair she had been sitting on.

"You've got to listen to me... " her pleads continued as she was taken, struggling, out of her front door and through the ever more fascinated crowd that had accumulated in the stairwell and as far as the three police cars parked outside the block of flats.

June 18th 1974; 16:40 hrs

William didn't remember the ambulance ride that took him to Greenbeck Hospital, he couldn't recall the words of comfort that were spoken to him by the staff on the ward as he was wheeled out to the ambulance to begin his journey to the mental hospital that would play such an important part in the rest of his life.

But he did remember being taken out of the ambulance and being confronted with an enormous red bricked edifice, the carefully mowed lawns on each side of the concrete path which led to the huge dome shaped double doors, reminiscent of a monastery or church. Either side of the door were enormous bayed windows and further than this were windows, stretching upwards for three floor and several hundred feet to the right and left of the doorway.

And flowerbeds... everywhere... flowerbeds... perfectly tended with perfect blooms... and not a weed in sight. Not normal... everywhere has weeds... everywhere on Earth that is. Where was this... someone had tried to recreate Earth, but they'd slipped up... too perfect you see... William knew, but he had to keep it to himself this time.

A man with a white tunic and dark grey trousers was waiting with a wheelchair as William was helped to leave the ambulance. One of the ambulance men steadied William by holding his elbow as he stepped out of the back of the vehicle and helped him into the wheelchair. A bag of toiletries and a change of clothes and pyjamas that his mother must have brought in to the General Hospital the night before were deposited, quite unceremoniously, on his lap.

Someone had put a brass plaque next to the entrance, which read "Greenbeck Hospital", but William knew better... this was no hospital... they were trying to trick him... it was a church... that was a church door

47

they had passed through, not a hospital door. The grey and white mosaic floor in the entrance clinched it… it was a church… he'd never seen a mosaic floor in a hospital before.

William seemed to be able to string his thoughts together better… yes… despite everything, he could see through it… see through what they were trying to do to him… this was where they brought people who resisted them… he had to be careful… he had to keep quiet about what he knew.

The huge square entrance hall that William found himself in (if that indeed was what it was) was nearly as imposing as the outside of the building. It was lined with numerous highly polished oak doors which seemed to provide exists in all directions, although to where, William couldn't tell. One huge set of half glazed double doors in particular stood out amongst the others and it was straight ahead. The glass was semi opaque and all William could see was indistinct and blurred moving shapes and the general noise of a lot of what looked like people going about their business. To his right was a formidable staircase, again, made of highly polished oak and leading to God knows where.

William's new found escort was engaged in a conversation with a grey suited middle aged man who had emerged from a door to William's left, which bore the legend "Senior Nursing Officer". Both were standing behind his wheelchair and both appeared to be concentrating on the contents of a light brown cardboard folder and all the while talking in whispers.

William was feeling increasingly nervous and his thoughts became more fragmented as they did when he was anxious, with thoughts entering and leaving his mind without even doing him the courtesy of telling him why they were there, what relevance they had to anything, or whether they would be back to explain themselves later.

The thoughts just came and came and the more they came, the less sense they made and the less sense they made, the more anxious William became and the more anxious William became, the more he began to become physically agitated, fidgeting in his wheelchair and darting his gaze from side to side.

William tried to keep focused, but the fragments of memories and the urgency of his fears wouldn't let that happen, but neither would the after effects of the paraldehyde help it

Visions of Mum at the bus stop… Dad said he'd buy a fridge… these are aliens… they want my brain… sitting on the floor watching the chimney sweep in Nan's front room... everybody's watching me... Grandpa's cutting the hedge... he was always cutting the hedge... but there was no sound of garden shears clicking... the top of that stair case is where their leaders are waiting... cold meat and chips for tea 'cause it's Monday and we've run out of pickle...

A steadying hand on his shoulder.

"Calm down son, you'll soon be on the ward." Then the mumbling to each other continued, but through the mumbling... there was Jack.

"They hide the people here that they can't convert, William"

But William didn't want to be "hidden".

He knew he was special.

He knew he had powers that others didn't have.

"Don't tell 'em anything about yourself..." Jack was there in an instant.

Hungry... the rain's making my hair wet, but no-one can feel the rain indoors except me... when I go through those doors, I'll never come out again... the 109 bus only went to Dansford, then late for school... William's thoughts became more fragmented... they've got listening devices... they can hear my thoughts.

Still the muttering behind his wheelchair, but now it began to move towards the double doors ahead.

"They're still trying to get to your brain!" Jack was insisting again.

The wheelchair was turned round unexpectedly to enable his escort to back through the double doors and as he did so, William glimpsed what appeared to him to be his last view of the outside world and as he saw the entrance hall, with people coming and going through the large entrance doors that he had been wheeled through only minutes earlier, he felt his knees drawing up to his chest and his head bent forward to meet them. As he did so, he felt the comforting involuntary rocking taking over.

William clutched, with increasing desperation, at his belongings, still in his lap and now seeming like his only link with his old, familiar life. He felt the pressure of a hundred thoughts competing for the attention of his conscious brain, with none of them able to put in more than just a fleeting, confusing appearance.

His feelings of desperation increased as he gazed at the almost street sized corridor in which he found himself. The walls comprised of ceramic tiles, like those found in old Victorian public toilets. The lower half of the walls comprised of brown tiles, with the upper half in white. The fluorescent strip lighting above his head betrayed the intervention of the twentieth century, but there was little else that spoke of anything modern.

There was even less to reassure him that he was going to be safe as his journey down the enormous corridor continued... Still huddled and rocking in the wheelchair, William stole cursory peeks from behind his drawn up knees at the unfamiliar and transient surroundings of the corridor.

There were people walking towards unseen destinations, some acknowledging each other, whilst still more progressed on their ways with apparently little interest in those around them. Women with papers and folders clasped tightly to their chests and yet more without such appendages but nevertheless with determined strides and downward glares, obviously betraying them as being in deep and as William perceived it, conspiratorial thought. Still more women appeared to be dressed as nurses, in a variety of colours, with most in a light blue colour dress with starched white aprons. A few had darker blue dresses and these women looked older than the rest and William assumed that they were in charge of something.

He noticed the men in particular.

They all wore the same non- descript grey trousers and some had quite shapeless jackets to match, although still more wore white tunics which extended to just below the waist and fastened by three or four buttons on the right shoulder, giving the wearers the appearance of being somewhat unkempt dentists. Like ants in a nest they appeared to be undistinguishable from each other and like the ants, they all appeared to have a purpose, although to the onlooker, the directions they were moving in looked chaotic as they suddenly left the cavernous walkway and disappeared through countless doors lining the corridor walls.

Still. William's escort propelled his charge forward.

"They're trying to make you believe it's a hospital, William," Jack was there. "All they want to do is to get inside your head and make you like all the others."

The surroundings added weight to Jack's words, not that Jack's words needed any help.

"This is where they bring people they haven't managed to convert with their machines, did you know that William?"

Footsteps... everywhere the echo of footsteps... and Jacks narrative that seemed in some way to confirm and heighten his own fears and suspicions.

"They've already got to your Mum, William. Where is she? They made sure

she wouldn't be here. Why isn't she here William? What have they got to hide?"

"I don't know... I don't know... I don't know!" Escaped Williams lips in a mumble as tears started to stream down his cheeks. His escort either didn't hear him or didn't care, but in any case, his journey continued.

"They all know why you're here." Jack was being persistent in his description of William's circumstances and predicament, but his words were unnecessary as William had already become aware of the knowing glances of the previously pre-occupied corridor population.

He began to shuffle his bottom in the wheelchair in readiness to make a run for it, but before he could do anything, his escort propelled the wheelchair to the left, paused for an instant before a large brown painted door, over which was a large glass panel which bore the legend "Tamworth Ward" in large and doubtlessly once clean white letters. He felt his wheelchair being turned a hundred and eighty degrees, giving William his last glimpse of the corridor and almost at the same time as he heard his escort unlock the door behind him, he felt himself being backed through it and into his worst nightmare.

June 18th 1974; 17:20hrs

As his wheelchair was turned around and the brakes were locked, William knew, even before Jack said anything, what the place really was. He was now in a place where they would try to take control of him and as he looked around, he could see little that would change his mind. Sat in his wheelchair whilst his escort entered a small office to his right. William took in his surroundings in a few brief seconds.

He found himself in a large room which had three huge arched bay windows lining the wall to his left side. The room must have been about one hundred and twenty feet long and around fifty feet wide. He could see thick wire mesh covering every window and the ageing, yellowing white gloss paint added to the depressing effect. The dirty green painted walls, heavily stained with tar and nicotine, were lined with uncomfortable looking torn brown and maroon vinyl covered armchairs, ripped to expose the foam which had been further picked at by everyone who sat on them. There were tables and chairs arranged near to the left hand wall. The worn grey linoleum floor covering was decorated with hundreds, if not thousands of cigarette burns and the high, dirty white ceilings and fluorescent lights encased in plastic covers (which appeared to double as insect graveyards), completed the depressing ensemble.

And of course there was the smell... a combination of stale and fresh cigarette smoke with more than just a hint of urine.

"Gimme a fag!" The smell had a voice and a body to go with it and he encountered all three embedded in what could loosely be called a man, now leaning over his right shoulder and with his face uncomfortably close to William's.

"Gimme a fag!" The intonation in the voice left sufficient doubt as to whether it was a question or a demand, but in any case William was too busy taking in the sight that confronted him to be worried about such distinctions.

Apart from the stench of tobacco from his breath and the stale urine from his clothes, the man appeared to have, if it was at all possible, even less going for him on the appearance front. He must have been between fifty and sixty years of age, unshaven for some days, and with unkempt grey hair adorning the back and sides of his head, with the top of his head being completely bald. The lines on his face and his rotting teeth and drooling, betrayed prolonged hardship, illness and chain smoking, not to mention years of medication.

"Gimme a fag!" This time with the word "fag" accompanied by a shower of saliva.

"That'll be you when they've finished with you." Jack provided the commentary to explain the scene.

"Leave him alone, Tom... he doesn't want to be bothered with the likes of you." A new voice now.

William felt the plastic bag containing his possessions being lifted from his lap and the male nurse responsible for its removable appeared in front of him. He offered William an arm to help him out of the wheelchair... or was it to reinforce to William that his journey had come to an end and that the wheelchair didn't do return visits to the outside world.

Jack had little doubt: *"Don't trust him, William... don't trust him."*

"My name's Dave," William focussed on the owner of the Welsh voice that had introduced himself and saw a large framed, round faced man in his twenties with dark hair and a goatee beard. The sides of his face hadn't been shaved for some days and his tortoise shell framed glasses completed his "intellectual revolutionary" appearance.

"Don't trust him… he'll get you… Don't tell him anything!" Jack was almost screaming at him now.

Williams muscles tensed as he involuntarily prepared to act on Jack's warning and as he did so, he felt Dave's grip tightening around his arm.

"Take it easy son…" Dave's voice carried the type of authority that sounded like it could deteriorate swiftly into aggression and his next words, shouted out, it appeared to the world in general, seemed to confirm Williams's suspicions.

"Can I have some help over here… now?"

Three male nurses in white tunics seemed to appear from nowhere, almost as if they'd expected to deal with the newcomer … one way or the other and were close by, just in case.

They positioned themselves around the wheelchair, but within a few seconds, another figure, this one in a white coat and clutching a buff coloured set of hospital notes to his chest, appeared in front of him.

"Hello, William," Was he expecting a reply? William avoided looking at the latest challenge to his survival.

"Tell him to fuck off!" Jack was certain of the response, but William kept silent and still avoided eye contact.

"My name is Dr Sellman… I'm Dr Trafford's Senior House Officer; I believe you met him earlier at the other hospital?" Dr Sellman which might, or might not have been an attempt at friendliness.

"They're laughing at you William… taking the piss." Jack gave his interpretation, but William looked up nevertheless and his gaze was met by the sandy haired, lanky houseman who was staring down at him. His eyebrows were knitted to give the unhelpful impression of confusion tinged with concern. There was something about him that reminded William of someone that he couldn't quite remember, but whoever it might have been, he didn't like him.

Without warning, William sprang from the chair and covered the five feet or so between him and the doctor in a fraction of a second and for an instant, got his hands round the doctor's neck, before being unceremoniously wrestled to the floor.

A barked order, presumably for medication, came from the now startled doctor and there was a flurry of activity from somewhere close, though hidden from William's position on the floor, staring up at the ceiling and being pinned down by four male nurses.

Trousers being forced over his hips and hands roughly turning him onto his side, the smell of ethyl alcohol as his skin was wiped... and then the sting of the injection and only now he became aware of voices directed at him, telling him to keep still, to stop struggling and worst of all to "be a good boy". William said nothing, but Jack had a comment for everything.

"Has he got anyone with him?" came a breathless question from one of his restrainers.

"They know you're on your own. They're taking the piss out of you."

"Nah... she went home to get some kip after our friend's little exploits last night."

"They sent her home so she didn't see anything."

"What did he do?"

"They're pretending they don't know... bastards!"

"Smashed up Casualty at King Edwards."

There was muted laughter around him.

"Richard!" Dr Sellman, who had now composed himself and was standing a safe ten feet away from the action, was addressing a much shorter and overweight middle aged man dressed in a grey suit who appeared to be the senior of the assembled male nurses... "Could you get 200mgs of Largactil... oral... for this guy?"

"Didn't catch that, Doctor." Came the response

"Could you please get 200mgs of Largactil, please?" Dr Sellman repeated his request.

"Still didn't get that, Doctor." came the response.

"Have you got a problem with my instruction, Mr Morgan?" The question was faltering despite Dr Sellman's intention to be assertive by dropping the informality of first names, but the effect was like an inadequate Ship's Captain attempting to negotiate his orders with an all-powerful and arrogant First Officer.

"I don't think so, Doctor... Four hundred milligrams of Largactil... wasn't it?" The Charge Nurse's response was self-assured, yet intimidating in its tone.

"I think you heard me perfectly well... Two hundred milligrams... please... now!"

The Charge Nurse, sweating unpleasantly from the effort of restraining his new patient gave a disdainful look in the direction of the now nervously assertive houseman and left William's right shoulder that he had been holding, to one of the other floor bound nurses, before heaving himself to his feet, departing through the office door behind William's head.

"Of course, Dr Sellman... whatever you say." The false respect and lack of sincerity in the Charge Nurse's voice was obvious for all to hear... especially Sellman himself, who was shuffling uncomfortably from foot to foot, with his face now a significantly deeper shade of red than his dishevelled tie.

As he reached the medicine trolley in the clinic room next to the office, Morgan was clear in his own mind what was needed, regardless of the instructions of the jumped up git of a houseman. He reached into his pocket for the medicine keys and opened the lid of the white metal trolley, reaching immediately for the large brown sticky bottle of Largactil, opened it and poured out 400mgs of the deep pink fluid into a medicine pot.

Placing the bottle back in the trolley, he unceremoniously slammed it shut and locked it before making his way out of the office.

"Two hundred milligrams, Dr Sellman." The Charge Nurse wafted the medicine pot in the air a few feet away from the houseman and so briefly that nothing could be gleaned from it about its volume.

Sellman, still adjusting his clothing from the recent affray, glared back, more than aware of the game he had just lost.

Richard Morgan, now kneeling at William's head, turned his attention to his hapless victim. "Now then, my lad, let's see if you can behave yourself for long enough to take this," and he thrust the deep pink liquid under William's nose "Or perhaps you'd like to stay on the floor... it's up to you... we can do this all day if we have to." A slimy grin accompanied this last speech, which told William, even in his confused state of mind, that this bloke could be trouble enough without the excuse of having a struggling teenager to contend with.

The grips on his arms, legs and abdomen slackened as William was allowed to prop himself up on one elbow, to accept the plastic cup which contained the medicine. He felt the eyes of his captors seeming to bore into him with gloating satisfaction and Jack confirmed his feelings.

"They're enjoying this... you make it too easy for them... you'll soon be one of them... not long now!!"

William briefly hesitated by keeping the medicine in his mouth as Jacks words struck home and was promptly rewarded with a nudge in his back.

"All of it!" The instruction carried a threat with it and William complied and swallowed without further thought… not even about Jack's words of caution.

Again, William's thoughts became more bizarre as his stress increased. Memories from his past mingled with paranoia… he was convinced that one of his captors was his cousin, Michael… but he couldn't see his face… the bus would be here in a minute… Dad needed to get ready for work… he mustn't encourage that ginger tomcat, it will only spray up everything… he had been taken to the aliens headquarters and was going to have his mind altered… where was mum… he was scared, petrified in fact… his Nan would have his tea ready… Wednesday… that was stew and dumplings… he felt sick… echoing noises in the background… men shouting… the smell of cooking, but nothing he was familiar with… it had to be alien food that they fed to the humans… he wanted to watch Coronation Street, even though he hated it, at least it was familiar, safe… the only programme protected from alien messages.

The radio in the background was giving instructions the whole time, telling his captors what to do… if he could only get to that radio and destroy it.

Looking around with quick and apparently random movements of his head, William had the appearance of trying to locate unknown sounds from a multitude of directions. To the team of restrainers, it just looked as if William was about to cause yet more mayhem.

Morgan's face was suddenly inches from William's, accompanied by a loudly whispered warning through clenched teeth.

"Don't even think about it!"

William froze, obviously much to the pleasure and satisfaction of the Charge Nurse, who gave a victorious smirk accompanied by a superior and condescending:

"There's a good boy!"

Jack was there. *"He'll see what a "good boy" you are when you stuff his so called medicine right up his fuckin' alien arse!"*

Morgan mistook William's distraction whilst listening to Jack as compliance with his command and proceeded, with a few others, to pull William to his feet.

"Are you going to behave yourself for the Doctor, William?" The question didn't really need an answer… it was more of a "putting the kid in his place" comment rather than an enquiry.

Arms led William into the office and guided him to a chair next to the desk, at which Dr Sellman was writing, so William allowed himself a cursory glance around the office. Like the area outside it was dominated by the tar stained green walls, but this time with numerous framed bits of cork which were straining under the weight of countless yellowing curled up notices randomly pinned over other yellowing curled up notices which had apparently lost their importance .

His brief reconnaissance was interrupted by Dr Sellman.

"What was all that about, eh?"

William sat, curled up in the chair, and rocking back and forth. He looked up, first to his right and then to his left at the two male nurses who stood either side of him.

And totally ignored the question.

"They're going to interrogate you... see what you know." Jacks commentary was predictable, but William heeded it, nevertheless.

Dr Sellman appeared to accept that he wasn't going to get an answer, picked up his pen and proceeded to write something on a blank sheet of paper on the desk at which he was sitting.

"I've read the reports from Casualty about what happened and all the things that your Mum told us, but I want you to tell me what's been happening."

A pause as Sellman awaited a response, during which he maintained a consistent stare in William's direction.

"Are you going to talk to me, William?"

Plenty of dialogue now, but not from William. Jack was in his element.

"He's got all the reports he needs... all the drivers of the cars that have been watching you, all the people you pass in the street... those people you thought were Nan and Grandpa...they've all sent in reports, they're all in that folder."

William's tension increased even more and he bit his lip and gazed around... giving the appearance of someone who was paying attention to someone other than the person expecting answers to their questions...in this case, Dr Sellman.

"Can you hear something apart from my voice, William?" Sheldon persisted. But before getting an answer, asked a further question that would serve as a reminder for future patient interviews to read their medical notes more diligently... before asking stupid questions that might possibly illicit an unwanted response.

"You don't mind if I call you "Billy", do you?"

The interview, one sided as it had been, ended with the help of five male nurse carrying William out of the office and up the stairs to a six bedded dormitory, where he was unceremoniously dumped on the middle one of three beds. Two of the nurses remained in the dormitory to ensure that William didn't cause any more problems, but by now the medication he had taken half an hour earlier was beginning to work.

William could just about make out something that sounded like Jack's voice somewhere deep in his brain, almost like a thought… but he couldn't make out the words, although he strained to hear them.

The early evening sun streamed through the huge bay window at the far end of the dormitory, somehow making William feel even more desperate and lonely. He was aware of the feeling, the emotion, but as always, his thoughts could add little realistic or logical substance to explain it. He looked around, his sight becoming hazy with the massive dose of Chlorpromazine that he had been given, but he could still make out the two empty beds with their diarrhoea coloured hospital counterpanes, one on either side of him and the three beds opposite, the foot of the middle one being leant on by his custodians.

Still the fragments of thoughts… still the tricks that his memory was playing, by mixing the past with present… making brief links that had no business being linked and all tied up in the messy wrapping of paranoia. His thoughts, his senses, his perceptions and even Jack now seemed to roll into one.

They weren't to be trusted, those two opposite… not even if one of them was Uncle Bill. He knew it was his Uncle Bill. Because of the way he was staring over his glasses… But why did he have someone else's face? His mother would be in soon, after she'd finished the washing up…

His brain was being drained by machines hidden around the room, so he started to recite equations… algebra always did the trick if you wanted to stop them getting into your brain. He started to mumble as though he was attempting an exorcism.

"If c plus 2 equals x squared minus 3, what is y?" It was important that they were complete nonsense so that the machines would blow a fuse trying to work them out.

He could never get on with Lowestoft, that must be it… the feeling… it was his Lowestoft feeling… why was he in Lowestoft? It didn't feel like a holiday.

"If D equals seventeen, then how much is Z squared?"

The colour of the bed covers were helping to brain wash people... he attempted to lift himself up on one elbow with the intention of jumping out of bed in order to pull them off the beds and throw them out of the window... but he simply hadn't the strength and his head ended up back on the pillow.

William fixed his now unco-operative glare on the "Uncle Bill" male nurse and as a final attempt to make sense of anything and with slurred speech, managed to utter "What have you done with Mum? Where is she? Can't anyone... can't... "

And then, finally, but not for the last time, the drug induced sleep overtook him.

June 18th 1974; 15:35hrs

Jean Phillips could remember little of her enforced journey to the police station. She'd managed to have the presence of mind to give the female officer her sister's telephone number and to give her details to the duty sergeant as she was led into the police station.

Now she sat, dazed and confused, in a police cell. The sergeant had told her that he would ring a solicitor for her... "Do you have a solicitor, Mrs Phillips?" ... "Why would I need a solicitor?" There was still blood under her fingernails.

What would her parents say? Did they know? What had her sister Mary told her daughter? Had she got to the school on time to collect her? How could she go back to the flat? Everyone would be talking about her... When would she go back?

Would she go back... ever?

"William... oh my God"

She leapt up from the bench where she had been sitting and rattled the iron bars of her cell and called, almost hysterically.

"I've got to go... help me! I've got to get to the hospital... Hello?"

Nothing.

"For Christ's sake, open this fucking door!"

Footsteps coming, then the appearance of a young faced constable carrying a large bunch of keys.

"Oh, thank God… you've got to let me out… my son's in hospital… he needs me… I'll come back afterwards" God, how bloody stupid did that sound… then some logic, but not much… "You can bail me or something, can't you? "

"Sorry, Mrs Phillips," But he didn't actually sound particularly apologetic, "Can't do that, I'm afraid."

"But you've got to. You don't understand." Her face was streaked with tears and her voice was sounding more hysterical by the second.

"Your solicitor will be here soon and then DS Blake will interview you… so you're going to have to wait… Do you understand what I'm saying, Mrs Phillips?"

She stared, unbelievingly at the Constable and then in very slow speech, spoken as if the policeman was either deaf or stupid.

"I… have… to… get… home… Don't you understand?!"

"We've made sure that your little girl was picked up and your sister knows that you probably won't be back tonight. What hospital is your son in?"

She screwed her eyes tight and shook her head as though she was trying to dislodge unwanted thoughts… "Eh… Greenbeck… but I don't know which ward he's on… Look, he needs me… I've got to go to him… Please!"

The Constable had clearly decided that repeating himself would be a waste of energy and turned on his heel and walked away, calling over his shoulder.

"Wait till your solicitor gets here, Mrs Phillips. We'll ring Greenbeck Hospital and let them know that you can't get there, apart from that, there's no more I can do until the solicitor arrives." With that, he closed the heavy metal cell door and locked it, leaving her alone with her thoughts. She sank back onto the bench and put her head in her hands and then, finally she thought of David, her husband and found herself muttering, as if he'd been lying in front of her …

"I hope you're in fucking agony, you bastard."

She heard the metal gate slam shut at the end of the corridor and the rattle of keys as it was locked.

Then silence.

Left to her own thoughts, Jean Phillips went down every blind alley which now appeared to be all that was left of her life. The tears had stopped and so, it appeared, had time. Her world, fragile as it had been, now lay in ruins and the future of her two children hung in the balance.

After what appeared to be an hour or so, the rattle of keys announced the return of two of her jailers, the constable accompanied by a WPC.

"OK, Mrs Phillips, your solicitor's here." The male constable announced as he unlocked the cell door.

She looked past the two officers and noticed, for the first time, a rather short, grey haired solicitor in a crumpled grey suit, grey stubble on his chin and a pair of half-moon glasses perched on the end of a rather unattractive hooked nose

"Hello, Mrs Phillips," The solicitor moved between the two officers and entered the cell, put his briefcase on the bench and extended his hand.

"Robert Sterling," ... then added, rather unnecessarily, "Solicitor."

Jean Phillips nodded, not even seeing Sterling's hand, which was subsequently taken back and more gainfully employed in extracting a notebook from the briefcase and a pen from his inside pocket. "You've got to help me," this being an extremely obvious thing to say, occurred to Sterling's new client almost as soon as she had said it.

"Actual bodily harm, grievous bodily harm, attempted murder," The now seated Sterling looked over his glasses. "And that's if he recovers. I need to have as much detail as possible... shall we start with some background details?"

Sterling appeared to ask an awful lot of irrelevant questions.

"How long have you known your husband?"

"How long have you been married?"

"What does your husband do for a living?"

"What shifts does he work?"

"How old are you children?"

The questions came thick and fast, with more and more of the questions attempting to establish background information. The questions eventually turned to the relationship itself, William and finally, an account of the last twenty four hours and in particular, the assault on her husband.

"So, Jean, you have told me that your husband had been abusive towards you and William for some years and on many occasions, this abuse was physical?"

"Yes, that's right." came the reply...

"Witnesses?"

"What?"

"Who witnessed these episodes? Who saw the bruises? Who heard the arguments?"

Jean Phillips just stared and shook her head slowly.

"Jean… You're going to have to give me something to work on here. You've been charged with causing actual bodily harm. Your neighbours saw you do it… we must work on your defence and the only hope that we have is to prove that you were provoked?"

"I was provoked!" Jeans retort was desperate.

Sterling stared at her, encouraging further disclosures with his look of expectation.

Silence. But then as her eyes settled on an unseen spot on the floor, she started to sob.

"I didn't want anyone to know… I just wanted to protect my children, and then leave him when they got older… no one needed to know. Before long there would have been social workers and then some do good bastard would have wanted to put them in care… I wasn't going to let that happen… can't you see that? Can't you bloody understand that much?" She was staring at her solicitor with wide moist red eyes now, with her teeth and fists clenched and awaited an answer that she knew would never come.

"Mrs Phillips… Jean… Unless you can convince a jury that you were provoked, you will almost certainly receive a custodial sentence. In any case, you will be remanded in custody until you appear before a magistrate tomorrow and because of the nature of the alleged offence, you may well be remanded in custody until your case is heard by the Crown Court. Do you understand me, Jean?"

She nodded in disbelief, before reassembling what was left of her thoughts, to ask, almost apologetically now about the thought which was uppermost in her mind.

"What's going to happen to my children?"

"I believe that your sister is happy to look after your daughter for the time being… Is that correct?"

"You know what I'm talking about… What happens if I go to prison? What happens to my kids if I go to prison?"

Sterling looked down as he closed his notebook and put it into his briefcase.

"One step at a time, Jean."

"No! Not one bloody step at a time… I've got to get out… Julie will be wondering where I am and William… he's been taken to that bloody looney bin and all you can say is "one fuckin' step at a time"!"

"I'll be with you during the police interview," Sterling was ignoring the outburst, letting his outstretched palm deal with it, as he got up to leave and Jean Phillips knew that the interview was at an end and that Sterling's description of possible custodial scenarios would turn out to be far more that guesswork.

June 19th 1974; 07:30 hrs

"Come on gents, time to get up…"
One of the white coated male nurses had entered the six bedded dormitory and was pulling the bedclothes from the beds in order to hasten their occupant's departure.

He clapped his hands as he left the dormitory, announcing his arrival in the adjacent dormitory.

The male nurse's less than delicate efforts at waking his charges had the effect of catapulting William back into consciousness. At first his thoughts would not come out from their hiding place and as he looked around the dormitory, it appeared to him that his entire brain was refusing to give him a commentary to explain what he was looking at.

Almost in reply to his frustration, fragments of thoughts began to rush into his mind like regurgitated, semi-digested food, but amongst them all, one thought pervaded all the others, namely that he was not at home.

Fear and panic as the thoughts became even less helpful, even more incomplete and yet mixed up with familiar memories triggered by odd bits of sensory cues that were now attacking his senses…

The echoing of every sound that conjured up flashbacks of morning assembly at his old Junior School… images of the holiday chalet at Gt. Yarmouth precipitated by sunlight streaming in through the windows… the multiple beds in the dormitory which dug up visions of the building he had once stayed during a biology field trip from school… the smell of porridge producing pictures of his Nan's houses… the aliens… messing with his mind… taking human form… the radio… he could hear music… but there were words in that music, although he couldn't quite make them out… someone or something was trying to mess with his brain… brainwashing… but why in Great Yarmouth? In his Nan's house?

Memories... but not to William... they were in the here and now... existing all at the same time... he was existing in so many places... but was it the past? Was the past present and future all the same? That was it... the aliens were making him travel in time and space... but as he came to be in one place and time, it didn't quite replace the previous one... he didn't quite travel there so much as experience the new location and its sensations superimpose itself on the previous one, making it sink into the background where he couldn't quite reach it and just as he was about to grasp it, it was gone...

Scared... so scared... just want to go home... why wouldn't they let him go home?

Jack knew... he always knew.

"Can you feel your mind being tampered with, William? Can you?"

Jack sounded almost smug; as though he was gloating... he had been right about the Aliens... right all along.

Jack renewed his attack... he knew when William wasn't paying attention... he knew when he was being blocked and he didn't like it... not at all.

"You can't ignore me, William... I'm your only friend... the only one you can trust." Jack sounded quite slimy in his insistence, but not for long...

"Listen to me, William," Almost aggressive now... *"Don't let them touch you... you'll become like one of them!"*

This last piece of advice coincided with William's horrified glare which was directed at the queue which had built up around the bathroom entrance opposite. It consisted of five men, all in ill-fitting pyjamas, barefoot, all with grey or greying hair with heads bowed and with little or no recognition or acknowledgement of anyone or anything around them.

The first and last in the queue were distinguishable from the others insofar as they were dribbling copious amounts of saliva on the floor where they stood. All were mindlessly hanging onto their toiletries, all of them looked as though they had previously died and had only partially been brought back to life... and none spoke... not to each other... but the mumblings were clearly audible from underneath the bowed heads, almost like monks reciting some meaningless and repetitive chant.

Jack hammered his point home.

"You don't want to end up like them... do you?"

Jack's words were irresistible, as they usually were, although the fragmentation continued, leaving William with only the consistency of the paranoia and a strong sense of what he didn't want, coupled with an inability, for that moment in time to do anything but lie there, screw his eyelids shut and sweat. He knew that Jack was right... had to be listened to... had to be obeyed... but for now, all he could do was lie there and sweat... with only his fear for company...

"I'd shift yer arse and get in the queue if I were you."

The voice sounded friendly and as such was unexpected and its arrival seemed to temporarily banish his unwanted feeling into the background. William opened his eyes and saw a back haired, moustached male nurse standing at the end of the bed.

"You're the guy that came in last night... William isn't it?"

Already Jim was moving away from the bed and the final part of his introduction was delivered as he looked over his shoulder as he went into the adjoining dormitory.

"My name's Jim, by the way... I've left your soap and towel on your locker... downstairs by eight o'clock."

And then, as an afterthought as it dawned on him that his new charge probably hadn't taken in a thing he'd been saying.

"I'll be back in a minute."

Jack didn't like him... William could feel his resentment... any minute he'd get a telling off from his auditory companion for the crime of thinking that Jim seemed OK... And it wasn't long before it came.

"What have I told you about trusting people... these people... these people who want to change you... these people who replaced Nan and Grandpa..." William could detect aggression and impatience in Jacks voice... *"are you really that stupid?!"*

William froze again, this time because of Jack's hostility... Jack's insistence... and his own self recriminations for beginning to trust the male nurse, but this time he was shaken out of it by the bed clothes being unceremoniously pulled from him by male nurse "one" ... "Deaf are we?" Sarcasm this time from the bed stripper.

William stared at him involuntarily as he drew his knees up to his chest.

"I could really do without this today." The male nurse one added impatience to sarcasm "Time... to... get... up!" This time as he moved away...

"Jesus...Where the fuck did they find him?" More to himself than anyone else, but deliberately loud enough for everyone to hear.

As William looked down he noticed for the first time that he was wearing an old, faded pair of striped pyjamas that he certainly had never seen before.

He stared at the locker to his right and saw a threadbare white towel, a shirt and some trousers and propped himself on one elbow to examine them, but had only just extended his hand to examine them when male nurse one returned to the verbal offensive from the other side of the dormitory where he was attempting to hasten the demise of the bathroom queue by pushing them through the door and at the same time pointing them towards a row of sinks as they became vacant.

"They're hospital ones... you pissed the others yesterday with your fun and games... now get up!"

William swung himself round and sat for a second on the side of the bed.

The radio was still playing... still giving out its incoherent warnings... and he could still feel Jack lurking in the background... but he nevertheless stood up and picked up the pile of clothes and towel and walked slowly towards the bathroom and joined the now diminishing queue.

The male nurse, Jim, returned as male nurse one announced his departure to return downstairs.

"Is someone coming in to bring you in some stuff?" Jim gesticulated towards the pile William was carrying.

With all the feelings welling up inside of him, with all the fear, all the anger... all the things that at least part of him wanted to say; all William could manage was...

"I don't know... I want to go home, now... please!"

Jim looked at him and came to the realisation that, knowing the Charge Nurse as he did, that William had probably been told nothing the night before and explanations now were going to be an uphill struggle that at best, would only skim the surface of this lad's comprehension.

But it had to be done.

"You can't go home yet, William. You have to stay in hospital so we can help you." Jim was genuinely sympathetic, but to little avail. On top of this, he knew, from experience, what the response would be.

"You can't keep me here... you're not the police... I'm going... " With this, William attempted to get past Jim in an attempt to leave the ward, but Jim blocked his way.

"This isn't a hospital... you're lying to me... you can't keep me here... I know what you're going to do to me... you can't stop me from going... "

William began flaying his arms at Jim in an attempt to get the nurse out of the way, but was only rewarded by the sound of an alarm bell, and seconds later by the arrival of six or seven male nurses. Jim still had an arm around William's waist as the response team arrive, felt William freeze as he registered the new arrivals, and used the opportunity to reason with him.

"Come on son... you don't want that lot to sit on you, do you?" He turned his attention to the approaching group. "It's OK... he's OK... he's OK... aren't you, William? Just got a bit jumpy... we're going to have a cup of tea and see what we can do, isn't that right, William?"

William nodded slowly and stopped struggling.

"You sure, Jim?" The male nurse at the front of the group wanted to make sure.

"Of course... no problem... is there, William?"

William nodded slowly, again.

The response team melted away, leaving Jim to guide William into the bathroom, staying with him until he emerged, dressed in the ill-fitting hospital clothes. The whole washing and dressing process was carried out in relative silence... except of course for Jack, who always had something to say.

"Bide your time, William... bide your time...we'll get out."

But, more than anything else, William was hungry and felt a sense of relief when Jim announced that they were going down to get some breakfast, and allowed himself to be guided down the stairs, through the door at the bottom... and into the ward...

June 19th 1974; 07:30 hrs

Jean Phillips wasn't woken by anyone... she hadn't slept as far as she could tell, although she had probably dozed a couple of times throughout the night. She laid on the narrow bed in the police cell, facing the wall... not moving. Even her tears had dried up.

The memory of the day before hadn't faded and neither had it been interrupted or obscured by other thoughts. Instead it had remained very clearly in her consciousness where every thought and action could be carefully and painfully dissected and analysed... over and over again. Alongside the replays were the recriminations, the guilt, and the desperation… why hadn't she walked away from him as she had done so many times in the past? Why now, when her children needed her most of all?

Time and time again the thoughts circled in her brain, but instead of feelings of familiarity and resolution, dread and fear were the only endpoints. The only conclusions she could reach was that the future could only be disastrous as a result of her actions.

Actions! She couldn't get away from the fact, she thought to herself yet again, that if she had left the bastard, told someone what was happening… in fact, done anything, then she wouldn't be in this shit now. If she had taken some action then her son might not be in the state he was in… her daughter wouldn't be wondering where her Mum was.

The whole thing… everything, was her fault. If she hadn't been so weak… if she hadn't have been so bloody stupid… so damn proud all the time, not wanting others to see the mess she had made of her life… of her family…

The sound of iron locks turning shook her out of her mesmerising cycle of thoughts and she turned to see a female police officer open her cell door.

"Breakfast, Mrs Phillips," the announcement coming as she placed the tray on the minute table next to where Jean was lying. "It's 7.30… you're due in court at 10am… how do you feel?" Genuine concern?

Jeans brain replied "What sort of stupid fucking question is that?" and "How the hell do you think I feel?" plus "What would you know with your smug little home life and husband, who cleans the car every Sunday instead of getting pissed down the pub? What the hell do you know? What do you care?"

But Jean's mouth almost meekly replied. "OK," Then she was able to shake herself to ask. "William, my son… is he OK? He's in hospital… " And rather unnecessarily… "He's been ill."

"I'm sorry, I don't know… I'll see what we can find out for you… what hospital was he in?" The officer wrote Jean's reply in a notebook.

The officer turned and left, locking the cell door behind her, making the noise that only an iron door closing on an iron door frame, with the loud turning of metal key in a primitive yet effective lock can make.

The finality of a cell door closing and being on the wrong side of it when the operation was complete, reinforced her thoughts and fears and she turned to face the wall again… barely even remembering why the officer had entered the cell in the first place.

William allowed himself to be guided into the ward dayroom, the scene of the previous evenings' activity.

The smell was of breakfast and stale cigarette smoke, but the view was one of desperation as he looked at, first one, then several other men in badly fitting clothes, heads bowed and shuffling around aimlessly. Some had some evidence of combed hair, others hadn't... some had been shaved, but most of them were smoking cigarettes right down to the filter, stubbing them out on the floor and then searching for a replacement, usually from a member of staff, but also by picking up dog-ends from the floor.

All of the men were carrying white, blue rimmed enamel mugs from which they drank with little ceremony. When they'd drained their cups they'd make their way to a male nurse standing behind a table and brandishing a huge teapot, from where he supplied refills, often accompanied by a comment or two and not always directed at the person he was serving.

"Tom... No more fags until after breakfast!"

"Jeffrey... I'm not waiting on you... come and get your own bloody tea!"

"There's a bloody ashtray over there... try using it!"

No niceties, no pleasantries, no gentleness... just orders barked out to a group of men who had somehow edged their way, by virtue of their illness, into some form of inferiority league which had been created by the very people charged with the task of caring for them.

"I want to go home... you can't keep me here... I want to go home... go home... go home." The words tumbled out of William's mouth as though he was vomiting his speech.

A guiding hand on his shoulder and... "Bring us a cup of tea for this lad in the office will you, Dave?" One of the nurses moved towards the teapot table, collected a clean mug and held it out to be filled.

"Let's go into the office for a chat." Jim was guiding William towards the nursing office, and Dave was following with the tea. For some reason, William allowed himself to be guided into the office and accepted the offer of a seat next to the desk. His tea was put in front of him and Dave stayed in the room, as Jim sat at the desk and opened a buff coloured folder.

"William... I need you to listen very carefully to what I am going to say to you. Do you understand?"

William nodded, although he didn't quite know what he was supposed to be understanding.

"Do you know where you are at the moment?"

"In an office." William replied unhelpfully.

"Yes, but where is the office?"

"He's trying to trap you, William... don't answer... he'll have your brain." Jack was there in a flash, but it was of little consequence, because as William became more nervous and agitated, so his thoughts prevented any logical answers, but he replied, he believed, rationally.

"In my Nan's kitchen... why did you take her over... what... ?"

Jim held his hand up in front of William.

"You're getting confused... I asked you where you thought you were and you told me that you are in your Nan's kitchen. Is that right?"

William stared at the nurse and nodded slowly, before adding "and I haven't done my maths homework because that driver on the bus was an alien."

"I see," Jim nodded serenely. "And do you ever hear voices?"

"Don't tell them about me... they'll think you're mad... don't tell him anymore!" Jack sounded almost scared by very insistent.

William shook his head and Jim acknowledged it with an "Mmmm."

"William, you are in a psychiatric hospital, Greenbeck Hospital to be precise."

William looked blankly, shook his head slowly. "I want to go home now."

"William, we need to sort you out, so I have to tell you that you are a detained patient under section 25 of the 1959 Mental Health Act, which means that we can detain you, with or without your consent for a period of one month for the purposes of observation. In other words, if you attempt to leave, we can stop you. Do you understand?"

"No... no... no... no... no, no, no... You're lying; you want me to be like you... "

Steadying hands on his shoulder now as William attempted to make a leap for the door.

"Keep calm, William. Remember that we can and will stop you from leaving"

William froze and eased himself back into his chair.

Jim continued "You will be assessed during this time and when the section has expired and if the doctor considers that you are well enough, then you can be discharged home… do you understand?"

This time, William nodded slowly.

"Good, now drink your tea and we'll go outside and get you some breakfast, OK?"

Dave put a hand under William's elbow in order to indicate to the new patient that it was time to leave the office and William complied.

"You're in enemy territory now, don't do anything stupid, there's too many of them," Jack was whispering almost as a commentary and very conspiratorially.

William moved towards the table with the tea pot, held out his cup and was surprised to see that the tea that came out of the tea pot already had milk added and when he tasted it, found that any choices he may have had regarding the addition of sugar had also been ignored.

Once again, his hunger came to the fore of his consciousness. A table which was some feet away had a large metal pot of very lumpy porridge, but more hopefully, a large battered tray of bacon and another of fried eggs, both almost submerged in copious amounts of fat. Dave, the male nurse was heaping large amounts of both bacon and eggs onto separate trays and taking them into a back room, which had the door open enough for William to see the Charge Nurse and his minions sat around a table in clear expectation of a hard earned pilfered breakfast to come.

But now and regardless of what anyone was doing, or wherever William perceived himself to be, or even despite any protestations that Jack may have made (which, incidentally, he didn't) William took his enamel plate plus breakfast to an isolated table and ate… and ate.

June 19th 1974; 10:20 hrs

The morning of June 19th 1974 was for Jean Phillips, the beginning of the rest of her life, such as it was turning out to be. Put another way, it was the day where just about every aspect of her life ceased to be self-determined.

Breakfast had been followed by instructions (or was it strongly worded advice) to take a shower, and get ready for court at ten o'clock. She had no option but to dress in the same old clothes she had been brought in with, but tried to make the best of them.

71

At 09.20, she had her wrists encased in handcuffs before being piled into a police van along with two female police officers, one on either side. Crazy recollections of Myra Hindley being dispatched in a similar police van, with almost fanatical photographers and members of the public giving chase… but not for her… just one photographer and reporter from a local paper… and they were unlucky because of the obligatory "photo proof" blanket which had been carelessly thrown over her head before she attempted the assisted five yard walk from the rear entrance to the police station to the back of the police van.

The journey to the court was a short one, and one which Jean was didn't seem to register… but there again, apart from the events leading up to her arrest, there wasn't much she could recall either. Suffice it to say that she was taken through the back entrance of the Magistrates Court and down a flight of stone stairs. At the bottom of the stairs they were greeted by a police officer who checked her particulars with her two escorts and proceeded to put her in a holding cell with only: "Your Solicitor will be down to see you in a few minutes." Before the now familiar metallic clang signified her continued imposed imprisonment commenced, following her excursion into the outside world…

Footsteps from the corridor outside announced Robert Sterling's arrival and as the cell door clattered open, Jean rose to greet him, almost in a begging posture with her hands wringing in front of her, a slightly bent back and a nervous, unwilling smile.

"Did you manage to get any sleep, Jean?" His opening gambit that she disposed of it quickly with a shake of the head and a "No… not really." Eyes down and another forced grin.

Sterling gestured for Jean to sit opposite him at the small table in middle of the cell. He unpacked some papers from his battered brown leather briefcase, put them on the table and turned his focus to Jean.

"Now then, Jean. You do realise that this is a Magistrates Court and all that will happen here is that they will commit you for trial at a later date in a Crown Court."

"No… I didn't… I mean… I think I did… I don't know what I thought," Jean was beginning to sweat, beginning to panic and Sterling picked this up and briefly laid a hand on hers.

"It really doesn't matter… Now… are you OK to carry on?"

Jean nodded and tried to look Sterling in the eye, as she issued yet another nervous grin.

Sterling continued. "Today, the court will just ask you to confirm your name and address and ask if you understand the charges against you, which is one of grievous bodily harm. Do you understand, Jean?"

"Will they let me go home... until I have to go to the Crown Court?"

Sterling looked her and this time it was his turn to avert his eyes and give a nervous grin.

"Jean, these are serious charges and if you are asking whether the Magistrate will grant bail, I'm afraid that the other side would oppose it strongly."

If Sterling had not looked at Jean Phillips he would probably have felt the increase in raw emotion anyway. His news had the same effect as pouring vinegar on an open wound and as he looked up he was confronted with the contorted face of his client as she now stood before him, supported by her clenched fists pushing down on the table, her face becoming drenched with tears.

"You've got to get me out... you've got to... I can't sta... " The last plea coming as she collapsed onto her chair in floods of tears and with her hands now covering her face. Sterling attempted to complete his brief as he heard the sound of approaching footsteps coming up the corridor.

"The Magistrate will put you on remand until you appear at Crown Court and will ask for reports from social workers and a psychiatrist."

Still crying, she managed to nod her head in some form of acknowledgement.

Sterling rose to leave, Jean reached out and grabbed his arm.

"The kids... what about William and Julie... did you ring the hospital about William? Is Julie OK?" She looked expectantly at Sterling.

"Sorry Jean... I meant to tell you but things ran away with us... Your Dad says that Julie was a bit tearful at first, but they'll be taking her to the park today to take her mind off things... and William... the hospital said that he's fine and had a restful night. So, I know it's easy for me to say, but try to stop worrying."

As Sterling walked out of the now open cell door, he reflected upon the utter stupidity of his last sentence and briefly closed his eyes as though to somehow prevent anyone seeing the truth... namely that as far as disasters and heartache, Jean Phillips and her children had barely scratched the surface.

The radio was playing somewhere in the background, still giving its sublingual messages, still changing all who listened. But others were giving messages on a much more audible level... namely the not so gentle tones of Dave, this time announcing "medicines".

Dave was helped considerably by the appearance of a white metal cabinet on wheels that he was pulling along and now stood, apparently ceremoniously outside the Nurses Office door. The ceremony consisted of the entire population of the ward moving slowly towards the trolley, without any prompting and forming an orderly queue.

"Without question... they can't even fight back... that's what they want to do with you... look at them... they take anything they're given... that's why the radio is always on... it's giving them instructions... you know it's true... you can feel it." Jack was in fine form.

William could feel it and that's the way it normally was. He could feel things. He knew when things weren't right. And right now... he felt like shit.

Sitting... watching... sweating and listening to Jack.

And as he listened, his awareness that his attempts at thinking, orientating and reasoning were meeting with failure. In their place was Jack. When Jack wasn't there, there was confusion and fragmentation.

Jack let him know what was what. And Jack was letting him know now. Giving him reasons for what he was seeing. Telling him what he must do.

Most of all, telling him what to do.

"William, can you come and get your medicines please?" Not Jack this time, but Dave.

The radio kept on... music, always music and the messages that were hidden in the music, underneath the music but impossible to pin down... but they was there... that's why all the others went and stood in the queue for their medicines... the radio had told them to comply...

"But we know, don't we, William? We know what that bastard, Dave, is really doing. You know what that radio is doing, don't you William?" Jack's commentary continued.

William's mouth was drying up and his skin was wet with sweat. He could feel his heart pounding as he looked around for the source of the music. He just had to find it.

"William, come and get your medicine, now." Impatience creeping into Dave's voice.

William stared in Dave's direction and saw what he was looking for. The radio. On the table just behind Dave and the medicine trolley.

William eased himself out of the chair and slowly walked towards the radio, his gaze fixed. It took Dave a few seconds to realise that William was not walking towards him as a reaction to his commands. Indeed, William was about three feet away from the left side of the trolley and walking with some determination and purpose towards the radio by the time anyone realised what was happening... and by that time it was too late.

The radio was a two feet by one foot lump of yellowing plastic that, along with the television, constituted well over ninety per cent of the patient's stimulation on a day to day basis. William made a grab for it, ripping the plug from the electric socket and raising it above his head before throwing it against the wall to his left. But even before the radio reached its final resting place, alarms were ringing and William found himself assailed on all sides and once again, taken to the floor in a full restraint.

But he didn't struggle or fight... he didn't have to... he'd destroyed one of their weapons... he had achieved a victory... but he was about to be re-acquainted with an adversary who was not the product of paranoia or hallucinations.

"We don't appear to be paying attention very well, do we, William?" The charge nurse, from the night before, was crouching down so that William could see him. He was now dressed in a dark grey suit which distinguished him from the other white tunic clad male nurses.

Richard Morgan leant even further forward and slapped Williams face in a mock friendly gesture... "We're not doing very well, are we Billy?"

William struggled and gritted his teeth in response to the mention of the hated abbreviation of his name.

"Oh, I am sorry, William..." Morgan's imitation of an apology was not meant to be convincing. "You don't like people calling you that, do you?"

William, now struggling more than ever, managed a saliva laden "No," in reply Morgan continued, this time doing an intentionally poor imitation of someone who cared.

"Now, we can't have you throwing your tantrums all over the place, can we William? I'm sure you wouldn't like us to get angry as well, now would you… eh?"

This final "eh" was accompanied by sniggers from his captors and was, for William, the death knoll for his immediate efforts to free himself. Instead, he just stared back at the Charge Nurse.

"That's good… I'm sure we understand each other… and I'm sure that you'll want to take your medicine like a good boy?"

All the time that the charge nurse had been talking, more male nurse were rushing to the scene of the disturbance, and taking in the scene, which appeared to be under control now stood in a circle around the restrained William.

Morgan didn't wait for a reply from his patient and called over his shoulder to Dave, who had regained his position behind the medicine trolley.

"Dave… I think I just heard our young friend here ask for some medication," Sniggers from the assembled group, "Or was it that he wants these gentlemen to help him calm down?" His face still close to William's, Morgan glanced around him in an exaggerated fashion so William could not fail to understand the threatening alternative to taking his medication.

More sniggers from the human circle.

"I think we can let our friend sit up now, so he can take his medicine."

Almost as one, the restraining arms seemed to melt away as the team of nurses complied with their instructions, but no-one made any attempt to help him to sit up. Gradually and with considerable trepidation because of the concerted and mocking gaze of the assembled audience, William eased himself up and sat cross legged in the middle of the circle, he was the new recruit, and Morgan was Arkala, but this cub-scout pack was more likely to lynch him rather than welcome him.

The Charge Nurse, who was now standing, kept his eyes looking down on William whilst extending his arm to his left, arrogantly expecting Dave to deliver the cup of medication to his hand without further ceremony… and upon delivery delivered his professional speech for the benefit of his assembled colleagues.

"Now then, William, if you take this medicine it will help you to relax… do you understand me?"

William nodded meekly… he was beginning to get used to this nonsense. If you annoyed them, they had to send you to sleep… they couldn't cope with him exposing their intentions, so there was no other way. He extended his hand and accepted the cup and after a few seconds hesitation, drained it in one go and, as if that particular action was an unspoken order, the circle began to disperse.

But Morgan crouched down and almost in a whisper, just a few inches away from William's ear, gave an alternative speech, this time for the benefit of no-one, apart from William and of course, his own over-inflated ego.

"Try that stunt again and I won't be so fuckin' nice the next time. You're on a section, sonny and you ain't going anywhere ... understand? So fuckin behave yourself next time or... well I'm sure we understand each other." This last bit with a sickly grin and again, the slapping of Williams cheeks in order to underline his superiority.

As Morgan slowly resumed his standing position, his comments intended for a more public reception re-commenced.

"Dave... I'm sure that Mr Phillips here would appreciate your company for a while."

Dave locked his medicine trolley, threw the keys to his Charge Nurse and walked over to William, who by this time, had got to his somewhat unsteady feet and was staring at his unwanted companion as he approached.

"Have a seat," Dave had grabbed the arm of a nearby green armchair, edged it towards William and gestured with a nod of his head for William to be seated and William slowly and reluctantly complied.

They know that you're different," Jack was there and William's attention was, for a moment, pulled away from Dave, before returning his gaze towards the male nurse, more intently this time, as Jack resumed his commentary.

"He knows you can hear me... he knows you're special." Jack persisted, William carried on staring, although Dave was oblivious as he thumbed through the newspaper he had picked up before seating himself on the corner of a nearby table.

The ward, seemingly unaffected by the radio incident, carried on as though nothing had happened. William was seated in the middle of one of the three windowed bays that comprised one side of the rectangular shaped ward. From his vantage point, he could see the comings and goings... or, to be more precise, the wanderings of the ward inhabitants. Of course, what he could see was no different to what anyone else could see, namely a group of seventeen male patients, all of whom were middle, or late middle aged, all looking moderately to very unkempt, all apparently unable to sit in one place for more than about thirty seconds at a time, and all walking with a shuffle and stooped gait that seemed to underline their desperation and lack of hope.

And then there were the cigarettes. Everywhere in the ward there was the stink of second hand smoke and the sight of patients smoking each cigarette with deep and rapid breathes until the filter and their own fingers began to burn, at which point they would let the dog-end drop to the floor before going in search of the next one. The entire floor which was once covered with drab green linoleum was now covered with drab green linoleum with hundreds upon hundreds of cigarette burns.

Meaningful contact between the patients was almost non- existent. The fact that human beings needed the presence and nearness of other humans seemed to be lost on this group of unfortunates, who couldn't even extend what was left of their social repartee to initiate or participate in conversation. The white coated nurses didn't appear to want to improve the situation, sitting around as they did, reading their newspapers or talking idly amongst themselves.

To any onlooker of this scene, it looked as though their only function was to give out and light cigarettes, tell inmates to get out of someone else's space, or to get into the toilet. Certainly, though, there appeared to be a real and vibrant interest in the nursing office, opposite to where William was sitting with all its various comings and goings. In fact, it would have proved a difficult task for anyone to have linked the activities in the office (which appeared to be continuous) with the care being given to the inmates, which looked as though it had no prospect of starting. In William's eyes, of course, the scene was not one of serious neglect, but rather one of sinister intent and actions. Such intents he would find difficult to verbalise, but he could feel the fear that his fragmented and paranoid thoughts precipitated and of course, he always had Jack to add an opaque clarity to his already confused brain.

He always had Jack to tell him what to do... who to trust... what to avoid and even to tell him what he was looking at. Jack knew that they were trying to get into his brain and knew how they would do it. It was Jack who first told William about the telepathic messages from the TV and radio. It was Jack who had first told him about the dangers of people calling him "Billy" and how it was a code to let them in.

At the moment, Jack was repeating himself, over and over again with every scene that William took in.

"See what I mean?" in response to seeing Tom shuffling up the ward with his trousers half way down to his ankles.

"See what I mean?" in response to William's attention being drawn to Ernie, a fifty year old who was sat in one of the green plastic chairs, noisily slurping (and spilling) a lukewarm cup of tea that he'd found on one of the tables.

"See what I mean?" in response to William's eyes settling on one of the male nurses, unceremoniously bundling Harry (a younger man with black, unkempt hair, black, bucked teeth and who laughed at thin air) into a toilet that he clearly had no intention of visiting by his own volition.

But it was of little use for Jack to give William any commands... not even simple ones. The medication was having its effect and William's legs were the first in line for the Chlorpromazine to do its job. He felt as though they wouldn't take his weight and even if they did, the rest of his body did not really want to put any form of effort into moving.

So he didn't.

And for once, Jack didn't seem to be on hand to object. He seemed to still be around... but at a distance, almost as though someone had told him to stand outside, but he was still attempting to speak and to put his point across.

But for now, it didn't seem so urgent. In fact, nothing he said was urgent.

And as William drifted into sleep, his last and unusually coherent thoughts were about his mother... where was she? Had she been hurt? Had they got to her? Why wasn't she here? William tried to open his eyes, to mumble something incoherent and to make an effort to get out of the chair. But hands held him back and it was only a few moments before he abandoned his pathetic attempts at liberation and went into a completely irresistible, if unnatural sleep.

June 19th 1974; 10:40 hrs

Jean Phillips found herself standing in the Magistrates Court, with a WPC sat next to her. The Magistrates bench to the right was occupied by all the types of person that she would normally be at considerable pains to avoid, but today she was being particularly unsuccessful in such a quest.

The proceeding began and ended with a speed that she would not, if she had been asked, have thought possible in a Court of Law, even if it was only a Magistrates Court.

She was asked to stand, confirm her name and the charges were read out, namely that she "did, on the 18th June 1974 cause injury to David James Phillips contrary to…" (she missed that bit) and was asked if she understood the charges. She could hardly comprehend that they were referring to her in their legalistic jargon, let alone be able to say that she understood the charges.

She looked blankly at the court official who was not altogether patiently waiting for an answer. He repeated his question and was still met with a blank expression, at which point Sterling leant over and whispered.

"Jean, do you understand the charges. You've got to reply."

By this time all eyes were on her, which made her feel ten times worse than she had done, but she nevertheless managed a stumbling "I suppose so… yes… look, what about my kids, I've… "

Sterling stepped in and muttered something about it not being the right time or place and that all she needed to do, she had done. Then and not for the first time, he wished he hadn't answered the telephone from the police station the day before asking him to see one Jean Phillips who was in need of a solicitor.

Pushing him away, the little self-control she had left (which was essentially only there in the first place because of the surreal nature of the situation) began to show signs of falling apart. Shoving Sterling's hand away again, she started to remonstrate with him, but within a second or two (and following much gesticulating by Sterling) she stopped and looked around her, and was confronted by the entire Magistrates Court staring at her. She mumbled an apology and within a minute or so was treated to the spectacle of watching her solicitor earning his fee (wherever that was going to come from) by asking for bail to be granted and the Magistrate earning his fee (if he got one) by refusing to grant it.

The Magistrate listened to a few legal arguments from Sterling and then a few more from the other side. The words "public safety", "best interests", "family needs", "unpredictable nature", "seriousness of the offence" and various other legal pivots were bounded around the courtroom. At which point there was a brief but intense period of mumbling between the three good citizens sat at the bench, before the magistrate looked over the rim of his glasses towards where Jean Phillips was still standing. "Jean Phillips, you will be remanded in custody for psychiatric and social work reports to be completed, then to appear at Crown Court at a later date. Bail denied."

And then he nodded to the WPC and that, obviously as far as he was concerned, was that. There was of course the subsequent disruption to proceedings as a now seriously unhinged Jean Phillips started to make an attempt to reach the Bench in order to make her point as forcefully as possible.

"You don't understand... I've got to get home... my daughter needs me... I've got to look after her." The two WPC's attempted to grab her arms in order to take her away, but through her struggling she managed to gain a temporary retrieve from the restraining arms, with a final "get off my fuckin' arms!"

"Sir... you've got to listen!" To no avail as the Magistrate and other bench inhabitants picked up their assorted papers and made for the door behind them, leaving the assorted minions who were left in the room to bring some form of order.

The WPC's had regained some control and were now attempting to pull her back by the arms and shoulders, but Jean hadn't finished.

"I'm fuckin'talking to you!" Now screaming as Sterling appeared in front of her and attempted to calm the situation.

"Jean... Mrs Phillips... this really isn't helping," Sterling was proving himself to be singularly useless in a crisis and earned a venomous "And you can fuck off as well... a lot of fuckin' help you were!"

She was now being pulled towards the door leading to the cells from where she had emerged only a quarter of an hour earlier, now screaming obscenities, now hysterical, but now most definitely on the wrong end of the struggle with her escorts attempts to remove her.

As she was bundled through the door and led to the cells, she twisted round as well as she could, only to see the remaining inhabitants of the magistrate's court staring at her, one or two shaking their heads in a nauseatingly condescending manner. Sheldon was one of them, now standing and looking in her direction, with his hand on his forehead as though a sudden and painful migraine had descended.

Even in her state of fear and agitation, though, she knew one thing, namely that they would go home, but she wouldn't... not for a long time... and William would now have to face the world alone.

81

Dripping fluid on his hand… the smell of tobacco that somehow failed to entirely disguise the stink of bad breath.

William opened his eyes and was confronted by Tom who had positioned himself about a foot away from his face and was drooling saliva over William's hand, which was resting on the arm of the chair.

Tom was busy going through William's pockets looking for fresh supplies of cigarettes before William jumped and instinctively pushed him away with such a force that Tom ended up as a startled heap on the floor. Just about everyone in the vicinity froze temporarily as a precursor to either leaping into another restraint, or just getting out of the way, but on this occasion a more reasoned intervention occurred because of the chance presence of a familiar face.

"It's OK… he's fine, he's fine," Jim had his hand on Dave's shoulder in order to prevent him from moving towards William.

"He's fine… fine, aren't you, William?"

William nodded as he recoiled in the chair and drew his knees up underneath his body.

"It's OK; he was only after a fag. Tom's harmless… aren't you, Tom?"

Tom, at this point was picking himself up off the floor and continuing the relentless search for his next cigarette and didn't bother attempting a reply, not that he was actually capable of any meaningful communication at the best of times.

"How are you doing, William?" Jim's question seemed caring enough and William managed a nod in reply as he invariably could to simple questions, but as the conversation continued, William's understanding and ability to reason took a characteristic nosedive, with only Jack and the paranoia providing any continuity.

"We need to…"

"Bastard, what does he mean "we"?!"

Where's Mum… he's a teacher… no homework to hand in…

"Sit down and have… "

"Don't you dare trust him… he controls the messages on the radio!"

Where did I put my donkey jacket… Uncle Bill's still driving buses…

"And do a bit of paperwork… "

"So they won't be able to trace you... just look at the evil in his eyes..."
Feel so afraid... so alone... don't want to be on holiday anymore...
"Talk to this bastard and you'll never go home again!"
"So we can figure out how... "
"He's trying to control you!"
Dad will be in soon... more arguments. Leave Mum alone!
"Best we can help you... "
"As if he doesn't fuckin' know!"

As the fragmentation became worse and Jack's condemnation of Jim became more vehement, William became more and distracted away from Jim and visibly strained to listen to Jack's commentary. As he did so, he shuffled uncomfortably in the chair and drew his knees up underneath his body.

"He can't hear me... he mustn't know about our conversations, William... he'll tell you you're mad and put electric wires in your head." Jack, as usual was graphic in his descriptions.

It was a few seconds before William realised that Jim had stopped talking and was now staring at him with, what appeared to be concern.

"Are you hearing voices, William?"

"Don't you dare say anything!"

Feeling so confused, so afraid... "You look as though you don't seem to be able to understand what I'm saying... is that because you can hear other voices?"

William made some token efforts to inappropriately nod in response to Jim's conversations, but was completely unconvincing if his intention had been to disguise his distraction. Jack was now less urgent in his words and tone and was successfully pulling William away from any reassurances that Jim had to offer.

"That's it, William. You're safe with me. I won't lie to you like the others do. I'll always tell you the truth. I'll always look after you. I'll always protect you. It's just me and you now, William." Jack seemed to know all the right things to say in order to calm him down.

It seemed to William that he really couldn't trust anyone else and that the only help he was going to get would come from his unseen mentor and part time friend, Jack.

Jim sat with William for another couple of minutes and tried once again to make an attempt at the well-guarded citadel that was William Phillips' consciousness. "William… William, will you talk to me? William… can you tell me what your voices are saying to you? William… ?"

Nothing except a blank stare from the huddled up figure on the chair.

Dr Sellman, who had just entered the ward, took a diversion away from his less than purposeful journey to the nursing office and came over to where Jim and William were apparently entirely locked out from each other's worlds.

"Any better?" The question begged a reply, but considering the short time since admission, it didn't carry much hope of a positive response.

Jim's voice, which had been increasing in loudness as he attempted to elicit responses from his increasingly distracted patient, altered his pitch as he stood to meet Sellman.

"Not really," Jim looked up, feigning intense concentration… "Although he hasn't attacked any radios or people for at least… oh, let me see, for an hour or so."

There was no malice in his voice or in his words… just a degree of hopelessness at the anticipation of the long road ahead and the real possibility that such a road to recovery may not exist at all.

"Has he talked to you about the voices?"

The male nurse shook his head. "No, but it's pretty obvious that their holding most of his attention. He barely speaks and behaves as though he's listening to something the whole time."

"And when you can get him to talk?"

"He tends to keep quiet as though he's afraid of saying something he shouldn't …but when he does say something it comes out in a rush before he clams up again. Movement is very quick, avoids eye contact and spends most of his time huddled in the chair and glaring all around him as though he's expecting someone to attack him any minutes." Jim's account told Sellman little that he hadn't already gleaned for himself.

"Drugs?" The question wasn't aimed at anything apart from eliminating the inevitably popular yet, in this case, mistaken diagnosis when a 19 year old shows symptoms of psychosis and generally bizarre behaviour.

Jim raised his eyebrows in mock surprise and pretended to seek clarification from the SHO.

"Gerald, am I to assume that you've struck up an alliance with our Charge Nurse Morgan?"

Sellman shook his head slowly.

"Look, I'm not trying to tell you what to do, but you really need to watch yourself before you think of crossing him again." Jim's voice had lowered and he looked around to make sure he wasn't being overheard.

Sellman looked shocked and disgusted, but still lowered his voice as if involved in a conspiracy. "So, I should just let him overdose, threaten and bully patients when he feels like it."

Jim shrugged his shoulders and avoided the searching glare of his colleague. "That's up to you... but you won't last five minutes and God knows you've only been here a fortnight."

"Thanks for the advice, but if it's all the same to you, we'll see what Dr Trafford has to say about it." Sellman obviously thought that evoking the big guns would put an end to the matter, but Jim just buried his face in his hands.

"You just don't get it do you? Morgan doesn't just work at Greenbeck... his IS Greenbeck. He's in everyone's pocket, the same as he father was when he ran this ward. As for Trafford, you might as well forget it, they're like blood brothers."

"Slight exaggeration, wouldn't you say?" Sellman was clearly sceptical.

Jim shrugged his shoulders as though to say; "Take it or leave it" but confined himself to "Just be careful, that's all."

William, in the meantime had resumed his rocking, seemingly unaware of the world and its problems, but nevertheless aware of his danger... albeit for all the wrong reasons.

June 19th 1974; 12:25 hrs

Sterling, plus overcoat and briefcase, were quite a formidable combination when they all tried to bundle through a door at the same time. When he was agitated and in a hurry, the doorframe barely survived the experience.

The smartly dressed middle aged lady receptionist with the religiously maintained perm was the only person in the reception area of Dankin, Dankin and Braithwaite not to jump in surprise at the unceremonious entrance of the solicitor and instead just looked over her glasses in polite and unspoken enquiry.

"Do I invite it? I mean, is there something that I do that attracts the sort of client who tries to attack the Bench?" As he approached the reception desk he made a grand play of lifting his briefcase and dumping it on the

85

previously uncluttered surface.

"I take it that Mrs Phillips presented somewhat of a challenge, Mr Sterling?" and then, by way of an explanation, "We received your message from the court to say that you had been delayed. Coffee? Or will you be going to lunch?"

"Coffee, definitely coffee, thank you, Sarah." Sterling appeared to visibly relax. "Did you get my message regarding her son, William at Greenbeck Hospital?"

Sarah reached for her note pad. Adjusted her glasses and read "He's been admitted to Male 4. I gave them a call and they said he had a quiet night but wouldn't give me any further details." She looked quizzically at Sterling in anticipation of some form of explanation, but all she got was another question.

"Did you manage to find out whether he is able to understand or deal with, or even be able to cope with the news about his mother?"

Sarah temporarily postponed her unspoken enquiry and once again referred to her notebook.

"I spoke to the Charge Nurse on the ward who told me that he couldn't give me any further information until William had been seen by his Consultant Psychiatrist – Dr Trafford." She slipped instantly back into her quizzical stare, this time with some success.

"William Phillips had some sort of breakdown. Came to a head over the last couple of days when he threw himself at a bus for no apparent reason. They took him to hospital to get him checked over and he assaulted the staff and virtually wrecked the place before they could sedate him. Anyway, it all ended with William being put on "section" and carted off to Greenbeck Hospital."

Sterling seemed to be on a roll, probably for his own benefit of being able to verbally summarise the case for the first time. "Meanwhile, it seemed all too much for "Mum", who seems to have gone completely overboard. You know the rest. Suffice it to say that she hasn't done herself any favours with today's performance." Sterling gave a false grin and raised his eyebrows to indicate that as far as further explanation was concerned, he was at a loss. "She even refused to see me afterwards. Ring up the prison where she's on remand and get me in to see her as soon as you can, please." Sarah duly made a note.

Sarah filled the void. "I rang the Hospital about Mr Phillips... They took

86

him to theatre this morning and he's back on the ward and "comfortable", whatever that means."

"In legal terms it probably means that Mrs Phillips will get a custodial sentence and lose both her kids. On the good side, she won't get done for murder or manslaughter, but I suspect that's of little consolation at the moment, she's already having herself hung drawn and quartered without any help from a Judge!"

Sterling left a respectful silence as if to allow his gloomy prediction to hit home and then resigned himself to getting on with the job in hand.

"Right, Sarah," he seemed to have shaken himself, at least partly, out of his gloom. "She's going to need a decent Barrister... see if John Hancock's available... this is right up his street and while you're at it, we need to get psychiatric reports ... See if Dr Cunningham would mind having a day out to the prison. Let's see if we can't get her sorted and salvage some of her life for her, although another display like todays and she can kiss that goodbye."

And with that, he retrieved his briefcase from the desk and made towards his office door to the right of the reception desk.

"At least we know that we don't have to worry about her son. We know he's in the right place!"

The door closed behind him, only to be opened a second later.

"Did you say you'd made the coffee?"

June 19th 1974; 15:20 hrs

Dr Trafford meandered onto the ward giving only the briefest of acknowledgements to the patients who tried to speak to him. On his way to the nursing office he glanced around him at his patients, possibly as a way of seeing how they were doing, or perhaps he was merely trying to remind himself who they were.

Trafford was the sort of Consultant who didn't believe in demonstrating unnecessary courtesies in places where he believed his word was law, so as usual, he didn't bother knocking on the ward office door before entering. Richard Morgan was sat behind his desk with his half smoked cigarette in his mouth, ash about to fall onto his desk. He removed it just in time and flicked it into an already overflowing ashtray as he looked up at his expected visitor.

"Good afternoon, Dr Trafford."

Trafford nodded as he went over to the metal trolley in the corner of the office and started extracting patient folders.

"Sellman arrived yet? I want to get on with the ward round as soon as possible." This last comment punctuated with a deliberate glance at his wristwatch. "How's he doing anyway?" Still Trafford didn't look up and Morgan didn't answer him. Obviously, Trafford needed to state the obvious.

"William Phillips. How is he?"

This time an answer was forthcoming. "Not too bad… bit like a fish out of water, but we'll look after him." Morgan was looking at the Consultant as he was speaking, although Trafford carried on with the task in hand and contented himself with a "Good… Good, yes. You do that." As he turned the pages of the set of medical notes he had retrieved from the trolley and carried on reading.

Whether it was the time it took for Trafford to answer, or just his own conniving mind waiting for an opportune moment, the meaning behind Morgan's next communication was unmistakable. Before he spoke, Morgan gave the beginnings of an almost nervous laugh, as if he was trying to disguise his intent and render it to a pile labelled "I didn't realise that was serious".

"Give him his due; he does listen to advice, like with that kid, William Phillips, last night."

Morgan left a gap in the conversation, being more than aware that Trafford would simply have to ask for further details. He wasn't disappointed.

"What about William Phillips last night?" Trafford turned away from his notes and look towards the Charge Nurse, who had lit another cigarette as if to celebrate being able to get the Consultant's attention.

"Sorry. Dr Trafford, I thought Dr Sellman would have told you."

"Told me "what" exactly. I haven't caught up with Sellman today; I've been on a domiciliary visit all morning. What's this about William Phillips?"

"Nothing much really. He got a bit spooked as we brought him into the ward yesterday afternoon and we had to restrain him and gave him something to calm him down a bit," and then he paused as if to reflect, but in reality he just wanted to make the next part of his narrative stand out, so that Trafford would ask for more details. "Just as well Dr Sellman was there, really."

Trafford took the bait "In what way?"

"Pardon," Morgan pretended that his previous comments had been so irrelevant that he needed to be reminded of what he had just said.

Trafford was growing impatient, "In what way was it "just as well" that Dr Sellman was there?"

"Oh, sorry, yes of course. He was able to prescribe some Chlorpromazine and to give him his due, when I told him he was giving too much, he wrote the correct dose up. Not all new doctors listen to advice like that."

"So what did he try to prescribe, then?" Trafford was definitely interested now.

"Four hundred milligrams instead of two hundred, I think, anyway… he soon put it right… no harm done eh?" Morgan carried on smoking as Trafford kept on looking at him over his glasses. The short silence was broken by Morgan

"Don't worry, Dr Trafford. Easy mistake. Anyone could have made it. We'll hold his hand for you."

Trafford didn't particularly like Morgan, but he was valuable. He knew all the "ins and outs" of the hospital like no-one else. Nothing escaped the man and if you needed anything arranging, fixing, sorting out of if you just needed to know what was going on, then Morgan was the man to go to. He kept a close eye on everyone who came into his world and made it his business to know theirs.

But to Trafford, he was so much more than an asset. Morgan made his job easier by scurrying around behind him, making phone calls for him, dealing with relatives that he couldn't be bothered with, covering for him when he was on the golf course, reminding him about engagements, changes to medication. Just about everything in fact. Put another way, having worked together for the last ten or eleven years, Morgan knew too much about Trafford for comfort.

So biting his tongue every time he wanted to tell him what a slimy back stabbing psychopath he was, was offset by the benefits of keeping him sweet and, of course preventing himself from becoming his next victim. And that was just what he was doing at the moment… biting his tongue. Trafford knew that Morgan didn't make "chance" remarks and any throw away comments he made were carefully calculated to elicit some response or other that could be used against the unfortunate victim when they were least expecting it. Whoever they were.

And so Trafford, nodded as if resigned to decisive action replied to the news of the alleged incident with "Thank you, Richard. You can leave it with me now."

Morgan began a token and insincere apology, "I'm sorry Dr Trafford, I do hope I haven't caused Dr Sellman any trouble. I… "

Trafford held his left hand up, which could have been construed as indicating to his Charge Nurse that all was well, but could equally have been a sign to make him shut up. In any case, the latter happened and that, Trafford mused, was a result and returned to his notes in silence as though to underline the fact that he had no wish for the "Sellman" topic to continue. After about five minutes of quiet, Trafford looked up and addressed Morgan again. "Thanks for taking the Phillips lad, by the way. I know he should have gone to an admission ward, but I really didn't have any choice because of the other place being closed for decorating."

Morgan gave his mouth a temporary respite from the cigarette and answered the Consultant with an obligatory "No problem."

"I know you said you had a spot of bother with him last night, but how's he been getting on apart from that?"

"To tell you the truth, he's been a bit of a bugger this morning as well… smashing the radio at breakfast and making a general nuisance of himself. He's got some strength too and I'm not altogether certain that he doesn't know what he's doing, at least some of the time."

Trafford had heard this speech before, many times before, in fact and he didn't like it any more now than the first time he'd heard it. He liked Morgan's attitude to mental illness even less, although, of course, it were one and the same thing.

"Are you perhaps, suggesting that Mr Phillips is not mentally ill, Richard?" Spoken whilst looking over the top of his glasses, Trafford had no intention of not letting Morgan know, in a thoroughly deniable fashion, just what he thought of his views.

Morgan picked up the hint immediately and was quick to deny any unprofessional intent in his statement. "Of course not, I was just trying to say that he seems to have got into this state very quickly and there's nothing from his GP to say there were any real problems. He's taken something, some nasty drug or other that he's got hold of, and he could be reacting badly just because we're telling him what to do, and he doesn't like it. He knows what you're saying to him." Morgan paused for a couple of seconds, as if to read Trafford's face for a reaction and when he didn't get the encouraging nod of agreement that he was looking for, decided to cut his losses with, "But of course, I could be wrong."

Trafford resumed his attempt to get a few crumbs of useful clinical details. "Any sign of distraction that would indicate auditory hallucinations?"

Morgan was about to answer in the negative, when the office door flew open and Sellman complete with flapping white coat, put in a breathless and somewhat flustered appearance. Trafford acknowledged the arrival of his houseman with another of his well-practiced raised eyebrow glares and was rewarded by saying "Sorry I'm late," from Sellman before he too, settled himself opposite Trafford on the other side of the medical notes trolley.

"Phillips?" Trafford's question was to the point and completely lost on his junior colleague.

"I'm sorry."

"What is your opinion of Mr William Phillips?" Trafford gave the full name of the patient in question, more out of sarcasm than an attempt to be helpful.

"Yes... yes... sorry, of course," Sellman fumbled through the notes trolley and then realised that Trafford was holding the notes in his outstretched hand.

"Eh, thank you... yes." and with that, opened the folder and began to summarize his own admission notes.

"I admitted William at five o'clock yesterday afternoon. He has a reported history of psychotic symptoms over the last year or so, culminating in what appeared to be a florid psychotic episode the night before last when he caused a road traffic accident and... "

Trafford had heard enough from his junior, who was not in his opinion, doing a particularly good job of proving Morgan wrong.

"Dr Sellman, could you tell me who saw this chap at King Edwards?"

Sellman looked at the note: "Eh? You did."

"Correct... So why are you telling me what I already know?"

Blank stare.

"Just give me your opinion of him. I presume you have seen him today."

"Yes, yes of course." Sellman felt expectantly more confident. Somewhere in Trafford's condescension and sarcasm was a suggestion, no matter how insignificant, that he was interested in his opinion.

"Well, he had a quiet night, but there again, we did have to give him a dose of Chlorpromazine to calm him down, last night." Sellman didn't think it was the right time to mention the incident with Morgan.

"So I hear. How much did you give him?" The question appeared to be asked in all innocence.

"Two hundred milligrams."

"I hear that he was quite disturbed. Didn't you think about giving a higher dose at all?"

Sellman suddenly realised that Morgan had got to Trafford before him and that he risked a childish slanging match if he made an open attempt to challenge what appeared to be Morgan's lies.

"Of course not. Two hundred milligrams is the recommended dose for sedation, and in any case, I had to be careful of side effects." He made his point as convincingly as possible.

Trafford allowed himself a cursory glance in Morgan's direction who, by this time had lit another cigarette and was staring out of the window, keeping his mouth shut, but his ears flapping.

Sellman continued. "He's showing distinct signs of distraction, probably indicating auditory hallucination although we can't get him to talk about it, as yet. Paranoia evident and probably linked to his voices in some way, if his behaviour's anything to go by. The radio seemed to get to him, as he made a bee line for it when he entered the day room and the staff that were near him report that he was staring in its general direction for some minutes earlier, and seemed to calm down as soon as he'd destroyed it."

Trafford was at last nodding his agreement, encouraging Sellman to continue. "And of course his catatonic rocking."

"Not much luck with getting him to talk, then?" Trafford's tone appeared to indicate a greater willingness to treat him as someone who possessed at least the beginnings of a valid opinion.

"No, but on the odd occasions that he has said something, it's been noticed that he avoids eye contact and speaks very quickly."

"And could you venture a provisional diagnosis, which is of course pending further observation... Any ideas?" Trafford had clearly made his mind up, and was playing the part of mentor to his houseman.

"I would say paranoid schizophrenia is the most likely probability," Sellman was sure he was on safe ground, and he soon gained the approval of the older doctor. Trafford nodded again and reinforced the opinion. "Yes, quite probably," and at this point glanced briefly over to Morgan to see if he was showing his irritation at the diagnosis, but if he was, he was covering it up well. "Yes, we'll carry on with the chlorpromazine and Orciprenaline and see how we go." Trafford removed his glasses and made it plain, as he gazed around the room, which he wished to have the attention of both Morgan and Sellman.

"We do have a bit of a complication with young William." Morgan stubbed out his cigarette, displacing some of the debris already occupying the ashtray, and looked up.

"It would seem that when Mrs Phillips returned home from being with William at King Edwards, as the police have put it, an incident occurred which had the end result of Mr Phillips being taken to hospital with stab wounds, and Mrs Phillips being taken into custody. She was due in Court this morning, but I haven't been able to catch up with what's been happening, yet" His ensuing short period of silence indicated that he wished to have some form of response and this came in the form of a question from Sellman.

"So, if Mrs Phillips is in prison, who will be his next of kin?"

"By law, that would have to be his father, but we don't know the severity of his injuries as yet." Trafford was thoughtful and addressed Sellman directly. "And I dare say that you have gleaned from the referral note from Dr Moyle at King Edwards, that there is at least a strong suspicion that the relationship between William and his father is far from harmonious, to such an extent that I wouldn't be surprised if this incident with the stabbing wasn't something to do with a dispute between Mr Phillips and his wife over William."

Morgan appeared to have discovered an answer to an unrevealed question. "So that's why we had a call from a Solicitor's Office asking about William's condition."

Trafford added his confirmation. "Just so, meanwhile, the social worker's getting in touch with the grandparents and we, or to be more precise, I have to make the decision as to whether William is in any fit state to be told anything at this time."

Sellman looked enquiringly at Trafford, but had to follow it up with "And?" in order to get a response.

Trafford took up the cue from his houseman. "And... I don't think that he is mentally well enough to be told at the moment. In the meantime, I think we'd better get on with the ward round," And with this he once again looked over his glasses towards Sellman. "Now that Dr Sellman has joined us!"

June 19th 1974; 16:05 hrs

"Can you come and have a chat with us, William?"

William moved his head to stare over at Trafford and for a moment, stopped rocking back and forth in his chair.

"He doesn't like me... He doesn't like you... You've got to be careful, so careful... If he thinks you're talking to me, he'll say that you're mad... Don't tell him about me!"

Jack seemed to be doing his utmost to protect William from the man now standing in the office doorway, if indeed he was a man.

"He's one of their leaders... He was at the other place, at the hospital. Don't believe him. Don't let him trick you..." Jack's pleadings couldn't be ignored and William returned to his rocking as he looked away from the Psychiatrist.

"William... could you come and have a chat to us please" This time Trafford moved to one side of the doorway and extended his arm into the office as if to remind William where it was. Almost as a reflex William uncurled his legs from under him, jumped up from the chair and walked briskly into the office and sat down on the opposite side of the desk, which was still occupied by Morgan.

Trafford closed the door and drew up a chair to face William, who, by this time, was once again experiencing a plethora of seemingly unrelated, irresistible and rapid- fire thoughts, all combined with Jack's commands. Trafford was aware of William's distraction, but chose to appear as though he was ignoring it for the time being.

"Now, William, you didn't want to say much to me yesterday when you were in the other hospital, can..." Trafford's words sank into the background as Jack attempted to take control of the interaction.

"Tell him to fuck off... stop fuckin' pretending... We know what he's trying to..."

Where's Mum... Jonathan got a detention today. Smell of chips... where's the paper?

"You try to tell me…"

"Fuckin' mind bending bastard … it's him that controls the radio."

It's a long walk if you miss the bus … has Lenny got my football cards, I only need Bobby Tambling… I don't like this guy.

"… why do you think you're here?"

"If you talk to him, he'll be able to tune into your mind."

I feel hungry, where's Mum…

"William… William, are you going to talk to me?" Trafford persisted and William just stared.

Jack was far more forthcoming. *"Fucking bastard… ignore him… he's alien, don't look at him!"*

William looked down in response to Jack's commands. "William, I know that you've been ill for some time," William's thoughts seemed to be pushed into the background by Jack. "Back on that track… telling you you're a fuckin' looney again."

"I remember being told that you are afraid of being taken over by aliens… is that right?"

Silence.

"William, we are trying to help you, but we can't do that unless you talk to us."

William quickly tucked his legs under his body and re-commenced his rocking, but this time, Trafford put his hand on his patient's shoulder to stop him moving. "William, stop moving… William!" This time with the beginnings of impatience from a man who disliked being ignored.

William stopped moving, but started again the moment Trafford removed his hand and sat back in his chair. So the hand went back to the shoulder in double quick time and again the impatience. "William!" This time he stopped and more out of reflex than anything else, looked at Trafford. For a moment, there were no other thoughts, not even Jack. Just for the briefest instant, he wasn't being bombarded with unconnected flashes or instructions.

"I want to go home… what have you done with my mother? I know what you're trying to do to me and you won't do it…" Then as suddenly as it had left him, the fragmented thoughts returned to prevent any further meaningful dialogue, but in any case, he knew that if he said any more, then Jack would get annoyed and that was something to be avoided.

Trafford, on the other hand, thought he had an opportunity to make some progress.

"Are you hearing voices, William?"

Again, the rocking and staring down at the floor.

Morgan decided, not altogether for clinical reasons, to add his contribution under the guise of giving his Consultant some help. "Could you tell us why you smashed the radio this morning, William?"

William had paid no attention to Morgan until this point, but now responded to the new inquisitor as though someone had shot a bolt of electricity through him, by shooting an unexpected glare at the charge nurse.

"You know… you know what it was doing, you knew all the time… did you think that I'd just let it poison me?" And then he looked down and recommenced his rocking as though he had instantly regretted his outburst.

"Is that what you think, William? That the radio was giving you messages that you didn't want to hear? Is that it?" Trafford seemed encouraged by William's little speech, but further reward was not to be immediately forthcoming.

Once again the silence and the rocking.

"Do you think that Dr Sellman or Mr Morgan here, or even I, am an alien, William?" With this, he gave a smile which was quickly copied by Morgan and Sellman.

A smile that was the very essence of food to William's paranoia, a smile that spelt conspiracy, secrets, plots… all it what you will, but it fitted, confirmed and justified William's fears and Jack was quick to add his opinions. *"Now do you see, William? They don't seem worried that you've discovered them. They think it's clever to laugh at you. They're laughing at you William, do you hear me, they're laughing at you!"*

William was turning his head slowly, in a winding motion, as if it was a TV aerial that was being adjusted in order to pick up the strongest possible signal, except that he was getting the message loudly and clearly from all quarters and without warning and in one motion, untucked his legs from under him and sprang over the desk at Morgan, managing to empty his ashtray and scatter an assortment of papers into the bargain. As his hands closed around Morgan's neck, the force of the leap across the desk sent both of them hurtling towards the floor as the chair was pushed back.

"You bastard… you fuckin' alien bastard!"

Everything seemed to happen in an instant, from Trafford flinging the office door open and yelling for help, to Sellman piling in through a jumble of upturned furniture in order to try and pull William from the struggling Morgan, to the response team taking control and pulling William off and onto the floor.

After a few "You ok, Richard?" type comments from all and sundry, Morgan picked himself up and tried to restore some semblance of order to his suit, tie, glasses, and of course, his ashtray, but before he could say anything, Trafford sidled up behind him with his own contribution.

"Our young friend doesn't seem to like you very much, Richard, or perhaps he's just playacting." Then, with clinical sarcasm, "Difficult to tell, really."

Morgan just gave a very insincere smile and without any further comment, carried on putting the office back together . Meanwhile, William was being coerced into taking the obligatory sedation, but this time in the form of an innocent looking blue tablet that Trafford had ordered.

"Sodium Amytal, 200mgs." Trafford read his prescription out loud, and then looked at both Sellman and Morgan over the rim of his glasses, as if addressing two delinquent schoolboys. "And, gentlemen, that's a "once only" dose… please note." He drew a deep breath in and as if to bring the matter of William and sedation to a close, he announced "And when you've sorted out Mr Phillips, perhaps we can get on with the ward round!"

June 19th 1974; 17:15 hrs

The prison van had stopped in the waiting area outside HMP Holshaw before being let through the tall wooden gates to the vehicle lock, where there were yet more delays while paperwork was checked. Eventually, Jean was ushered off the van with a load of other women, most of whom seemed to be accepting their fate rather more readily that she was.

The women were loud, and weren't obviously fazed by the female prison officers who were barking orders at them in order to begin the reception process. Lined up in a queue now they presented their outstretched wrists, without being prompted, for one of the officers to remove their handcuffs, before being directed into a separate area where each one was searched, their personal belongings catalogued and put into storage.

This new and unwelcome world filled Jean with fear and apprehension and as she attempted to gain some reassurance, so the situation just got worse.

"How long will I be here?" she asked as the cuffs were removed.

"Until you go to Court again." came the reply.

"When will that be?" she persisted.

"They must have told you that today. Your solicitor must have discussed things with you before you came here."

"I told him I didn't want to see him, so he went."

"Listen, Phillips," The officer made some attempt at explanation. "This is the reception area, if you want to ask questions, wait until you get to the wing. But if it's any help, you're here on remand pending reports, and that's usually at least 4 weeks. Next."

Jean attempted to continue the conversation, but to no avail as the officer was now busying herself removing the next set of handcuffs.

"In here please," Another officer. A smaller room with a desk and two officers.

"Take your clothes off and put them over there."

"Why… I don't need to be searched. Why?"

"Just do it, Phillips. It's procedure. Everyone has it done." There was no tone of conciliation or sympathy in the officer's voice, just mild irritation at being delayed in her task.

She removed her clothes slowly and put them in a pile as she was told. One officer went through each item of clothing one by one, whilst the other carried out a more intimate search and Jean felt, not for the first time, the sting of tears welling up in her eyes as the indignity just went on and on.

Once dressed, she was photographed her possessions removed and signed for and then taken to sit in front of the prison doctor, for what was, in the very loosest sense of the term, a medical. Finally she was put into a locked waiting area with the other women who had similarly been processed and instantly she became the object of their curiosity.

"What didn't you do?!" The sarcasm was reflective of a humour tinged with cynicism rather than anything more malicious.

Jean looked around and made eye contact with a young girl in her mid-twenties with long dark hair. She was sitting on the bench opposite and was leaning forward with her arms folded and tucked across her stomach as though she was cold. By the look of her eyes, she was expecting an answer.

"I… I had a fight with my husband and he… he got… I mean… I hurt him." Jean managed to stutter her way through the reply.

"How exactly do you mean?" The follow up question was inevitable and Jean was aware of all the women in the room waiting for her to give some more detail.

"I stabbed him."

Clapping and whooping from three or four of the women including the original enquirer, but as they noticed Jean averting her eyes and apparently becoming upset, they quietened down and the girl with the long hair moved over to Jean and put an arm round her shoulder in an attempt to comfort her.

"What's your name honey?"

Jean managed to splutter her name through her tears and was rewarded with a reciprocated disclosure.

"I'm Sandy… you alright now?"

Jean nodded and in the absence of anything more appropriate, wiped her nose on her sleeve.

"Did you kill 'im?"

Jean shook her head and realising she was in a room with women who would appreciate her gesture, followed it up with "worse luck" and sure enough, earned the verbal approval of all those present. This was obviously the ice-breaker as brief introductions followed and Jean learned that she was sharing the space with mainly shoplifters and prostitutes, but much to her surprise, she felt, for the first time that day, more at ease.

"You got kids? I've got a kid. Me Mum's got him while I'm in 'ere… What about you?"

There just wasn't an answer. Not a simple answer anyway. Not one that even went a fraction of the way to describing what was going on in her mind in response to the word "kids". She just stared back and felt her insides churn at the thought losing them. All she was capable of doing at that moment was to nod dumbly and mumble, "Two… boy and a girl… "

Sandy's arm tightened around Jean's shoulder in an attempt to further console her and her eyes searched the room for some form of assistance in the task. Some looked down, one or two others chipped in with "They'll be alright luv" and similar comments. But Jean knew what she knew and couldn't even begin to explain why things simply wouldn't "be alright".

The group of women were spared the necessity to further exercise their reluctant counselling skills by the loud unlocking of the cell door and the instruction, by one of the officers, to move out. On their way out they were issued with their bedding and led through countless locking and unlocking of iron gates, down grim cell lined passageways, eventually beginning to lose one or two of their number every few yards as they reached their allocated cells.

The officer in front of her stopped and turned to face her, whilst at the same time extending her left arm into the open cell door.

"In here, Phillips... Dawson... you've got a new cellmate... show her the ropes... it's her first time."

There was no response from the overweight mass on the top bunk. Not even a shift of position to acknowledge the newcomer.

When Jean turned round to look, the officer was gone, taking what was left of the straggly band of new inmates with her. Jean looked around her, but it really didn't take more than a few seconds. The cell was about ten feet deep and eight or nine feet wide, but the bunks up against the left hand wall took up nearly half the space. On the right side of the cell were a small table and two wooden chairs. Straight ahead of her was a small barred window, about six feet from the ground. The walls were brown Victorian tiles from the floor to mid-way up the wall where they appeared to lose interest and give in to the dull, chipped, green painted brickwork.

And then there was the smell. Feet and stale cigarette smoke, plus a few other indefinable.

"Are you just goin' to stand there like a fuckin' idiot?" The overweight body on the top bunk still lying on her side facing the wall, spoke for the first time. "Do you smoke?"

"No... No I don't." Was that a polite enquiry or did she want one?

"Well I do, so you'll 'ave to fuckin' well put up with it. The last stupid cow complained 'cause she 'ad" (and here she attempted to emulate what she obviously considered to be a refined accent) "a very bad chest that is made so much worse by tobacco smoke"... fuck 'er!"

"It really doesn't bother me." Jean lied as well as she could.

"All the same if it does." and with this she turned onto her back and accompanied the move with a conspicuously loud fart for good measure.

"I'm Dora... do you snore? I hate fuckin' snorers."

"No... Well, I don't think so anyway."

"Don't you fuckin' know?!" But it really wasn't a question that demanded an answer.

Jean put her bundle of bedclothes and provisions onto the lower bunk and sat down next to it, her hands resting on her knees and looked around again, but it didn't get any better.

"Telly's on downstairs til nine... go an' get yer dinner in about ten minutes... it's fuckin' shit, but it's 'ot... 'bout all you can say for it."

Jean took these comments as either an unwarranted olive branch or a formal orientation to prison routine, or both, and managed a "Cheers, Dora" in acknowledgement and was rewarded with a grunt in response.

Julie would be at her parent's house now, having her dinner. It was Friday. They always had boiled eggs and bread and butter on Fridays, because they always spent Friday afternoon's up the High Street, since Dad retired and didn't want to cook when they got home in the afternoon.

Then her thoughts raced into panic and guilt. "I'm... not... there... for my little girl. She'll wonder where I am... She'll miss waking up at home and helping me with the shopping tomorrow... What are they going to tell her? How her evil mum tried to kill her Dad... Is that what they'll say?" The pain was more than she'd ever had to endure in her life. It was all engulfing and unbearable, and the thoughts didn't just come into her head once or twice, that would have been too easy. Instead they lurked until the beginnings of reason could be felt before returning with a vengeance. Reason gave up the fight, so she was left with its unsavoury alternative.

She couldn't dismiss it; couldn't turn her thoughts to other things because nothing else mattered. She just kept playing it back, almost as though the hurt was irresistible. So she pondered. Not a reasoning type of pondering, but more the sort of pondering that destroys... a malignant pondering that just wouldn't respond to any form of logic that would offer any respite from its inevitable destination.

And William. What about William. He hadn't been right for so long... well over a year now, and what did she do about it... one bloody visit to the Doctor and that was it... and then she did her usual... hid it because she knew everyone would say that it was her fault... her fault for marrying that bastard... her fault for staying with him... her fault for being a rotten bloody mother... her fault for not knowing what to do and now... and now her family was in bits, her son had been committed to a looney bin... her daughter would believe her mother was an evil murdering bitch who had deserted her... and that's always assuming she can even remember

101

who her mother was after being in prison for years.

And because of what?

Jean fucking Phillips. That's what. The guilt and fear went through her like spikes, tearing at her insides. There was no way out… she was guilty, she'd already admitted that, all they needed to know was how many years she was going to get, then they might just as well throw away the key and forget about her. How many years of turmoil, how many years away from her children? She wouldn't let them come and see her here. The thought was unbearable. They'll never want to see her again. Mum and Dad won't even be alive by the time she gets out. Life as she knew it had ended and there was no way back.

Humiliation, loneliness, guilt: they all rolled into one. No way out. No resolution. No hope.

She lost track of time for a while, during which a strange calmness came over her, a calmness that only came when conclusions have been reached, when actions can, albeit incompletely, be planned and when uncertainty has been removed. The tears were no more, the resolution was complete, as if out of thin air… and so obvious… so very obvious… just a couple of bits missing, but that would come.

She felt the bunk above her head move violently and two stinking feet appeared next to her left shoulder. Dora jumped down, put on a pair of plimsolls and looked over her shoulder at her new and unwelcome cellmate.

"You coming to get to get fed." but she didn't wait for a reply before she waddled out of the cell door and down to the communal area.

Jean sat and returned to her new found ponderings… the ponderings that were now far from depressing, just irresistible and inevitable and in a strange way comforting. She felt as though she didn't need to worry about anything anymore. Not even her children… they were safe. They weren't her responsibility any more, she'd forfeited that privilege.

As she sat on her bunk, Jean could hear the clatter of meal time paraphernalia and the voices of what seemed to be hundreds of women coming from somewhere outside the cell. Somehow though, despite its volume and what should have been its obtrusiveness, the goings on in the dining area seemed safely distant from her, not part of her world, somehow detached. Her body seemed to be in a sort of slow motion, as though every muscle had not only relaxed, but were also unwilling to give her any significant help in doing anything. She felt as though she just wanted to sit and stare and do little else. Even thinking was off the agenda.

"Phillips," One of the officers was standing at her cell door, and although Jean could hear her, she didn't immediately think that the name being called had anything to do with her.

"Phillips, go and get your meal."

Jean finally looked up and stared at the officer. "Yes, I will, thank you." With that, she got up and slowly followed the officer along the metal gangway and stairs and down to where it seemed that countless women were sat on long benches set at equally long tables. The noise was deafening and briefly Jean wondered how it was possible to do any eating and drinking and make that much noise at the same time. The thought somehow amused her and she found herself almost laughing at the silliness of it.

She turned to her left and saw a long line of equally vociferous women queuing up for their food and after staring absently at them for a couple of minutes, joined the women who had obviously eaten all they needed and had spoken all they wanted to and were now returning along the various gangways and stairs to their various cells.

Somehow, although she couldn't remember making a conscious effort to remember her cell number, or even its route to the dining area, Jean managed to find her way back without any difficulty and resumed her position on her bunk. Her cellmate, she guessed, would be one of those women downstairs that would probably be eating and talking more than most, so she would probably be on her own for some time. Not that it was any particular importance, but she appreciated the fact that she didn't have to try and be pleasant towards people that she didn't particularly wish to be pleasant to.

She stared. And as she stared into that numbing space commonly known as thin air, her muscles once again relaxed and she was once again able to sink into a nothingness where the world of the last couple of days couldn't intrude and she found herself fleeting in and out of the most stupid and inane thoughts. When was the last time they painted the walls... they could do with another lick of paint... Did they have other colours? This table could do with a bit of a scrub...

Her thoughts, although changing and flitting, couldn't seem to go any deeper, as though the trivia was safeguarding her brain from thinking about home or even her children. But of course, such an analysis was rapidly becoming out of bounds to her and nothing was preventing it more that her own defences which had presented her with such clear, but as yet incomplete resolutions that, even so, were her greatest source of comfort.

She allowed herself to summarise without going to the effort of trying to work out what or who exactly would be alright. She was content with her ridiculously incomplete conclusion that everything would be OK. She returned to her musings, and as she did, she turned her attention to the pile of kit that had been issued to her in the reception area and with her right hand still slumped in apparent lethargy and resting on her knee, slowly picked her way through it with her left hand.

How many times has that towel been through the wash? They have to be so careful in places like this, boil them probably, that's why they feel so rough. Not rinsed properly either.

She carried on slowly rifling through the pile and pick up the bar of soap and raised it to her nose, sniffed and returned it to the pile as she recognised the smell of soap that her mother used to clean her father's shirt collars. She picked up the toothpaste, which rather unimaginatively had "toothpaste" written on it. Jean opened it and wasn't altogether surprised to find that it didn't have any stripes on it, smelled of mint and was white. She replaced the cap and put it down again.

As she got to the pile of bedclothes, she wondered if anyone had ever asked for a second blanket or pillow and her thought was rewarded with a picture of a scene from "Oliver" only this time Oliver was a woman prisoner asking for more bedding. She grinned to herself at the absurdity of the picture and continued her slow and deliberate exploration.

She picked up the roll of toilet paper, the type that scratches your arse and doubles (always assuming it hasn't been used for anything else) as tracing paper for the kids. She put it down with a little disdain but no particular surprise at its inclusion as "prison issue".

Jean turned her attention to the last two objects. As she picked up the white plastic toothbrush she found herself thinking how crazy it was that you could go out and commit the most dreadful crime and the prison authorities were worried about whether you could clean your teeth or not! Just how stupid was that? But as she held the toothbrush she realised that prison had given her some help with a quite separate problem. She carried on fingering the cheap plastic and mused about its qualities, its suitability for purpose, and its usefulness for all sorts of things and found herself inwardly smiling at the possibility of the last piece of her very personal jigsaw being in her hands.

She put the toothbrush down as though it was made of porcelain and set about exploring the final object. A black plastic comb made of equally cheap plastic, but to Jean it was so much more. It was God given, another justification for her own thoughts and the path that she must tread. As with the toothbrush, she ran her fingers up and down its length before returning it to rest next to its plastic soul mate.

Outside the cell the clatter of enamel mugs and metal plates continued to compete with the incessant chatter and now this was joined by the sound of moving benches against concrete floors and the television being switched on. But still she sat and stared at the wall, before once again reaching over to pick up the toothbrush. She ran her fingers almost remotely along its stem before she gripped it with both hands and sharply snapped it in half. She looked down at her handiwork. The toothbrush had broken clean into two halves, with the edges of each broken piece being almost flat and square. She looked and stared before carefully putting the pieces down and picking up the plastic comb. She repeated the operation again, culminating in a similarly broken comb. This time, however, she examined the damaged edges with appreciably more satisfaction before putting the pieces carefully in her pocket.

It was as though she felt that she could now continue to carry on with the solitary domestic chore which she needed to do in the cell, namely making up her bunk ready for the night. This she did with care and a degree of disproportionate precision, before sitting down again. This time to wait.

June 19th 1974; 20:30 hrs

George came downstairs to what was sure to be a discussion that no parent ever wishes to have. Certainly, he didn't pretend to know how to cope with the situation, but he knew that his wife would expect some sort of wisdom to be forthcoming. That was fine, but he also knew that whatever decisions they reached, it would be wrong for someone they loved and at this moment, he would rather that things just drifted along for a while, preferably without him having to make any decisions.

"Is Julie asleep yet?"

"No, not yet." he lied to buy himself a little more time knowing his wife wouldn't say anything until she could be certain that their granddaughter wouldn't be able to overhear the conversation.

"She must be asleep by now; you were up there for ages with her."

"You can go and check if you like." George figured that a couple of minutes would be better than nothing.

It was less than two minutes by the time his wife Irene re-entered the dining room with the not unexpected news. "She's snoring her head off!"

"Really?"

Irene picked up the cups of tea that she had made and handed one to her husband, now firmly ensconced in his chair and busy opening his third packet of cigarettes of the day.

"Yes really!"

Irene closed the dining room door and sat opposite her husband.

"Tell me again, exactly what Mr Sterling said to you when you rang this afternoon."

"He said that Jean had got hysterical at the Magistrates Court when they told her that she'd be remanded in custody while they get her looked at by a psychiatrist, or something like that anyway."

"And you say that he thinks that she'll be in prison for a couple of months?"

"No… he said about a month," George corrected his wife who was renowned for her ability to expand a problem to at least double its size.

"Even so… " And that part of Irene's sentence was left unfinished, as she really wanted to get to grips with the next bit. "And what happens if she's found guilty?"

George slowed his speech, lent forward in his chair. "My dear, there is no "if" to it. She has already confessed, and half the block of flats," (by which George meant Doris and Sid Brownlow) "saw her do it! Of course she'll be found bloody guilty!"

"There's no need to swear, George… I only want to get the picture right in my own mind."

"Yes, I know, I'm sorry." George apologised more to prevent further repercussions of being impatient rather than out of genuine regret. "Anyway, Mr Sterling has said that he may have something to work with if he can find evidence to support her statement. He wouldn't go into detail, obviously, but he indicated that if he could prove that she was provoked, then a Judge would be more lenient. Of course another alternative would be to prove that she was of a disturbed mind when she did it." George knew the response the last statement would get and was not disappointed.

"So if he can prove that our daughter's is as big a nutcase as her son, then all will be OK. Is that what you're trying to say?"

"Darling, I'm not trying to say anything. I'm just repeating what Mr Sterling said to me. Anyway to answer your question, if none of that works, she could get up to three years and obviously, the authorities would need to decide what would be best for Julie." And with this he raised his eyebrows and looked his wife in the eye, at least satisfied that he'd now broached the subject.

"I don't know what to tell the poor kid now… as it is, I had to pick her up from Heather's because she'd worked herself up into a state… God alone knows what she'll be like if they decide to put her into care. " Irene went quiet, as though trying to search for alternatives, but all that came were tears.

"I won't let them take her… I won't." The sobbing bordered on hysteria as Irene had, in her mind, her granddaughter taken into care and adopted.

George went to her side and knelt as he put his arm around her and was his usual down to earth person that she loved (and sometimes hated) so much.

"You're getting ahead of yourself a bit aren't you, old girl? She'll probably be back in a few weeks and we can sort things out from there. Sterling seems like a decent sort. I'm sure that he'll do the job."

Irene nodded through the sobs and blew her nose on her husband's handkerchief which he kept readily available for such occasions and as a sign that things could be resolved, he went to make another cup of tea and remained completely unconvinced that anything apart from a disastrous outcome would be possible.

Who on earth would let a woman who had tried to kill her husband ever have her kids back?

Who would believe her stories about David, particularly when there was no-one to back up her account of their life together? She hadn't even told her own parents (and that hurt more than anything).

And what about William? What the bloody hell had happened there? Was he on something and she'd protected him? In any case she should have insisted on something being done a lot sooner. Not the sort of motherly behaviour that the authorities would be impressed by. He mused about his daughter's possible motive for not taking more action than she had "I thought he was just being a teenager" or perhaps "I couldn't face people knowing that my son is in an asylum" or even "I thought it would go away on its own". George mentally reproached himself for even thinking that his daughter would have said such things, even to herself.

But he knew that other people would think the same as he had done and wouldn't be so willing to talk themselves into a more reasonable explanation.

January 19th 1974; 22:45 hrs

Dora had returned to the cell nearly ninety minutes earlier, had made her entrance with her usual blend of swearing, farting and fag smoke and had retired to the upper bunk for a well-earned rest following her latest bout of flatulence and active avoidance of all social graces. Lights out had been 45 minutes earlier, half an hour after an officer had locked the cell door and Jean was now lying, wide awake on the lower bunk.

Still waiting, listening.

Outside, she could hear the sound of footsteps on the iron stairwells and landings and the daunting sound of observation hatches being systematically opened and shut on each cell door in turn. In her mind's eye she could visualise an officer making her way towards the cell she was occupying. The progress seemed so painfully slow and several times Jean thought that the observation hatch on her cell door would be the next to open, but had been mistaken and then had to change her visualisation of the officers progress to take account of her error.

As it turned out, Jean found herself unable to predict the event at all, so that when the hatch did eventually open, it almost came as a shock. The suddenness and the lack of care with which it was shut jolted her system but as the footsteps moved away from the door she returned to her almost mesmerized state of concentration.

Counting seconds.

Turning seconds into minutes.

Calculating.

Nearly, so very nearly correct. She had counted 3,423 seconds, just over 57minutes, before she heard the rhythmic sound of footsteps approaching and the hatches being opened and closed (this time with more care). Nearly an hour between rounds. But could she depend on it?

She started counting again; starting at ten seconds to account for the time it had taken her to readjust her thoughts back into counting mode. Outside she could hear someone coughing, someone cursing at her cellmate for snoring, but little else. Inside her own cell, she was being serenaded by Dora's presumably deniable snoring and grunting.

Five hundred and sixty one, five hundred and sixty two... still she counted.

The echo of a cell door banging shut and the jangle of keys somewhere in the distance.

Six hundred and twenty six, six hundred and twenty seven, and counting.

The snoring from the bunk above was reaching almost biblical proportions. Just right. In fact, perfect.

Seven hundred, eight hundred... still counting.

Her counting seemed to maintain its minor inaccuracy, as around fifty seven minutes from when the observation hatch last closed, the sound of footsteps could be heard again. One minute and four and a half minutes later, the next round started.

The conclusion was not a remarkable one to arrive at, but it gave Jean a certain amount of satisfaction. The rounds were carried out every hour and were more or less predictable. That was comforting to know.

It must have been three hours since she had started counting, so she calculated, it must be around one o'clock in the morning by now. She reached to her right side where she had placed both the broken comb and toothbrush under the blanket.

Still the constant snoring from the bunk above.

Slowly and deliberately and without diverting her gaze to the objects of her attention, she felt the sharp edges of the broken implements with a degree of satisfaction. Feeling them in turn, comparing them in turn, judging and calculating in her own mind their suitability for the purpose which she intended them for.

As she felt the edges, she found herself forming a more precise plan of action. A greater guarantee of success. Failure would be unthinkable, unbearable, humiliating. She had to succeed. First time, no doubt about it, it had to be at the first attempt or not at all,

Again she fingered the edges. They weren't as sharp as you'd expect a knife to be, they were just sharp. Quite good enough for piercing, but not for splicing through anything. You'd need a knife for that.

Piercing. That should do the trick as long as she didn't try to splice anything. That should work OK. As long as she didn't try and cut in the traditional sense of the word. This would need to be more of a digging and opening, but she could see that speed was going be important need to be lengthways, not across. Across wouldn't work, even if that was the way everyone used.

Holding the broken plastic in the palm of her right hand, she extended her index finger to caress her left hand, then her arm, and lastly and with most attention, her wrist. The exercise was not without its frustrations and after a minute or so, she laid the fragments of plastic on her stomach allowing more fingers to be freed up to carry out their task.

The extra deployment did the trick and she found what she was searching for. She spent some time moving her fingers around the object of her exploration before she was satisfied that she knew, almost without thinking, its location, its extent, its feel and indeed its very predictability.

Very satisfying, but a tinge of sorrow. Can't be helped. Everything's gone too far. A life in this place, a life or tortured thoughts. A life without her kids.

She could see Julie. She could see William and I her mind she knew that would be the only place she would be able to see them… ever.

And in her mind.

Her senses seemed to be aware of everything at once. The smell of the prison, the distant echoes of iron gates being shut, and bunches of keys jangling for attention on heavy duty key rings as one of their number was selected for their only task in life… to turn a lock… to incarcerate people.

She shuddered at the mere thought of this existence, this alternative existence.

She listened to distant footsteps, now knowing that they were not due to tread the gangway outside her cell for at least another fifty minutes or so, but it really didn't matter that much… they wouldn't be able to see anything anyway.

And when they did finally get to see anything, it would be too late.

Once again she extended her fingers to her left wrist, but this time without fumbling, and without any hesitation they found their target. First time.

Now she could retrieve the shards of plastic, safe in the knowledge that

110

she wouldn't need to put them down again before her goal was achieved, or she failed utterly and condemned herself to a life of living misery in this place, being watched every minute… just in case.

But that wouldn't happen. She wouldn't let it happen.

July 20th 1974; 11:50 hrs

His knowledge of his location continued to fluctuate and as he struggled to orientate himself, so the confusion increased. One thing was certain, although not to William and that was the greater the unfamiliarity of the surroundings, the more disjointed his thought processes became.

At home, at school, at his Uncle Bill's house… bits of all these places but bits of none of them. It seemed that he had only just arrived at this place, but that he'd been there for as long as he could remember. Bits of memory once again became as one with current perceptions. Past thoughts and sensations were being resurrected by things that he could see and hear now and on their journey through his disordered thoughts, violated the barriers between past and present. The real and imagined became indistinguishable from each other, resolved and given meaning only through his own paranoia and hallucinations.

The smell though, that wasn't familiar, but the longer he sat there the less he noticed it. It was like watching a film, and the film could be part of his world and he knew that he could even choose to enter the film.

He knew that, because he had already entered the film, somehow… but he didn't have a clue as to how to leave and just to make things worse, he knew that it shouldn't be real… but it was. All too real, and he was inside it… living it.

Everything around William confirmed the danger he felt himself to be in. All around him were signs of alien activity, of covert messages being transmitted and his captors conspiring to mentally torture their charges. All around him, where once he would have seen objects and things for what they appeared to be, now he saw conspiracy and fear in everything he looked at, felt and heard.

But worst of all, were those that wore the white tunics. And their leader, the older one in the suit. What had they done to these people? Was the human garbage that he saw drooling, smoking and shuffling around incessantly, the results of their fumbling attempts at brainwashing that had gone badly wrong?

"The same will happen to you, William." Jack was, as usual, uncompromising in his opinions.

But what would happen? Again William experienced the fear without the coherent thoughts of just a few moments earlier. He couldn't work out where he was, although in the back of his mind, wherever that was, he had some form of recollection of being brought there.

But he knew things. He realised that much. He realised things that he wasn't supposed to know. Things that were forbidden to even think about. And it had something to do with this lot, this bunch of aliens. That was it! They were aliens!

But his homework, what had it to do with his homework. Uncle Bill thought he was quite bright, but the holiday chalet was so cold at night. He hadn't been right about that.

Again his thoughts jumped and flitted, defying all attempts or desire for continuity.

And then his attention was wrenched into focus by a raised voice somewhere to his left.

"Go and fuckin' drool over someone else, for Christ's sake!"

He turned to try and locate the cause of the disturbance. It didn't take long to find it, as his eyes were drawn to a scene being played out by the office door.

The one they called "Dave" was in the process of pushing the old man Tom, away from him and as a result, Tom was sent reeling to the floor. The look of utter disgust on Dave's face left William stunned, even in his disorientated state of mind.

Anyone could see that Tom could barely shuffle from one chair to the next at the best of times and as William watched in horror as he hit the floor, it struck him that cruelty was cruelty, whether it came from an alien or human. The distinction was irrelevant.

William continued to watch as Dave stepped over the prostrate Tom, who now had the almost comic appearance of an upturned tortoise, but even this view of his obviously distressed charge escaped Dave's notice as he made his point to a small gaggle of three highly amused white coated staff over by one of the windows. "Dirty git dribbled all down my fuckin' coat!" And then, looking back at the still struggling Tom. "Filthy bastard."

Laughter.

"They're not human. Humans don't do that." Jack stated the obvious, but William was unable to focus on the "ins and outs" of who was what. He was only aware of what was wrong.

And this was wrong.

Unwittingly, he drew his knees up underneath his body and once again recommenced his rocking, as he always did when he felt scared or threatened. But this time, it just drew attention to himself and that from a quarter where attention was most certainly unwelcome.

Morgan was stood in the doorway to his office, observing his kingdom with some degree of satisfaction and amusement.

"Seems like you've set Mr Phillips off again, Dave." Nodding his head towards William.

It raised a few smiles, but that was all, so Morgan decided to further provoke the ward's latest floorshow, sauntered over to where William was sitting and stared down at him.

"Mummy not been in to see you today, Billy."

William stiffened at the name and mention of his mother.

Morgan looked over to the two male nurses who were sat at a table a few yards behind where William was sitting.

"Mother's as fucking mad as he is." At this William made an attempt to jump out of the chair, but Morgan pre-empted him and with a hand on his shoulder, pushed him back into the chair. To add to the contemptuous act, Morgan didn't even take his eyes away from the direction of his colleagues to look at William. He carried on his carefully contrived speech.

"Runs in the family, you know. Mummy decided to stick a knife into his old man. In the nick, isn't she Billy?"

William made another attempt to get up, but the restraining hand remained. Morgan's audience, in the meantime, sat up and took notice at what was quite obviously some welcome gossip to lighten their day, while Morgan himself continued his performance but looking down at William, this time and ensuring that he was in a position to maintain eye contact with him, sarcastically feigned shock and remorse.

"Oh, I'm so sorry, Bil… I mean William. That must have slipped out! I don't think I was supposed to tell you about your dear "Mummy"… never mind." He patted William on the shoulder and walked back to his office, his face engulfed in a smug grin.

William's head began to reel even more. He couldn't do anything with the information about his Mother. It was a lie; she would come, if they let her. But if he could stop the messages, if he could just work out why the stairs at the end of the dayroom only went up, but didn't seem to come down. Uncle bill would tell them. Why didn't that Green Line bus stop at Leigh any more. The toy bricks were not enough, not enough to build a bridge, so he couldn't get out.

He looked around. It was lunch time and he was being told to queue for his medicines. Medicines that would clear out his brain and replace his thoughts with alien ones.

William got up and queued and shuffled behind the other men as they gradually had their turn at the pink medicine. As he shuffled, he looked over to the table where they were dishing up the lunches and saw Dave carry the enormous steaming metal teapot, minus its lid, to the table and proceed to pour in a pint of milk and a cupful of sugar, stir it and replace the lid.

Jack had something to say about that. "They can't let people choose… it spoils the brainwashing!"

The queue got nearer to the medicine trolley and William focussed on the other men taking their pink medicine without question. He knew that after lunchtime he would need to go to the shops to buy some spam for his father's sandwiches to take to work, but he had to change these clothes. He couldn't remember where they came from, or why he was wearing them. Someone else's. That was it. His turn for the pink medicine. He took it without question. Without knowing why he'd taken it without question. Time to join the next queue. This time for lunch. He felt safer in a queue even though he didn't want to be in one.

Jack didn't say much about the queues. It was if they were the only thing that William could cope with independently of Jack and something about that gave him a sort of quiet satisfaction. But the queues soon dissolved and William was left to take his meal back to a table. Charlie, a tall, grey and unshaven man of about forty was occupying the only table that had any spare chairs, so William was left with little option other than to gain a mealtime companion.

"You a soldier?" The question from Charlie came as a surprise.

"Eh, no." William was at least certain of that.

"I'm a soldier." Charlie seemed as though he really didn't need to engage in any conversation, he'd carry on talking, regardless. "I'm on sick leave.

Injured." Charlie's voice lowered. "Got to get back to my lads," he looked around to make sure that no-one was listening. "They can't do without me, but the CO here," Nodding towards the office, "…says I've got to stay until fully recovered." This time, Charlie took a large mouthful of food from his plate, obviously content in the belief that he'd got his point across to a likeminded soul.

But of course, he hadn't.

Instead, his audience of one became re-engulfed in his own paranoid and deluded perceptions, aided and abetted by his constant yet persistently unseen companion.

"*He's mad. Completely bloody mad. They've made him insane with their machines. Their brainwashing. That's what's done it. That's what they want to do to you. That's what they've done to your family. You're next, William.*" Jack seemed to be almost enthusiastic in his warning.

Charlie had started talking again, but Jack was far more compelling… far more urgent, so Charlie took a back seat as far as William's attention was concerned. He had to go, to leave this place. To go home. Home was in the next room and he thought he could smell his Grandpa's cigarette… he must be here, wasn't this the factory where his Dad worked? But it was a restroom in the factory? He'd be out in a minute when he'd finished his tea. They've got Mum, he knew that. The bus was due, but he had to make sure he got on the bus with the right number, otherwise he'd never get to school and then he'd be in trouble.

"*You've got to make your move; you've got to go before they take your brain.*" Jack was in the familiar territory of giving William yet another irresistible command.

"Of course they've hidden my uniform. Must find it." Charlie was well and truly talking to himself now and William was looking around him, at the sight of mealtime. The sight was not a pleasant one.

Everywhere he looked, he could see tables of men busily engaged in feeding themselves, bent over their plates and shovelling the food into their mouths without ceremony and certainly without care. Much of it ended up decorating various parts of their faces, chins, shirts and surrounding surfaces, with some falling to the floor via one piece or other of their clothing. There seemed to be little attempt to clear it away; save for the occasional sleeve that was pressed into service to wipe the odd mouth here and there. Only their slurping of the sweet milky tea, somehow made to sound even worse by being drank from chipped enamel mugs, interrupted the disgusting spectacle that was mealtime.

All around, in what doubled as a dayroom and dining area, was the sound of cutlery and plates, as well as the occasional comments from the group of men who had served up the meal that had remained standing and talking to each other by the long table that had been put outside the office.

"You dirty bugger, Tom. Wipe your mouth, for Christ's sake!"

"Henry… Henry!" No response, so Dave made his way over to his table in order to make his point. "Henry, get away from Richard's plate. Eat your own bloody food!"

The scene got even worse with the pudding, which was some form of jam sponge with custard. Like the first course, only some of it ended up in the place it was supposed to go, with the remainder causing even more mayhem than the rest of the meal had done.

On a couple of the other tables, rather less lunchtime debauchery was going on, with some semblance of table manners being exhibited, but no matter where William looked, one thing stood out more than anything else, even to his confused mind.

No one was having conversations.

In fact, it appeared to William that the brief exchange with Charlie that he had been involved with, was for this place, unusual in the extreme and indeed, the one thing that cut through the mess that was William's thoughts was the all engulfing feeling of isolation.

But without conversation or direction, the inmates all seemed to know when to move and where to move to and even what to do when they got there. As the men finished their meals, none of them remained seated. They all picked up their plates and cups and one by one, moved towards to the serving table at the front, which had now been adorned with a plastic bucket and a bowl. As the men approached the table, they formed a queue, almost by instinct and tipped the remnants of their meal into the bucket, deposited their cutlery into the bowl and their plates onto the growing pile of other plates, before collecting another mugful of the milky tea from the battered metal teapot.

But their almost robotic behaviour went on for a bit longer. Once they had finished their clearing up duties, they kept moving towards one of the other white coated men that had dished up the lunch. This time though, it wasn't food or medications that were being doled out, but something far more important.

Cigarettes!

William could see the now familiar white and red packets of Players No 10 cigarettes on the table. They were being given out, one cigarette at a time, to each person in the shuffling queue of addicts… given out, almost in silence and being held between dark brown tobacco stained fingers before being lit, this being the signal for the now replenished smokers, to leave the queue and find a corner to retreat into.

William could make little sense of what he was looking at and could make even less sense of where he was and the reasons for why he was there. But he did recognise the simple lack of human warmth, the lack of interaction, but most of all he felt fearful of those who wore the white tunics or the grey suits. They appeared to be in control, to have power over the others and that, apparently for no one's benefit except their own.

In short, he felt scared. And that was not good, because whenever that happened, Jack was quick to add his commentary and give his orders.

"They've got no brains left, William. They've had everything taken away. That's what's going to happen to you… you've got to get out, William. Get out!"

He felt scared… so scared. He surveyed the scene around him and fixed his stare on a door over to his left where he had observed people entering and leaving. Slowly, he got up and began to wander, looking around him all the time.

He couldn't risk being caught. He was going home. He was going to see his mother. He was going to see Julie. His sister, Julie! What had happened to Julie? Why was he prevented from thinking about Julie? He hadn't thought about Julie. Someone must be stopping him from thinking about her. They must have got her as well. That's how they can do it. They get inside someone's brain and tune in… and that blocks anyone from thinking about them… and so everyone forgets about them. Then they go on to the next one… and the next one and then they dump what's left in this place.

But William was still strong and he knew the tricks they were up to. Very clever… very clever indeed… but he was up to it. He could beat it, with Jacks help, he could beat it… he just had to get out of here… wherever "here" was.

He continued to wander, seemingly without purpose, but all the time with the door in mind. No-one would bother him. He knew that much.

They only bothered you when they wanted a cigarette. Still he wandered. Still looking around him.

He was there. At the door. He just had to go through the door and he'd be free. Slowly and deliberately he put his hands to the door to push it open. Both hands now.

Locked!

"I wouldn't do that if I were you, Billy boy." Morgan's voice brought him to the stark realisation that he had dropped his guard to concentrate on the door and now he had been caught. Morgan was just a few yards away and stood with his arms crossed and a humourless grin on his face. The rest of his staff were at least sixty or seventy feet away, oblivious to the scene that was about to be played out and certainly unable to hear Morgan's comments.

"Did we have a few dodgy ciggies... eh? Did one of your little friends give you some tasty blotting paper to suck on... eh...? Well, did they, Billy Boy? And poor little Billy couldn't cope with it, was that it?" Morgan's voice was full of contempt and sarcasm, but William was still standing in front of the door, his hands on the handle and at least to anyone who was watching, not rising to the bait.

But Jack was responding and while he was responding, William was listening.

"Fucking arsehole... he's saying you're on drugs... that's his excuse for bringing you here!"

"Thought Mummy could take you to the doctor to make your poorly head all better? Is that it Billy?" Morgan was calculating in his sarcasm, building the tension with every word.

"Fucking bastard's got Mum and Julie... Now he wants you... he wants your brain, William... do you hear me? He's destroyed your world and now he wants you... just look at him... smug bastard!!"

"Go on Billy boy... try the door again," Morgan's mock encouragement had the desired effect and William rattled the door again.

Jack was still aiming his abuse towards Morgan, but his words were beginning to fuse together and take a back seat to his own feelings of contempt and hatred towards this man. His thoughts, although disorganised in time and space, were becoming focussed and concentrated by the sheer hatred of the smug, lying murdering bastard before him.

He stopped rattling the door, but kept his hands where they were and his

118

eyes firmly fixed on Morgan.

And as Morgan looked back there was just the beginning of fear in his eyes. A fear that was born out of the realisation that he had pushed too far and the sort of fear that only a coward experiences.

In William's eyes however, there was only intent and rage and although the silent exchange only lasted a matter of seconds, it was enough to convey the gist of the situation, but too brief for Morgan to avoid the consequences.

Morgan fell backwards over a chair with William's hands firmly gripping his neck and the noise of crashing furniture along with Morgan's attempts to call for help, produced the predictable rush of white coated figures to the scene.

Hands grabbed at William from every angle and wrenched him away from Morgan's neck. In an instant, he found himself being pinned down on his back, arms and legs immobilised, but it didn't stop him from struggling and spitting at his human restrainers.

"Someone grab his bloody head!" The cry from one of the men that had got in the way of his phlegm. His head was grabbed and held and at the same time he felt his trousers being yanked off... and then his balls being grabbed through the fabric of his underpants and twisted until he felt a sharp pain.

His violent and intentional contortions and spitting ceased suddenly as he felt the hand slowly twisting and pulling at his scrotal sack. Laughter around him. The act of inflicting pain in this way certainly caused some amusement... but William wasn't laughing.

"Are we going to be a good boy, now?!" Morgan again.

William stayed absolutely stock still... again isolated laughter.

The hand was removed from his scrotum and the hands that were holding his head and limbs melted away and, as if on cue, the door unlocked and in walked Dr Sellman. He was confronted with a scene that spoke for itself and immediately turned and looked quizzically in Morgan's direction, who in response to the unspoken question, through his arms out and with a spectacularly unconvincing explanation, announced. "He just went for me for no reason!"

All eyes settled on Sellman, waiting for the next part of the dialogue, but instead, he just looked down and waited for the crowd, including William to melt away. When he and Morgan were the only two left at the scene,

Sellman asked his question:

"Well, what did you say to him? What started it off?"

"As I said, he just went for me." Morgan's eye contact was just a little bit too convincing and after a few seconds of silence, Sellman turned on his heel and disappeared back through the door, locking it behind him, before he made off purposely down the corridor.

Morgan watched the Houseman disappear through the door, before he turned and walked back towards his office and in response to a quizzical look from Dave announced. "He should keep his fucking nose out of what he doesn't understand."

And with that, he disappeared into his office, slamming the door behind him.

June 20th 1974; 12:35 hrs

Sarah could hear the unmistakeable sound of Sterling's footsteps coming up the stairs and searched through her notebook until she found the entry she was looking for. As the solicitor burst through the door with his usual disregard for anyone who may have been on the other side of it, she was ready with the message, now transcribed onto a separate scrap of paper.

Sterling took the paper and without reading it, looked enquiringly at his receptionist.

"The Governor at Holshaw Prison called at about ten o'clock this morning and I told him that you had gone straight to court and that you wouldn't be returning until lunchtime. He was most insistent that you returned his call as soon as you came in."

Sterling took the note and bustled into his office, not bothering to shut the door behind him and dumped his coat and briefcase. Not bothering to come back out, he leaned forward from his seat in order to call out to his receptionist. "Sarah, could you get Holshaw on the line please?"

"It's ringing for you."

Half a minute's silence, then Sterling's part of the conversation could be clearly heard.

"Ah, yes... could you put me through to the Governor... he is expecting my call... Robert Sterling... solicitor... thank you."

Then a few seconds later.

"Good afternoon Governor, Robert Sterling here, I believe you called..."

"Yes that's right, I am representing Mrs Phillips."

A few seconds silence, then Sterling's tone changed noticeably.

"And when did this happen?"

His responses were now coming thick and fast to what he was obviously finding to be distressing news.

"Yes, I appreciate that, I was in court."

"Let me put it another way: when did she actually do it?"

"And you found her when?"

"And no-one noticed until then? Didn't anyone check?"

"For God's sake, man, it was her first night in prison!"

A longer silence this time.

"Well, what did she use to do it with? Didn't anyone search her?"

Another protracted silence.

"Oh my God!"

"Didn't her cellmate notice anything?!"

A shorter silence this time.

"I presume you'll be having an enquiry?"

"And the next of kin?"

"No, I wouldn't think he would, no."

"Thank you for letting me know."

And then the sound of the receiver being replaced, followed by the creaking of floor boards as Sterling made his way back into the reception area, glasses in his hand and head bowed. He sat down heavily on one the seats at the reception desk normally reserved for clients and ploughed right into the part of the Governor's account that he'd found to be more unbelievable than anything else.

"She'd been dead for at least five hours before they found her... I just can't believe that, five bloody hours!"

Sarah stopped what she was doing, looked up and waited for Sterling to return to a more logical starting point, as she knew he would, eventually.

"Five hours... what the hell did they think they were doing?

The question was rhetorical, and needed no reply.

"I mean, even you know the state she'd got herself into yesterday... I knew, you knew, the court certainly knew. Apparently the only people who bloody ignored it were the damn prison!"

"I presume she killed herself?" Sarah felt that she needed to prompt him in order to make some sense of what she was hearing.

121

"Yes, sorry, yes she did. Apparently she was quite calm when she arrived at the prison. The prison staff, the doctor, no-one, in fact, no-one identified her as being a suicide risk, but they should have done. It was her first night in a prison, for God's sake... What the hell were they thinking of?"

"Perhaps if you told me what did happened?"

"Of course, sorry. She was deemed to be alright when they left her in the cell to get herself sorted out. She didn't leave the landing to collect her meal or a drink and no one made any attempt to check if she was OK, but she is reported to have been sitting on her bunk and responding when spoken to when they were banged up for the night."

"So, by what you're saying, she killed herself in the night?" Sarah was doing her best to find out exactly what had happened, without sounding impatient.

"They found her when they unlocked the cell at about seven o'clock this morning. She was lying on her back, covered with a blanket... obviously dead for some time. When they pulled the blanket away, they found that she was lying in a pool of blood. The mattress was completely saturated, and the Governor tells me that much of the blood was congealed and according to preliminary medical reports, she had been dead for at least five hours."

Sarah was about to ask the obvious, but Sterling pre-empted her as he continued.

"In one hand, they found the broken handle of a plastic toothbrush and in the other hand; they found the remnants of a broken plastic comb. She'd used both of them to gouge at her wrists until she found what she was looking for, namely her arteries. According to the governor, by the state of the wounds, she had obviously been trying for some time before she reached her goal. Apparently the skin on her wrists was ripped to shreds."

Sterling fell into silence and Sarah didn't feel as though she wanted any more detail, but almost instinctively, she asked. "What about her kids? Has anyone told them?"

"I really don't know, but in any case, the Governor has assured me that they've taken care of that side of things. Mr Phillips is still not well enough to be told, so under the circumstances, her parents have been informed. More than that, I really can't say. Normally in such cases, I would have to say that our responsibility is at an end, but in this regard, her son is being detained under Section and the "next of kin" issue will have some relevance, so I will call the Almoners office at Greenbeck. Then it's up to them."

"Was she really facing a long sentence? Surely the mitigating circumstances and…"

Sterling put his hand up to prevent Sarah from stating what had been going round in his mind since the day before, but was now too uncomfortable to hear someone verbalise.

"With the right defence and a sympathetic judge, she could have been out in a few months, or she may even have got a suspended sentence, but…" and leaving the sentence deliberately incomplete, he threw out his arms as a gesture of helplessness. As if to underline the fact that he considered the matter to be closed Sterling got up and walked towards his office.

"So that's it!" Sarah sounded almost indignant.

Sterling didn't even bother to turn his head towards his receptionist. "Unless I receive instructions from the family to the contrary, yes. That, as you put it, is it." This last part of his reply being accompanied by the closing of his office door, with him firmly on the other side of it.

June 20th 1974; 16:20 hrs

Trafford was distinctly unhappy. Not only did he find himself being summoned, which he felt was beneath him, but he'd been summoned to an office on the opposite side of the hospital to his own. To make matters even worse, he had hoped to have been on the golf course by now.

And all of that because Margaret Page had said that she needed to see him urgently. That was the worst part of all. The contempt in which he held the hospital social worker was probably no different to the contempt he had for just about everyone else. The major difference between Margaret Page and everyone else was that she wasn't afraid of standing up to him and had a far lower opinion of him than he had of her.

He didn't bother knocking. He never did. Instead, he barged into her office without any regard to anyone's privacy and of course, with his characteristic lack of manners and social niceties.

Margaret Page was busily occupied, as luck would have it, watering her plants rather than mopping up someone's tears and didn't even look towards the door as it flew open. No one else but Trafford would enter someone's office in such a manner, so she didn't feel the need to check the identity of her visitor. Apart from anything else, she knew that it would annoy Trafford if she carried on with her task.

She was right. Trafford just had to lay eyes on that short, dumpy, odious woman with the pudding basin cut grey hair, in order for him to feel an appreciable rise in his blood pressure. Not to be acknowledged as he walked in, pushed it up to dangerous levels. He helped himself to a seat at her desk and she turned briefly away from her horticultural labours.

"Do take a seat, Dr Trafford."

And with this she put down the jug of water she had been using and walked over to her desk. Her sensible shoes and white coat both had an appearance that further annoyed Trafford and as her well healed footwear made contact with the wooden floor, Trafford was, at the back of his mind, aware that he didn't even like the sound she made when she wasn't even speaking!

"Thank you very much for coming, Dr Trafford. I wouldn't have called you over if the matter hadn't been so urgent."

"Well?" Trafford was unconvinced as to the reality of what the social worker was referring to as "urgent".

"I've had a telephone call from a Mr Robert Sterling, who apparently has been representing William Phillips' mother, Jean Phillips in the matter of an alleged assault on her husband."

"And?" This time the mention of the William Phillips' name sparked a little more interest.

"And it would seem that, as you know, she spent last night in prison and was found dead in her cell early this morning, having cut her wrists," Miss Page looked at Trafford to see if there was a response, and was slightly reassured at the momentary look of shock on his face, but didn't wait for a response before she continued. "I presume that you didn't tell William Phillips about his mother being in prison."

"That's correct. As I told you yesterday, his mental condition is too unstable to handle that sort of information. I planned to monitor his progress, and if and when… " Then he broke off the sentence as he realised that he was giving the social worker the courtesy of a conversation. "Anyway, I explained all this yesterday. I'll keep it under review and when the time is right, I'll let you know, but for now, he has a serious mental illness and is receiving treatment."

The psychiatrist clearly thought the conversation was over and had already risen from the chair to leave, when Miss Page beckoned him to resume his position.

"I'm sure, Dr Trafford, that you know perfectly well that it's not just a case of whether you tell him about his mother or not. That decision, as his consultant, will under the circumstances, have to rest with you."

"So what's the problem?"

"The problem," The social worker continued. "is that we need to discuss the issue of the next of kin because, apart from anything else, you have him detained under Section 25 and as I am sure you are aware, the next of kin should be involved, or at least informed of the decisions you make. Not to mention, of course, that they have the right to appeal against the Section that has been imposed."

"Obviously… and I have to say, Miss Page, if this is your idea of "important", then I think this meeting is at an end," and with that he once again attempted to leave the room, only to be motioned back to his seat, which he returned to with some irritation, but Miss Page ignored him and continued anyway. "Or of course, the conduct of the Section itself," and at this point, she held his gaze, until Trafford shifted uncomfortably in his chair and attempted to brazen it out.

"If you've got a point to make, kindly do so."

"In the first place, Dr Trafford, I'm sure you are well aware that William Phillips' father is currently recovering from a serious assault and is unable to fulfil any obligations or rights he has with regard to his son, under the terms of the Mental Health Act. What you almost certainly don't know, is that I have had a conversation with my colleague at the hospital where William's father is being treated. The gist of this conversation is that it would seem as though he wishes to relinquish those responsibilities."

"I beg your pardon?" Trafford seemed at least partly interested.

"Put another way, his father doesn't want to have anything to do with him."

"So, isn't there anyone else who can be classed as "next of kin"? There must be someone, anyway… that's your job to sort out, not mine, so if you'll excuse me." Trafford made his third attempt to leave, but only succeeded in being unsuccessful again.

"It is possible that his grandparents will agree, but as I'm sure you'll appreciate, they're currently looking after Mrs Phillips young daughter and they are struggling to come to terms with their loss."

"I feel as though I should be asking the question; 'What are you getting at?'"

"I just wanted to put you in the picture regarding Mrs Phillips and I'm sure that you fully agree that we need to ensure that William Phillips' best interests are represented,"

Trafford nodded, grunted and started to leave again, only to be stopped in his tracks by the beginning of Miss Page's next sentence... which something told him, would turn out to be the real reason for the meeting

"I couldn't help noticing though," the almoner paused to allow Trafford to resume his position, "That when you were talking about Mr Phillips a few moments ago, you mentioned that you would see how his treatment progressed, or am I mistaken?"

"No, you're not mistaken, why? What's your point?"

"My point, Dr Trafford, is that William Phillips is being detained under Section 25 and I'm sure that you don't need me to tell you that Section 25 only allows you to detain and assess him, without his consent."

"Are you suggesting that I am treating him without his consent?" Trafford was indignant, but only because someone had dared to question his integrity.

"As I said, I'm concerned only with his best interests and of course, if you're telling me that... "

Trafford leaned forward with his elbow on the desk and not for the first time, glared at the lady almoner. "I am telling you. Now, if there is nothing else... "

This time, Trafford didn't make the mistake of trying to leave and was saved the effort of re-seating himself as Miss Page still continued to make her points.

"Well, I'm glad to have had your reassurance," Although she was making a point of looking anything but glad or reassured, "And you'll be placing him on Section 26 if the treatment becomes a problem?"

"Of course!"

"And I daresay that you are making every effort to move him onto a more suitable admission ward at the very earliest opportunity. I'm sure that Mr Morgan would appreciate not being distracted from his important work with his long stay gentlemen, by having the level of disruption that Mr Phillips has brought with him."

This time, Trafford did get up, moved towards the door, and on his way through, looked over his shoulder. "That is out of my hands and it could be weeks before we move him. In any case, I'll thank you not to interfere with clinical matters."

And with that, he finally managed to escape through the door, slamming it behind him. As he made his way up the corridor, his mind was filled, not only with contempt for the irritating Margaret Page and a wish that her fast approaching retirement would somehow become more imminent. More especially, though, he felt a deep resentment that someone had gone behind his back and involved a third party.

Someone had been talking to her and that level of disloyalty he wouldn't tolerate.

June 25th 1974; 14:05 hrs

Someone had wiped the dining chairs after lunch and had moved them into a large circle, in the middle of the day room. Various members of the unkempt and wandering population obviously felt that they needed to try them out in their new positions, only to get up a few moments later and wander off.

William surveyed the scene from the chair in the middle bay window that he'd adopted since day one. Every day he sat there and watched.

He watched the old men wandering and smoking.

He watched the men that were referred to as "staff" or "nurses", who just seemed to talk to each other or sit in the office.

He watched the comings and goings of different people through the locked door and he saw the man they called Morgan, strutting around the place.

He watched the one who called himself Jim, who seemed to want to sit down and talk to the old men, and was always smiling.

All these things he observed, but they remained as separate events, with little or no obvious connections except those that his own ideations had created. Apart from Charlie, who he liked (mainly because he would sit and talk with him at mealtimes), the only reassurance or comfort he felt in this place was when the randomness of people's actions and movements ceased and it was time for everyone to do the same thing at the same time.

He felt safe in a queue.

You didn't have to talk to anyone, not even to ask the reason for queuing in the first place. It just happened. All you needed to do was to stand there until you were at the front of the queue and whatever it was you were queuing for, happened. It was the only structure to the day in this place that he seemed to be able to deal with, without having to think.

He'd even started smoking because of a queue that he'd joined one day after his meal. At the time, he'd joined the queue, or so he thought, because Jack had told him to and after all, it wasn't as though he'd never tried cigarettes before.

"They'll pick on you if you do things differently from the others, they'll clear your brain and make you like the old men."

But strangely, Jack didn't seem to be quite as vocal as usual. William knew that he was there, but couldn't always hear what he had to say, except when he was frightened, or someone was annoying him… then he could hear him.

He had been told by the nurses that he was in a hospital, but that couldn't be true. He wasn't ill. This wasn't a hospital. The old men weren't ill, in his mind, someone had damaged their brains. William knew that he was in an alien place and that he was always in danger. He had to keep quiet. Not tell them anything. If you told them something they could follow the thought trail back into your brain and once they did that, you were changed for good.

They'd told him time and time again that he couldn't leave, couldn't go home. Where were his mother and sister? Why had he been left here? It had to be because they didn't know where he was. He couldn't remember the answers he'd been given, but they were all lies. But he could remember bits of one conversation.

A woman came to see him yesterday. A grey haired old lady in a smart white coat and old fashioned shoes had sat and talked to him and asked him all sorts of questions and smiled a lot. But she'd said the same as all the others, that he couldn't go home yet, that he was ill, that he couldn't go home yet. He seemed to recall that she'd said something about coming back to see him when he was better. That was when he'd asked about his Mum and Julie.

Someone else had come to see him yesterday. He said he was "Grandpa" he looked like his Grandpa, he even sounded like him. But it wasn't him. It couldn't be him. It was someone they made to look like him. He tried to talk about home and asked if William was feeling better. But William wouldn't speak to him. He was obviously an imposter because he'd cried. Grandpa never cried. He'd left, saying he'd be back soon.

A few more memory fragments began to linger in his mind, especially over the last day or so and particularly during Jack's silent periods.

Fragments? More like feelings.

There was no difference, not really and still his thoughts jumped from one thing to another. The only difference now was that as his thoughts jumped, he was slightly more aware that he couldn't hold onto what he had been thinking about a few seconds earlier.

And of course, there was still the radio. The radio and the television, to be precise. They bothered him. They were still giving out their messages, but he seemed to be the only one to hear them and therefore, the only one to be bothered by them. William couldn't say exactly what the messages were, not word for word, but he knew that they were trying to get him to tell the staff about everything he knew about the brainwashing. He also knew that if he did that, they would have won. So he hummed. When he hummed, he found the messages couldn't get through. He didn't give it a second thought as to how it looked to anyone else and he wouldn't have given a damn anyway.

He just hummed to himself. Whenever the television or radio was on, he hummed. Hummed and rocked

He was humming and rocking when Jim came over and asked him to come and sit in the circle of chairs. He stopped rocking and just sat and stared for a few moments, then reluctantly got out of his chair and stood motionless, looking around him. Whether for his benefit or not, someone turned off the radio, William stopped humming and nervously moved towards the chairs where several of the others had already taken their places.

Moving around the circle and with his head partly bowed and tilted one side, he looked around to find a seat that didn't have any neighbours, went over to it and curling his legs underneath him, he sat down with his arms wrapped around his chest as though he was struggling to keep warm.

It wasn't long before most of the chairs in the circle were filled, including a few of them by nurses. William heard the office door open behind him and looked round to see Trafford making his way to one of the empty seats and watched him sit down next to a little man called Arnold, who appeared to take little or no notice of the Consultant's arrival.

"Now then, gentlemen, who would like to start off the meeting. Has anyone got anything they'd like to share with the rest of us?"

Trafford wasn't exactly met with silence, but had to wait a few minutes before any of the assorted grunts or noises were directed towards responding to his request.

Charlie was first to speak, and stood up in true military fashion to do so. "When can I have my uniform back, Dr Trafford? I need it back. I'm better now... I really am." And then he sat down as abruptly as he had stood up.

"Now, I think that we've talked about your uniform a little while ago and we said... well, can you remember what we said, Charlie?"

Charlie stood up again and with his head slightly bowed. "We... you said... you said that I was still poorly and that... and that I couldn't have my... "

Trafford cut in, almost sympathetically. "Don't have," he corrected... "You don't have a uniform."

"Yes, I... I don't have a uniform, Dr Trafford." Then he sat down, very gradually as though he'd been inflicted with a slow puncture and was deflating.

Trafford kept looking at him until he had settled back into his seat before he continued.

"Thank you for that Charlie; we'll have another little chat presently. Now, has anyone else got something they want to talk about?"

A hand went up to the left of where William was seated and he noticed that the little balding man in the rather stained and battered brown tweed jacket was nervously indicating that he had something to say. Trafford looked in his direction and smiled.

"Yes, Edward, what would you like to say?"

"I don't know where to look for my cat, she's gone missing, you know, I don't know where to look and I've got to find her... I'm so worried." He began to get upset, tears rolling down his cheeks. "You've got to help me find her!"

Trafford motioned to Jim with his eyes and the male nurse went over and gently extracted Edward from the meeting.

"I wanna fag." Tom didn't say much and what he did say was accompanied by a shower of saliva that cascaded down the stubble on his chin. But he wasn't one to be left out of such occasions and was given one, more to keep him quiet than anything else, and the meeting continued.

130

"Why are you trying to brainwash me?"

William's voice even caught Trafford by surprise. It usually took much more effort than this to get him to say anything.

"That's an interesting question, William. Do you believe that we are trying to brainwash you? Who exactly is trying to do this to you, do you think?"

William shot glances to just about every point in the circle, before his eyes came back to rest on Trafford. He'd blown his cover and could feel Jack trying to stop him he, but he was too late… much too late.

"You are… you and them." And with this, William pointed to the rest of the staff who were peppered around the room. "You're all doing it!"

"Don't… Don't say anything!" Jack could just be heard and William hesitated for a few seconds in response.

"And how do you think we're doing that, William?"

His response was to curl up even tighter and re-commence his rocking, but he kept on staring at Trafford as though he was hoping for some form of explanation… or even a confrontation.

He got neither; instead he got another question from the psychiatrist.

"It's good to hear you speak at last, William. Perhaps you'd like to tell everyone about yourself. I'm sure that we'd all like to get to know you a bit better."

Nothing. Nothing apart from staring and rocking.

"Don't you want to say anymore today, William?"

"I want to go to the shops. When can we go to the shops?" The little man, Arnold, thought he'd fill the void left by William's silence and started to straighten his gravy and custard stained tie in anticipation of a shop visit.

Everyone ignored him.

"William, are you going to carry on talking to us?" Trafford was anxious to keep his young patient talking, but by this time he was staring intently at Morgan, who was stood in the office doorway, arms crossed and looking in his direction. He felt the tension rise and his thoughts to further fragment… and that triggered Jack to add his contribution. *"They think you're mad. He thinks you're mad… Why did you speak to them? Why.. ?"*

"I want to buy a new tie at the shop." Arnold wasn't going to be ignored and got up to leave the circle, only to pulled back down to his seat by one of the male nurses.

Tom's cigarette had burned down to his fingers and he was now going round the circle in search of a replacement and Charlie had crossed his arms and legs, sunk his chin to his chest and disengaged with the world.

"William!" Trafford made one last attempt, but knew when he'd encountered a lost cause. He looked around, took a cigarette from a pack of ten that he'd quietly extracted from his inside pocket and lit it. By this time, the circle had disintegrated into anarchy and Trafford decided that he'd got as much mileage as he could from his weekly attempt at group therapy and departed for the nursing office.

Morgan had shifted his position marginally, as his consultant brushed past him on his way. The lack of sincerity and concern in his voice wasn't unintentional, but it jarred the nerves, nevertheless.

"I noticed that Dr Sellman didn't join us today. I do hope he's OK."

Trafford looked up from the medical notes trolley that he'd just started rummaging through and looked over his glasses at the charge nurse.

"As I'm sure you'll be aware, Dr Sellman has, regrettably, decided to pursue a career in psycho -geriatrics at St. Mary's and I believe, takes up his post this week."

Morgan smiled to himself and he couldn't resist letting Trafford know that he understood perfectly the how's and why's of the junior doctors sudden departure.

"Well, Dr Trafford all I can say is that Dr Sellman is a lucky young man to have someone such as yourself helping him with his career moves. It always helps to have someone putting in a good word in the right places."

Trafford didn't even extend Morgan the courtesy of replying to his obviously inflammatory statement, but his next comment put his message without any doubt.

"Don't you have something you should be getting on with? I'm sure that I can manage to ask for help if I need it!"

And with that, Morgan moved himself from the doorway he'd been supporting and busied himself on the ward, primarily finding someone to make his tea and then watching the dismantling of the circle of chairs. More especially, he was watching William, who was still occupying one of them, still tucked up and looking quite pathetic now that everyone else had gone back to their wanderings. As he approached his young patient, William looked up and for a second their eyes met, but the contact was quickly broken by William who recommenced bowed head posture.

"He's the one… He's the bastard you've got to watch… He's the one who's trying to break you… He controls the radios and television… Don't let him know anything… he can follow your thoughts back into your brain… he's already been listening to you… and now he's trying to get in… can you feel it? Can you?" Jack's message was uncompromising. William stopped rocking and once again looked at Morgan, who gave his own uncompromising and misguided interpretation of the events of the afternoon.

"Nearly said too much, did we Billy boy… eh? Mustn't let on why we stood in front of the bus. Eh?" Morgan drew up a chair, obviously intent on making his views known, whether William wanted to hear them or not.

"You see, Billy… oh I'm sorry, William," Morgan's apology was anything but convincing and he continued. "You see, people just don't go mad overnight. You're not sane one day and cracked the next."

William's mind was racing and the pressure to say everything at once was becoming irresistible, but not in a pleasant way. It didn't occur to him that when he did speak that the jumbled thoughts and misguided perceptions would all come out as complete nonsense.

"I'm not listening to you, my mind is not in my body… you can't get at it… you ask my Uncle Bill… He does all the shopping… I'm not supposed to stay out late… Mum will go mad if I'm not home and my records can't play anymore. I don't want to be here. Here… here… I can't do my homework… not like Lenny, he cheats… at football… You're trying to get me… To brainwash me… "

Morgan held his hand up, as if to tell William to shut up, and continued. "Did you know that you can't go mad overnight? Well, did you?" No response. "See Tom over there? He was barking for years before he came in here. So was your friend Charlie. Terrible isn't it?" Morgan left a gap in his narrative before he continued, as if to allow William to absorb the information.

"Don't speak to him, if you speak he will follow your brain patterns and get into your head. You shouldn't have said anything!" William tilted his head slightly in order to pay attention to Jack, but Morgan just carried right on.

"All of 'em. Got the records in my office. All of them. Notes that thick." He held up his thumb and forefinger as if to demonstrate to William just how thick the notes were. "Backwards and forwards to their doctors for years before they ended up here. Could see it a mile off that they were going round the bend… But you… Mr William Phillips… the first anyone

133

knows about you is when you decide to have a chat with a fucking bus! And before that… nothing. No history, no symptoms… bugger all. And why was that… eh? Why do you think that no one picked it up?"

William didn't respond, and Jack was being uncharacteristically quiet.

Morgan leaned forward and continued in lower tones as if to share a secret. "Because, Billy boy, there wasn't anything wrong, was there… eh? Bugger all. And you know it, don't you? And now you've fucked up your brain with drugs, and expect us to clean up the mess, eh… isn't that right?" Morgan's voice lowered even further, as he got up to leave, delivering his parting shots as he rose from his chair. "Well, I've got no time for brats like you, that do this sort of thing to themselves… Got it? If it had been left to me, I would have had you chucked in a cell and thrown the key away then you could babble all your crap to the nice policeman instead, and see how far you would have got if you tried to hit one of them."

"I'm going home… I want to go home." William was almost pleading with the charge nurse, but William's distress was totally lost on Morgan.

"Home! Home! You ain't going anywhere. And whose fault is that? Can you guess? Your mother couldn't deal with you, won't have to any more … but, of course, I'd better not say any more about "Mummy", had I? Just in case I tell you any little secrets that I'm not supposed to tell you." Morgan, on seeing Trafford emerge from the office, walked away with a swagger, obviously pleased with himself that he had made his point, even though his patient was in no state to comprehend all of his words.

He'd only walked fifteen yards or so towards his office when he was met by Dave who had taken on the mantle of tea monitor and was now brandishing a steaming cup which he handed to Morgan. Trafford was on his way out of the ward, having seen, but not heard the exchange between his Charge Nurse and the young patient.

"Glad to see that you're trying to make some headway with William. Did you manage to get any more out of him?" Morgan felt a deep satisfaction every time Trafford showed how stupid he was.

"Afraid not, Dr Trafford, but we'll keep on trying."

"Well, let me know if there are any changes. I've still got our social worker on my back." Trafford started to make his way out of the ward, hesitated and looked back over his shoulder. "I'm having to share Dr McKenzie's SHO until I appoint Sellman's replacement, so don't bother him unless you really need to."

Morgan again began to walk back to the office, only stopping briefly to circumvent Tom, who'd intentionally stood in his way to get another cigarette. Morgan didn't even acknowledge him, except to throw his arms out as he walked around him to prevent being grabbed.

"And someone chuck Tom in the bath, he's pissed himself again." He reached for his own cigarette, lit it and blew the smoke into Tom's face and watched as two of his staff pulled a reluctant Tom in the direction of the bathroom.

July 3rd 1974; 15:15 hrs

George and Irene's lounge was always hot in the summer. That's why they always opened the French windows, although George used to say that they only ever opened them to impress the neighbours. Everyone, except Irene, laughed whenever he said that. Especially Jean. The laugh that could light up a room and everyone in it. But it had been so long since he'd last saw her laugh. Really laugh, that was.

Jean. That was all gone now. The bubbly little girl who always put a smile on the face of anyone she met was gone. George kept thinking that they'd hear her key in the latch any minute and she'd come walking through the door, just as she always did.

And William. He seemed to be more dead than his mother. A sort of living death. George tried to replace the image of the unkempt young man he'd seen in the hospital with one of the baby that he'd held in his arms, of the boy who always had his nose in a book and anxious to get his homework just right. So neat and tidy.

And questions! There were times when it seemed that he'd never stop asking questions. And there was always one to replace the one he'd just asked. George felt the tears coming again, as he saw his grandson's eyes looking into his and tried to block the memory of the two or three times he'd told him not to ask anymore and to go and watch the television.

He'd give anything for just another day of questions.

Once the tears started, he couldn't stop them. He could see his daughter in the pretty yellow dress she'd worn at her 18st birthday party. He could see William holding his baby sister when Jean had brought her home from the maternity hospital. He could feel the affection that they both gave so freely and now he could feel it being snuffed out... taken away. So cruel.

And William didn't even recognise him. Wouldn't talk to him. He couldn't even tell him about his Mum. For God's sake, the boy had just lost his mother and he didn't even know. Did he know or realise anything anymore? He didn't look as though he did. He'd sat on that bloody ward, with his grandson, surrounded by a load of old men. William had been wearing some tatty old clothes that the ward had given him and when he'd asked if he could bring in William's own clothes, his request was met with regretful smiles and comments such as "They'll only get lost," or "The hospital laundry ruins everything," or some such crap.

He'd taken William a few of his favourite books and they said that they would give them to him when he felt better. And when the bloody hell would that be? That poor bugger's got nothing from home, no possessions, no photos. Nothing to make him feel better. Nothing to remind him that they still loved him.

Dr Trafford had been sympathetic, but there are only so many ways that you can say "Wait and see." Only so many ways of saying "We don't know."

But George knew. He knew that a couple of years ago he had the most wonderful daughter and grandchildren he could ever have wished for. If only she hadn't married that bastard. They would have coped. Again the guilt. He hadn't known that she was carrying William. He didn't even ask her what the rush to get married was. It didn't occur to him that she'd tried to hide the truth because she didn't want to hurt her Dad.

So she married him. And now she was gone. Because of him, she was gone. Once more he closed his eyes and held out his hand, somehow hoping that Jean would hold onto it, just for a second, so he could tell her that he loved her more than he'd ever told her. Hoping that somehow, she could return from wherever it was that she'd gone to, so that he could say sorry for all the mistakes he'd made, for anything he hadn't given her, but most of all, for not being there on the night in the prison when she must have felt so alone, so desperate.

George could bear the pain of that thought less than any other. Almost instinctively, he lit another cigarette and got out of his chair to go and make some tea. As he got to the lounge door, he listened. No sound. Irene had gone to lie down after taking one of the tablets that Dr Preston had given her to help her to relax.

He moved quietly into the kitchen and put the kettle on, being careful not to make any noise, mostly because he needed some time. Just a bit more time. He could barely cope with his own distress and was finding it more difficult to give any comfort to his wife when he felt as desperate as he did right now.

He finished making the tea and returned to his chair in the lounge. Looking out at his garden he was gripped with a feeling of complete futility. What was the point in anything? When you can lose so much in so little time, what was the point?

They wouldn't even let them bury her. Wouldn't let them say goodbye properly. Not until the coroner gives his permission. Not until then. Shouldn't be long, they said in the coroner's office, probably next week when the hearing starts again. Then, they said, he could make all the arrangements.

They'd made it sound as though he was going to pick up a pair of trousers that had been on order.

He pulled his thoughts back. What the hell was he thinking of. He was going through some logical set of motions that he was expected to go through. The process that he had to show to everyone as being completed. But this was his daughter, his little girl, not someone you read in the paper. Not something Mrs Holmes had told you about that had happened in the street.

It was Jean lying on that slab. Waiting for their permission. She was alone when she died, and she was alone now. He should be there... but they said it was best if he waited for the funeral.

The funeral. How would Julie be at the funeral? They'd talked about not letting her go, but surely that would just make things worse for her? Wasn't it bad enough losing her Mum, let alone not being able to say goodbye? Poor kid had cried herself to sleep every night for her Mum and her brother. Every bloody night. He felt so helpless. No, not helpless: useless. There was nothing he could say, nothing he could do.

So useless.

He remembered the conversations, so many of them. The conversations in whispered tones about William. He'd listened and done little else. Why hadn't he done something? Anything. What was it that Dr Trafford had said? "Wasn't responding to treatment," and "Serious mental illness," but worst of all, he wasn't "hopeful". William was going to go to university, he was bright, all his teachers agreed. He was so good at maths... the only one in the family that was.

So bright.

How come he wasn't bright anymore? Jean had been so proud of him. It must have destroyed her to see him gradually losing his mind. Was that the real reason why she killed herself… ? They said that her mind was unbalanced. Was that the reason? He should have done something to stop it happening and now it was too late.

Too late.

As his thoughts turned to David Phillips, his blame and grief didn't budge, instead, they stayed firmly on his shoulders. But contempt and hatred, that was a different matter. Those he put exactly where they were deserved. He had pushed her and neglected his family and because of his ignorance and arrogance, Jean was dead. He'd fought with his son when he should have been helping him.

Jean should have killed him when she had the chance; God knows the result couldn't have been any worse.

He'd actually been to visit him in hospital. He'd been dreading it, but it had to be done, they were looking after his daughter. He was her legal parent. They had things to discuss, things to arrange, but it didn't work out that way. He'd ignored any mention of his wife and referred to William as his "looney son" Then he dropped his bombshell when he said that he was going to start a new life and didn't even want anything to do with his daughter. Bastard. When he went back to the hospital the next day to reason with his son-in-law, he was met with the news that he'd discharged himself the day before. When he went to the flat and let himself in with Jean's spare key, he found that the bugger had taken all his clothes. Taken them and gone.

So that was that. If only he'd gone a month ago. How can you just walk away like that? How?

So why hadn't he stepped in to stop it? He should have persuaded her to come and live at home with the kids and divorce the bastard. But he hadn't stepped in. He hadn't done anything

Julie would be home in a minute. She was at her aunt's house for the afternoon to give Irene a break. She wants to know where her brother has gone, wants to know why she can't go and see him. But Greenbeck's not the sort of place to take a little girl. It would break her heart even more to see her brother like that, especially in a place like that.

She thinks that she's lost the people she loved because she'd done

138

something wrong and they won't come back until she's been good. Poor kid is so obedient and quiet nowadays, just not normal for a little girl that, a couple of months ago, was into everything. And now she's started wetting the bed again. She breaks her heart over that, poor kid.

And poor Irene doesn't know what to say to her. Doesn't know what to say to anyone. It was easier for her to tell people that her daughter had died (with more than a few adjustments, it was true), than to tell them about William being in a nuthouse. She'd even used to say to the kids when they were young… "If we don't go on holiday soon, I'll end up in Greenbeck!" Or "If you kids don't give it a rest, they'll end up putting me in Greenbeck!"

It's what people used to say around here. It didn't mean anything, but it was a sort of way of dealing with what people dreaded most. Going round the bend. Being "taken away". And now William had been "taken away".

Poor Irene was torn in so many different directions, all of them full of blackness and hopelessness. She couldn't come to terms with the disgrace of having her daughters' suicide, her imprisonment, her failed marriage and worst of all, her grandson being in a mental hospital. Worse still was the guilt at giving in to the feelings of disgrace and embarrassment for the people she loved so dearly. All that grief, hammering at her door, just waiting for a chance, getting in the never ending queue of emotions and conflicts, waiting for a chance to introduce itself, to announce its position as the supreme pain that would need to be experienced before any healing could take place.

Poor, darling Irene.

Irene had come downstairs and walked over to where George was sitting. Slowly she sank to her knees and touched her husband's cheek.

The little restraint and composure that George may have had up until then, disappeared in those few seconds and as the floodgates opened, Irene held him tight and tried to comfort the man who prided himself on always being able to keep it together. He cried. But Irene didn't know that so many of his tears were for her. For the road ahead which would be filled with mind destroying grief, as she came to terms with the reality of what had happened.

As he had.

Today was unusual. Very unusual. Some things were the same, but some things weren't. William didn't know what was unusual; he just knew that he felt uncomfortable. He couldn't string together the sequence of events for that day… even though his day was only a couple of days old.

He was sat where he always sat, in the brown chair in the middle bay. He could hear Henry, in the bay to his left, playing snooker, on his own, on the snooker table with the threadbare base. Henry always played snooker.

The radio was on. He didn't like the radio. Sometimes he felt as though it was giving messages. But he didn't know what they were, or, for that matter, who they were meant for. He just didn't like it.

But that wasn't much different to any other day that he heard the radio, except, of course, he could now stop the radio from invading his brain. But that was now a memory of things past, memories that he could now only access as fears without really remembering the concrete events that would back them up.

The queues had been the same.

The queue for the sink to have a wash.

The queue for his medicine.

The queue for his breakfast.

The queue for a cigarette.

All those queues. William didn't think about the queues. He just joined them. There was no particular memory of waiting in the queues.

No, it wasn't the queues. In any case, William couldn't be that analytical. The routine of the day just happened. Every day, it just happened and you did it. It was comfortable. A bit of him, somewhere resented it. But it was comfortable.

Breakfast was breakfast. William could remember his meals. But breakfast didn't take much remembering anyway. Porridge during the week and bacon at the weekend. He remembered that.

It was getting hot. The sun streamed through the huge bay windows, making the dayroom hot and uncomfortable, but William only noticed such things if it became unbearable. There wasn't anything out of the ordinary that he would have been able to remember, and indeed, he wasn't trying to. He was just aware of the feeling of something making him feel uncomfortable.

"Looking smart, today, William!" Jim was passing by his chair and as usual, he was the only one to say anything that wasn't an instruction or a comment. He felt more comfortable with Jim than he did with any of the others. Jim didn't seem to want anything from him and wasn't a threat, although he still didn't trust him. But there again, William didn't trust anyone.

William looked down at himself and slowly ran his hands down his shirt and looked again at the properly ironed grey trousers that he was wearing. The shirt had all the buttons sewn on and his face felt softer than it usually did. He remembered that someone had stood with him while he shaved, and had taken the trouble to find him some decent clothes. Somewhere in the back of his mind, he recalled that he had been impatient about getting dressed, about having to wait whilst shirts and trousers were discarded because they were in a bad state of repair. That was unusual and almost completed wasted time as far as William was concerned, as all he really wanted to do was to go downstairs a have his breakfast and cigarette.

But it wasn't that. That happened sometimes when Jim was there. The dressing and shaving thing that is. He always took longer than the others. But the shaving and dressing didn't give the feeling of being unusual. It just made him feel better.

As his hand came to rest by the side of his leg, it encountered something that was half down the side of the chair. Slowly he retrieved it, and found that it was an envelope, and he turned it over, he soon remembered that it was his. He read the envelope for maybe the tenth time that morning, as if it held a revelation so startling that it had to be read repeatedly to be believed.

Mr William Phillips
c/o Tamworth Ward
Greenbeck Hospital,
Dennysford Road,
Bassford, Essex.

He read it slowly to himself, but although the revelation was stirring deep in his subconscious, he was only aware of recognising the name and knowing it belonged to him. Slowly he turned the envelope around. Someone had written on the back.

Sender: Mr and Mrs Cranford
28, Honeybush Road,

Dews Park
Bassford,
Essex.

Nan and Grandpa. He recognised the name and address and who they belonged to, but couldn't seem to do anything with the information. It just briefly rattled around his brain, seemingly unable to find any emotional doors to open before finding a part of his mind where it could stay, out of sight and unobtrusively.

He fingered the top edge of the envelope that had been opened. He remembered opening it. Jim had given him the envelope after he'd finished his breakfast. He remembered that. He'd opened the envelope.

Still he fingered the opened end of the envelope, turned it over again and read his name, turned it back again, fingered the edge and ventured to touch the contents of the envelope before slowly extracting it. Carefully, he put the now empty envelope on his lap and turned his attention to the contents that he was holding between his finger and thumb.

It was a card.

Carefully he turned it over, and read the legend, now being aware that he had already read it before that morning.

Happy Birthday
Grandson

He read it several times, as if having difficulty in fully taking in the simple message, before he opened the card. As he read, it was as though he was back watching the film once again, about someone whose birthday it was, that had received a birthday card from his grandparents. Invading his perception, just as the sea invade the beach, was the thoughts that nit was him. It was his card.

His birthday.

His Nan and Grandpa.

But just like the sea on the hot, dry sand, it sinks in so you can't see it anymore. And he was back watching the film. But it was the sort of film that made you feel uncomfortable, even though you know it's just a film. And he felt uncomfortable now, as he read:

Dear William
Hope you have a Happy Birthday.
Get better soon. We all love and miss you. We'll being in to see you soon
Love from
Nan, Grandpa, and Julie xxxxxx

Julie had written her name herself and its childlike precision stood out from the rest of the writing.

Get better soon!

He wasn't ill! He tried to think the problem through, but was met with the usual fragmentation and couldn't get far with the task.

If he was ill, he shouldn't be at school. He had to get Lucozade if he was ill. There was no Lucozade. He couldn't be ill. Mum would be there. Mum is there. She's outside. Somewhere. Must find a pen. Must write down the homework... forgot my homework book. Mum had to sign it. Ill. Julie went to the Doctor's. Mum took her.

He became aware of Jim standing next to him. He'd been watching from over by the snooker table and had noticed William becoming visibly more agitated as he'd been reading his card and came over.

"You OK, William?"

He nodded, although the meaning of "OK" was rather lost on him in the absence of any form of useful template to use with term.

Jim sat down next to William and reached down the other side of the chair and retrieved another envelope, this time with different handwriting. William took hold the envelope and picked up the other one from his lap and compared them before reaching into the second opened envelope to take out another card, this one wishing him a happy birthday from Auntie Maggie and Uncle Bill.

William stared and felt disturbingly emotional as the names stirred snatches of memories from a time when everything was safe. Memories that were incomplete, that had, in the main been infested by paranoia and delusions... but not all, and not for long. Fleetingly he could see his Uncle Bill and his Grandpa laughing together at Christmas and Uncle Bill coming to see Mum and Julie when they got home.

"Where's Mum? She said she'd be back. What have you done to her?"

He felt as though he could hear a voice in the distance, but no matter how much he strained to listen to it, he couldn't make out the words.

But the question didn't need an answer. William had left reality to journey back into his disordered world where past and present, delusions and paranoia all rubbed shoulders.

But even so, thirty seconds of coherent thought and actions was an improvement. But only slight and it occurred to Jim that such marginal improvement might just be as much as they could achieve. With a feeling of frustration, he rose from his chair and made his way back to the snooker table, where Henry was deep in conversation with someone that no one else but him could see. As he walked into the adjacent bay where Arnold was standing, he saw William sit up and stiffen and when he followed his gaze he found that, not surprisingly, he'd spotted Morgan, who was stood, in his usual position, in the office doorway, staring at the young patient.

The visual exchange was interrupted by the arrival of a visitor to the ward, Alan Wallace, who was a psychiatrist from one of the Admission Wards. He strode over to where Morgan was standing, said something and Morgan pointed in William's direction. Wallace's eyes took their cue from Morgan's raised arm and looked in the same direction, said something else to Morgan, who retreated into the office, only to re-emerge with a buff coloured folder of medical notes. Wallace took them, checked the name and made his way over to where William was sitting.

"Mr William Phillips?" The black suited Consultant was smiling as he stood next to William's chair. William looked up at the new arrival. Wallace's sharp features and blond hair reminded him of someone, but he had trouble remembering and as he tried to, the memory just went further away.

"My name's Dr Wallace. Can we have a little chat in the office?"

William didn't move. Just stared. Wallace tried again.

"What about if I leave the door open when we're in there? Would that be OK?"

Still nothing. Jim, who had been watching the exchange, made his way over and put a hand on Williams shoulder.

"Do you want me to come with you, William? No one else in the office. Just Dr Wallace, me and you." And with that he shot a glance towards the Charge Nurse who had resumed his position in the office doorway, fully aware of what was being said and the attention that was being focussed on him.

William looked again at the charge nurse, who gave a wry grin and

144

moved out of the doorway with a sweeping gesture of his arm to indicate that the office was empty.

Both Wallace and Jim began to slowly move towards the office and William, in his usual manner, jumped up from his chair, made it to the office and sat down before the others reached the doorway. As they entered the door, Jim looked in Morgan's direction and their eyes met with anything but mutual admiration.

Wallace seated himself behind the desk, and Jim stood unobtrusively in the corner of the office. William was sat opposite Wallace, his arms stretched and gripping his knees with his hands. And of course, there was the almost inevitable rocking.

"Are you nervous, William?" Wallace seemed to want to know, but William didn't trust his motives. Was he trying to get inside his brain? Was he part of the conspiracy?

In the absence of a reply, Wallace abandoned that line of enquiry and decided to try another approach.

"Dr Trafford has asked me to come and see you, because you've been with us for a while and we need to decide what we can do to help you."

William said nothing so Wallace carried on regardless.

"Can you tell me the name of this place?"

William looked to be slightly bemused by the question, so Wallace asked it again in a different way.

"William, do you know where you are?"

"In a camp."

"What sort of camp?"

Silence.

"What sort of camp do you think it is, William?"

"A brain camp."

"And what's a "brain camp"? Can you tell me, William?"

William recommenced his rocking and looked down at his hands. But again, the silence.

"William, can you tell what a brain camp is?"

Silence and rocking. Wallace decided to change tactics.

"I understand that it's your birthday today. Is that right, William?"

The memory of the envelopes was still fresh in his mind. "Mum didn't send me anything."

William could just make out the sound of Jack's voice in the distance.

145

"They'll get into your brain!" He strained to listen, but couldn't make out any more words, although he was sure Jack was still there.

Wallace noticed William's distraction.

"Can you hear a voice apart from mine, William?"

His guard dropped, William nodded, but then looked up at the psychiatrist.

"No... No voices."

"Do you ever hear a voice when you can't see anyone there with you?" Then to give William the impression that it wasn't saying anything new if he admitted to the hallucinations.

"It must be frightening for you to hear voices."

"It's not."

"Is it not? What do they say to you? Do they tell you to do things?"

"Sometimes."

"What sort of things do they tell you to do, William?"

"He!"

"Oh, it's a "he" is it?"

Silence.

"Do you know who he is? Do you recognise his voice?"

"You're trying to brainwash me."

"Am I, William? Is that why you call this a brain camp?"

"It is a brain camp."

"Is that your name for this hospital, William?"

"It's not a hospital. They say it's a hospital, but it's a brain camp."

"So can you remember why you were brought here?"

"I hurt my head. They wanted to take my thoughts out of my head."

"Why would they want to do that, William?"

"My homework isn't finished."

"Your homework isn't finished. Why would that make someone want to take your thoughts?"

"Grandpa goes to the pub on Thursdays."

"Does he really, William? William, could you tell me more about the voices you hear?"

"I don't like music lessons. I don't want to go."

"You don't want to go to music lessons? Does the voice tell you not to go?"

"I've got a stereo in my bedroom."

146

"William, can you tell me what year it is?"

Silence.

"Can you tell me what day it is? What day is it today, William?"

"It's my birthday."

"That's right, William, it's your birthday today. Well done. Can you tell me how old you are today?"

Silence.

"How old are you today, William?"

"I don't have my bus pass. I can't get on the bus without my bus pass."

"Why do you want to get on a bus, William?"

"He's following your thoughts; he's following them back into your brain!"

Rocking. Straining to hear Jack and rocking. The distraction was not lost on Wallace, who had been waiting for exactly the sort of behaviour that William was exhibiting.

"Can you hear something? Can you hear someone else talking to you, William?"

Silence. Hand wringing and rocking. But no Jack, at least not that he could hear.

Wallace decided to try another angle and put a page of arithmetic in front of William.

"I'm told that you're very good at maths, William. Is that right? Is it right that you're good with figures?"

The briefest of familiarities touched his brain as he viewed the mathematical symbols in the arithmetical problems… Without hesitation, William picked up the pencil that was lying on the desk and started making marks on the paper… and then it was gone.

Wallace looked at the paper with the two times table sums on it and the few completely (apparently) random marks that William had made and carried on his examination.

"So, can you tell me what you've been doing today?"

But, by this time, the luxury of only partly fragmented thoughts, which had been temporarily brought about by a change of activity had once again given way to his more usual cognitive chaos.

"My Uncle Bill's got a white car." William was now well and truly back into his incoherent catatonic state and Wallace knew that there was little point in pursuing any further attempts aimed at establishing progress or any type of consistently coherent thought.

"OK, William. Thank you for talking to me."

Nothing.

"Thank you for talking to me. I'm afraid that you're still quite poorly and that we'll need to keep you in hospital for a while longer. We'll try changing your medication. Do you understand what I'm saying to you William?"

Through the jumble, William's brain, as if by instinct, managed to extract the information that it really didn't want to hear and he jumped out of the chair, left the office and returned to his chair in the middle bay, clearly agitated and rocking more than ever.

Neither Jim nor Wallace made any move to stop him and after watching William resume his seat outside, Jim sat on the now vacated chair opposite the psychiatrist, who by this time was busily engaged in writing up his notes and filling out the forms needed to continue William's detention at Greenbeck. Without looking up at the male nurse who was clearly waiting to hear his opinion, Wallace gave his verdict.

"Quite obvious schizophrenia with paranoia. I totally agree with Dr Trafford. I don't suppose you've seen much improvement since he was admitted?"

Jim wasn't expecting a question or to be asked for his opinion and it took him a couple of seconds to collect his thoughts.

"Eh… no, well, not really. I mean, he's not as aggressive as he was."

Wallace looked up. "I should think not, with the amount of Chloromazine we're pumping into him." and with that, Wallace glanced at the prescription chart to the left of the notes he was writing. "And Sodium Amytal!" Wallace looked up enquiringly and the staff nurse.

"He only had that a couple of times, when he was really agitated. Dr Trafford originally ordered it as a "once only" but we had to get it written up again a couple of days later."

Wallace kept looking, waiting for Jim to continue his account of William's non progress.

"Still persists with the story about having his brain changed and he's mentioned aliens a couple of times. He still seems to think that he's getting messages from the television and radio and we have to be really careful about the news and weather in particular. He did throw the ward radio just after he was admitted."

"So do you think he hears voices that tell him things, apart from the

148

radio and television, that is?" Wallace picked up on the distraction he'd noticed during his interview with William.

"Almost a hundred per cent certain that he does, although he's always been reluctant to talk about it." Jim felt as though he was on solid ground, but he felt as though he needed to back his statement up with more information.

"He shows signs of auditory hallucinations quite a lot. We've all seen him grinning to himself for no apparent reason and to stopping what he's doing as though he's straining to listen."

Wallace was making note of Jim's information. "So you don't know what the voices are saying?"

"No."

"Or whether the voice is someone he's known in the past? Someone who's died? Someone he knows now?"

Jim shook his head. "Can't help, I'm afraid."

"It doesn't really make much difference, although it would possibly have helped to get the bottom of why he does some of the things he does... never mind." Wallace put the cap back on his fountain pen and closed the folder of notes in which he'd been writing, got up to leave, but then, made another comment, almost as an aside. "So what's happening about telling him about his mother? Any news?"

"The almoner... social worker, or whatever you call them now, she's coming to see him later today, now that you've seen him, to do her bit of the Section papers, but she won't say anything to him, mainly because we're still waiting for Dr Trafford to give his OK."

"I see. Well, there's nothing we can do about that, then." Wallace was now quite dismissive of the problem, almost as though he wouldn't let himself become concerned about another consultants' patient. As if to punctuate the end of the encounter, he placed his pen in his inside pocket and made his way towards the exit.

"Anyway, that little problem aside, find out when Miss Page is coming to see Mr Phillips, would you please? She's got to sign the Section papers."

"Good morning, Dr Wallace." Morgan was standing at the door and as the consultant approached, he unlocked and opened it. Wallace nodded to acknowledge the greeting and left. As Morgan locked the door behind, he turned to Jim.

"I presume that our Dr Wallace found Mr Phillips to be an interesting case."

Jim stared at his charge nurse and leaned towards him. "What is your problem with William Phillips?"

"Problem. What do you mean, problem?" Morgan feigned shock at the mere suggestion that his attitude could be anything but professional and began walking back to the office, with his staff nurse following, determined to get some answers.

"If, of course, you're referring to my dislike of a spoilt little shit that we have to patch up and put back together, then, yes. I have a problem with that. These fucking kids can do what they like and rely on someone else to pick up the fucking pieces afterwards." Morgan was quite vehement in his opinion.

Jim knitted his eyebrows in a not quite genuine expression of puzzlement. "And just what do you mean by "do what they like"? The kid's ill. Anyone can see that!"

"Did I say he wasn't ill? When did I say that? Of course he's ill. That's not the point. It's how he got himself into this state that I'm talking about."

"And?" Jim persisted as they got back to the office and shut the door so they wouldn't be easily disturbed. Morgan sat behind his desk and lit a cigarette. "And what?"

"And what do you think made him ill?"

"Now, even a fucking do gooder like you should be able to see that. Drugs. Obvious. It's his own fault and should be left to fucking wallow in it. Or perhaps you think that it's OK to go round and beat the shit out of anyone he wants to... Do you?"

Jim wasn't surprised at the answer, nor was he particularly affected by being dubbed a do gooder. What he did feel was a mixture of disgust and resignation, and surprised even himself as he continued. "So let's get this straight," Jim knew what he was walking into and what sort of response he'd get, but he had to give a sort of summary of Morgan's approach to his patients for his own piece of mind, that his sense of disbelief was nothing short of normal. "So, William Phillips is here because he's taken LSD, Tom and Henry are ill because they're weak willed bastards who couldn't be bothered to take control of their lives, Charlie's a pathetic man who'd probably go round fucking little boys if he had half the chance," Jim quoted from one of Morgan's more famous labelling efforts. "Shall I go on?!"

Morgan drew hard on his cigarette and sat back in his chair and gave one of his renowned sarcastic and smug grins. "Well, well! Jim Overton's having a little tantrum is he?! Do you have a point to your little outburst?! Trying to impress someone, perhaps?"

"Why do you do this job, Morgan? What is it that keeps you going? Is it the power? Is it?" Jim was in full flow and was now leaning forward on the desk. All he really wanted to do was to wipe that self-satisfied grin from Morgan's smug little face.

Morgan flicked his ash into the ashtray, then placing both hands on the edge of the desk, leaned forward as if to match his staff nurses' position. "You see, Jim, that's where we differ. There's you on the one hand, young, pie in the sky ideals and thinking you're the best mental nurse ever created. And then there's me, older, wiser, knows what's what and can do the job twice as well as you could... and that's with both fucking eyes closed."

He held Jim's gaze for a few seconds, until he was satisfied that his insults had been absorbed, then sat back in his chair and continued his opinionated oratory. "You see, these bits of sub human shit depend on people like me to keep them alive. They don't give a damn about what I think, and they certainly couldn't give a toss about Trafford's fancy made up diagnosis... "

Morgan stubbed out his cigarette, and immediately lit another.

"... because all they are, is a bunch of fucking looneys. A ward full of feeble losers who can't even wipe their own fucking mouths without us helping them." Morgan stood up to indicate to his staff nurse that the exchange was nearing its conclusion. "In fact, I'll tell you why they're here. Shall I? Really?"

Jim hadn't changed his position and glared back at the charge nurse without speaking.

Morgan lowered his voice, as though he was about to divulge a secret. "They're here because no one has the guts to do us all a favour and put the poor bastards out of their misery!" As Morgan walked around his desk and past Jim, he stopped and leant towards the younger man's ear: "Such a pity you won't be staying to help these poor helpless people... Enjoy yourself, mopping up the shitty arses on geriatrics!"

Jim felt the bolt hit him out of the blue and turned to Morgan. "You what?! You can't do that. I've got a contract. You can't just move me like that!"

"Must have slipped my mind," Morgan feigned deep concern. "Sorry about that, but concerns have been raised about your suitability to work in such a challenging environment as this, particularly from your colleagues who've been terribly concerned about you. Isn't that right, Dave?"

Jim swung round to see the male nurse standing in the doorway, with a cigarette hanging from his mouth. "Oh, absolutely, Mr Morgan. Deep concern, but so sorry to lose you." Dave was even more mocking and less sincere than Morgan. Jim shot glances at both of them and stormed out of the office and seconds later, out of the ward, but despite the drama of his exit, he knew that there was nothing he could do against a man who had something on just about everyone who mattered at Greenbeck.

By the time he managed to get a meeting with the chief male nurse later that afternoon, he'd already been well and truly stitched up and was facing accusations of incompetence. He didn't need to ask where it had originated and for that reason he didn't stand any chance of being heard.

You could hate him as much as you liked, but when Morgan told you that you were finished, it was always time to go.

August 26th 1974; 14:00 hrs

George really didn't want to be at Greenbeck. Not even as a visitor. He didn't want to be there and he certainly didn't want to see his grandson being kept there. But it was his birthday and he couldn't let William be on his own. Not on his birthday.

God knows, no one else would come to see him.

Irene couldn't deal with it. Julie was too young and just about every other relative had gone quiet since Jean's death. Friends were more or less none existent, largely thanks to David and his disgusting rudeness towards anyone that Jean had tried to befriend.

So, George was the only link that William had with home and he felt the responsibility weighing heavily on his shoulders. To make things worse, he felt as useless as it was possible to feel. His Grandson wasn't getting any better and he didn't seem to recognise his own Grandpa, or perhaps, for some reason, he just couldn't acknowledge him. Who knows? Half the time, he talked gibberish and the rest of the time he just rocked backwards and forwards. Catatonia, they called it, as if giving it a name made it any easier to bear.

But they could put all the names they liked to what William was doing and it didn't make an ounce of difference. He wasn't getting any better, and all their medicines weren't doing a bloody thing. No good whatsoever, except he hadn't actually attacked anyone lately, but there again, until they took him to casualty on that night in June, he'd never attacked anyone in his life.

As George approached Margaret Page's office he found himself hesitating. Sure enough, he was expected. He was even early, but it occurred to him that this was probably going to be the latest in a long line of encounters where he was going to be told things that he simply didn't want to hear. Even worse than that, he knew that he was the only person left to listen, the only person who came back to see William and it seemed that he was the only person that stood between William remaining as part of the family, or being completely alone. He shuddered with that last thought and braced himself as he knocked on the office door.

"Come in." Miss Page's voice rang out and he was briefly put in mind of a headmistress beckoning one of her pupils to enter.

George pushed the door open and was met with the sight of the social worker making her way round her desk to greet him with an outstretched hand.

"Thank you for coming, Mr Cranford. Do have a seat." She beckoned George to one of two easy chairs, situated with a coffee table to the left side of her desk.

As he sat down, it was obvious to the social worker that George was apprehensive about either being at the hospital or the visit to his grandson that was about to take place or both.

"I'm sure that William will be pleased that you've come to see him on his birthday."

Being confronted with officialdom was not a situation that George felt comfortable with. Added to this was his own sense of guilt and helplessness at not being able to do more to help his grandson and he immediately became defensive. "I try to get here every couple of weeks, although I don't know what good I'm doing… he does even acknowledge that I'm there half the time and as for… "

Miss Page put her hand up and smiled in order to stop George from rambling any further, recognising his words for what they were and to indicate that she could understand his feelings of helplessness.

"I'm sure that William does know that you've come to see him, but his illness makes it difficult or even impossible for him to respond as he used to. He really is very ill, Mr Coleman, but I'm sure you've been told that already by Dr Trafford."

"I've been told that by just about everyone, but it doesn't help us understand how he got into this state in the first place, I mean, is it anything to do with his father? They didn't get on you know? And how long will it be before he'll be well enough to come home, not that we're going to be much use to him at our ages, but we'll do everything we can…" Every concern and every question just came tumbling out before Miss Page put her hand up for a second time.

"Mr Coleman. One question at a time! Firstly, no-one is at all sure about the causes of schizophrenia, but what we do know is that generally, if it starts this early, it's difficult to treat."

"So you're telling me the same thing that Dr Trafford told me and I don't want to appear rude, but aren't you saying that the condition can't be cured? I mean, he'll never get any better than this? Is that it?" George was becoming clearly agitated at this point, and his questions became more direct. "Miss Page, tell me please. We need to know. We need to know without words like "difficult to treat" and "unlikely" and "serious" and "very ill". Is he ever going to get better? And what's he going to be like if he doesn't? Just tell me in plain honest English!"

Miss Page made no attempt to stop the frustrated tirade, but instead sat with an expressionless face until he'd finished and then, with a deep sigh, prepared to deal with a relative who, quite clearly, wouldn't be palmed off with platitudes.

"Mr Coleman, I do appreciate that you and your wife must be very worried, but I'm sure you understand that I'm only the almoner or hospital social worker to be more precise nowadays. I can only reiterate what you've already been told. There are very isolated and rare cases where it has been reported that the condition has apparently disappeared and no further treatment is needed but as Dr Trafford has told you, it may be possible to control some or nearly all of the symptoms or it may be the case that William won't respond to treatment. As far as the relationship with his father, I'm afraid that I really don't know but for what it's worth, I've never heard of anything like that being a factor before."

George sighed, but he persisted. "So will he need treatment for the rest of his life? Can he come home?"

"To answer your second question first, I'm afraid that, in the opinion of a second psychiatrist, Dr Wallace, the section that William is detained under, Section 26, has today been renewed." She paused briefly to examined George's questioning expression before she continued. "This is because, in both Dr Trafford's and Dr Wallace's opinions, William has not responded sufficiently to treatment and he remains a danger to himself and possibly others. And as I indicated, he will probably always require medication to control his symptoms, but to what extent that can be achieved is impossible to say at the moment. I'm so sorry that I can't be more positive, but I feel that you wouldn't thank me for falsely building your hopes up."

The blunt approach had an obvious effect on George and he sat for a few seconds in silence. Even though he'd expected the news about the renewed Section and he'd been told more or less everything else before, for some reason he felt as though he'd just been hit by a sledge hammer. Over the past few weeks he had lived through nightmares that he didn't even know existed and now as he regained his composure, he felt the need to clear and deal with what had been on his mind since the first day he had visited William at Greenbeck.

"So, did the other patients on William's ward start off like he has? Is that what he'll be like in years to come? How long will it be before that happens? I mean will he know... do they know anything about it? My God, I... I can't believe I'm even thinking this!" None of these questions needed an answer and none was forthcoming. The tears started to prick and the more he tried to stop them, the more he could see visions of William in a few years.

Forever the professional, Miss Page was ready with the box of tissues, which George accepted with a nod of acknowledgement and she then proceeded to fill the silence by answering the question she suspected that George would be asking next. "I know that there have been major problems with the plumbing and electrics on the ward that he's supposed to be transferred to. Age of the building, I'm afraid, so I can't give you a date for his transfer, but I am assured that it won't be long now."

George nodded and blew his nose, before taking issue with her last statement. "I seem to remember being told that when he was admitted," and giving his nose one more wipe, "In fact, I've been told that just about every time that I've visited!"

Acutely aware that there was no possible answer that would bring that particular topic to a satisfactory conclusion, Miss Page decided it was time to progress the conversation and to tackle a more pressing problem.

"One more thing did emerge from Dr Wallace's visit this morning."

"And that is?" George had recovered his composure and had reluctantly accepted the change of subject.

Miss Page looked down at her hands, which were clasped in front of her on the desk and took an involuntary deep breath, as if to prepare her visitor for an unpleasant subject. "Dr Wallace has had a conversation with Dr Trafford concerning the best time to talk to William about his mother's death."

"You've all been telling me all along that William is too ill to be able to deal with it. What's changed now? You can't tell me that his condition has improved from last time I was here, or is there something else I should know?"

"No… no… there's nothing, I assure you. It was just that Dr Wallace and I'm sure Dr Trafford, feel that although they were hoping for more of an improvement in William's condition before the subject was broached, that we now have to consider his right to be told and whether it's right to delay it any longer."

George looked puzzled but his voice displayed exacerbation. "Now hold on Miss Page. When I said that the boy had a right to be told about his mother, Dr Trafford prevented me from telling him. Now you tell me that he's changed his mind, is that right?"

Miss Page clearly felt uncomfortable, but tried to deal with, what was turning out to be, a difficult encounter. "Yes, but as I believe I've already said, they had hoped… "

"Yes I know. An 'improvement in his condition', I remember, thank you." Both George and Miss Price seemed to know instinctively that further exchanges would be unproductive and would only serve to cause more frustration. Instead, George was beginning to visualise the picture of his grandson's reaction to the news of his mother's death, combined with rehearsals of the words he would use to give him the news.

Words just weren't needed and Miss Page stood up and walked round to the side of the desk where George had already began to rise from his chair. Extending her arm towards the office door, she asked the inevitable and overdue question. "Are you ready to go to the ward and talk to William?"

August 26th 1974; 14:35 hrs

William was not stupid. He was mentally ill… but not stupid. In fact, he was intelligent. He was certainly intelligent enough to know that if one of the nurses humiliated of threatened him and he retaliated, then he would be sat on and made to take yet more medicine. So he didn't respond. He learned to keep himself as safe as possible. That didn't mean that he was any further down the line of being able to understand his predicament or even to be aware of exactly where he was.

William knew that he wasn't at home and that he wasn't surrounded by the familiarity of what home represented. In fact, his perception of strangeness, of being somewhere he simply didn't want to be was one of the few enduring features of his thought processes. That and of course, the almost ever present paranoia. His fears and beliefs about aliens were a little less urgent, but the paranoia and fear of just about everyone he came in contact with, remained.

William could make connections, cause and effect connections and he always had been able to, no matter how ill he was. Sometimes the connections between things and events were born from his paranoia or hallucinations, but often, they weren't. If he kicked off, a load of men in white jackets would jump on him. If he ever mentioned Jack, which he only ever had done when he was being panicked by other people and it just slipped out, it seemed as though he had told them what they wanted to hear. When he had admitted to hearing Jack's voice, they seemed to get more interested in him.

William didn't trust people that took an interest in him, so he wouldn't tell them anything.

But the queues helped. The queues and the daily routines. He seemed to feel less agitated when he was lining up for his medicine, or dinner, or of course, his cigarette. Nobody asked the men to form a queue. They just happened. As they saw the medicine trolley arrive, a queue formed. When the table was put in place at meal times, a queue formed. When it was time to clear away plates, a queue formed. When it was time for cigarettes, a queue formed. No arguments and no jostling for places. Just queues. Just pure, unadulterated conditioning.

It was as though William believed that he would come to no harm as long as he joined the queues.

And for the time in between the queues? Time just seemed to pass. William had his chair, which was where, apart from being in a queue, that he felt safest. And there he sat. Passing time. His thoughts seemed to reach a lot of dead ends and they still jumped from one thing to another, but his attention span had increased marginally, so at least he could engage in a very elementary conversation for a short period and only then if someone else persisted in getting him to respond to simple questions. He would only initiate dialogue when he needed something and that was unusual. In any case, after half a minute or so, his thoughts still flew off in different directions.

Tom was having one of his extended wanders. In fact, most of his waking hours were spent shuffling round the ward with his head bowed and dribbling, or to be more precise, dribbling and as long as he could get one, smoking as well. Shuffling was bad enough, but Tom's shuffling always looked peculiar. He didn't shuffle quite like anyone else on the ward. Tom had jumped out of a first floor window a couple of years earlier and had snapped both of his ankles as he landed on his feet.

When they took him to hospital, they'd put both his legs in Plaster of Paris, but when he'd returned to Greenbeck, instead of following the instructions to keep him off his feet for a few days, they'd just let him walk before the plaster had dried. So his bones set. They'd set in completely the wrong position, but they'd set.

And now, all he could do was to shuffle on his insteps, with his feet splayed outwards. No one knew for sure if he had any pain and because he had so much trouble speaking, no one particularly bothered about it. In fact, just about everyone ignored him, except of course, for some of the staff, who seemed to take some form of pleasure in humiliating him.

William didn't humiliate Tom at all. He never told Tom to "go away" or "piss off", or anything like it. In fact, William felt strangely comfortable and safe when Tom was there. That was on the occasions when he actually sat down, like now. Tom's clothes were in their usual post meal mess and as was often the case, no one had shaved him. He sat in the armchair that was opposite William and about ten feet away. Neither spoke, but there again, they never did.

William could smell shit and it wasn't him. He looked up towards his newly arrived companion, but Tom didn't seem that bothered about having messed himself. The smell was awful and seemed to occupy every square inch of atmosphere, and didn't escape Morgan's nostrils as he walked past. He turned his nose up in a contemptuous and exaggerated display of disgust, and as he slowly walked back to his office called out.

"Dave, get a couple of the others and clean him up, he's crapped himself."

Dave and two other male nurses drained their tea cups got up from the table where they had been sitting and reluctantly wandered over to where Tom was sitting. "Christ almighty Tom, what a fucking stink!" Dave joined in with Morgan's disdainful expression of disgust and was joined by the others.

"I'll get the bath ready and you two can bring him through." Dave took control and opted for the easy option, a move that wasn't entirely lost on his colleagues.

"Thanks mate, we'll do the same for you some time!" The male nurse, Paul, spoke for both of the Tom bearing duo as Dave disappeared through the door at the end of the dayroom which led to the patient's bathroom. Positioning themselves either side of the chair and grabbing Tom under the arms, they pulled him to his feet with little finesse. As he grunted his disapproval, their only response was to pull him along a bit harder, a bit quicker, until they too disappeared through the door at the end of the day room.

William had watched the whole process of escorting until they had disappeared from sight, and had felt strangely apprehensive and nervous and Jack jumped in to give his interpretation.

"They're taking him to get a bit more of his brain… it's what they do… they're going to take a bit more, William. They're taking him to a special room where they do those things!"

William didn't hear Jack so much these days and when he did, he couldn't always understand or quite hear what he was saying. But he did this time. Loud and clear.

"If you don't believe me, go and look for yourself… Go on! "

William could hear the sound of raised voices from what he thought of as the bathroom. Slowly he uncurled his feet from underneath him and leaned forward on his chair. He looked around him, his thoughts temporarily held together by adrenaline and rose cautiously and walked towards the doorway that Tom and his escorts had disappeared into. The noises from the bathroom were a combination of laughter and jibes from the nurses and protests from Tom. It was Paul's voice that rose above the others.

"For Christ's sake keep him still. The shit's caked on around his bollocks!"

William was creeping up to his destination, but even with what he was hearing, he was unclear as to why he wanted to look or indeed, what he wanted to look at.

They hadn't even bothered to close the door and as William edged forward he could clearly see Tom's naked back. He was standing in the bath with a male nurse on either side of the bath, holding his arms and bending him slightly forward with his legs apart. Behind him, Dave now with his sleeves rolled up, had his hands in the water and was obviously cleaning something. Within seconds it became obvious that the something was a wooden floor brush, which Dave used to get the remaining faeces from Tom's nether regions.

Tom was yelling out and although his words couldn't be understood, the emotion, the anger and the indignity behind them should have been obvious to anyone who could hear him.

William didn't hear Jack, maybe Jack had nothing to say, or perhaps Tom's cries were drowning out Jack's words. He just felt nauseated by what he saw. He couldn't put it into context, he wasn't able to view it as nurse doing things to patients, but he was able to recognise cruelty and he felt sick.

As he backed away, his mind began to race again… aliens… human prisoners… wanted to go home… needed to write something… want to go Grandpa… Julie will be waking up after her afternoon nap… Go back to the chair…

He was affected by what he had seen, even though, a few minutes later, he would be unable to put into words exactly what he had been confronted with. The feeling of fear was there, whether he could articulate or not. As he reached his chair, he could feel the beginnings of reassurance, but at the same time, he was noticeably disturbed by his experience, tucking his feet underneath him as he sat and rocked.

It was some minutes before William was shaken out of his almost trance like state by a familiar voice. "Hello, William," and then with more hesitance. "Happy Birthday."

He looked up and to his right and made eye contact with his Grandpa and in that moment, both of them felt the faintest glimmer of what they once had. William's paranoia and ideations wouldn't allow him to hold, explore and enjoy the feeling. He couldn't get past, through or over the thoughts in his head.

He wanted to, he so wanted to, but he couldn't. Instead, all that he could muster was a feint, and somehow foreign smile, and an even less familiar and very formal. "Thank you," before he looked away and started rocking again.

George hung on to the feeling a little longer and was clearly emotional as he tried to smile and carry on the conversation.

"Did they give you your cards?" George's eyes searched and William responded by reaching down the side of the chair, but seemed almost surprised when he retrieved the cards and envelopes.

"Nan sends her love, and says that she'll try and get in to see you soon."

William was looking at his cards again and didn't seem to acknowledge his grandfather's conversation.

"Did you get Uncle Bill's card? He said he'd sent you one."

William appeared to respond by looking at both the cards and handing one of them to George, who made an exaggerated gesture of relief that it had arrived. "Ah, that's good! Julie sends you a big hug and keeps asking when her brother… "

"Where's Mum? What have they done to her? Where is she?"

"You know what they've done to her, don't you, William?" Jack's voice was there and adding fuel to the fire.

George's eyes looked to one side and for the first time, William noticed that his grandfather wasn't alone. Standing about ten feet to his left was a short grey haired lady in a white starched coat. As George looked up at her, she slowly walked over to William and sat next to him.

"William, I'm afraid your Grandpa's got some bad news for you. Do you understand what I'm saying to you?"

"Yes… yes, I do… where's Mum? It's about Mum, isn't it?"

"Yes, I'm afraid it is William." George stopped talking and looked at the almoner for her approval. She nodded her assent, and he carried on. "Your Mum had a bad accident, William. Do you understand? A very bad accident indeed."

"They've got her, just like I said. They've got her. That's why she hasn't been here to see you!" Jack was in no doubt.

"They got her, didn't they?" It was obvious that William was doing something with the information that George had given to him. It was also obvious that he was not hearing the news as it should have been heard.

"Who do you mean, William?" George was temporarily distracted from the task in hand by the strangeness of his grandson's reply.

"All of them. They've got all of them."

"I'm sorry William, but I don't know what you mean?"

Jack was there in an instant.

"Of course he knows. They sent him. They altered him…"

William was becoming confused and held his fists to his ears as though he was trying not to listen, although which messages he was trying to block wasn't certain, especially to William himself. "William!" George persisted, but William just withdrew further and further in himself, or at least, that what it seemed like. He tried again. "William, we need to talk about your Mum. Do you understand, William?"

"You didn't come with us when we went to Lowestoft."

"No, William, but that was years ago. Why do you want to talk about that now?"

"Mr Grainger said that I've got to cover my books, or I'll be in trouble."

George was silenced by the sudden randomness in William's conversation and the sight of his grandson sitting huddled and rocking in the chair was more than George could handle. As he turned to the social worker, it was obvious by the look on her face that the news they had come to the ward to give would have to wait for another day. Reluctantly, and with a sigh, George got up from his chair, touched his huddled grandson on the shoulder and made his way towards the door, nodding to the still seated Miss Page on his way past. Dave, having completed his task with Tom in the bathroom, was waiting to unlock the door and George passed through without words and without looking back.

Miss Page continued to sit for another minute or so, before she rose to sit in the chair that George had vacated. Gently, she touched William on the shoulder. "William, will you talk to me for a moment? I'd really like that."

Nothing.

"William, you don't seem very happy today. Is that right?"

William momentarily moved his head to look in the social workers direction before resuming his position. She repeated the question, but before she could get any form of response, a clearly agitated Tom came bustling up and planted himself next to her.

"Hello Tom! How are you?"

Tom said nothing, but just stood there, seemingly content at being close to someone and most uncharacteristically, not shuffling off in search of the next cigarette. Miss Page tried to find a reason, and probed. "That's not like you Tom. Is it? You don't normally stand still for more than a half a minute."

"Bath!" Tom could manage to say that much, but little else was intelligible. He seemed clearly agitated, but the social worker had no way of knowing about the events in the bathroom under half an hour earlier and proceeded to entirely miss the point.

"That's nice, Tom. Are you nice and clean now?"

Tom didn't persist. He couldn't. Not yet and certainly not verbally.

"Fag!"

"I'm sorry, Tom, I don't smoke. Go and ask in the office over there." As she pointed Tom in the direction of the office, she was a little surprised to see him shuffle off in the opposite direction to his cigarette supply. With a shrug, she continued with her efforts with William.

"You normally have a little chat with me when I come to the ward. Are you feeling a bit muddled today?"

Nothing.

"Are you hearing lots of things that are upsetting you, William?"

Nothing.

"Shall I go and leave you in peace, and I'll come and see you again in the week?

Nothing.

Slowly, she got up to leave, and with a final reassuring hand on his shoulder, walked towards the office door. Upon entering, she found Morgan, with the obligatory cigarette in his mouth, sat behind his desk.

"Good afternoon, Richard"

"Miss Page." Morgan's acknowledgement of his visitor was less than enthusiastic and he underlined his attitude by carrying on with his paperwork, without bothering to look up, but the social worker was used to Morgan's manners and carried on regardless.

"William Phillips' Grandfather and I have just tried to broach the subject of his Mother's death, but we really didn't get anywhere with him. He seems disturbed by something. I can usually have a reasonably normal chat with him for a short period before he disappears back into his confusion and voices, but we couldn't even get that far today. Any idea why?"

163

Morgan just shrugged his shoulders, dislodging some ash from his burning cigarette. Brushing it away from the paper he was writing on, he looked up for the first time.

"No idea. He goes like that sometimes", Morgan had little time for the social worker, or any social worker for that matter. And it showed in his voice and his manner.

"I see… " Although she plainly didn't. "So you can't throw any light on why he seems so nervous?"

"Sorry?"

"Yes, I suppose you are. Well maybe you can tell me when he's going to be transferred; his family are getting rather impatient that it's taking so long."

Morgan stopped what he was doing, removed his glasses and looked up at the social worker.

"I'm informed that they are going to start the moves in a couple of days, but it will take a few days to move forty patients, so count on it being a slow process. In fact, you'll probably retire before that happens." Morgan shot a falsely quizzical look at Miss Page. "Remind me when that is?"

"Next month."

"Ah yes, September, I remember now. You'll be sadly missed." This last comment was said with little feeling and was accompanied by Morgan putting his glasses back on his nose and resuming his paper work. Miss Page remained where she was, saying nothing and eventually, Morgan looked up, clearly irritated. "Was there something else?"

"William Phillips' Section Papers… where are they?" Her voice matched Morgan's for irritation and disdain. Without speaking, Morgan pointed with his pen in the direction of a shelf by the door, which was home to a few piles of papers. Without any further reference to Morgan, she found what she was looking for and took them to the medical notes trolley to complete her part in the process of detaining William.

Administrative duties complete, Miss Page replaced the top on her fountain pen and left the office.

"Fucking do gooder!" was Morgan's only comment, as be put stubbed out his cigarette and made his way into the ward, only to bump into Tom, who was back to shuffling and on his way to purloin another cigarette.

"You smell a bit sweeter. Had a good arse scrub have we?" The last comment being accompanied with one of his mocking smiles and

164

demeaning cheek slapping. Tom didn't respond well, with the experience obviously still fresh in his mind and let out a phlegm ridden roar, much to the amusement of the charge nurse and his staff.

"Naughty boy, Tom. Now you know we don't like tempers here. Don't you?" Morgan was in his element and thoroughly enjoying the encounter. "You know what I think? I think that you don't deserve a cigarette now."

Another roar.

"That's two tempers, Tom. Very naughty, Tom. That means no cigarettes for two hours." Then his tone altered, obviously tiring of the game. "Now piss off and get out of my sight." Morgan turned and surveyed his kingdom before walking slowly over to where William was still sitting. Slowly and deliberately he sat down in the chair vacated by William's grandfather.

"Well, birthday boy. You've had a busy day!"

William glared at Morgan from under his eyebrow.

"At least someone came to see you, although Christ knows why!" Morgan reached over to William's chair and took the birthday cards from their hiding place next to William's thigh. Slowly he opened them and with mock interest, began his torment.

"Nan and Grandpa? Uncle Bill?" He stopped reading and looked over his glasses at William.

"Didn't we get one from Mummy, eh? Did Mummy forget little William's birthday?"

William's mind began to race and jump, but it maintained a common thread of hate towards his tormenter.

Morgan could see his agitation and decided to have just a little bit more fun. He looked at William with a sarcastic imitation of remorse.

"Oh, I'm so sorry, Billy boy. Mummy can't send you cards anymore, can she? Mummy can't do anything anymore, can she?"

Jack's voice was no longer as muffled or distant and although it wasn't as clear as it had been before, the words were plain enough.

"He's taken her brain... washed it. He enjoyed doing it, William. Did you know that? You'll never see her again. Did you know that William?!"

William felt that his head was going to burst with the messages it was receiving and the hatred and sadness that was there. There, but without almost without coherent thought. Missing his mother and hating the man in front of him were emotions that he couldn't separate and Jack's words kept ringing in his ears.

But Morgan hadn't finished. To him it was a game. To him, William was another loony that he had power over. Another crackpot who was only there because of their own stupidity and weak mindedness. To Morgan, William Phillips deserved it and to a man whose only reasons for doing the job were the wage slip and the power it gave him over those who couldn't fight back, he was good afternoon sport.

Morgan put his hand to his mouth, mimicking the action of someone who had said something that they shouldn't have done. "Oops. Sorry about that, you don't like that name do you William? Silly me. Still, at least Mummy won't be telling me off, will she? Eh?!"

Again, the hand went up to his mouth. "Oh, there I go again, saying things I shouldn't."

No thoughts that he could put his finger on anymore. Just the red of anger and the pure simple and untangled emotion that he must silence the person who was hurting him and his mother so much, William's knuckles tightened on the arms of the chair as he watched Morgan get up from his chair.

"Oh well. Can't stop chatting to you all day, Mr Phillips. Got work to do," Then as an afterthought. "Not that you'd know much about that, would you?"

The last comment was said under his breath, but loudly enough to be heard. William followed Morgan with his eyes. His relief at knowing that his tormentor had moved didn't outweigh the feelings he had to hurt him. To damage him as Morgan had damaged his mother.

He stared in Morgan's direction as he made his way back towards his office.

The replacement radio was still sending him messages. He couldn't make out what they were, but he did know that it was one of Morgan's brain washing tools, and he also knew they were directed towards him.

"He's going to get you too, William. You know that. He'll get you!" Jack didn't hesitate to jump in with his contribution.

Morgan altered his path to go over to Tom, who was searching for dog ends from the floor. He stood and watched as Tom struggled to keep his balance as he bent down to the floor. As he watched him stagger to his feet, he moved closer and reached into his pocket for his cigarettes and lighter. He had Tom's immediate attention. Slowly he took one of his cigarettes out of the packet before closing it and putting it slowly and deliberately back into his pocket, not taking his eyes away from Tom for a second.

Still William watched. Still the anger.

Tom, for his part, was following every move that Morgan made. As Morgan stood, still staring at Tom, and with the unlit cigarette in his hand, he called out to his colleagues who had resumed their tea drinking and smoking at a nearby table.

"What do you think, lads? Shall we let Tom have a fag?"

Laughter, as the lads around the table saw that the afternoon's entertainment was continuing.

William didn't register the scene that was being played out. All he knew was what Jack was telling him to do.

"He's going to get you, William. He hurt Mum, he took her brain away. He's going to do the same to you. You've got to stop him." William uncurled his legs from under him and began to rise from his chair. Twenty metres away, the scene with Tom was continuing.

Morgan stared at Tom, who for his part, was staring at the cigarette in Morgan's hand. Slowly and deliberately, he lifted his arm so that the cigarette was level with Tom's head. Keeping the cigarette in Tom's view the whole time, he brought his other hand, the one with the lighter, into Tom's line of vision. For a few seconds, there was no movement between them, until quite suddenly, Morgan put the cigarette into his mouth, lit it and blew the smoke into Tom's face. Without even taking the cigarette out, Morgan delivered his parting shot. "I don't think so Tom, do you? How does it feel to be a non-smoker, Tom?"

More laughter from the table, particularly as Tom let out a frustrated growl at the charge nurse. Even more laughter as he made a grab for the cigarette, still firmly lodged in Morgan's mouth, and stumbled to the floor as Morgan casually stepped back to avoid him.

Morgan walked over to the table, and milked the incident for all he could. "Did I say something to upset him?"

More laughter. "You bastard, Richard. Do you want a cup?" Ever faithful Dave was there with the teapot. "You can talk, Dave. You've just cleaned his arse with a fucking floor brush!" More laughter.

Morgan sat with the rest of his staff, but William didn't even see the others. His eyes only saw the thing they called Morgan, the alien that kept on tormenting him. The thing that took his Mother. Still the radio played its now unintelligible messages. Still trying to fry his brain.

"Go on, William. You know what you've got to do. Go on!" Jack spurred him on as he walked slowly towards the table, his eyes fixed on the source of his anger and pain. His mind intent on its task, although he was incapable of planning how he would achieve his aim, if stopping his pain could be construed as an aim. More of an instinct. An instinct to survive.

Eighteen metres... sixteen metres. Morgan was still laughing and joking. Still with his back to him. Fifteen metres... thirteen... eleven... still engrossed in his story telling. Eight metres, seven... still slowly, still Morgan and his cronies didn't look away from their table. Six metre, five, four. William even hated the bastard alien from the back. Three metres... then...

Even as William felt the muscles tense in his arms and legs as his body braced itself for the onslaught, he was stopped in midstream by a sudden movement to his left. He only became aware of what it was as Tom, who was being ignored by all and sundry as he always was, lifted one of the dining chairs above his head and brought it crashing down onto Morgan's skull, send him crashing, unconscious to the floor amongst a sea of upturned chairs and startled nurses. Single mindedly, Tom reached down and picked up the remnants of Morgan's still lit cigarette and was about to put it to his mouth when he was jumped on from all sides and taken to the floor.

William froze and watched as Tom was bundled to the floor, and after what seemed like a few seconds he heard the ward entrance door being hurriedly unlocked, followed by the bustle of the obligatory white tunic brigade who had come to join in the fun. Seeing the prostrate figure of Tom being held down caused even more confusion than the site of Morgan lying unconscious and face down in a pool of blood, just a few yards away.

William was still watching as he and the other patients who had gathered around the scene were ushered away. In William's case, only far as his chair, from where he still had a good view.

The scene was chaotic, with half the nurses dealing with a now completely harmless Tom and the other half standing around Morgan playing the part of innocent bystanders as one of their number was presumably rendering some form of first aid to the unconscious charge nurse.

William was still watching some time later as Morgan was lifted onto an ambulance stretcher and carried away. The aliens could be defeated! All he needed to do was to think about something and it would happen. They couldn't get to his brain while he had this power.

168

"So why did it take the incident with the bus for someone to notice that he was this ill, I mean, what the hell did his family think they were doing?"

Trafford looked over the rim of his glasses at the young charge nurse and silently wondered which took more energy to endure, the bigotry of the now hospitalised Morgan, or the raw and sometimes misguided enthusiasm of the newly promoted John Winson, who was leaning his overweight frame self-righteously against the notes trolley.

"I mean, none of this should have happened. You can't tell me that the guy suddenly started talking to buses without any warning!"

Trafford held his hand up to let Winson know that he should be taking a breath and engaging common sense before he said anything else. "Nothing is ever that simple, John. You should know that. Anyway, if there was ever a family that have paid a price for trying to deal with their own problems it's got to be this one."

Winson waited for the psychiatrist to add to his statement, but he really knew that when Trafford went silent, it was not for effect, but rather that he had said all he was going to say on the matter. He shuffled a little uncomfortably before trying a different approach. "Has anyone told him about his mother?"

"The hospital social worker was dealing with that and she reported that she had made an effort, with his grandfather, to break the news to him, but little success. When I spoke to William just a couple of days ago before we moved him to this ward, he seemed to somehow know that she'd died." Trafford took off his glasses and began to absently clean them with his handkerchief. "I'm not altogether certain whether that's part of his psychosis and he'd be thinking that whether she was alive or dead. Or perhaps Richard Morgan let something slip that he shouldn't have done. I don't know. The fact is he seems to know."

"So, how far have we got with him? Has there been any improvement since he was admitted in June?"

"Some," Trafford didn't sound very convinced. "He seems to be less agitated and at least can follow a conversation and respond appropriately for a little while until his thoughts start to fly off in different directions and then we get the characteristic gibberish. His paranoia, if you look at his behaviour and the way he looks around him, still plays a major part in his illness."

"So what now?" Winson, largely through not knowing the psychiatrist and his over inflated ego, was being bold with his questions and Trafford, for now at least, was doing him the courtesy of replying.

"I think we've given the Chlorpromazine long enough and we can't really increase it any more than we have done. That leaves us with Thioridazine. We'll give that a try." With a flourish of his pen, Trafford wrote the prescription got up from the desk and brushed past the bearded charge nurse, indicating that he was not prepared to enter into any further discussion.

"And goodbye to you too!" Winson's comments were uttered under his breath as Trafford made his way out of the ward.

Winson walked into the dayroom, which still smelt of paint and looked around him. Rose Villa was not part of the original Victorian hospital, but had been built in the grounds in the 50's. It was a self-contained building on its own, with several others like it nearby. The building itself was much less imposing than Tamworth Ward and inside, its lower ceilings (and of course, new paintwork) were less depressing. The dayroom was about sixty feet square, with the usual plastic covered easy chairs in a line against every wall. The almost compulsory smell of cigarette smoke hung in the air, despite the open windows.

The patients were generally either sitting and rocking or wandering around with little purpose. They were rather younger, on average, than they had been on Tamworth Ward, but an onlooker could be forgiven for thinking that it was just a waiting area for eventual admission to one of the long stay wards. For now, though, they mostly comprised of patients who had returned from their temporary lodging in other wards during Rose Villa's refurbishment and for all of them this was either their first admission to a mental hospital, or they had been re-admitted due to a relapse in their condition.

Schizophrenics, manic depressives, a couple of attempted suicides, a couple of nervous breakdowns and probably a couple of imponderables and that was John Winson's ward. Twenty five of them in all. As he watched, he couldn't help but notice how little they spoke to each other, how much they appeared to be in their own worlds, their own spheres of torment. Noticing was about as far as the process went for Winson. He wasn't cruel or inconsiderate; he was simply used to seeing patients behaving like that. Fact of life. In his early days as a mental nurse he'd tried to get them to do jigsaws, but they used to get up and walk away. He used to get them books to read, but they just held them up in front of their eyes to keep him happy, just long enough for the next cigarette to come around.

Waste of time really. He cared about them. He made sure they had their medicines on time. Made sure they had their physical needs looked after. He seemed to spend half his working life on the phone to the laundry or the stores, or the kitchen. Of course he cared. But what else could he do apart from keep them safe, comfortable and of course, medicated. They had their group sessions, of course, but that didn't achieve much for most of them. It was all he could do to keep them seated, let alone anything else.

As he looked around him though, it didn't occur to him for a second that not only didn't the patients talk to each other very much, but his staff didn't talk to them much either, beyond giving instructions or asking questions. No one ever passed the time of day or talked purely for the sake of it.

As for William, he'd wasted no time in claiming his territory in the dayroom in the form of a regular and jealously guarded chair. As he sat there now, he fixed his stare on Winson who was standing at the entrance to the dayroom. Like the other one, the one they called Morgan, he wore the grey suit, but he was somehow more subtle, less threatening, although Jack was insistent. *"He's one of them William He's not to be trusted. He's just like all the rest!"*

It seemed that every time he saw Winson, Jack was issuing his warning. And every time that Jack gave his warnings, William listened. He was listening now. Although Jack was more distant and sometimes less coherent than he had been in the past, he still listened. Couldn't help it. Didn't want to.

He was in another of the mind altering areas. He just had to look around him to see that. The chairs, the lino covered floor, the male nurses in white tunics. The paint work was different though, having cream walls and yellow paintwork. The victims were younger than they had been in the last place, but still they walked around with heads bowed. Still they moved from seat to seat and still they queued for meals and medicines. Although it was a bit less formal, it was recognisably similar and strangely comfortable.

He shared a dormitory with three other men, who had barely said

171

anything to him since he got there. Christopher was middle aged and spent much of his day huddled up and weeping. Graham was about twenty years old and would at least talk when spoken to, but avoided people as much as he could, spending most of the day smiling and laughing to himself. Peter talked all day. William couldn't see who he was talking to, but he kept talking nevertheless. Peter seemed to latch onto him for some reason and William was aware of Peter being of no threat to him. They'd already taken all the brain they wanted to take from Peter.

Jack was always insistent that it was William's turn next, so it was best not to talk to anyone unless he needed to, otherwise they might be able to follow his thought trail back into his brain and then that would be the end. Like his mother, it would be the end.

So William just waited and watched. He watched Anthony, the young thin man with the black mop of greasy hair as he darted back and forth. Always in a hurry, never sitting for more than a few seconds. He watched Sean as he just sat in his chair and stared out of the window. He watched Ivor, who didn't seem like the others as he kept talking to the nurse, asking them questions, sometimes smiling, sometimes frowning, but almost always talking to himself when he wasn't talking to others. He'd tried to talk to William, but Jack had told him to ignore him because he was an undercover alien. Clever!

Most of all though, he watched the men in white tunics and the one in the grey suit in particular, the one who called himself John. Then there was Rob, the short one with the Irish accent and Jeff, the middle aged one with the grey hair who spent most of his time in the office with John.

This was the area where they softened people up. They got them to drop their defences so they could get into their victims brains a lot easier and in less time. That's why they had the women in this place. Dressed in blue check dresses and calling themselves nurses, but that didn't fool someone as clever as William. Jack had spotted the trick right away and warned him. *"They've made themselves look like women to try and get you to talk to them… Don't go near them… they've picked up your thoughts about your mother and they sense that women can soften you up. Don't go near them!"*

But William already knew. He already knew about the short pretty one with blond hair. They'd made her look young, but he knew. He could recognise the Morgan alien anyway, no matter what the disguise was. It was certain. This girl they called Christine was Morgan. How could they think that he was so stupid that he couldn't work that one out!

William couldn't identify the older female alien, the one they called Irene, but he would… in time.

So, for now, William watched and waited. He did everything he was told to do. He got up when he was told to get up, he queued up when it was the time to queue, he eat when it was time to eat, smoked whenever he could get hold of cigarettes, and went to bed like a lamb when he was told to do so. He even took his medicines when they gave them to him, although Jack would get angry and not talk to him after he'd taken them.

In between doing what he was told to do, he just sat and watched and waited. He didn't really know what he was waiting for, but he waited nevertheless.

December 2nd 1974; 15:45 hrs

William was standing. Standing and looking out of the window. He did that sometimes, or rather he did that sometimes lately. He stared out the window at the overcast and drab looking day. He could see the other buildings, including the huge Victorian edifice that was the original Greenbeck Hospital, and the smaller villas in the grounds. They told him that he was ill and was in hospital, but he wasn't convinced and certainly didn't trust them. Who'd ever heard of a hospital with locked doors? Who'd ever heard of a hospital where no one ever when home?

"Did your Grandpa come in today to see you, William?" The Irish accent announced the enquirer and William turned to see Rob who was busying himself with a load of books that someone had just left on the floor.

It took a few seconds for the message to reach where it was supposed to go to and for a response to be formed. All the time, William was aware of other thoughts trying to interfere with his answer, competing for the window of opportunity to muddle him. But he was learning. He was learning to hold the thoughts back. He was learning how to concentrate. He was, above all, learning how to appear as though there was nothing wrong.

"Yes… yes, he did."

Having got an answer to his question and apparently satisfied that his patient was at least one step better than merely just breathing, Rob moved on to his next bit of tidying, at the other side of the day room. William stared after him for a few moments, before returning to look out of the window. He'd been standing there for over half an hour, in fact since his Grandpa had left. He had watched him walk up to the big building, looking back once or twice to wave as he went. William was still holding the bar of Cadbury's chocolate that he'd brought, unwilling to let it go, lest he should lose it. Reluctant to eat it as it seemed that of he did so, then a part of the memory of seeing his Grandpa would be lost forever.

William continued to stare out of the window. The day was nearly over and the light was fading. As he watched the gardeners packing up their tools for the day, his attention wandered to what had been the rectangular flowerbeds, now skilfully dug over and weeded. Dug over and weeded to leave the earth raised in the middle of the beds and neatly edged, ready for life to return in the Spring. They looked somehow sad, as though the promise of life was simply too distant to be convincing. They looked like winter graves and as the light faded, they looked ever more sinister. But they were irresistible and William found himself continuing to stare and even too wonder at who it was that was buried there.

William argued with himself and even muttered under his breath as if in response to his thoughts, almost as if they were real voices. Or were they real voices. There was no one there, so the voices couldn't be real. Or could they? Sometimes the thoughts seemed to be so compelling, so real that they had to be coming from somewhere. They couldn't be coming from inside his head. Could they? He had a friend once. He thought he had a friend, he sometimes thought that he came to visit him sometimes, but when he looked he wasn't there. He thought his name had been Jack and he thought he could hear him sometimes, in the background, almost as an echo to his thoughts. Whenever he heard it, or thought he heard it, he felt compelled to stop what he was doing and try to make out the words.

But he couldn't make out what it was saying. Not really, but every time he thought he heard something it was when he was trying to think of something, to remember something, or when he was getting nervous or worried. Like the other day Christopher had hit Rob and they called the team to deal with it. William could have sworn that the voice had been there and had strained to hear it. And then it was gone.

The radio made him feel uncomfortable. As he continued to stare at the graves, now deserted and in a half light, it was as though the radio knew his feelings. The music made him sadder, as though he was in some way linked to the radio station. Somehow, a part of it, or was it trying to tell him things that he just didn't want to hear. Things in the music that no one else could hear. Things that were just aimed at him. Still they turned it on. Morning, noon and night the bloody thing churned on. Sometimes, it had nothing to say to him, and even when it did, he couldn't make it out.

There was a radio once. Vaguely in the past he could remember a radio that gave him messages and someone had silenced it. Was it him? He didn't know. Couldn't tell. The memory just wouldn't give him the details he craved for. Wouldn't give him the answers he wanted. When did it happen? Yesterday? Last week? Last month? William didn't know. Everyday seemed the same. Except Saturday and Sunday. Bacon for breakfast on Saturday and Sunday, then back to everyday being the same.

Every once in a while, someone tried to get him to do something. Some jigsaw puzzle, or book, but he'd just fiddle with it for a few seconds before returning to the more comfortable and less strenuous inactivity broken up by the even more comfortable routine. So difficult to concentrate, although he never consciously thought about it. If the task wasn't routine and needed to be thought through, then it simply didn't happen. It was so much easier and indeed so much more compelling to do nothing than it was to try something new.

"William," It was John who had approached him from behind and now had a hand on William's shoulder.

William turned round to see Winson indicating towards the office. "Dr Trafford would like to see you for a minute. Nothing to worry about." The last comment was a complete waste of breath as William began to instantly, instinctively and groundlessly worry, as he began to follow the charge nurse to the nursing office to find Trafford sat behind the desk, with his glasses characteristically perched on the end of his nose and his fountain pen poised above a pile of prescription sheets.

"Good afternoon, William. Take a seat."

William bent his knees slowly, as if in trepidation, eased himself onto the seat opposite Trafford and after meticulously putting his chocolate in his shirt pocket, sat still with his hands firmly placed on his thighs.

Trafford noticed his young patient's apprehension, and tried to go at least a little way to reassure him. "There's nothing to worry about, William. You should be used to this by now; after all, we see each other every week, don't we?"

175

William attempted a smile which wasn't altogether convincing and after a couple of seconds of reflection, Trafford decided that the reassuring approach was a waste of time, or, to be more accurate, a lot of effort for very little return.

"So how are you feeling then, William?"

William didn't answer immediately. Should he be feeling ill? Why was he asking "how are you feeling"? Why did he want to know?

Trafford decided to rephrase the question in order to increase his chances of gaining a response.

"Are you OK today?"

A nod for a reply.

"Do you remember a chat we had a few weeks ago about where you are? The place you are in at the moment. Do you remember where you are?"

Another nod.

"Good. Can you tell us, then? Where are you?"

"In John's office."

A grin from the charge nurse who was standing by the trolley and even Trafford had the beginnings of a smile.

"No, not this room. This place. All the buildings you see when you look out of the window. What's it called?"

So they were watching him. When he was sitting. When he looked out at the gardens, they were watching him. He knew they'd been watching him. Something had always told him he was being watched. Trafford repeated the question. "What's the name of this place?"

"Greendale Hospital."

"That's very good, William, but it's Greenbeck hospital, not Greendale."

"Greenbeck Hospital." William repeated the name.

"And do you remember why you came into hospital?"

Silence.

"Do you remember why you came into hospital, William?"

"I hurt my head."

"Yes, that's right. That's why you went to casualty. But do you remember why you came here?"

"Because they painted it to look nice."

Another grin from Winson, but only persistence from Trafford.

"Not quite. Why did you come into this hospital?"

William searched from an answer, but his experiences, since he didn't know when, simply couldn't provide it. He couldn't coherently synthesise any events that would match the question with an answer.

"Do you remember when you first came into Tamworth Ward? Do you remember anything about that?"

"They all jumped on me and held me on the floor."

"Yes, they did. And why do you think that happened?"

"Because I'd been bad."

"Well, yes, you were a little bit aggressive, and we had to give you some medicine. Do you remember that?"

This time, a nod, but William plainly found the memory disturbing. Trafford repeated his question again. "So do you remember why you came into this hospital?"

"Because I hurt someone."

"Did you?" The reply took Trafford by surprise, so he allowed himself to be distracted away from his line of questioning in order to explore further.

"Who did you hurt, William?"

William looked down at the floor and didn't reply.

"Who did you hurt, William? Can you tell me?"

"Mum."

Trafford and Winson exchanged glances, aware that the discussion was entering areas that William had previously been unable or unwilling to explore.

"In what way do you think you hurt your mother?"

More looking down, shuffling and rubbing his thighs.

"William. Can you tell how you think you hurt your mother?"

"I left her and they got her and I knew they'd get her and I knew they'd kill her and if I'd have been there I could have stopped them getting her. I was her bodyguard, I was her protector and I went away and they got her and now she's dead and it's my fault. My fault and she's dead and it's my fault." The words came tumbling out as if they were out of control. All the time, William was getting more and more agitated and was beginning to rock in his chair.

Trafford persisted. "Who do you think "got her" William? Can you tell me that?"

Something deep inside him told William that he'd already said too much. He knew that he'd said too much and that they would somehow be able to do something with his words, something with his thoughts, but he didn't know what. Didn't know how. Uncle Bill would know, but he was at school and had been painting the front door before they went to the beach.

Thoughts jumbling. Coming and going, mismatching now and just not making sense. William knew now that they didn't make sense and it was distressing him... and it showed. He made to get up and leave, but Winson put his hand on his shoulder and he reluctantly bent his knees to sit down. On the periphery of his thoughts, he barely perceived a voice, or was it his own thoughts... the voice sounded familiar. Sounded like someone he'd known, but not known. Sounded like Jack. But he couldn't remember what Jack looked like, only that he'd been there and used to tell him things, but his memory was muddled. Or was it his own thoughts... he strained to listen nevertheless. Or was it straining to concentrate on his own thoughts? *"They... brain... don't speak... danger, danger."* Sweating now. Sweating from his own agitation. Sweating because of his own internal struggle to pay attention to a voice that couldn't be there, but at the same time, thoughts that he knew couldn't be his. Again the rocking.

The office had gone quiet as William looked up and saw both Winson and Trafford looking at him with concerned expressions. It was Trafford that broke the silence.

"Are you OK?"

William stared back for a moment before nodding, but no one was convinced, least of all William who felt scared and confused and if he could have recognised it, very paranoid.

"William, it looked to me as though you were trying to listen to something a moment ago. Did you hear a voice, perhaps? A voice that didn't belong to either John or me. Did you hear something?" Trafford's voice and manner oozed reassurance that it would be absolutely the right thing to do to confide in him.

"Mmmm?" Trafford tried to prompt a response.

"Hide it... follow thoughts... think you're mad... hurt you... " Thoughts or voice, it didn't seem to matter. The words were compelling wherever they came from. In the background, outside the office, he could still hear the radio. Irritating radio. More than irritating... frightening but he didn't know why.

"No... No, nothing." William's delayed response was unconvincing, but it wasn't pursued. Winson approached him from the side and presented him with a medicine pot of red liquid.

"Don't want it."

"I think you should take it William. It will help you to relax."

As if the words from the psychiatrist had triggered some form of response mechanism in his brain, William immediately and without thinking, discarded his objection and quickly swallowed the fluid and eagerly accepted the cigarette which Winson offered.

Drawing excessively and rapidly on the cigarette he appeared to regain a little composure, and Trafford continued, anxious not to waste the opportunity to gain some insight into William's thinking.

"So to go back to what we were talking about originally. Why do you think that you were admitted to Greenbeck Hospital," Then anticipating further misinterpretations. "To this hospital, here."

Connections admitted… hospital… snippets of previous conversations. Conversations that he couldn't understand, things that had been repeated time and time again without explanation. Things that stuck in his brain without any conscious realisation or understanding. Just words that fitted the question he'd been confronted with. "Because I was ill."

"Yes, that's right. You were ill. Do you remember now? You're here because you've been ill." William responded to the approving tone of voice and the irresistible facial expressions that led to only one compatible response, even to his disturbed thought processes.

"Yes. I remember." It seemed as though the answer had been the correct one, because Trafford didn't pursue it any further, but went down another route entirely.

"Did your Grandpa come and see you today?"

William nodded.

"I see he bought you some chocolate."

William looked at the bar in his shirt pocket as though the psychiatrist had reminded him of something important that he had temporarily forgotten.

"I want to go home… I don't like it here… I want to go home."

Tears now. Rocking and tears.

"Now William, you're doing really well. You're a lot better than when you came to us, but you're not quite well enough to go home yet. We've just got to make sure that all your medicines are right and that you are well enough, and then we'll talk about going home. Is that OK?"

In fact, it didn't really matter if it was OK or not, because that was

Trafford's last words on the subject, and as he looked down to write in the notes, Winson assisted William to his feet. It wasn't often that the charge nurse felt as he did now, but there was something about William that somehow made him feel less than useless. To see his torment, his battle between reality and psychosis was heart wrenching. There was nothing that could be said. The medicine would hopefully have its effect eventually, but as the weeks went by, it was looking less likely that William Phillips would ever see an end to his career as a psychiatric patient, and if he did, how much of William Phillips would be left to enjoy life.

For now, Winson confined himself. "Come on mate, time for a cup of tea?"

And that at least, was something normal.

March 15th 1975; 15:30 hrs

"Are you serious?" George looked incredulously in Trafford's direction. With no response from Trafford other than a stare over his half-moon spectacles, he switched his glare to the petite young hospital social worker, Sue Hunt who was sitting to one side of the desk.

"Tell me you're not serious?" Sue had a habit of flicking the fringe of her long black hair out of her eyes and she was doing this now, much to George's irrational annoyance. He tried a third time.

"Did I hear you correctly when you said that you want to discharge my grandson?"

"That's correct." Trafford had apparently found his voice again. "I'm sure you'll agree that he's much better than when he came to us in June of last year."

George responded as though he'd been asked a trick question. "Well… yes, he's certainly a lot better than when he came in here, but… " Trafford had won a concession and wasn't going to let it go.

"And I'm sure that you appreciate that this may be as well as he will get, at least for the time being?"

Another trick question? This time he didn't answer, but waited for further and greater particulars that would quantify Trafford's idea of "better" and "well", but instead, his silence was answered by the social worker.

"That is, of course, if your wife and you can cope. Miss Page obviously told me about your circumstances before she left, so I know that you already have one child to look after."

"Julie," George interrupted with some indignation. "She's called Julie."

The social worker looked sheepish at her own lack of sensitivity. "Julie. Yes, sorry, of course."

Trafford stepped into the embarrassing breach. "As you know, we've changed his medication and I'm sure you'll agree that William does seem to be a lot better. His mental illness, his psychosis, is now a lot more manageable and of course, he's a lot calmer now."

George looked puzzled. "But you've told me up till now that he couldn't come home even if he wanted to because he was a detained patient. How can you tell me now that he can come and live with us? I don't understand you."

"I'm sure you remember a discussion we had a few weeks ago regarding our decision not to renew his Section 25."

"I remember the charge nurse speaking to me about Section papers, but I just thought that it was another change like the one you did before. What was it, turning a section 25 into a section 26, or was that the other way round?"

Trafford didn't have the patience to further extend his explanation and instead, confined himself with the present. "Quite different! This time, we've decided that William no longer presents a danger to himself or other people and hence, should not be detained. He is now classed as a voluntary patient."

"So he doesn't need any more treatment?"

Trafford realised that his explanation should have been more complete and proceeded to backtrack.

"No, no, I think you misunderstand. Before, William was detained under a section of the Mental Health Act, which meant that we could give him treatment and detain him against his will. That was done, as we explained at the time, because we had good reason to believe that he had no insight into his illness and would attempt to leave the hospital having refused treatment. Removing his detained status means that he is receiving treatment voluntarily and realises the need for hospitalisation. Of course, it also means that we have achieved a degree of symptomatic control in order to achieve this, but it certainly doesn't mean that he no longer requires treatment. He still requires treatment and probably always will, in one form or another."

George didn't look or sound very convinced. "So, are you telling me that he understands about his illness and the medication, and the importance of taking it?"

"I believe that he has some insights along those lines." Trafford tried not to commit himself.

"I don't think that's quite what I meant. Does he know, in fact while we're on the subject, do you know what the consequences of him not taking his medication actually are?"

Trafford clearly didn't appreciate being lumped together with a psychotic patient's understanding of symptoms, and after a highly restrained raise of his eyebrows, continued.

"William understands that he's been ill and that the medicine is going to help to prevent the symptoms from returning."

"And does he know he's been ill because you've told him, or because he genuinely understands?" George pressed his point, and he could see that the psychiatrist was getting a little fidgety.

"I'm sure that both would be true, although the discussions I have had with William would suggest a level of understanding, albeit very basic. Naturally, your wife and you would have a key part to play in supporting him and ensuring he takes his medication."

George glanced over to the social worker, who evidently prepared for some resistance on George's part, was instantly ready with.

"Of course, if you're prepared to have him home."

"And what other home has he got? You're giving me almost no option whatsoever. You know that William has nowhere else to go and no one else to care for him. And while I'm on the subject of there being no one else to care for him, we don't know how he'll react when he finds that his mother isn't there!"

"I don't think that should be much of a problem, after all, he seems to have accepted the news and understood that she died. I don't think there'll be much of a problem." And indeed, to Sue Hunt, there really wasn't a problem, that is, until George dropped his bombshell. "I'm sorry." George was getting more disturbed by the second. "And who was it who gave my Grandson the news about my daughter? When was this? Why wasn't I consulted?"

"I was given to believe that it was you who had told him, Mr Coleman, back in... " Trafford rifled through William's medical notes. "August, I believe." Trafford whipped off his glasses and met George's stare.

"And what does it say in your notes about this event?" Sarcasm and impatience was beginning to creep into his voice.

Trafford replaced his glasses and looked down at the notes again. "Ah yes, here it is. August 26th of last year, I made an entry that I had a discussion with Dr Wallace and Miss Page regarding this very issue. Apparently, you had quite a debate with her on this subject." Again the spectacle removing exercise followed by the stare.

"And the result of this debate was?" George already knew the answer, but the question just had to be asked. Again, Trafford's glasses went back on his nose and he rummaged through the notes once again. "I can see an entry that I made some weeks later, where I mention that he had broached the subject of his mother's death, and that he appeared to be making it part of his delusions."

George almost completely ignored the consultant. "Would it surprise you to know that I haven't told him?"

"I'm sure that Miss Page had said something about you both going to talk to William about his mother, at about the time referred to by Trafford." Sue Hunt seemed suddenly very unsure of her facts, despite her words.

George shook his head. "I had the conversation with Miss Page in this very office in August. We discussed the subject of telling William about his mother's death and we went to the ward with every intention of doing just that. But he simply wasn't well enough, and what's more, I rang the ward when I got home, and discussed it with the charge nurse… why don't you ask him?"

"If you're referring to Mr Morgan, then I'm afraid he's still on sick leave!" Trafford evidently thought that he could be off the hook and continued. "Although I'm sure that he would not have intentionally have said anything out of turn, it does seem most likely that either he or one of his nurses may have said something to William about his mother."

"So, in other words, you don't know!" George's patience had been tested over these last few months and never more so than now, listening to people who seemed to think that they could be ignorant, at will, of other people's feelings.

"As I said, Mr Coleman, there are no entries in the notes to say when your Grandson was told the news." Trafford could obviously not see the need for further discussion.

"And that, as far as you're concerned, is it? Someone, you think, has told my grandson about his mother, but you don't know who, you don't know when and because nobody has bothered to make an entry in his notes, you don't even know what was said."

Sue Hunt decided to try and bail the consultant out of the mess he'd just dug himself into, but didn't make a very good job of it. "I'm sure that whoever told William the news only considered his best interests."

"You do, do you? And how did you work that out without even knowing who told him?" George's glare silenced the social worker and when he was satisfied that her completely meaningless contribution was over, he once again turned his attention to Trafford. "So, Dr, you don't know whether he knows or not, and the best you can say is that he may, or may not have invented his mother's death as part of his illness?"

Trafford simply wasn't accustomed to being challenged in this way. Most of the relatives he saw accepted what they were told without argument and he found that even pretending to be humble a most unedifying experience, but he was left with no choice. "I'm afraid that I can't throw any more light on the subject, Mr Coleman." Then with a monumental effort. "I do apologise."

George knew that any further debate on the subject would be a waste of time, so he returned to more general matters concerning William's mental illness. "So what symptoms does he have now that we should be aware of?"

Trafford visibly relaxed at the change of subject. "Well, naturally, with schizophrenia, there are disordered thoughts in which disjointed thoughts, mixed up with memories, come and go, and will often make little sense to either the patient or anyone having a conversation with them."

"And how "disordered" are my Grandson's thoughts now?"

"Oh, greatly improved compared to what they were like when he first came to us. We can now have a quite a good conversation with him for a few minutes before he becomes distracted, although that's probably poor concentration."

It was obvious to George there was a marked difference of perception surrounding the concept of "greatly improved". As far as George was concerned, "greatly improved" when applied to illness, meant that the pain was nearly gone, the vomiting had stopped or the cough had eased. What it didn't mean was that the boy who should have gone to University can only now pass the time of day with someone for five minutes, before he looks blankly into space, or walks away. Clearly, if he was going to be of any help to William, he needed to change his way of thinking and that included lowering his expectations that he might have otherwise had, to a depressingly low level.

"So, will he be able to do a job, or go to college?"

"I think we have to see how we go, Mr Coleman, but I have to tell you that, there is a possibility that William has improved as much as he ever will, although of course, with time it is possible that he will be almost symptom free and I do have many patients who are employed and can lead quite normal lives."

George finished the unspoken ending to the sentence. "... and many others who can't and don't!"

"I take your point, but that doesn't mean that your grandson will be one of them. He may go on to live a relatively independent life."

"And there again, he may not... look... if we are to look after William properly, I need to know precisely what to expect and all you've given me is a load of "mights" and "might nots"!"

Trafford sat back in his chair. "Schizophrenia is a disorder where the personality is fragmented. Thoughts are usually muddled and appear to be random. As a result, concentration is impaired and they often have other symptoms such as paranoia and hallucinations in the form of hearing voices or even seeing things. On top of all this, they may experience other delusions and beliefs which seriously affect their behaviour. In Williams' case, we know that his beliefs centred around being taken over or controlled in some way, and that he was hearing voices that were telling him to do things."

This, at least was getting somewhere. This at least was giving him something to go on, but too much was being left unexplained and as he attempted to make further headway, uncertainty piled on uncertainty.

"So what causes it?"

"We don't know."

"Will his symptoms get any worse?"

"Difficult to say, but they might well do."

"What are the chances of William making a full recovery?"

"Difficult to say, but generally, we can only control the symptoms, not cure the condition."

"How long will he need to be taking medication for?"

"Possibly for the rest of his life, but it's impossible to say."

"So, in short, you can't really say if he's got this for life, or whether it will go away, or if we are going to have to stand over him while he takes his medicines umpteen times a day. Is that right?"

"I'm afraid that there is a good deal of uncertainty involved," Trafford saw no reason to make the situation any worse by being falsely optimistic. "Your point regarding the medication is unduly pessimistic. If he does have difficulty complying with medication, he can have it every couple of weeks by, what we call a depot injection."

George held his hands up in protest. "He's petrified of needles, always has been!"

"Well of course, if he sticks to his medicine as he's supposed to, then we may be able to do without the depot injections, at least for a while." Trafford was confident that he'd got past the dangerous bits of the conversation and Sue Hunt was nodding in agreement to everything he said, obviously relieved that Trafford had been taking the flack rather than her.

"And if he doesn't?" George asked the question that he already knew the answer to.

"If he doesn't, it is most likely that his condition will relapse, and we'll have a repeat of the past few months... or worse."

"Or of course there is a chance that the disorder will correct itself?" but George's question was met by a look from the psychiatrist that pre-emptied his answer.

"Of course there's always the possibility, but... "

George completed the sentence. "Don't count on it!"

"Precisely!"

There apparently being little further to say, a brief and rather awkward silence followed, broken, to Trafford's irritation, by George returning to a point that he hoped had been buried.

"And from our conversation, I can't "count on" your opinion as to whether he knows about his mother or whether he's just deluded?"

Trafford prepared to say something or other either in defence or explanation, but George wasn't in the least bit interested and as he stood to leave, he extended both his palms towards Trafford in order to silence him.

"Forget it. We'll cope with it in our own way and then, if I'm the only person who knows what he's been told, then I've done better than you lot!" Then in reply to the young social workers' unspoken question that her poised pen and diary page flicking was announcing,

"I need to prepare a few things at home first, but I'll be back to take William home on Thursday."

Both Trafford and Sue Hunt got up as George moved towards the door, both clearly relieved that the encounter had come to an end. Trafford extended his hand to George and before he could stop himself, he instinctively shook the Consultant's hand, although every fibre of his being remonstrated with him for giving any indication that he either liked, respected or even less, was grateful to the psychiatrist. Sue Hunt, on the other hand decided not to push her luck any further and confined herself to a nervous smile, which was barely reciprocated.

As George closed the door behind him, Trafford collected his papers. "If there's one thing I can't abide, it's rudeness!" He too exited the social workers office, leaving Sue Hunt with her pen and diary still trying to get together and her mouth and eyes wide open, astounded at the parting comments from the rudest and most ever arrogant man she had the misfortune to encounter.

March 15th 1975; 18:15 hrs

George wasn't enjoying his tea. Irene wasn't enjoying hers either. Julie was busy attacking her boiled egg and didn't really have any idea about what was going on apart from the fact that her grandparents were whispering very loudly at each other.

"So that's it! He comes to live here, and that's it!" Irene found it difficult to contain her frustration and confusion.

"What could I do?" George found himself almost apologising to his wife. "We're all he's got, and besides, if you could have seen the sort of patients that… "

"Don't go through that one again… you know I couldn't face seeing him."

"I know, you couldn't face seeing him in that place, but that's why I had to make a decision, I had… "

Irene added her own ending to George's sentence. "You "had to" ask me what I thought first, or didn't you think of that?"

"What I thought about was our Grandson… Jean's son and I couldn't bear to see him in that place week after week, being left to rot, being treated like a lump of horsemeat." The tears began to prick and Irene put her hand over his, realising that the man who had taken on so much could take no more. Instinctively, she looked to her left where Julie was still mopping up the remainder of her egg with her bread and butter soldiers and knew that her husband had been left with no choice.

"Is Grandpa crying, Nan?" Julie asked the question with as little gravity as she would have done if she had asked about a programme on the television. "Is he missing Mummy again?"

"No, darling, Grandpa's just very tired." As she spoke, it occurred to Irene that she had developed a talent for providing her granddaughter with erroneous explanations. Julie barely thought about her grandmother's statement and obviously considered that the matter had reached an adequate conclusion, reached for her drink and asked to leave the table.

"Do you think she'll be pleased to see her brother?" George asked the question with some amount of trepidation and it was met with his wife's raised eyebrows. He didn't need a verbal accompaniment and carefully drafted his reply out loud. "Yes, I know it's going to be difficult for all of us and I know that William isn't the same lad he was a couple of years ago, but he'll get a whole lot better when he's surrounded by... " He didn't get any further.

"When he's living in a place that isn't the home he was brought up in, when he tries to live his life without Jean, when he knows that his father, useless as he was, has deserted him and his sister. How the hell can we say who'll be pleased to see who? And what about us, eh?" Their eyes met and George knew what was coming next.

"For God's sake, Georgie, what will happen to them if anything happens to us? Have you thought about that?" No reply. "No, of course you haven't. We had all this discussion when we agreed to look after Julie. Well it won't go away, darling, it just won't."

"I know, I know." George had to reluctantly agree with his wife, but she was determined to make sure that her point struck home.

"No, I don't think you do, I really don't think you do. You're sixty seven next birthday and I'm sixty four. Anything could happen to us. And probably will do before too long. What happens then? Have you thought of that? Could one of us cope on our own?"

George looked down, finding it impossible to come out with any reply that would provide Irene with the reassurances she needed. They simply weren't there to be had and the direction of the conversation changed in the absence of any further meaningful answers.

"So what's the next step? Have they given us any help or advice?"

George decided that the time for dressing the problem up had come to an end and what he really needed at this time was for Irene to know the extent of the task ahead and not to panic or dissolve. He simply had to take the chance.

"Precious little of either, I'm afraid. His diagnosis is about the only thing that they can tell us. Apart from that, according to his consultant, he may get a bit better than he is now, but he doesn't think he will. He doesn't hold out a lot of hope, from what he was saying, that William will be able to carry on his life as before and he might well get ill again, particularly if he doesn't take his medicine."

Irene sat with her mouth slightly open and slowly shaking her head.

"According to him, his thinking can be muddled and he has a problem with concentration. To put it another way, he'll find it difficult to keep his mind on something unless it's quite short or simple."

"So this schizophrenia has damaged his intelligence, then?" Irene was finding the whole subject difficult to grasp.

"No, no, apparently not at all. He's still intelligent, the same as he always was, but he has a problem with his concentration, as I said."

"So if you've got schizophrenia, you won't be able to concentrate, is that it?"

George was on uncertain ground and he was aware that he was filling in gaps in a way that he really wasn't comfortable with.

"William's symptoms have been difficult to control and Dr Trafford has had to change his medication and keep on increasing it until he's better."

"Well?"

"Well according to Trafford, his condition has been quite resistant to treatment and he hasn't managed to get the symptoms completely under control. Added to that, William's on a high dose of whatever it is and that makes him a bit knocked off… if you get my meaning?"

Irene was still looking blank. "No, not really."

George thought and then had to admit. "No. Nor do I really, but they assure me that he's well enough to come home and I'm sure that we can do a better job than they've done. God knows, we couldn't do much worse!"

"What do you mean "couldn't do much worse"?"

"To be honest, they don't seem to know anything. The interview I had with Trafford and that Social Worker girl was a waste of bloody time. They didn't even know if William had been told about Jean's death. How bloody disgusting is that?"

Another surprised look from Irene, so George made an attempt to continue. "I said to Trafford, if… "

"So, let me get this straight," Irene couldn't help herself from interrupting and George couldn't help feeling uncomfortable. "William doesn't know about Jean's death, but the hospital thinks he does? Is that it?"

"Well, according to Trafford, he did know, but there again he was convinced that I'd told him, but obviously, I hadn't. In fact, as you know, I was waiting for the right time to broach the subject when… "

"So what makes him think that he knew? He must have had some reason for thinking that, or was he talking out of his backside?"

"Well, apparently, whenever he's spoken to William, it's William himself who says that his Mum's dead, so presumably that's why he believed that he knew, but in the next breath he was telling me that his belief about Jean's death could be part of his illness and nothing to do with what actually happened." George left a gap in the conversation so that his wife could have time to fully get to grips with what he had been saying, but Irene didn't need or want reflective silences.

"So, does he know or doesn't he?"

"Well," George gathered himself, "the only way I could find that out was to talk to William myself."

"And?"

"Well, after I finished with my meeting with those two, waste of bloody time that was, I went to the ward to see William. I gave him his bar of chocolate and a bit of chat and then I brought up the subject of Jean."

"How? What did you say?"

"I asked him if anyone had talked to him about his Mum." At this point George paused for a couple of seconds, narrowing his eyes as if he was trying to reluctantly recapture an unpleasant memory. "He stared at me at first and gave me a tiny nod, so small I almost missed it and then he looked away and started rocking, you know, like he used to do when he first got ill."

"So he isn't well enough to come home if he's doing that."

"The Charge Nurse said not to worry and that he's still upset about losing his Mum and that it was nothing to worry about."

Irene's stare said it all, but most of all, it said "I don't believe it!" but out loud, she said "What exactly did you say to him?"

"Well, after I asked him if anyone had spoken to him about Jean, I asked him if he knew that she had died and he nodded again… but he carried on rocking. He was obviously upset."

"Did he say anything? I mean did he give you any clue as to what he knew, or who told him?" Irene persisted in her interrogation and George was doing his best, not to sound as intolerant as he felt.

"Honey, it's not like that." George took a deep breath and corrected himself. "He's not like that, he just doesn't tell you things like that, not without a lot of coaxing. If you'd seen him in hospital you'd understand."

Irene shot him a glance that told him that he was pushing his luck by mentioning the fact that she didn't feel able to visit William in Greenbeck Hospital, but he carried on regardless. "He's not the same as he was. I asked him, of course I asked him who had told him, but he just kept saying "she's dead, she's dead," over and over again. As for his father, when I said to him that Dave had gone, all he said was "Good… I hate him," and that was that. All I can think of is that someone has already told him."

"But they don't know who?" Irene's question was rather unnecessary.

"No," George's irritation at Greenbeck Hospital was beginning to become evident as he became sarcastic. "Probably the same person that introduced him to the pleasures of smoking!"

"So Dr Trafford thinks that William's beliefs about his Mother may be a part of his illness. Is that what you're telling me?" but she didn't take breath for long enough to get an answer. "I don't understand. Sounds a load of rubbish to me. How the hell has he come up with that one?" Irene wasn't really asking the question, rather than expressing her frustration. George nevertheless threw his arms out in exacerbation as though he was expected to provide an expert opinion about something, about which he had little or no knowledge.

"And what about Julie? Hasn't that poor kid been through enough without seeing her brother in that state?" Irene was in full flow and any answers would be of little avail. "And who's going to keep an eye on him? Who's going to make sure he takes his medicine? God knows how many times a day? You won't be able to run down the road to Heather and Roger anymore, they'll be moving in the next few weeks and then we'll be on our

191

own with nobody to turn to!"

"We'll get it sorted out, you'll see, it'll be fine." George wasn't convincing anyone, least of all himself and Irene's eyes and mouth were getting wider with each passing second. "Anyway, we've got a week or so to sort things out."

No reply. Just the wide eyed stare.

George had run out of reassuring platitudes. He'd drained every explanation from his intellect until there were none left and he felt as though his emotions were in a deep freeze and in fear of being thawed out and brought back to life.

He knew that he was the only stable person in William's life and he didn't relish the responsibility. He would get it wrong. Sooner or later he would get it wrong mainly because there was no way of getting it right, not really. When that day came, the day he did or said the wrong thing at the wrong time, the day he missed a sign that William was becoming ill again, the day that William didn't take his medication... on any one of those days he would let William down... and then what? Hand it all over to Irene who couldn't even talk about mental illness without getting upset? Hope that nothing goes wrong for another fifteen years until Julie is able to deal with it? Put William back into that Victorian excuse for a hospital?

George reached out over the table and put his hand over Irene's. "Don't worry, honey. There's nothing for you to worry about, I promise." And Irene faced with the choice of being realistic or unrealistic chose the latter and believed him.

March 23rd 1975; 22:45 hrs

William had taken up residence in the box room. That was the room that he always slept in when he stayed over on Thursday nights. At least, that what he used to do, when things had been different. Today was Saturday. He felt as though he knew it was Saturday not because anyone had told him, but rather because it just felt like a Saturday. To William, even if he had his eyes closed all day and no-one spoke to him, he would know what day of the week it was. They all felt different. He could almost smell the day, to perceive it in such a way that every sense he had would rush to back up his instinctual knowledge.

It just didn't seem right being at Nan and Grandpa's house on a Saturday night. Someone had brought loads of stuff from his old bedroom at home and put it in the box room. It didn't seem right. Didn't feel right. Many things didn't feel right. Julie didn't feel right; well, not to look at anyway. Somehow, she looked different to how he remembered her, although that didn't matter, and William craved her attention, unconditional and uncomplicated as it was. When she didn't give it, he found it hard to get his thoughts into enough order to put his feelings into words, or to do anything to get her attention back. Except the dolly. Whenever William picked up Julie's dolly, she took it as a sign that her big brother was going to play with her, but it rarely lasted very long and William would just end up with half a dozen assorted dolls and teddy bears on his lap, with little or no ability to enter into his sisters playful make believe world.

But now he was stood by the window and looking out at the almost deserted street. Houses almost as far as he could see, all of them in terraces and all of them looking the same, with bits of differences here and there as there owners had tried to signal to the world that they were individuals by planting fuchsia bushes in the front garden instead of roses and painting the window frames with sunset yellow gloss instead of magnolia. William liked that sort of detail. He couldn't do much with it, but he felt comfortable just looking at something that for some reason appealed to something deep inside of him.

He liked to look at differences. Differences made him feel more comfortable. Houses that were the same colour made him feel uncomfortable. Things being the same as something else reminded him of something that he could not quite get from his brain. Something that made him feel deeply uneasy. Looking at the street now made him feel uneasy. Bathed in its orangey yellow street lights made everything look more "the same" than in the daylight.

William had gone up to his little room at just after nine o'clock after his Grandpa had given him his medicine and he'd been standing, staring out of the window ever since.

Of course, he didn't have to go to his room at all. He could have watched television. He could have read the newspaper, but he felt more at ease going to his room after his medication. It was what he had grown used to over the past year and in any case, he didn't miss his cigarettes when he was upstairs. They didn't let him smoke in the dormitory when he was in hospital and his grandparents wouldn't allow him to take his cigarettes to his bedroom and in a funny sort of way, William found that easier to live with than if he had not been able to smoke downstairs.

He had a radio in his room, but he never listened to it, it made him feel somehow uncomfortable. It seemed to make him anxious, put his nerves on edge. It wasn't too bad in the mornings. He could cope with it then, but as the day wore on it made him depressed and even a bit muddled, but that was OK, he just turned it off and that got rid of most of the problem.

Most, but not all.

He'd still go back to it, even after he went to bed and tentatively turn it on, very quietly and only for a few seconds or so, in case he missed something. He didn't really have much idea about what he would be missing. He wasn't worried about missing a programme, or a familiar DJ or anything like that. He remembered the incident with the radio when he was in hospital, but Dr Trafford had told him about the whole paranoia thing and all about his delusions and how they weren't real, just part of his illness.

He still didn't like the radio though and remained suspicious of it even though he told himself that he was being stupid and that Dr Trafford was right. Dr Trafford had said that it was all in his mind and that no-one was trying to get him. There was nothing there to be afraid of. There were no aliens trying to take control of him. That's what Dr Trafford had said. He had a mental illness and that was the reason why he got so muddled, why he was afraid and suspicious all the time.

But if that was the case, where had his mother gone? That bastard, Richard Morgan had told him that the reason she hadn't come to see him in hospital was that she was dead. Said she'd killed herself because he'd been on drugs. But he'd never taken drugs.

But she was dead, that much was certain. Everyone seemed to know she was dead. Trafford, Grandpa, that Social Worker Woman... all of them. Everyone seemed to want to talk to him about Mum, but he didn't want to talk. It was bad enough knowing she was dead without having to talk to people about it. But it wasn't his fault. She was alive when he had last seen her. He hadn't done anything wrong. He just wanted to protect her, to look after her and everyone wanted him to talk about her.

Something had happened to her. Something that no-one wanted to talk about. They just wanted him to talk. Someone had killed her... or something had killed her.

Jack would have had something to say; or rather he did have something to say. But Jack was just part of his illness, part of his delusions. Jack hadn't been real. The memory of his voice was just a blur. But he knew that he would have said something about Mum. He would have said something about how she died, but it wouldn't have been real. Or would it?

William laid down on his bed and stared up at the ceiling. It wasn't real. Jack hadn't been real. His illness wasn't real. Had they made that up, Trafford and the others? He turned his head towards the far wall and for some reason fixed his gaze on a piece of paper that he'd screwed up and had tried to throw it into his waste paper bin earlier. He'd missed, and it was next to the bin, on the floor.

As he stared at it, he felt a strong compulsion to get up and put it into the bin. It was so necessary to move it, but he didn't want to put it in the bin. He didn't want to get off his bed, but still he stared at it. He just had to get up and move it, but he didn't want to. But he had to.

Still he resisted. He didn't have to move it if he didn't want to move it. It didn't matter, did it?

Move it. Get up and move it.

No!

Get up and move it!

No, no, no.

Move it, put it into the bin!

No, no, no, no

He began to sweat with the effort of resisting the thought. But it was more than a thought. It was almost irresistible. It was irresistible. But he would resist it. He would have to resist it. Who knows what would happen if he gave into it.

Move it, put it into the bin!

No!

Sweating. The effort of resisting increased. He couldn't stop looking at the paper. Maybe he could will it into the bin that would mean that he wouldn't have to move in order to put it into the bin. He concentrated even more. His eyes began to hurt with the effort of staring.

Move it, put it into the bin!

No!

He wouldn't move. If he moved, he would give into it. If he gave into it, he could be taken over. He would be lost. But that was part of his illness.

195

Wasn't it. This illness that made him think all the wrong things. The illness that made him muddled. That was his illness, being muddled.

Move it, put it into the bin.

No, no, no, no, NO!

William felt his leg muscles become tense as if they were preparing to leave the bed and follow the command. The effort of stopping his legs from tensing was every bit as strenuous as making them lift weights.

Move it, put it into the bin!

No!

The sweating became more perfuse. His shirt was sticking to his back and felt cold. He could see the clock on the wall and noticed the time. It was ten minutes to two in the morning. He'd been lying there for about three hours. Resisting the temptation to move the paper for three hours.

Again and again the thought came.

Move it, put it into the bin!

Go away... just go away!

"Move it, put it into the bin, William."

Jack! It was Jack. But was Jack real? Of course he wasn't real.

"William, put it into the bin," Jack insisted, but William didn't want to listen. Wouldn't listen. How could you listen to something that wasn't there?

He hummed to himself. He sung to himself. He sung "Union Man" but he couldn't remember any more than the first verse. So he hummed bits and sang the verse that he knew in between the humming. That seemed to put an end to Jack, but it couldn't put an end to something that didn't exist in the first place. He didn't exist, but every time he stopped humming and singing, the thought came back and he fancied that along with the thoughts he could hear Jack, but there again; it might have been his imagination.

"William, pick it up."

He reached to his bedside table where he had his record player. Without taking his eyes off the paper, he turned on the record player and moved the arm onto the LP that was on the turntable. He didn't care about the song or whether he particularly wanted to hear it or not. "Someday, we'll be together" The Supremes sang out, but the rest of the house didn't appreciate that he had to have noise to get rid of the thoughts, the voices that weren't there. At least, they didn't seem to appreciate it at nearly half past two in the morning.

Banging on the wall from his grandparent's room. He turned the volume down in response. Still he stared. And stared. The music continued. "... never meant to be, love child," Diana Ross' voice continued despite the protests from next door. As he concentrated on the words, the thought diminished, but it didn't disappear, it just became a bit more tolerable.

"Move it..."

"Born in poverty, a love child," Easier to resist now.

"William..." Go away, you don't exist... go away...

And so it carried on. As the music continued, the compulsion and the thoughts took second place... just. He felt tiredness creeping up on him. But still he focussed on the paper. "... if you feel like loving me... " Eyelids becoming heavier "... I'll second that emotion... "

The clicking noise made by the stylus signalling that the record had finished, but the arm hadn't been able to return to its resting place. Round and round it went, making its clicking noise. The sun was shining through the window and William blinked in an attempt to acclimatise to the unexpected light. He'd fallen asleep hours earlier, but now, the reason for his anguish the night before seemed to recede into the background, reduce in importance.

The paper was still on the floor. The bin was still next to it. Irene walked into his room, as she did every morning and moved over to the window and opened the curtains more fully.

"You didn't get undressed to get into bed last night, William. Are you alright?"

He nodded, and threw in a "Mmm" for good measure.

"Grandpa and Julie are already having their breakfast. Up you get." The last part of her morning greeting was accompanied by a change in her tone as she bent over to put the screwed up sheet of paper into the bin. "See you downstairs in a minute!"

April 2nd 1975; 14:30 hrs

William hadn't made the decision to go shopping, that was made by Irene who, taking her courage in both hands, decided that enough was enough and that normality needed to break out without any further hesitation. William still wasn't right in her eyes, but who knows if he ever would be. Certainly not the hospital in any case.

197

So she decided that life must go on and the sooner the better. If William was to ever get any better, such an improvement would not be achieved by sitting in his room or watching the television all the time. He needed to get going, start doing things. Start living. She stopped short of thinking that all he needed to do was to give himself a bloody good talking to, but that piece of good, old fashioned homely advice was in the background somewhere, as yet unspoken.

It was a long walk to the High Street and she felt exhausted before she even started.

"Put your shoes on, William, put your coat on, William, get a handkerchief, William." He needed reminding of just about everything and it wasn't because he was stupid, far from it. It was just that he was somehow dulled, blunted, not with it. Call it what you want, but a part of the William that she once knew wasn't there anymore. Or rather that's how it appeared to her. Or was it that he simply couldn't be bothered. Or perhaps he was just missing Jean, although he hadn't even talked about her since he'd come home.

Maybe it was David. He'd just disappeared from his life, but surely he'd be glad to see the back of his father. They never got on anyway. Simply nothing to miss. Couldn't be that.

Who knows?

She simply couldn't walk with William in complete silence. She felt strange anyway, with this being the first time they'd ever really spent any time alone with each other since he'd been home. She had to talk about something that wasn't related to what he wanted for tea, or reminders to do things. She'd tiptoed around him since his discharge. She'd made sure that he had his medicines, and cooked his meals, and washed his clothes, but nothing any deeper than that.

They used to be so close. William would come to stay on Thursday nights to give Jean a bit of a break, and they'd always looked forward to him staying as much as William enjoyed being there. They'd always have a bit of a chat about this and that. School, home, David. Anything really. William had always known that whatever he said when he was in their house, it wouldn't go any further.

So walking the mile or so to the High Street in silence, with William looking down at his feet the whole time, was a decidedly uncomfortable experience.

"Are you alright, William?" It wasn't much, but it was a start.

"Yes Nan... yes, fine thanks."

Well that didn't go very far.

Mrs Holmes had, of course offered her advice on how to deal with him. She'd been at the front door the day after he'd come home, not that she didn't know everything anyway. She'd been virtually camped out in the front garden since the day Jean had attacked David. Always there to offer her advice. Strange that she always knew someone who'd had a similar problem. Even stranger that she ever knew about anything because she never stopped talking for long enough for anyone to get a word in edgeways. But she managed it somehow and always had some advice for just about anything that didn't concern her.

"Of course, it's nothing to do with me and tell me to mind my own business, but... " This was her opening gambit for just about every piece of advice, the same as "I'm not getting involved... it's nothing to do with me," was her closing salvo whenever she felt that someone actually would tell her to shut up. "But I don't think it's right that he should be let out."

Irene had carried on listening. She didn't want to listen, of course and it didn't immediately occur to her that even having Mrs Holmes anywhere near her was about the same as sending a telegram to the News of the World. But still she had listened.

"I mean, do you remember Mrs Curtis' daughter?" Mrs Holmes' questions never need a reply and in any case, she would have found it difficult to have stopped talking in order to hear the reply, at least, not while she was talking about anything as meaty as a neighbour's grandson being released from the local loony bin. Mrs Holmes carried on her narrative. "Well, her husband, can't remember his name... " She hesitated as though searching the files in one of the lesser accessible filing cabinets in her brain, but soon gave up the task. "Anyway, he went for her one night and they carted him off to... you know... " Knowing looks to which Irene had nodded. "Never came out. Best place for him. I said to Mrs Curtis at the time, I said to her: "you don't want him home, you never know if he'll go for you or one of the kiddies!" Well, you don't, do you?"

Irene remembered the conversation well. Perhaps she'd been right. Perhaps William should be put away and never let out. She shrugged and tried to put the thought out of his head and concentrated on William. Again the distraction, this time about William. He'd hit God knows how many people when he was in hospital. They used to hold him down because he was so violent. Hold him down to give him his medication, George had told her. Should he be home?

Safe. Was she safe? Strangely enough she didn't fear an outburst and couldn't altogether get her head around William being violent. She feared the unpredictability. She feared the fact that she knew so little about his illness and no one could tell her anything for certain. If he'd got asthma, they would have given him an inhaler and told him to keep away from pollen and then he'd be alright.

But this! This was different. They didn't know this and couldn't say that. She felt as though she was feeling her way in the fog, with nothing on either side of her to hang on to.

"Do you feel lonely, William?"

William didn't look up. "No."

"Well that's good." Irene could have kicked herself for being so lame. She had another go.

"You must miss Mum a lot?"

"Yes. She's not here anymore. I wasn't careful." The answer took Irene completely by surprise and for a few seconds they just carried on walking in silence as she managed to get her thoughts together.

"What do you mean, William?"

No reply. She approached from a different angle.

"Do you think it was your fault, William?"

William nodded but said nothing.

"Why do you think it was your fault?"

"I wasn't careful. I should have been careful."

Irene was none the wiser. "Careful about what?"

"About protecting her."

Again the genuine puzzlement. "Protect from who?"

William didn't answer and Irene was feeling out of her depth. They walked in silence for another couple of minutes while Irene tried to figure out whether William was talking about protecting his mother from David or something else, but had to weigh up whether it was possible to ask such a direct question without causing him too much upset.

She decided she could.

"Was it your Dad that you were trying to protect her from?"

"No, but he knew what was happening. He knew she couldn't deal with it. Now he's gone too. He doesn't matter. I hated him."

This could mean anything. It could be that William was more in touch with reality than anyone thought, or he could mean something else entirely.

"Deal with what? What did she have to deal with, William?"

"I don't know. People. People that wanted to change her."

"Why would they want to do that? Do you think people didn't like her, or do you think she did something wrong?" Irene was getting more confused than ever and her questions were just tumbling out, one after the other.

"They wanted to make her like them. They all thought she had to change, but I knew better. I knew she had to stay as she was. That's why she died, because she wouldn't let them change her. I wasn't there to stop it."

Irene thought that she finally understood. It was to do with David. She knew it. William was blaming himself because he couldn't protect her. He couldn't do anything about the way he was with people who tried to be close or friendly towards Jean. People who thought she should change. Be harder, leave him. So that was it.

To Irene, that was what a good son would always try to do. Protect their mother from harm. Nothing wrong with that. As they walked, she touched his arm to reassure him and said no more about it. In her eyes, William understood far more than George, or the hospital for that matter, had thought that he understood. There was no point in pushing it any further and causing even more upset.

As they finally reached the High Street, William appeared to be a bit more animated. Looking at all the cars as they went past and seemingly taking more of an interest in the people they were passing. As they went into the bank, William stationed himself at the end of the row of counters while Irene drew out some money. Perhaps it was because of the conversation they had just been having, but the way William was standing there, looking at everyone as they came into the bank, reminded her of a bodyguard, protecting something or someone.

How sweet!

As they left the bank together, it occurred to Irene that all William needed was time. Time and encouragement. She guided William into Woolworths and straight to the cafeteria. When he was younger he always liked it when she bought him a sausage roll in Woolworths and as she queued, she looked over to where William was sitting and reminded herself that all he need was a bit of tender loving care.

As William sat at the table, he felt agitated, but he couldn't put his finger on it. Not quite anyway. Looking at the people in the cars and in the bank had made him feel uncomfortable and he didn't know why. A part of him felt threatened. Was this him or was it the illness. He remained vigilant nevertheless. Just in case.

May 28th 1975; 21:15 hrs

George had an early night, as he always did when he had one of his bad headaches. He'd been in bed for over an hour leaving Irene to supervise William's night time medication, although quite why she had to stand there and watch him take his medicine was beyond her.

Even through his blinding migraine, George felt that he just had to say it. "Don't forget William's medicine." Always the red syrup and the little yellow tablet. Why on earth George was so obsessed, she couldn't tell. William always measured out his own medicine and got out the yellow tablet. He didn't need prompting every inch of the way, just a bit of reminding about when to take it, that was all.

They'd been to the hospital today. Not to Greenbeck Hospital, but to the general hospital where Dr Trafford had an outpatient clinic. They'd seen one of his Registrars, but Irene couldn't remember his name, not that it mattered. He'd said that William seemed to be doing OK, although William had been a bit jumpy. Dr someone or another had asked whether William was taking his medication and Irene had assured him that he had, but then he said he was going to increase it a bit anyway because it didn't look as though he was having enough. Then he muttered something about William being prescribed the maximum dose and that they'd need to keep an eye on it and made another appointment for a months' time.

All that and taking William to get a new pair of shoes afterwards and picking Julie up from school and George is the one to get a migraine!

Irene thought about her day as she sat in the dining room watching the television. She could hear William mooching around the kitchen and she shot a glance at the clock on the mantelpiece.

"It's time to take your medicine and tablet, William!"

No reply.

"William!"

"OK, I'm doing it."

"Well done! Are you going to bed then?"

"In a minute."

Irene carried on watching the television, safe in the knowledge that William had taken his medicine and William made his way upstairs, safe in the knowledge that for the fifth time that week, he'd tipped medicine, that he didn't need, down the sink.

June 28th 1975; 23:20 hrs

Staring out of his bedroom window. Just standing and staring. William couldn't afford to take chances, not with the amount of cars that were going up and down the street and everyone that walked by the house were all acting strangely, either walking too fast as if pretending that they weren't keeping an eye on the house, or being much more blatant and looking into the windows of the house as they walked by.

"Babylove, Oh babylove, I need you oh I... " Diana Ross and the Supremes were playing as usual, in the background on the Tandy stereo. He was protected as long as that record was playing. Nobody could get him.

Still he stood and watched. He didn't quite know what he was afraid of, but he knew that there was something about the people in cars especially. He couldn't concentrate on the problem sufficiently to put any substance to the fear, but he knew that if he kept watch as long as he could stay awake, then he would be safe.

"... you treat me right... " Still it droned on. He looked briefly over to his digital radio alarm clock beside his bed. It was covered in black insulating tape so it couldn't be turned on. Just to make sure, he'd unplugged it and taped over the socket. If he didn't cover them up, something could enter the room while he wasn't looking. Nothing could get through the socket that he had his stereo plugged into, because he'd know if anything tried. He listened.

"... someday, we'll be together... " The record was playing what it should do and the Supremes were singing all the right words. If anything entered through that socket, then the words would change and he would be warned.

His thoughts were coming thick and fast and jumped around, bouncing from one thing to another, so much so that his Nan had to keep on telling him to slow down when he spoke. But that was good. That was how it should be. The medicine made him sluggish, slowed him down.

They said that he was ill. He wasn't ill. He felt fine, never felt better in fact. The shaking he used to get when he took the medicine was gone. Never better.

He returned his gaze to the street outside, and surveyed the scene. Satisfied that there were no dangers, he reluctantly tore himself away and picked up the insulating tape from the windowsill and pulling his bed away from the wall, he taped over the spare electrical socket that wasn't being used for his stereo. Quickly, he pushed the bed back against the wall and continued his vigil by the window.

It was beginning to rain outside. That kept them in their cars. That was good. That was safer, but still no reason to relax his guard, but at least now he could think about things while they were distracted.

Think about things, or get his mind straight? Or perhaps to be able to pay attention to whatever it was he needed to pay attention to. Whatever one it was, he strived to search for whatever it was that was gnawing away at him. He felt alone, isolated, but that was fine. That was the way it had to be if he was to protect himself. Protect himself from what?

From who?

This place he was in. It was safe until all other places fell, but what then? And was this place really safe? Where was this place? Everyone told him that it was his grandparent's house, but he really wasn't so sure. In fact, he wasn't certain of anything anymore, but that didn't matter. Not really, not as long as he was able to keep the danger at bay.

But if this wasn't his grandparents house… his thoughts started to jump… why did the rose look so neat when he never saw anyone prune them? There were no blue roses, probably because of all the traffic, yes that was it, the cars again. But Grandpa would be annoyed, especially since he'd missed the boxing on Grandstand. That wasn't like him, to miss boxing. Was it him that missed the boxing? It couldn't be. He wouldn't miss the boxing.

"… wanna say, wanna say, wanna say, someday, we'll be together…" Still the songs played, and still the thoughts kept jumping.

Mum wasn't there. They said she was dead. He knew she was dead. They took her away and did it. She didn't like the traffic, she always moaned about all the cars. They knew. He knew that she was trying to protect him.

Yes, that was it. It was her trying to protect him, not the other way round. Trying to protect him from the people in the cars.

Why didn't he know this earlier? They must have both been undercover and hadn't been told about each other in case they'd been caught and tortured. That was it.

Things were not the same, the blue roses that weren't there, Julie living in this house. And the feeling. Feeling like Sunday when it wasn't Sunday at all. Manipulating time. That's what they could do. But William knew. He knew what they were up to.

But who were they. Who were the people living in this house. He was being guarded. He known that for some time. Being guarded and watched because they hoped that he'd give them information that might help them get to other people. There had to be others like him. Others that knew what he did. Others who were working undercover, blind towards each other because it was the only safe way to be. He had to be careful.

So careful, lest he give himself away. All that responsibility and for one so young. He couldn't share it with anyone. He couldn't give himself away, not even to those other people in the house, the ones that looked like his grandparents. Especially not to them. He knew now.

The man they called George worked for Trafford and he was their ringleader. Why couldn't he see that before?

The rain continued outside and he strained, through the raindrop smeared window, to follow the progress of the car that was slowly passing the house. He followed it with his eyes until it turned into another road and kept on staring, convinced that it was a trick and that would stop the car when it was out of sight and creep back towards the house, but after a few minutes he managed to convince himself that the danger had passed.

The green shirt didn't help. Green attracted them. The thought was useless without action and he quickly tore off his green shirt, threw it under the bed and resumed his vigil.

All clear. The record came to an end and William reached over to play it again, taking care to complete the operation as quickly as possible.

Outside the rain came down heavier than ever and as it made more noise hitting the window, William felt safer. He had to be so careful all the time, but at least for now, he could let his guard down a little. Just for a few moments.

Movement on the stairs. Nan going to bed? If he opened the door and looked and he was seen, that would give him away. Tell them that he wasn't sleeping. He had to keep undercover. He pressed his ear to his door so that he could hear the activity on the landing. A door was being opened. Voices. "You still awake?" His Nan's voice. "Now come on, time to put your book down and go to sleep, you'll never get up for school in the morning."

A child's voice replied, but he couldn't make out the words. Julie.

Closing of her bedroom door.

Footsteps across the landing.

"Are you in bed, William?" Without waiting for a reply, she continued. "Keep your music down, Julie can't sleep. See you in the morning."

William briefly considered not answering, but remembered to be inconspicuous. He remembered not to arouse suspicion.

"OK… see you in the morning." He reached over to turn the volume down a couple of notches.

The sound of the bathroom door being opened. At least that what it sounded like. The sound of the bolt as she locked the door. Waiting. Two minutes or so later, the bolt again, the door opening. In his mind's eye, William was visually predicting the next action and a couple of seconds later, his prediction reassuringly came true as he heard her open her bedroom door and close it behind her.

He listened for another couple of seconds, before he reached over and turned the volume down to a barely audible level, opened his door and crept very quickly downstairs, checked the front and back door to make sure they were locked, opened the living room and dining room door to ensure that no windows had been left open, before quietly closing both doors and running silently upstairs, into his room and noiselessly shutting the door behind them. Having accomplished his aim of ensuring that the house was secure, he turned up the volume on the stereo but not so high as to bring attention to him and again took up his position at the window.

Again, William's thoughts turned to his mother and how he had been unable to protect her. It was too easy to let them in, and he wasn't going to make the same mistake again. He didn't know exactly what they had done to her and his thoughts became more florid, disjointed and fantastic as he tried to speculate. It had something to do with the flat they were living in, the echo's on the stairwell, they were linked to the radio in the flat, a sort of feedback that stole thoughts and washed brains, but he was saved because his mother had fixed it so that he went undercover into their headquarters,

206

the place they called Greenbeck.

Clever, very clever.

July 29th 1975; 13:40 hrs

The long walk to the High Street. Turning right from Gordon Road to Elliot Road and straight on, past the church on the corner and on towards the shops.

Nothing was right. William had to be so careful. He was being watched. He had to be so inconspicuous, but everyone in the cars stared at him as they rode past and it seemed to him that some of them slowed down to get a better look at him and his Nan. William acted as though it didn't bother him and just carried on walking. Walking past the church on the corner, he noticed that even the people tending the graves looked up as they went by. Tentatively he looked behind them to make sure that they weren't being followed.

The High Street was uncharacteristically quiet and those people that were out and about were dodging the rain and concentrating on avoiding puddles, barely looking up to notice William and Irene. That was good, for a start.

To many people, the rain filled sky, the half-light and the sad looking, empty shops would have been a depressing sight. The reflection of the shop lights on the wet pavement completed the dismal picture, although to William, it meant that no-one was interested in him and that was just what he needed.

This was much safer than if the sun was shining. Even the drivers were being distracted away from looking at him. That was even better, but it couldn't continue. Sooner or later they would go into a shop and that was where the danger would lay. To make things even worse, Irene always went into shops in the High Street on the same day, at the same time every week. Worst of all, she would visit the shops in the same order, and wouldn't dream of doing anything differently. First of all she would go to the bank and that would always involve spending excessive amounts of time talking to one cashier or the other. They all seemed to know her and most of her business and William feared that one day she would tell them things that she shouldn't be telling them.

Then it was on to MacFisheries to buy her bacon and cheese. Always she looked and picked up this piece of cheese or that, but she'd always choose the same variety and portion size of cheese, week after week. Today was no exception.

From one aisle to another, Irene sauntered, looking at this and that. When he'd been well, William had been unable to work out quite why she needed to look at so many things in a supermarket that she apparently had no intention of buying. Now he was ill, he still didn't know, but his emotions were becoming fragile with the anxiety of watching someone he loved, being totally oblivious to the danger she was in and it was as though it was only William that knew it.

Didn't she see what he saw? Surely she couldn't miss it. The supermarket was much emptier than usual, presumably because the rain was preventing people from venturing out to the shops, but they were still there. The people who were watching them.

Watching them!

There were much fewer of them, but they were there nevertheless. His grandmother though, couldn't, or wouldn't be distracted from her browsing. William dropped back a step or so, making himself less conspicuous as he continually looked in all directions for signs of danger. Danger that he knew was there.

Supermarkets were always difficult, particularly this one. Too many people and too many places to jump out from. Some of them had children. That made their cover even more convincing, but William wasn't fooled. Eventually Irene found the cheese she was looking for and put it in the basket before going in search of the bacon a few yards away. At least when she was picking up something that she was actually going to buy, the little attention she was paying to William evaporated, leaving him free to carry out his surveillance without being continually questioned.

"Are you alright, William?" "What's wrong, William?" "Aren't you well, William?"

Always the questions.

But he was forgetting himself. He had to keep watch and he had to keep his mind clear. Quite literally clear. You never know who's tuning into your thoughts, or what they will do with them once they've managed to get hold of them.

"I think you're fed up with shopping, aren't you, William? That's your trouble. You need something else to occupy you. Never mind, nearly finished, then we'll go to Woolworths for a drink and something to eat. That OK?"

A lot of words that didn't really need an answer, but William managed a fleeting and quite unconvincing smile with an "OK" in response and was rewarded with the briefest of indications that she was at last, going to speed up and complete the shopping, but that illusion only lasted as far as the bacon.

On the bacon display came the inherent dilemmas of whether to choose back, collar, gammon or streaky, not to mention the time consuming and apparently insurmountable choice between smoked and unsmoked. As his grandmother picked over the various bacon products on offer, William carried out yet another survey of the scene, only this time he felt his heart miss a beat. Something was wrong, although he couldn't recognise what it was at first. As he looked to the other side of the isle to where the egg display had always been, there was now cooking oil and a few other things, but no eggs. He looked around again, and spotted the egg display some yards further on.

The display wasn't where it normally was. It had been moved. It had been moved, or someone had made a mistake, got a detail wrong, thought that no one would notice. Whatever the reason, it wasn't where it should be. And it wasn't for the first time that he'd detected little glitches in their system, but it was usually just a part of a shelf here and there that had different products on it. Nothing as major as this.

William's thoughts, which had been devoted to the detection of danger from the people around them, now hurtled towards a bigger picture.

Someone had made a mistake, but with what?

It was the rain. Just as William and his grandmother could walk around in the rain, safe in the knowledge that it stopped them from being detected, so it could work the other way round. It could mask things that they were doing, such as replacing real places like shops with cleverly made copies and then luring in innocent people. How many people had fallen for this one and never returned to their homes?

How could he have been so stupid?

They knew they were coming. That was the trouble. They knew the day and time when William and his grandmother would go shopping. It was the same every week. It made it too easy for them. As he looked on from a few paces away, he realised with horror that his thoughts were transmitting. He didn't know where they were being transmitted to, but that wasn't important for now, all that mattered was that he had allowed his thoughts to become strong and they could pick that up and follow them back to him.

He had to clear his mind. He had to think of more mundane things that wouldn't be strong enough to be transmitted. Getting up this morning, Julie's dolls and Grandpa cleaning his shoes.

They were in a replica supermarket and were going to be trapped there!

His bedroom wallpaper. His dinner last night. His Mum telling him to get ready for school.

His Mum! They'd already got her, the bastards. He'd taken his eye off her and they'd taken her! Thoughts getting too strong again, emotions transmitting at a high frequency that could be picked up a mile away.

Clear. Keep it clear. Mothers Pride bread, his damp trousers from the rain, the red handle of the supermarket trolley his grandmother was pushing. Think boring. Think low key, they can't follow that back to his brain.

He thought that she would never move away from the bacon, but eventually her decisions were made and movement re-commenced. Slow to the point of being agonising, they made their way to the check-outs. William didn't recognise any of the girls at the tills. They'd been replaced. Yet more evidence. Everywhere around him was evidence.

Sweating now, as he stood in the queue. Three women ahead of them. All with baskets, none with trolleys. William looked behind and all around him. No one approaching, but the girl at the next checkout was looking at him.

Quickly, he looked away and pretended to look at the contents of his grandmother's basket.

A bottle of orange, a pound of cheese, half a pound of unsmoked back bacon. Keep it boring. The checkout girl had probably already been picking up his thoughts and even now was trying to pick up the frequency again so she could follow them into his brain.

The woman being served in his queue was about sixty years old and behaving as though she'd never been in a supermarket in her life. As she unloaded her basket at a speed that would have done credit to lame tortoise, William's anxiety increased.

Keep calm. Keep clear, but then a voice that sounded as though it was coming from over his shoulder.

"She's not shopping, William. She's only here to get you and Nan."

William hurled round on his heel, but there was nobody there.

"What's wrong, William?" His grandmother couldn't help but notice the suddenness of his movement and he realised that he had inadvertently brought attention to himself.

"Nothing. Just thought I heard something; that's all."

His grandmother looked at his face. "You're sweating! Are you OK?"

Quickly, William jolted himself back. "Fine, just a bit hot. It's too warm in here."

"Mmm… " She didn't altogether believe him, but the explanation would do for now.

The woman at the front of the queue was putting her shopping into her bag, with an almost obsessive attention to detail. In went a packet of biscuits, then half taken out, turned around the other way and put back in. The same with the half a pound of butter. And then the eggs. In fact, long after the checkout girl had finished her part of the process, she was still packing. Then, to make things worse, she kept looking around for items she'd already packed.

"She's stalling to give them time to pick up your thoughts!"

The assistant had finished putting the old lady's shopping through the till, saw the speed of the packing and obviously came to the conclusion that to tell her how much was owed would, if attempted too soon, cause untold complications. After a delay which had the entire queue hopping from foot to foot, the girl finally took a chance.

"That'll be one pound sixty seven and a half pence, please." Then she had to say it again in order to prompt the search for the purse.

Eventually, she managed to prize the oversized purse from her handbag and opened it. As she rummaged around in its apparently endless compartments, the contents appeared to be a complete surprise to her, although to most in the queue, including the girl at the till, it soon became apparent that decimalisation still hadn't caught up with her. Their suspicions were confirmed within a few seconds as she tipped the assorted coins out onto the counter. "Take what you need, dear!" Thereafter, she appeared to divorce herself from further involvement in the transaction.

William was watching the performance with everyone else, but his observations were interrupted by his constant vigilance of the surrounding area, particularly behind him where he felt that attack was most likely. To him, the excruciatingly slow progress caused by the elderly woman with her currency issues was a deliberate ploy to enable someone to latch on to his thoughts. It was designed to make him agitated... made his thoughts stand out, made them easier to trace.

"Now I want one pound and sixty seven and a half pence, so... " The assistant was explaining her actions to the old lady, slowly and loudly.

"They're getting close to your thoughts, William!" Again the voice, but William now knew it was Jack and didn't bother turning round to see where it came from.

"So if I take this one and... " The decimal currency lesson was continuing.

"If you stand here, they'll get a fix on you and get into your brain."

William looked around with even more urgency and moved from foot to foot to such an extent that he began to attract the attention of his grandmother.

"What's wrong, William. Do you want to go to the toilet?"

He was aware that he'd been spoken to, but didn't know what had been said.

"Pardon... I'm sorry... what did you say?"

"Toilet! Do you need to go to the toilet? You're hopping from one foot to the other."

"They're nearly onto you now, William!" Jack wouldn't go away.

"To where... what did you say?"

"To the toilet, William, are you... "

"... and then I take two of these, making another twenty pence."

"They're staring at you now, staring because they've found your frequency. You've got to move from here, William!"

"... and one of these little ones, and that makes... "

"William, did you hear what I said? Is there something wrong?"

No reply, because by the time she had finished the sentence, William had unceremoniously grabbed the wire basket his grandmother was holding and sped off to an empty till some distance away, leaving her startled, but reluctantly following her grandson. Impatiently he tipped the bacon, cheese and orange onto the checkout conveyer belt.

"This one's quicker!" He announced in an attempt to disguise his real motive for his sudden action, but by now, the only person who wasn't staring at him was the old lady who was examining the two shiny coins that she'd been given as change.

"What on earth's wrong with you, William? Why are you being so impatient?" His grandmother, clearly flustered at the suddenness of his actions, along with his disturbing level of distraction, finally caught up with him at the till.

Now that he had done Jack's bidding, William knew that he would disappear into the background. In the brief respite from trying to pay attention to several things at once, he turned his attention to Irene and tried to smooth things over.

"I'm fine… really, just a bit hot, that's all."

Still Irene stared at him. "Well you don't look right to me!"

And although no-one spoke, it didn't look as though anyone else at the check-outs thought he looked right either.

August 3rd 1975; 16:35 hrs

George and Irene were returning home from a visit to the GP for George's regular checkup for his high blood pressure. The surgery was close to the High Street and with Julie at her friend's house for tea and William at home, they were both making the most of the rare hour or so of privacy.

"I know, I know… I've seen him behave like that a lot over the last week or so," George was responding to Irene's description of William in the supermarket a couple of days earlier, "but what I can't understand is how he could get like this so quickly, particularly when he's taking his medication so regularly."

"Don't ask me, I'm not a doctor, and in any case, you told me that Dr Trafford had said that this could happen." Irene was defensive and it showed.

"Yes, he did say that, but it's only been a few weeks and… "

"And what? It's obvious to me that he wasn't well enough to come home in the first place."

It didn't seem right to George, but he didn't even want to scratch the surface for an explanation that would cause him more grief than he already had. All the same, he felt responsible and although he'd not been in a position to do anything that would have involved a great deal of effort over the last few weeks, he couldn't help feeling that he shouldn't have been so dependent on Irene to look after William.

It had, after all, been his decision to have him home. He had been the one who'd taken the responsibility for his grandson. He shouldn't have left it to someone else, not even Irene.

In fact, especially not Irene, but he had little choice in the matter.

"Your blood pressure is dangerously high, Mr Coleman." He could still hear Dr Taylor's words a few weeks earlier. "Ignore it for much longer and it'll be too late." Taylor had completed his warning and with a flourish of his pen, completed the prescription to go with it.

He was told to rest and he had. No longer did he get up at seven in some misguided belief that it kept him healthy to maintain the early morning routine he used to have before he retired. A nap after lunch and to bed before nine and that, along with trying to lose a bit of weight and taking his tablets, that was supposed to keep his blood pressure under control. Reducing the amount of stress and worry was the final part of the prescription, but one that stood little chance of success, particularly as his visit to the GP had been a mere three days following William's discharge from Greenbeck.

Irene had needed a crash course in caring for someone with a mental illness, but the only person who could do that, barely understood it himself. Except the medicine. That was the easy part and he'd reminded her of it so often that it was beginning to spark tension between them. So after a few days he didn't say anything about making sure that William took his medicine. Didn't say anything, but he checked the bottle every day to make sure that William had been taking it and sure enough, the level kept going down as it should have done.

But it still didn't seem right and he was not altogether convinced by the inference of the decreasing volume of medicine. Neither was he convinced that Irene had done exactly what she had so vehemently claimed, but he simply couldn't face a row, not at the moment.

George decided that a more subtle approach would be less stressful. "Maybe I could have a bit of a chat with him, try to find out what's going on in that head of his, see if we can do anything to help him. What do you think?"

"Why are you asking me?" A sharp reply, born out of a mixture of frustration and retaliation in response to her suspicion that George was in some way blaming her for William's deterioration.

"No reason other than wanting your opinion." George was trying to prevent what he knew would be coming next, but he tried in vain.

"You obviously think I'm incapable of looking after him. I obviously need your supervision, don't I? Well now you can bloody well do it yourself!"

George couldn't find any more words. Not for the first time in their marriage, the speed with which Irene responded to the heart worn very firmly on his sleeve had floored him, and all he could manage was a feeble response. "I didn't mean… " But he didn't get any further as Irene was in full flow.

"Well, try thinking before you speak! You're the same with William; all you can do is nag the poor boy." George, by this point, would have normally turned off and resigned himself to an evening of prolonged and bad tempered silences, but Irene's last salvo caused the hairs on the back of his neck to stand up and demanded a challenge.

"Nag! What do you mean, "nag"?"

"You know bloody well what I mean. I wouldn't be surprised if his behavior now isn't down to you standing behind him every minute. You don't give the boy any space at all. That's half his problem, thinking everyone's watching him the whole time. That's what that whole business was about in the supermarket. The boy needs a bit of space… a bit of trust… fat chance of that with you on his back the whole bloody time."

George now thought he knew what he had suspected for some time and would have to bring some calm to the situation if he was to find the reason for William's worsening condition. Their conversation had taken them to the top of their road and George felt the familiar pangs of dread at what he would find when he got home.

"Maybe I am overprotective and perhaps I can be overbearing." His conciliatory words were as divisive, as his question.

"That's probably why he gets annoyed with me when I give him his medicine? Is he the same with you?"

Irene sensed that common sense was about to break out. She'd made her point and this was one of those rare occasions when George would see reason.

"No, he doesn't. Ever. Do you know why?"

George gave a barely audible grunt that approximated to "No."

"Well, I'll tell you. I trust him more than you do. I remind him to take his medicine and he takes it. Simple. No fuss… no bother… no… "

George stopped walking and held his hand up, the surprised look on his face being as genuine as his earlier humility.

215

"So, all you do, is to remind him to take it and he gets on with it. No fuss!"

"That's right. Trust is obviously something that you're not familiar with, but I trust him to take it and it's as simple as that."

"So you just tell him to take it and he does it, without you watching him take it?"

George opened the front garden gate, but neither of them went through it, as Irene's tone of triumph turned to one of doubt.

"Yes, of course. It's not necessary. Is it? I mean, we've got to trust him, haven't we?"

George just looked at his wife and shook his head, letting her walk through the gate ahead of him, as he fished around in his jacket pocket for his front door key. Irene was still exploring the rights and wrongs of the trust issue, but George was being confronted with a more practical problem.

The key turned as normal, but as he tried to open the door, something stopped him. He examined the key and repeated the operation, this time exerting more force as he tried to push it open. This time, however, the door gave way, but with a loud tearing or ripping noise which announced its liberation from the door frame. Tentatively George and Irene entered the hallway and George fumbled for the light switch. Looking behind them at the front door, they saw that someone had put masking tape around the small gaps between the door and the doorframe. The large amounts of masking tape remnants which were now hanging down were testimony to the thorough job that had been done.

"William!" No reply, but the ever present drone of Diana Ross and the Supremes came floating down the stairs.

"William, we're home."

Still nothing, so George tried a much louder appeal.

"William!"

The sound of a bedroom door being opened and the corresponding increase in volume from the record player, but still no response from William, so Irene decided to have a go.

"William, what's been happening down here?"

"… reflections of the way we used to be… " Diana Ross's words seemed to echo the situation.

Footsteps across the landing and William's face appeared over the bannister rail, but still he didn't speak.

George's turn. "Why all the masking tape, William? Why have you put tape all around the front door?"

As they both looked up, they saw William shrug his shoulders and it didn't take a massive leap of insight on either of their parts to come to the realization that there couldn't be a rational answer and any further attempts to get one would be a waste of breath.

"Let's see if we can sort things out," George's remark was meant to entice him downstairs, but when William didn't move or speak, he had little alternative other than to go upstairs himself.

William still didn't move a muscle and didn't even look at his Grandfather as he approached, but became more animated as George moved the bedroom.

"… aint no mountain high enough, aint no river wide… "

"Shall we turn the music down a bit while we have a chat?" But as he made a move towards the record player, William leapt forward. Putting himself between his Grandfather and the volume control. Although it wasn't particularly warm and he was only wearing a T-shirt, William was sweating profusely.

"No… no, don't do that. Please don't do that."

The sound of panic in William's voice took George completely off guard, and he jumped back in surprise, although after a couple of seconds, he composed himself enough to challenge William's reaction.

"Why… what is it you're afraid of? Why can't I turn the music down?"

"You can't, that's all… you can't… you mustn't… understand?" William's voice was getting louder and his words, more pleading, but his sudden outburst caught George off guard and lost for words.

"Do you understand?" William was almost screaming at him now. "Do you understand?"

"… To keep me from you… "

George nodded his head, but William held his position a few inches from his face, his glare a mixture of fear and menace. They were still in that position when Irene called upstairs.

"George! I think you'd better come and have a look down here."

William wasn't going to move from his guarding position in front of the record player, neither was he going to be the first to break eye contact.

"George… I need you downstairs… now!"

Reluctantly, he pulled himself away and without answering his wife, made his way downstairs and into the front room where she was standing. In the weeks that followed, he would see the picture of his previously pin neat and orderly lounge every time he closed his eyes.

"I'm so sorry, Georgie… it's all my fault…I know it's my fault… I should have made sure he took his medicine… I'm so sorry… " The words were coming thick and fast as she sobbed, but George barely heard her.

The net curtains had been pulled to one side and the windows taped over with masking tape. The three piece suite had been piled up in front of the windows, barricade style. The television had been systematically dissected with its innards spread all over the carpet and its cabinet smashed to pieces and piled up in the corner. The old radio which had stood in the opposite corner of the room had suffered a similar fate and as he stared in horror, the sight of the plugs which William had cut from the television and radio which had been carefully placed next to each other on the windowsill, somehow struck him as ridiculous. After all, without the plugs, the appliances couldn't work. Why do anything else to them? That wasn't logical.

"… never meant to be, a love child, born in poverty, a love… " Diana Ross carried on regardless.

Even in the chaos, George found himself remonstrating with himself for even considering anything that was remotely logical. Logic simply didn't enter into it, unless of course you were William, in which case everything probably made perfect sense, but the thoughts and fears that led to such mayhem couldn't even be imagined.

"George!" By now Irene's voice was betraying her upset and confusion. "George, come and look in here."

George covered the distance within a couple of seconds and stood with his wife in the dining room. Instinctively she reached for George's hand and squeezed it as they surveyed the scene together. As with the lounge, there were copious amounts of masking tape around the windows and it also had the added benefit of the upturned dining table pushed up against the French doors.

William appeared behind them and far from being apologetic, seemed well satisfied with his handiwork. "Nobody can get in, I made sure of that… and don't worry… they won't get in upstairs either… "

"… different from the rest, a… " The music droned on, not respecting the devastation being felt by at least two people being forced to listen to it.

George and Irene shot urgent glances at each other, before George disappeared back upstairs and within seconds had confirmed his Grandson's words. Julie's bedroom and their own had received the same thorough treatment. As he stood and stared, he knew that there was little he could do. Mere words were just not enough and in fact, the wrong words, which would be so easy to use at the moment, could make things so much worse.

And floating upstairs came all the wrong words.

"William, you should have taken your medicine... you promised me you'd taken it... whenever I asked you said you'd taken it... now look at what you've done... you'll be back in hospital at this rate... " Then through the sobs, "I trusted you... I thought we trusted each other!" More sobbing. William was just standing there, next to her with his hand on her shoulder as though he'd told it to go there but failed to give it any further instructions. His head was tilted to one side as though he was trying to pay attention to something and he was muttering inaudibly to himself.

And that's how they were as George reached the bottom of the stairs. For a just a fleeting moment he put his arms around both of them, possibly out of resignation, more probably out of love, but almost certainly because he really didn't know what else to do.

An ending had been reached. Whether it was a final ending, or the closing of a particular troublesome chapter, George could only guess. For the present, though, with evening approaching, the situation seemed, if that were possible, even worse. He moved himself away from the inconsolable and unreachable pair at the bottom of the stairs. Decisively now, he picked up the phone receiver and dialed Bill's number. If ever he needed his brother it was now, and all he needed to say was "William" and "ill again" and Bill was in the car almost before he'd put the phone down and after another call, and before long, Julie was too busy getting ready for the unexpected adventure that was sleeping at her best friend's house to bother about anything else.

Then the phone call for the ambulance. To be more precise, the call to the GP surgery so that they could tell him to ring Greenbeck Hospital, who told him to ring the GP who then told him to ring an ambulance, only to be told that it wasn't an emergency and to phone his GP to arrange an admission with Greenbeck, followed by the phone call to the taxi company, purely on the belief that if they presented themselves at casualty, then someone would do something.

He needn't have bothered.

With the Supremes as an almost deafening background noise and while George had been making his phone calls, William had rediscovered the masking tape, had brushed past him and was busy re-taping the front door, but not before a still sobbing Irene had run through it, almost causing Mrs Holmes, who had stationed herself at the Coleman's gate, serious damage as she bulldozed her way past and into the sanity and order of the street.

Thereafter, as if it hadn't already, the whole situation took on a life of its own, at least partly as a result Mrs Holmes, who had quickly composed herself, taken charge of the situation and whisked a confused Irene into her house.

Bill pulled up outside the house and bustled up the front garden path and rang the bell. For his effort he was treated to a cocktail of Tamla Motown music, the sound of masking tape being torn away from the door and his brother's voice. "William, now move away, let me open the door… " Eventually the door opened revealing a usually unflappable George looking anything but calm as he tried to prevent William from doing whatever it was he was trying to do.

"Thank God you're here, Bill… come in. As you can… " He didn't get a chance to finish his sentence. Behind Bill's vehicle, a police car and van had pulled up and disgorged six officers, all of whom seemed rather too large to get through the gate, but they managed it.

"We've had a call from a… " The sergeant consulted his notebook: "a neighbour who has reported a disturbance at this address. Can we come in, sir?

"Taxi for Mr Coleman!" Another new arrival announced, who had little or no interest in the chaos in front of them.

"Were you going somewhere, George?" Bill was puzzled.

"No… well, yes, it was for William to go to hospital."

"What, William getting a cab. Are you sure that's a good idea in his state?"

"No, not on his own… it was to take him to hospital." George didn't know who to talk to first.

"… Babylove, oh baby love, I need you, oh I need… "

"Can we turn the music off, sir?" The sergeant was addressing William, presumably because he probably thought that George was rather too old to listen to Diana Ross and the Supremes. It was George though, who answered and quickly.

"No, please don't do that. That's not a good idea, officer."

"And you would be?"

"Coleman. George Coleman. Look, I don't think that's…" But the sergeant was in no mood to do anything while the music was playing and with a nod of his head indicated to one of his officers to find the offending machine and turn it off.

"Cab for Mr Coleman!"

George turned his attention away from the sergeant for a second in order to deal with the cab driver, but was immediately distracted back by a loud thud produced by an officer being rugby tackled on the stairs by William.

"I told you not to turn the music off, didn't I? What the hell do you think… " But his words were lost as three officers piled in to pull William off their colleague.

"I take it you don't want the cab anymore?" But the question didn't need, or indeed get, an answer and the cab driver decided to cut his losses and left, brushing past Irene who was re-entering the front garden following her session of emotional first aid, ably administered by Mrs Holmes. George turned his attention to her as she appeared by his side, just inside the front door.

"So, who the hell called the police?" This was all he could manage before once again attempting to interfere with police business. "Is this really necessary? The boy's mentally ill. Sergeant, you shouldn't be doing this… he needs to be in a hospital."

"Then perhaps you should have called an ambulance, sir."

"I did, but they told me to contact my GP."

"And," The policeman sounded more impatient than ever.

"And they told me to contact Greenbeck Hospital where he'd been a patient."

"And,"

"And they told me to ring our doctor," George didn't wait for another "and". "So I rang for a cab so we could try to get him seen in casualty."

The sergeant temporarily saw reason. "So that was the cab that just left?"

"It was! Now, perhaps you'll let us get him to where we were going to in the first place!"

William, by this time had been allowed to sit on the stairs, having been allowed up from under the pile of officers and was still looking determined about something or other and judging by the lack of Diana Ross, it was probably that.

"I'm afraid it's not quite that simple, sir. I'm sure that you're aware that we are responding to a call regarding a disturbance and willful damage to property at this address?"

"So you've already said," George was on the brink of completely losing patience, "But I don't wish to press charges and since it's my property, that's all there is to it. Surely?"

"That's true enough, Mr Coleman, but we still have the issue of the causing a public disturbance issue to deal with, although in... " The sergeants words were cut off in mid-sentence as William, obviously determined to turn the music back on, had tried to bolt back upstairs without waiting to see if the officer standing in is way would move. As he was once again bundled over, one of the officers looked over to the sergeant who gave a nod and started to go out of the front door, only stopping to give the briefest of explanations to a wide mouthed George.

"And of course, assaulting a police officer in the execution of his duties..." George opened his mouth to speak, but was cut off with the sergeants last word on the subject. "... Twice!"

The doors of the police van were opened and William firmly held and handcuffed was physically encouraged to get in.

George was left, standing on the pavement, with gaggles of onlookers and a completely dumfounded brother being his only company. As he turned towards his house, his eyes met Irene's and though he didn't say anything at all, he got the answer to the question his whole being was asking. "I didn't know! I didn't... I didn't know she was going to call the police... she must have thought she was helping!" At that point, George heard a front door close and looked across to see the hall light of the Holmes' household being turned off almost immediately after.

August 4th 1975; 07:00 hrs

"How come nobody told me he was being readmitted?" Dave wasn't impressed, but as Rose Villa's latest charge nurse he was still trying to impress Trafford, so his comments were merely being hurled at his minions during the morning handover from the night staff.

"Police surgeon and on-call psychiatrist at about eleven o'clock last night. Trafford agreed to it apparently. Why, is there a problem with him?" The night staff nurse, had been around for more years than it was comfortable for her remember and everyone in the office could tell by her expression that the real question she was asking was "Is there a genuine problem with this man, or can't you be arsed with him?" After all, Dave Hicks' reputation as Morgan's deputy and sidekick was well known.

"I remember this guy from Tamworth Ward... one big management problem from start to finish... and now we've got him back... great!" Dave had no intention of trying to hide his disdain.

"Was this the guy who went for Morgan?" The question came from one of the assembled nurses.

"He wasn't the one who put him in hospital, if that's what you mean, but he went for him a few times." Dave wasn't unaware of the knowing looks between members of his team and countered the unspoken questions. "Without any provocation!"

The would-be cynics were, for the time being, silenced before they'd even said a word, so Dave continued his narrative. "Tried to have a chat to an oncoming bus and nearly got himself killed!" The looks on the faces of his audience clearly indicated that they wanted to hear more. "Believes that radios and tellys are giving him messages and tries to smash them. Did it on Tamworth. Took eight of us to hold him down."

At this point, he turned his attention back to the night staff nurse again. "So why's he back this time?"

"Apparently he trashed the house he was living in, smashed the telly and had a go at a couple of coppers who were called to the scene. They carted him off to the police station and it was the police surgeon that contacted Trafford."

"So, presumably there must have been some sort of warning that something wasn't right. You can't tell me that there were no signs before this happened!" Dave was showing his intolerance of anyone who wasn't a psychiatric nurse and decided to inject a dose of sarcasm as well "Don't tell me. Someone called him Billy. That usually does it, fucking wanker."

"Playing music all night, being very jumpy, distracted. That's about it, but his Grandpa thought he might not be taking his medication." The staff nurse referred to the set of notes in front of her.

"Oh surprise, surprise! But if there was going to be anyone who'd think that they could do things better than we did, it's him, self-righteous bastard. Used to sit on the ward and look down his nose at the staff and now we find he can't even follow a simple bloody instruction to make sure his grandson takes his medicine. And now we're going to have to pick up the pieces again, these people just make you want to puke."

Dave was being just a little too enthusiastic in his character assassination, but now he'd started, he wasn't going to stop. "Morgan probably had it right all along. He used to say that that the boy had done it to himself with drugs and that he was spoilt fucking rotten into the bargain. Whole fucking family's cracked. His mother tried to kill his father, then she topped herself when they took her to prison. Fucking cracked. And the old man's probably as nutty as the rest. I can't believe that Trafford thought that anyone in that family would do as they were told."

The night staff nurse decided to act for the defence, mainly because someone had to in the face of such a vindictive and sustained attack. "The way I remember it was that he probably wasn't stable enough to be discharged in the first place and that Trafford should have kept hold of him for a lot longer. Seems to me that this would have happened sooner or later anyway because the treatment simply wasn't working."

Dave really didn't appreciated having his bigotry diluted by anyone. "And what did you have to do with it? You never worked with him."

"Actually, I did a few nights here just before he was discharged and I did a few on Tamworth when he was there."

"Hardly call that "working with him" would you?" Dave was anxious to regain the high ground that he believed was his by right.

It was quite obvious to everyone in the office that the question neither needed or deserved an answer. Without even looking at the slightly ruffled charge nurse, the night nurse picked up her carrier bag from the side of the desk. "I'm off to my bed." She made her way out of the office and into the ward area.

She paused briefly at the curled up rocking figure of the new admission. "I'll see you tonight, William." But she knew that no response would be forthcoming.

And there wasn't.

Jack was always suspicious and always giving out his warnings about not trusting anyone. *"He's only come to make sure you're still locked up... so you can't protect Julie and Nan. They've already got to him... You can't trust him."* But William still felt different, nicely different, when he saw him coming on to the ward, despite Jack and his warnings. William wanted him to be there and his Grandpa always seemed pleased enough to see him and that should have been enough.

"He won't let you go home. They're all in danger and he won't let you protect them." Jack wasn't happy with William's visitor.

"I don't why know I can't come home. I want to come home and do my homework. I don't like this camp, I can't see the horses. Why can't I see them? I like my chocolate... have you got a fag? I want a fag... "

His visitor was visibly confused at the rapid and confusing verbal onslaught and tried to cover his discomfiture by smiling awkwardly and holding his hands up, as if surrendering.

William eagerly accepted a cigarette and drew on it eagerly as it was lit.

"He's trying to make you say things so he can get into your brain!" William's fear of being altered was something that George knew only too well and as he listened to the disembodied voice, his knees drew up and he started to rock as an almost automatic response.

"Aren't you going to talk to me anymore, William?"

No eye contact. No words. No response. Just rocking and incessant puffing on the cigarette, which, after only a minute or so, had been smoked almost down to the filter.

William felt the need for closeness that only his grandfather was willing to give, but more than that, his instinct was to avoid an altered mind. A mind that was able to get into his brain and cause havoc.

"Do you want me to go, William?"

William stopped smoking for a few seconds, turned his head and for a moment there was a flashback to an earlier time, or to be more precise, earlier emotions of familiarity, safety and closeness... then it was gone and Jack filled the void.

"He wants to trap you... wants to get into your brain!" At Jacks words William looked away and resumed his rocking.

In enemy territory now... lost to the world... must stay alert... look away from the radio, eye contact could mean death…

"Stay close to my words, William, you're in so much danger. Don't talk, they will follow your words into your mind!" William let the spent cigarette drop into the tin ashtray balanced on the arm of his chair without even looking at what he was doing.

As his visitor left, he turned to see William clutching his newly acquired half pound bar of Cadbury's to his chest as though his very life, as he'd once known it, depended on it. As William heard the sound of the ward door being unlocked he turned to watch his Grandpa slowly making his way past the male nurse who had temporarily taken on the role of gatekeeper and not for the first time, felt as though they would never see each other again.

Christmas Day 1975; 11:10 hrs

Bacon for breakfast and paper hats to wear as they queued.

Bits of tinsel in their hair. Christmas? That's what they said it was. Christmas?

"Happy Christmas!" They all said as though it was a reason to get up. More of a reason than normal. But it could be less of a reason.

Paper chains and loads of tinsel, all held up with sticky tape. Who were they trying to fool? A Christmas tree by the office door and lights that went on and off. The ones they had at home didn't go on and off unless you kept flicking the switch at the wall. No, these weren't real Christmas lights. The ones at home were real ones. They were all odd ones that had been replaced over the years, but they were real lights which had given him an excitement that was his alone. The excitement of seeing the green fairylights on the green needles of the Christmas tree. The bright orange light that lit up the small presents resting on the branches. He'd sit for hours imagining the excitement of the Christmas morning to come.

That was Christmas. Not this.

His Mother. He missed her. Missed her so much. She wouldn't leave him at Christmas. She'd be making mince pies and sausage rolls. That was Christmas. Uncle Bill coming round on Christmas Eve and Nan and Grandpa on Boxing Day. That's Christmas.

Not this.

Eric was busy putting things away, moving everything from where it was, to somewhere else. Eric always did that. He always did it quickly and today he was tidying all the tinsel.

Might not be Christmas at all, but all the staff seemed to be happy. Happier than usual. They'd all been told the same thing; look happy as though it's Christmas. Was it Christmas? William kept thinking it must be, but Jack had other ideas.

"*They're trying to catch you off guard so they can get in. Don't let them, don't believe them!*" It couldn't be Christmas. It would be different if was Christmas. But was it different? It didn't feel like it, it didn't smell like it. His mother would be here if it was Christmas. There would be a pillowcase of presents if it was Christmas.

Rodney was sitting in his chair just a few feet away from William. He was sat with his legs crossed and talking to himself as he always did, but nobody could make out the words.

"*He's clever, that one.*" Jack had said many times. "*They can't follow what he says back into his brain.*" William couldn't help but feel a certain kinship with a fellow resister, although, of course, they never talked about it. In fact they never talked at all. Never had.

William sat on the same chair in the same place. Always the same, never any different and no one ever said that he shouldn't, so he carried on sitting there day after day and week after week. He only moved to queue and to eat. He was careful to go to the toilet, if he could, at the same times, because he knew that the more often he left the chair, the easier it was to be trapped.

That's what they'd done to Martin. That's what Jack had said. That's why he cried all the time. Cried and rocked backwards and forwards. A woman came to see him every week. Someone had said it was his Mum, but William had his suspicions. She came through the doorway. He'd no way of knowing whether she existed on the other side of the door. Unlikely that she did.

Martin didn't seem to think it was Christmas. Nor did Eric. Nor did Rodney.

But Danny did. Danny was covered in tinsel and was excited, but there again, he was always excited about something. Today it was because someone had said it was Christmas.

The sound of the ward door being unlocked and one of the male nurses coming in. Did they exist on the other side of the door, or did they materialize as they seemed to pass through the doorway? The other side of the door was where the real humans were, if there were any left. He'd seen people walking around outside and they looked like the people that came through the door and the people that went out looked like the ones that had walked away from the building.

William wasn't convinced. Not at all.

"Watch the door, William... watch and wait. Your time is coming... watch and wait... " Jack was certain about the course of action.

Sitting in the dayroom with six or seven others, but still alone. Unconnected. He couldn't connect with other minds, they'd find out, they'd be able to trace it.

So he just sat and looked. Sat in the same place. Looked at the same things, week in week out. Except today. Today is Christmas, so they said.

William looked down at his lap and re-examined the torn Christmas paper and the soap and deodorant that had been inside. The label said 'Happy Xmas from the Friends of Greenbeck Hospital'.

"Clever. And where's Grandpa if it's Christmas?" Jack added his weight to the "it can't be Christmas" argument and even though William knew that if it was really Christmas that his Grandpa wouldn't be able to get to the hospital because he didn't drive, it made no difference.

It couldn't be Christmas Day and that was that.

March 18th 1976; 14:30 hrs

"Can't say I'm sorry. So why isn't he coming?" Trafford hadn't even bothered to remove his glasses or even to look up from the medical notes he was reading.

Sue Hunt stood and waited in vain for a more courteous and attentive response, but in its absence, carried on anyway. "His wife rang me to say he'd been taken into hospital last night. He's apparently very ill."

Trafford had the decency to look up and to even look a little concerned. "What's wrong with him, did she say?"

"He's had a stroke, by all accounts. His wife sounded devastated."

"Yes, I would think she would be. From what I could see, he was the one who made all the decisions." Trafford blundered his way through what he probably believed to be empathy or sympathy, or some such thing, leaving the social worker aghast.

After a couple of seconds, she composed herself enough to continue. "He was coming to talk to you about his grandson's condition. Did you want me to pass anything on to his wife, or did you want to talk to her yourself?"

"To say what in particular?" It looked to Sue as though Trafford was going to make her work for every ounce of detail, but Trafford had no such intentions in that direction.

"There's nothing to tell her. The lad hasn't got any worse and I suspect it will be some time before we can even think about discharging him again, but now that Mr Coleman is out of the picture, I can't see us sending him there. So if you want to translate that into your Social Worker language when you talk to her, be my guest." Trafford clearly thought the discussion had ended, but the social worker didn't move.

"So what shall I tell her? Do you plan to renew his Section? I've got to be able to tell her something. I can't just tell her what you've told me… no matter what language I use!

Trafford looked up, removed his glasses and sat back in his chair and just for a short while took on the air of someone who had just realized how unreasonable he'd been. "We've come a long way in psychiatry over the past twenty years. Chorpromazine and Thiorodiazine work wonders for a lot of patients. They help to keep the symptoms down to a manageable level. You know that. William Phillips though, has been tried on both. I've had him on the maximum dose of each of them and still his symptoms persist. Probably the best that can be achieved is that we can reduce his hallucinations and make him a bit less paranoid. As for his ability to concentrate and to string his thoughts together for anything like a reasonable timespan, well, you've spoken to him, you've heard his conversation go all over the place after a couple of minutes or even less."

Sue saw the chance to take advantage of the psychiatrist's rare moment of humility. "So, did you know this before you discharged him? You didn't sound this pessimistic when you spoke to his grandfather before you sent him home. So what's changed?"

Trafford leaned forward and replaced his glasses as his period of tolerance approached its conclusion. "I have to make decisions, Miss Hunt, based on whether the patient is well enough to be able to cope at home. Not whether they're cured. Not whether they'll relapse or not. Not whether they'll get into Oxford, or to be able to give an eloquent speech to the Trade Union Congress! In short, Miss Hunt, I'm concerned whether they can cope!"

The social worker tried to interject, but Trafford was in full flow. "And every now and then, someone goes home, or comes off their section or both and has problems. But, Miss Hunt, if we didn't send these patient's home, I daresay, we'd have you and your breed bleating about keeping people in mental hospitals under false pretenses!"

"I'm sure you di... " But Trafford bulldozed his way to have the last word.

"So perhaps, Miss Hunt, when you decide to ring Mrs Coleman, you'd like to bear in mind that her grandson will remain on section for as long as he remains a risk to himself or other people and the small chance this patient had of having a modicum of relief from his symptoms went out of the window when they decided to let him pour his medicine down the sink!"

Sue knew she was losing any possibility of any further reasoned discussion, but managed to force out: "Yes but..." before Trafford delivered his final salvo. "If she wants to speak to me, or if you can't handle it, you can make an appointment for her to see me. Now if there's nothing else?"

Sue knew defeat when she saw it, and without any further attempt at dialogue, turned on her heel and left Trafford pretending to work on the folder of notes on his desk.

August 3rd 1976; 14:35 hrs

"So what do they do all day?" Rachel Strong simply wouldn't give it a rest. Questions! Always questions. The fascination of having a young female student nurse on the ward, was wearing very thin indeed and that was after only one day.

Dave thought he knew what she meant and resented the implication that he might not be running his ward as well as he should do. He stalled for time. "What do you mean "do all day"?"

"I mean: what do they do all day? The patients, that is."

Dave shifted uncomfortably in his seat. "Well, we have group sessions, ward rounds... " The list stood little chance of growing and he was temporarily grateful that Rachel didn't make him search for any more by filling the void between "ward rounds" and a non-existent third activity.

"So, how often do they have group sessions?" Her pen was poised over her notebook.

"Every Wednesday afternoon." The expression in Dave's voice suggested to Rachel that he evidently thought that such a timetable was more than adequate, but whatever he meant, it didn't impress Rachel enough to write anything.

"And they last how long?"

"About an hour, or so." Dave obviously thought he'd said enough, but Rachel wouldn't let the subject drop.

"So that's all that happens all week?"

Dave was starting to get impatient. "I don't recall saying that. Obviously, other things happen like the Consultant's round and the Houseman's rounds."

"But surely those are the doctor's activities, not the patient's activities?" Rachel's irritation began manifest itself through sarcasm. "Surely they must do something else?"

"Of course they do. When we get time, we take them for a walk in the grounds, if it's safe enough to take them out." At this point the look on the charge nurse's face indicated that either he thought he'd given a perfectly adequate and faultless answer, or that any further dialogue on the subject would cause him undue effort. In either case, Rachel persisted. "Anything else?" She still hadn't written anything.

"Rachel, you don't seem to understand mental illness, and since you're only here for a few weeks secondment from King Edward's Hospital, I wouldn't expect you get to grips with the way we do things." Dave was condescending to say the least and his attempts to divert her away from asking questions were failing more with every word he uttered.

"So is that all the activities they're given to do?"

"Rachel, you just don't understand what you're asking. You keep on about activities, when half our patients can barely have a conversation for more than a couple of minutes or so without getting completely mixed up, and give them a book to read and they wouldn't know what to do with it." Dave's smiled and clearly believed that he'd given a good account of himself and his views about mental illness. "And of course, they could always play pool, we've got a table and if they want to buy some sweets or fags, we can take them to the hospital shop in the main building."

"How often does that happen?"

"Well, the shop's open on Tuesday and Thursday afternoons. We usually take at least one or two of the patients over there every week, if we get the time."

"So there are probably some weeks when no-one gets to go to the shop, is that right?"

"Rachel, you simply don't understand that I'm responsible for the safety of these patients and whenever one of them wants to go out, I have to send a member of staff with them and I won't let the ward become short staffed for the sake of someone wanting to sit next to a bloody rose bush in the grounds. Now, I'm sure you've got a lot of things to be getting on with." Dave rose from his chair and without any real need to, started tidying the bookcase behind his desk.

It took a while, but eventually, Rachel took the hint and left the office. Standing in the office doorway, she tucked her notebook into her uniform pocket and looked out onto the ward dayroom and, not for the first time, her gaze fell on the stocky, disheveled figure sat next to the window. His brown hair was uncombed, and fell over his eyes. He sat with his knees drawn up to his chin and was rocking backwards and forwards, whilst concentrating on smoking his cigarette.

His fingers were heavily stained with nicotine and his clothes were ill fitting that looked and indeed were hospital issue that had been through the unrelenting hospital laundry on countless occasions and had lost numerous buttons on the way.

Rachel guessed that the pathetic looking focus of her attention was about twenty seven or twenty eight years old. She hadn't had time to read his notes but knew from the handover that morning that his name was William Phillips, and that he was a paranoid schizophrenic. Pete, one of the staff nurses, was standing a few yards away and she walked over to him in the hope that he was going to be more forthcoming with information than his charge nurse had been.

"How long has Mr Phillips been in hospital?"

Pete thought for a moment. "A few months this time and about a year before that."

"Couldn't they cope with him at home? Did he relapse?"

"They couldn't be bothered to make sure he took his medicine, by all accounts, but from what I hear, his head still had at least two people living in it when he was discharged, so it's not surprising he came back."

"Was he normal when he was younger? I mean, when did anyone notice?"

"Yeah, sure he was normal. Supposed to be really bright. University material and all that. Couple of years ago his family noticed him becoming more isolated… distracted, strange, afraid of his own shadow. They thought it was him just being a teenager, at first."

Rachel was intrigued. "So what started it? Something must have set it off. Surely you're not sane one minute and insane the next!"

"Obviously!"

"So did anything trigger it off?"

Pete was beginning to get impatient with the barrage of questions, not least of all because he suspected that he was reaching the boundaries of his knowledge and that he stood a good chance of appearing to be a complete idiot in front of the student nurse. He lit a cigarette and collected a couple of empty cups from a nearby table and as he walked past Rachel on his way to the kitchen and gave, what he hoped to be his final words on the subject.

"Richard Morgan thought he'd been taking drugs, but who knows?"

Rachel followed her colleague into the kitchen. "Who's Richard Morgan?"

"Used to be the charge nurse on Tamworth Ward. Funny bugger. Anyway, he's not here anymore."

"Has he left?"

"You could say that. He was invalided out."

"How did that happen?"

"Well he… it doesn't matter."

Rachel looked at her colleague for a few seconds and realizing that no further answers were imminent on the subject of Richard Morgan, she returned to talking about William Phillips.

"So he didn't take drugs? William, that is."

"Who knows? Anyway, you can't say that schizophrenia happens because of this or that. It's just not like catching a cold. It just happens." The last part of the sentence was accompanied by a shrug of the shoulders.

"And he won't get any better?" Rachel asked the question but didn't expect much of an answer and her expectations were fulfilled as her colleague turned and looked out of the kitchen door in William's direction.

"Look at him. What do you think?" He didn't wait for an answer as he brushed past Rachel and made his way to the office.

"So how the fuck did he get out? Dave was not happy and neither were the staff in his office, all of whom were avoiding eye contact with him.

"Well?"

"I don't think I locked the door behind me when I came back from the hospital shop." Rachel was as honest as she was inquisitive and although the atmosphere in the office immediately turned from apprehension to irritation, it was tempered with a sizable helping of relief that someone was taking the blame.

Dave glared at the student nurse but, almost as though realizing it wouldn't achieve anything, settled for a resigned sigh to show his exacerbation.

"And when did this happen? I presume you can remember that, even if you can't remember to turn a key in a lock!"

Having a room full of people staring in her direction was enough to shake Rachel's usual composure. "Well… twenty minutes, maybe half an hour, I don't remember exactly… sorry!"

"Didn't it occur to you to tell someone, or perhaps you didn't you think it was important enough to mention, eh?" Dave didn't really need to say anymore, but he simply couldn't stop. "What the fuck did you think you were doing, for Christ's sake?"

"Look, I didn't do it on purpose and it could only have been unlocked for a couple of minutes before I realized what I'd done and I didn't see anyone go out, so… "

"So you didn't take your eyes off the door, is that right?"

"No, I didn't say that."

"No, you didn't, did you? So why are you telling me this crap about not seeing William Phillips go through the door? Obviously you didn't see him go, you were probably too busy asking stupid fucking questions to pay attention to what you should have been doing, namely locking the bloody door behind you."

"Look, I'm sorry, OK. I can't say any more than that." Rachel was clearly upset at the verbal onslaught she'd just received in front of everyone. Dave picked up the phone, his gaze still fixed on the object of his contempt and keeping his eyes firmly in her direction as he spoke to the hospital switchboard. "Dave Hicks here, Charge Nurse on Rose Villa. Can you get me the local nick on the line. Yes, I'll wait." Dave covered the mouthpiece.

"And you, young lady, will give me a full description of what he was wearing… now!"

Rachel hurriedly took out her now infamous pen and notebook and started to scribble, pausing only briefly to search her memory for more details, but she was obviously not quick enough for the charge nurse. "Don't tell me you can't remember what he was wearing!"

"Yes, of course… it's just that… " There was little use in finishing the sentence, partly because she'd recalled what she'd been trying to remember, but mostly because she knew that she was trying to reason with a complete bastard who simply had an excuse to dislike her even more than he had done before the incident. She quickly tore the page from her notebook and handed it to Hicks, who was still waiting to be connected to the police.

"Now you can go and explain to the Senior Nursing Officer how you managed to lose a sectioned patient, and hope that someone manages to bring him back before he does any damage." Then, almost as an afterthought: "or, for that matter, before anyone does any damage to him!"

Rachel turned and left the office, but Hick's couldn't resist one last dig. "And try to remember to lock the bloody door behind you this time!"

"Bit hard on her, weren't you, Dave? We've all done it. Even you, I seem to remember!" Pete had remained in the office after Rachel and the others had left. Once again, Hicks covered the mouthpiece and grinned. "Sure, but it's put that little "know it all bitch" in her place, hasn't it?"

Pete smiled and nodded. Dave was an evil sod, but he was a good laugh.

"Hello, this is Charge Nurse Hicks from Rose Villa, Greenbeck Hospital. I'd like to report a missing patient."

August 5th 1976; 18:45 hrs

From his vantage point from behind a bush in the grounds, William fixed his stare on the hospital gates. Cars were leaving the hospital at the end of the day and there didn't seem to be anyone at the gate checking who was leaving. He'd been hiding for nearly an hour, waiting for his chance to get through the gates without being noticed and since there was no one opening or closing the gates, it was only a matter of time. On other side of the gates William could see the road and heavy traffic flowing in either direction.

"You've got to stay undercover, William. They're all looking for you now. All

235

those cars. Looking for you!" Jack sounded certain.

William stared at the cars. The cars and their occupants. All trying to find him. They'd always known who he was. They'd always tried to find him, so they could change him. They'd already taken his mother and his Grandpa and God knows who else.

Now he needed to go. Needed to leave their headquarters where he'd been lying low. He needed to work undercover. Had to work things out. Stop his thoughts from being detected, work out the mathematics and identify the equation he needed to solve. But not yet, and not while it was light. They could trace his thoughts when it was light. When it was light and there was cloud cover. Cautiously, William stared up at the sky. It was overcast, so it was dangerous. He had to be so careful.

The traffic was beginning to thin out and William looked around. The coast was clear and there were no cars at the gate. Bowing low and running at the same time, William made a dash for the gate and made it as far as another bush, this one being just in front of the left stone pillar of the gateway. He was right next to the road that led to the outside. Another car approached the gate and William peeped through the branches of the bush and caught a brief glimpse of Trafford behind the wheel of his green Jaguar as he sailed past to join the rest of the rush hour traffic.

"Their controller has gone. They can't do anything without him. He controls all the machines. It's safe to go, as soon as there's a gap in the traffic!" Jack sounded urgent.

William looked back into the hospital grounds, and couldn't see any more vehicles approaching. Looking out to the road, he saw a yellow lorry approaching. The colour yellow always took power away from them. Made it safe. Wait for it to go past and make a run for it. Use its yellow energy to stay hidden.

One last look and he emerged from behind the bush, dashed through the gates and went in the direction that the yellow lorry had taken. Loads of people were out. They would all be looking for him, he had to be careful, keep his head down. The yellow protection would soon wear off.

19:20 hrs

"Just keep on walking. Keep looking at the ground so they can't make eye contact!" Jack was helping him all the way, but even so, William didn't really

have much of a clue as to where he was. He just had to keep on walking. Keep walking and keep hidden. Darting in and out of shop doorways when he saw cars coming towards him. Looking down at the ground when anyone approached. It would be safer when the clouds thinned and when the light faded, but it looked as though that wouldn't happen for some time.

19:45 hrs

More shops now. Shops that looked familiar. But did they look familiar because someone had made them look that way, or because he really recognized them. It was impossible to tell. Maybe they'd started their mind tricks and just made him believe they were familiar.

"Just keep on walking, that'll fool them... don't fall for their tricks. If you keep on walking they won't be able to keep up the illusions, their power cells will be drained if you don't take the bait."

It fitted the mathematics. Jacks advice helped to balance the equation. But it didn't do the whole job. Not quite. If he could just complete the task and balance the equation it would create a clearing through their detection machines. It would make it safe.

From the safety of a shop doorway, William carried out a thorough visual search of the immediate area.

"It'll fit into place if you can find the sequence. Look for the sequence, William. You'll know it when you see it. The power within will tell you." Jack's voice sounded excited and hopeful.

Woolworths. Marks and Spencers. Kentons. No, that didn't give him the right feeling. Didn't balance the equation. Another sweep of the vicinity. He had to know by instinct. Like listening through a stethoscope against a safe door as the barrels fell into place with the dullest of thuds when the dial is carefully turned. That's how he'd know, only he wouldn't hear it. He'd feel it.

Woolworths, FineFare, Marks and Spencers, Williams and Glynns Bank... no, not quite, but his mind felt at least one barrel falling into place that hadn't with the previous sweep. That meant that Woolworths was wrong.

Finefare, Marks and Spencers, Williams and Glynns Bank, C&A's.

Two barrels in place! That meant that two were wrong and two were right. Try taking one away and putting another one in: John Colliers, Marks and Spencers, Williams & Glynns Bank, C&A's.

Three barrels! Delaying any further searches, William looked around to make sure he was safe and soon found what he'd suspected. He'd been seen! Parked over the road was a white Ford Cortina and behind the wheel sat a middle aged man smoking a cigarette, looking in his direction. William looked away, he had to break the contact before his brain was invaded.

The equation would change the longer he spent concentrating on something else. Cautiously he looked up. The car was still there, but the driver was busy opening one of the rear doors for a woman to get in.

"You can't stand here... you've got to move... someone else will find you!" Jack's urgency hadn't abated, but the search for the missing part of the equation had to go on. But did it? Would it protect him? In any case, he couldn't find it and didn't know where to look. Could it be found here, or was it something he hadn't thought of?"

Grandpa. Hadn't seen him for ages. Did he have the answer? Was that why he came to visit? He could have been the missing protection. No one ever used to speak to him while he was there. Was that because they were scared of him, because they knew he had power?"

It started to rain. The people in the street started to quicken their paces to escape the drizzle. Heads down and rushing. Perfect. Too pre-occupied to notice. Too busy to detect his thoughts.

Searching for colours now. Yellow was good, but there was no yellow nearby. Yellow was good protection but it soon evaporated. Soon disappeared. You had to be quick before it went, but there was no yellow here.

"You're too exposed, William. Running won't save you. Won't save anything!" Urgency to desperation. Jack never gave any warning of such changes. It just happened.

Crossing the road. The screech of a car and a cursing driver. No matter.

Grandpa didn't come anymore. They'd got to him. They'd stopped him from coming.

Soaking wet, hair plastered to his forehead. Search for the colour for protection. The personal colour he could use. Yellow wouldn't work for long, not to build a decent, strong force field around him. Grandpa knew, but they had him now. But did they know his secret?.

Away from the big shops now, but still walking, still dodging into doorways to avoid prying eyes. Still lost, but it was so important to keep going. The way to stop running was to find the colour. The colour would encase him in a bubble of safety.

The streets were quieter now, not so many cars or people, but those that were there stared at him. They knew. They would be sending in their reports.

"Stop running and hide. Find somewhere away from their gaze. Find it quickly!" Once more, the urgency from Jack.

20:25 hrs

Crouching in a front garden between a privet hedge and a low wall. The foliage enthusiastically gave up the raindrops they'd been holding onto and gave William a further drenching.

People walking past, but they couldn't see him. Keeping all thoughts away in case they were followed back into his brain, but now he could see the colour of the front door that he hadn't noticed as he jumped behind the wall. Jack had meant him to find this house. Jack had shown him the sign he needed.

Purple! It had to be purple to fit. To protect. The door was purple but it was a door and a door wouldn't do it. Wouldn't do the job he needed to be done.

The rain was coming down heavier than ever and the street was getting emptier. The motorists were concentrating on trying to see through rain and wiper obscured windscreens and wouldn't even notice him unless he got really close and that was something he wasn't going to do.

"Look around, make sure the coast is clear... ready now... ready... now go!" Jack was adding his comments to what William was looking at. In one swift move he'd moved out from behind the privet, cleared the wall and was back on the pavement.

Rows of houses. Road after road of houses. No familiar landmarks, but it didn't matter. It was better this way, they couldn't locate you if you were lost, it confused their sensors. Grandpa knew their secrets; he'd been trying to tell him every time he visited. He knew that now, but now he wasn't there anymore.

More houses and still the rain poured. On the other side of the road was a bus shelter. An empty bus shelter. Need to keep dry for a few minutes, a few seconds.

"Stay away from their sight!" Jack's warning prevented any move to cross the road to keep dry. Just keep on walking. The houses were different now, smaller, not so well kept. Loads of cars parked on either side of the street. That's how they protected themselves against prying eyes. They formed rows of cars and vans.

Instinctively now, turning left into a wider street with fewer parked cars, but danger was all around, all the time. Stopping at a narrow alleyway and taking refuge. The people in the cars couldn't see him. Rain easing and cloud cover lifting, safer but not safe enough. Need to remember the past, remembering the past gives immunity. Mum, remember Mum before they got her. Mum when she came back with baby Julie, the day it snowed after dinner. Nan's egg and chips on Thursday's and Uncle Bill on the beach.

All gone now. No. Get rid of that thought, they can trace it too easily. *"Blank it out!"* Jack had picked up the thought and wasn't at all happy. *"Find the protection. You know what to find!"*

Looking out from his hiding place in the alley way, the way looked clear. Cold and wet, but it was beginning to get dark and the sky was clear. Just one more thing to achieve a near perfect safety. The equation needed to be balanced and if it wasn't, then there would be no harmony, no safety and everyone who hadn't been altered would be in danger.

Walking cautiously out of the alleyway, away from the temporary sanctuary and into the open street. No moving cars to be seen. The parked cars on either side of the road had spaces between them. Their protection was incomplete.

Looking to the left, houses and more houses. To the right, houses… houses and hope. Hope in the form of a sign. A sign with a light.

Walking towards it now. Getting nearer, the sign becoming clearer. Drizzle starting again. Pace quickening. Thoughts racing.

21:10 hrs

Standing at the end of the row of houses, looking at the petrol station. Two cars filling up, their drivers looking around, apparently innocently, but anyone who had eyes to see knew that they were scanning the area. One after the other they replaced the petrol nozzles into their holsters and made their way into the kiosk, emerging a couple of minutes later and driving away.

The rain coming down heavier now. More urgency needed. Moving quickly towards the kiosk, a man and women behind the counter. Complete the equation with the purple. If they were unaltered, they'd understand.

"Yes, can I help you?"

August 7th 1976; 14:40 hrs

"Say that again!" Trafford's registrar, Max Arbury, wasn't being difficult or sarcastic. He just couldn't be certain he'd heard it right.

"The police got a call from a petrol station in… "

Arbury held his hand up and shook his head, indicating that Hicks could fast forward that bit.

"Sorry Max, er, ah yes." The charge nurse referred to the notes, although he didn't need to. "He rummaged around the sweet counter in the petrol station. The bloke behind the counter asked him what he wanted, at which point William became quite aggressive, telling the bloke that if he didn't know, then he couldn't be real… or something like that."

"And what happened then?"

"Well then he, William that is, stared this guy straight in the eyes and carried on rummaging through the chocolate. Then he said something like "you can't follow my thoughts, you can still be saved", before looking down at the handful of chocolate bars he'd picked up and throwing most of them on the floor. That's when the other assistant called the police."

"And what did he do with the rest? The ones he didn't throw on the floor?" Arbury was still trying to encourage the charge nurse to get to the point.

"Ah, yes, I see what you mean now. Well he unwrapped the chocolate, kept the foil wrapping from about twenty bars and stuffed them underneath his shirt."

"And the chocolate bars?"

"Oh, those? He threw them away. Police got there a few minutes later as he was leaving the petrol station."

Arbury was beginning to get a little impatient at having to dig every last detail from the charge nurse. "And then?"

"Well, obviously he looked a bit suspicious with no coat and being soaking wet and the police stopped him and arrested him."

"Yes, but what happened when they arrested him?"

Dave Hicks referred to his notes again. "According to the police account, he just turned towards them when they called out, held his arms loosely by his side, closed his eyes and smiled. Oh, yes, he was nodding the whole time and just kept repeating that the purple would protect him, whatever that means."

"Could it be that the wrappers he tucked into his shirt were from Cadbury's chocolate?" Arbury felt it necessary to state the obvious.

"Well, yes. Yes they were. Oh, I see, Yes, well anyway, then they called us because he matched the description we'd rang through and we sent some lads to the police station to pick him up. And that's it!"

"Prescription sheet?" The registrar expected colleagues to keep up with the obvious at least, but he knew that with Charge Nurse Hicks, it wasn't a battle worth fighting and resigned himself to getting on with what he had to do.

"Going to increase his medication?" Dave Hicks was fairly certain of his ground and was quite surprised by the registrar's response.

"Actually, I'm going to stop it and try him on haloperidol and see how he goes. When Dr Trafford returns from leave, we'll give it a few weeks and review it again."

"I don't understand. He came off the chlorpromazine because it wasn't very effective, now you're saying that the Thioridazine isn't working either. What's to say that haloperidol won't be useless as well?"

"How long have you known him?" Arbury carried on writing, making it plain that any answers from the charge nurse would not have the slightest effect on his course of action.

"Since he came in to Tamworth ward. I remember... " But Arbury was only interested in making his point and had no desire whatsoever to go down memory lane with Dave Hicks.

"Any better, is he? Any better at all?"

Hicks didn't have to think about that one. "No. Well, he did seem to get better for a while, otherwise we wouldn't have sent him home, but now he seems to be worse than ever."

"Exactly. It would appear that although our Mr Phillips seemed to have improved before he was discharged, he hadn't stabilised as much as everyone had thought and now, unfortunately, his medication would seem to be making his psychosis worse instead of better."

"Is that possible?"

"Oh yes! Rare I'll grant you, but it happens, and as you've probably gathered, it is quite possible that his condition is substantially resistant to treatment."

"But I thought the relapse was due to him not taking his medication?"

Arbury saw a chance to stamp his clinical authority on the situation. "Perhaps it was, or perhaps it would have happened anyway. Who knows? One thing at least is certain and that is that he is more psychotic now than ever he was, but tell me, have you noticed anything else about him since he was readmitted from home?"

"Like what?"

"Like any other changes. I've only been here for a couple of months. You know him far better than I do."

Hicks thought for a moment. He considered two things, both at the same time. The first thing he thought about was whether there actually had been any changes. More importantly, the thought occurred to him that Arbury knew what changes there had been and just wanted to find out if he knew what they were!

"He's put on a few pounds?"

"OK, so how much has he put on?" It seemed like a common sense type of question to ask a nurse.

"How do I know? Quite a lot, I suppose." Hicks sounded indignant.

"Well surely you must weigh your patients?" Arbury sounded amazed at the charge nurse's answer.

"Well, probably. When he was originally admitted, perhaps. Look, I'm a psychiatric nurse, I'm concerned about mental illness, it's not my job to…"

Arbury had heard enough. "So whose job is it? Or perhaps your ward doesn't have a set of scales, because it's not your job to use them, eh?"

The look on Hicks' face told the registrar that he wouldn't get any further with that particular form of questioning, so he tried another. "I suppose you've noticed that the medication isn't working? You must have noticed that his psychosis is getting worse? Hasn't it occurred to you to watch for any side effects, such as weight gain?"

Hicks nodded, so Arbury continued. "At the last ward round before Dr Trafford went on leave, we discussed his medication and as you know, there was some debate as to the advisability of commencing him on haloperidol, the conclusion being that it was at least worth a try. I daresay you will also recall that you managed to lose Mr Phillips before I could change it!"

Adam, one of the patients, tapped on the office door and poked his head in, his eyes fixed on a small package on the desk in front of the charge nurse. "Can I have my parcel? Pete said I'd got a parcel and that you had it and can I have it please?" The words tumbled out so fast that they rolled into one. It was as though Adam had been practicing the request for some time and now he'd managed it, he stood ringing his hands and looking down at the floor. Dave was in no mood to be bothered with trivia, or patients, for that matter. "When I'm ready to give it to you, I'll let you know. Shut the door on your way out, I'm busy!"

Arbury looked up briefly and stared at Hicks, as though he was confirming to himself his opinion of the charge nurse and his novel approach to care and compassion. Rapidly returning to the task in hand, he completed his rewriting of the prescription sheet, put his pen back into his top pocket and began to leave the office, but couldn't resist a parting shot. "Perhaps now we've changed it, you'll be good enough to hang on to him long enough for him to take it." He didn't wait for a response and turned on his heel and left.

Pete had been just outside the office during the exchange and as the doctor left the ward, he made his way into the office to where Hicks was sitting, smoking a cigarette and seething.

"Fucking arrogant bastard. Thinks he can come in here tell us how to do our jobs, well he knows fuck all about anything."

"Fucked you off, hasn't he?" Pete stated the obvious.

Hicks ignored the comments and reluctantly gave his orders. "Get that bloody student nurse to find some weighing scales and a blood pressure machine and tell her to do some observations on William. Perhaps she can manage that without asking too many bloody questions."

"Anything else apart from weight and blood pressure, or is that it?"

"Why don't you ask "know it all" fucking Rachel? Maybe she'd like to turn it into a project!"

Pete took the hint and went in search of Rachel, while Hicks sat back in his office chair and lit a second cigarette from the smoldering remains of the previous one. It seemed that William Phillips would keep on giving him aggravation, but deep inside he knew that he would simply have to learn to live with it.

244

William Phillips wasn't going anywhere in a hurry. He'd seen it many times before, but it never ceased to occur to him quite what an understatement the term "treatment resistant" actually was.

In fact it wasn't so much a term as it was a life sentence and Hicks had a pretty good idea where the sentence would be served.

August 24th 1976; 10:30 hrs

"Would you like to play a game of Snakes and Ladders with me, William?"

In between frequent periods of walking around the ward and smoking, William would sit in his favorite chair and smoke. There didn't seem to be any direction in anything he did. When he wandered around, it seemed that it was done with some sort of determination, a purpose, but it wasn't. He'd jump up from his chair, walk rather quickly round the ward and return to his original position without having done anything or spoken to anyone.

Unless, of course, it was time to queue up for something.

For the moment, though, William was in one of his sitting down periods and the clinical psychologist took his chance while he could. He extracted the game from the bag he was carrying. He wasn't going to take the chance of William jumping up and disappearing whilst he went to look for it.

William nodded and seemed to be interested in the process of setting the board up. Ian watched carefully as William extended his tar stained fingers into the box to extract the dice.

"How are you today?" Ian wanted to engage him in a conversation, no matter how basic.

"I'm OK."

"That's good. You remember me, don't you? I'm Ian McDonald, the psychologist. Yes?"

William nodded, but in such a way that neither confirmed nor denied his recognition.

"Have you got a cigarette?"

"No, I'm afraid I haven't. What colour counters do you want to have?"

William didn't answer, but just pointed to the red one in the psychologists left palm.

Ian proceeded to put both the counters at the start of the game board and handed the dice to William, who proceeded to shake the dice and let

245

them fall onto the board. Ian waited for him to move the counter, but he had to prompt him. "William you've thrown a five."

It seemed as though William was waiting for either permission, or confirmation of what he should do, but having been told, he moved his counter the five spaces on the board. Ian took his turn and moved his counter accordingly.

"What did you have for breakfast this morning, William?"

"Porridge. I always have porridge."

It wasn't much of a thread, but Ian took it as a starting point. "Do you like porridge, or isn't there anything else to eat?"

"I like it." William spoke as he followed Ian's prompt to take his turn.

"Well that's good, but don't you ever want to have something different?" Ian took his turn and moved his counter up a ladder on the board, all the time taking care to observe whether William was able to follow his move and the conversation.

"We have bacon on Sundays," William was looking at Ian as he spoke and his brief enthusiasm to tell his visitor about his world had an almost schoolboy enthusiasm about it, but his response was at the cost of doing anything about his move.

"That's good. Your turn, William." Another throw of the dice, this time followed by an unprompted move of the counter, but a move in the wrong direction up a snake.

"You only go down snakes, you go up ladders." Ian explained and William appeared to examine the board carefully, but made no attempt to move his counter to where it should have been. This task fell to Ian.

"Have you got a cigarette?"

"No William, I told you that I didn't smoke."

Ian started to take his turn, but hadn't completed it by the time William jumped up and disappeared in the direction of the toilet, only to emerge a couple of minutes later. Instead of returning to his game with Ian, he started walking round the dayroom, picking up any object he came across, looking at it briefly and putting it down and moving on to the next object. After a minute or so, he returned to his seat, but made no attempt to take his turn.

"Your turn, William." Ian made no mention of his meanderings and was surprised when his patient tossed the dice and move the counter correctly and without hesitation, almost as though he'd had enough of

Ian's surreptitious analysis and wanted to make the point that he really wasn't an idiot and could play Snakes and Ladders perfectly well.

"Well done, William. My turn."

William started to get up again, but this time, Ian challenged him.

"Aren't you going to carry on with our game, William?"

He sat down again and watched as Ian took his turn.

"What do you enjoy doing, William?"

No reply, so Ian decided to put it another way. "What do you like to do with your time?"

William shrugged his shoulders and the psychologist realized what a bloody stupid question it had been.

"Do you like to read?"

William took his turn without prompting, landed on a snake and folded to board in half, leaving no doubt that the game was at an end.

"OK, so we won't play that anymore!" Ian cleared the game away and put it into its bag. "Is it OK if we just sit here and have a chat?"

William nodded. He still seemed restless, but Ian carried on anyway. "Does your Nan come and visit you very often?" The psychologist had no intention of collecting erroneous information about the visiting habits of grandparents, he knew that anyway. What he really needed to do was to explore William's grip on reality.

"Sometimes," William looked down at his lap.

"Well that's good, isn't it? When was the last time she came to see you?"

William didn't have to think about it. "Saturday."

"She came on Saturday? And did she bring you anything when she visited?"

William showed the beginnings of a smile. "She brought me some chocolate."

"Wow! Did you eat it all?"

"I ate it before my tea."

"So you didn't want your tea on Saturday?" Ian's comment came with a reciprocated smile.

William looked up and just for a few seconds, established eye contact. "Yes I did. And I had seconds!"

"You obviously like your food then!"

Eye contact broken again. "Yeah. Can I have a cigarette?"

"Sorry William, I don't smoke. We'll get you one in a minute, OK?"

Another nod and again his gaze returned to his lap.

"So does your Nan tell you all about what's happening at home?" Ian genuinely didn't know the answer to this and was anxious to find out how William viewed his predicament.

William nodded and Ian mentally kicked himself for asking a closed question that got him precisely nowhere. "So what's happening at home then? Can you tell me?"

"Grandpa died."

"Yes, I know. I'm sorry. That was some time ago, though, wasn't it?"

"Last year. He died last year."

"You miss him, don't you?"

Again the nod, followed by a short silence. "Can I go to the shop?"

The request caught Ian off guard, but he recovered quickly and tried to pull the conversation back. "Gary's taking you to the shop later, William. We were talking about your Grandpa."

William nodded and stared at the ground again.

"Well, for instance, what sort of things did you do together before you came into hospital? Can you remember?"

"He used to help me with my homework. He was good at maths."

"Is that right? I hear that you're very good at maths too."

Again, the briefest of smiles and eye contact, but it only lasted a second or so and then he was up and away, this time to a table a few yards away where he picked up an old book and without looking at it, put it down again.

"William, will you come and sit down and talk to me a bit more?"

Nothing.

"Please." William returned to his seat.

"I'm going to be a teacher."

"Well that's good. What are you going to teach? Do you know?"

"Maths," The answer was unsurprising, but William was showing distinct signs of distraction and before Ian could ask anymore, his conversation began to show signs of his thoughts becoming fragmented and muddled. "I've got some money in the office."

Ian decided to follow the flow to see if it would lead anyway, or whether it would deteriorate into a load of jumbled and outwardly unrelated commentaries.

"And what are you going to do with your money. You're going to the shop with Gary later, aren't you?"

William started fiddling around with his socks. "I couldn't find any grey ones!"

"Do you like to wear grey socks, William?"

"Have you got a cigarette?"

"No, I don't smoke." Ian decided that following William's lead was going nowhere "So you said you wanted to be a maths teacher. Is that right?"

"I'm going to be a maths teacher." William corrected the psychologist.

"Sorry! So how are you going to be a maths teacher? Don't you need to go to University to do that?"

"You can send them a letter, then I can be a maths teacher."

"Don't you think they'll expect you to have passed your "A" Levels or something?"

"It's my birthday today." Another change of direction, but one that could yield useful information.

"I know! How old are you today?" Ian looked genuinely happy that William had shared the information with him.

"Twenty two." The answer was quite spontaneous.

"Did you get any cards today?"

"Can I have a cigarette?"

Ian finally decided that he was wasting his breath explaining that he didn't smoke and just ignored the request altogether, and repeated his question instead. "William, did you get any cards today?"

This time a response as he rummaged around his pockets and produced three crumpled and folded birthday cards, with three folded envelopes from separate pockets. As he handed them to the psychologist he added his commentary. "That one's from Nan. That one's from Julie, she's my sister and that one's from Uncle Bill."

"That's great! Are any... " But Ian couldn't finish his sentence before William was off again, this time straightening a few chairs at the table, as if in preparation of the next meal.

Ian waited patiently, knowing by now that William would return to his seat and sure enough, after about half a minute, his patience was rewarded.

"So, William. Can you tell me why you're here?" The psychologist decided to see if he had better luck in a different direction.

William began fiddling with the birthday cards that Ian had placed on the table next to his chair. "Because I'm ill."

"OK. Can you tell me about your illness?"

"I've got schizophrenia."

"Can you tell…" But there was no time to finish the question as William had jumped up again, this time making his way towards one of the male nurses who was busy handing out cigarettes. Having finally got what he wanted, he returned to his seat, curled his legs underneath him and dragged almost desperately on the cigarette, putting Ian in mind of a lion taking its kill away from the pack before devouring it.

"We were talking about your schizophrenia, William. Can you tell about what happens when your schizophrenia gets worse? What's it like?"

The smoking continued, but no answer was forthcoming, so the question was re-phrased. "What does it feel like when you get ill with your schizophrenia? Do you hear voices or see things that other people can't see?"

This time a nod.

"Which is it? Do you hear things or see things?"

"I hear things." William looked most reluctant to volunteer information, but Ian knew that if there was to be any prospect of rehabilitation, no matter how marginal, he needed to know how much insight William had into his condition.

"Hear things. Sometimes."

"Are you hearing anything at the moment?"

"No."

"Do you hear things very often?"

"Sometimes," The almost inevitable reply. Another stupid bloody question! Ian mentally kicked himself again for asking a question that could only result in the conversation going round in circles.

"What is it you hear? Is it a male or female voice?"

"Male."

"It's a man, yes?" Ian sought confirmation. He was getting somewhere.

"Yes."

"Do you know who this man is?"

"Yes," William was literally only giving minimal answers and the psychologist knew that his attention span wouldn't last much longer, particularly if he had a sniff of lunch to further distract him.

"Does he have a name, William? Can you tell me?"

Near the end of his cigarette now, William appeared to ignore the question, so another approach was needed. "Is it someone in your family you can hear?"

"No."

"Have you ever met this person? Is it someone you've known in the past?"

Silence, but Ian let it continue for a few seconds this time and his patience was rewarded.

"Jack. His name's Jack. Jack." William was clearly uncomfortable about his disclosure and started to stuff the birthday cards and envelopes back into his pockets, as though preparing to leave.

"OK. Thank you for telling me that, William. Does it make you feel bad to talk about it? About Jack?"

William nodded and was looking in any direction except towards the psychologist.

"What sort of things does Jack say to you, William? Can you tell me that?"

"He tells me all about people."

"Anything about me?"

"No, I don't hear things anymore."

"Ever?"

William seemed to be reluctant to confirm or deny hearing voices and curled up into an even tighter position by crossing his arms and bending his head.

"Nan's coming to see me after lunch."

"Well that's good. Did she tell you that?"

William unstuffed the cards from his trouser pocket and handed one of them to Ian to read.

"OK, William, I'm not doubting you." He handed the card back having read the message promising a visit on the afternoon of his birthday.

"So does Jack ever tell you to do things?"

A nod.

"What sort of things?"

"Can I have a cigarette?"

"What sort of things does the voice tell you to do, William?"

Silence. Another approach needed. "Do you like listening to the radio, William?"

"I like music."

"You like to listen to music on the radio, is that right?"

"Sometimes. Sometimes it makes me angry."

"Why's that, William?"

Another silence.

"Can you hear voices when the radio is on?"

"No. Sometimes it stops me hearing things."

"What things?"

"Things that aren't really there."

"Is Jack really there?"

Silence again.

"Is Jack real, or is it just in your head?"

"In my head. It's my schizophrenia."

"Well done, William. Yes, that's right, it's an hallucination. Not really there. So does the music help you to block the hallucinations?"

"Sometimes. Sometimes it makes me scared."

"Scared! Why's that? What are you scared of, can you tell me?"

"Don't know." Another short excursion to tidy the chairs around the table followed before he returned to his chair and resumed his position.

"I miss Mum. She died and I miss her. It's lunch time in a minute."

"I know it's nearly lunchtime. Do you know what's for lunch today, William?"

Certain ground here. William asked what was for lunch several times during the morning. "Sausages and mash and gravy." Being asked a question on which he was certain of his ground seemed to brighten his mood and he smiled and sought eye contact, albeit very briefly.

"Yes, I heard about your Mum. It must make you very sad."

"Julie likes me to hold her dolls while she dresses them up!"

"Is that your sister?"

A nod.

"Has she come to see you in hospital?"

"Nan says she's too young. I want to live in the park. Can you live in the park?"

"What park are you talking about, William?"

No reply.

"Uncle Bill's got a Rover. Can I have a cigarette?"

In the background, the sound of the tables being moved into position and cutlery and plates being put out. It was pointless carrying on with the interview with the distraction of lunch ever looming. Ian finished writing

252

his entry in his notes. He'd got a lot further than he'd expected before William's thoughts and concentration began to wander.

That was something at least.

Inevitably, William, after a few seconds of waiting for everything to be put into place, was again out of his chair, this time to take his place at the head of the meal queue. Ian watched the queue form behind William and not for the first time in his career, felt a sense of professional impotence. Immediately behind William was Eric, reaching out on either side of him to move or rearrange anything he could lay his hands on. Next in line was Hugh, painfully shy and would only queue in such a way as to hide behind others as he plainly hated being looked at, by anyone. Then there was Rodney, head bowed and having what looked like an intense discussion with himself.

Ian got up from his chair and moved towards the office. Time to turn off and be professional again, although he couldn't stop himself seeing, in his mind's eye, William, Hugh, Rodney and at least half a dozen other patients as they would have been twenty or thirty years ago, running around a playground, looking forward to birthdays and Christmas, first days at school. As he snapped himself away from the vision, the contrast between the hope of life to come, that had once existed for all of them was replaced with the sight of hopelessness and a future of institutionalization, or to coin one of Dr Trafford's favourite terms, "prolonged supportive care".

Pete was sat behind the desk in the office and look up as the psychologist entered. "That looked like an uphill struggle!"

"Well at least he talked to me. I should be grateful for that at least."

"So who won?"

"I beg your pardon?" The question took Ian off guard.

"The Snakes and Ladders. Who won?"

"Oh, sorry, yes, I see. Neither of us. We didn't finish the game."

"Well, there's a surprise!" Pete began to tidy the desk, as though he expected any further discussion regarding William Phillips to be short lived.

"Actually, he did a lot better than I'd been led to believe he would."

Pete stopped his desk tidying. "We are talking about the same William Phillips? What's the verdict?"

Ian quite rightly detected no sign of malice or cruelty in Pete's voice and gave a wry smile. "Well, as you'd expect, not brilliant. But he's a bit more "with it" than I'd been led to believe. For instance, he's quite orientated and knows where he is. He's orientated in time, although, of course, it's his birthday, so there's things like birthday cards to remind him, but even so. He can hold a conversation, of sorts, for a short time, but his attention span is seriously impaired."

Pete repeated his earlier question. "So what's the verdict?"

"Well, for what it's worth, it's possible that the haloperidol has helped him, but not dramatically, so, long term? Not terribly hopeful, although he possibly has a little insight as to why he's here."

"In what way?" Pete was genuinely surprised.

"Well, it's the old dilemma. Is he saying that he's mentally ill and the voices are part of the illness, because that's what he's been told, or does he actually know he's ill? Difficult to tell after just one session."

"What are the odds? It doesn't make any difference, if he's too ill to look after himself that's the end of it, isn't it?"

"In terms of rehabilitation, if he has true insight into his illness, it will help him to know when to get help if his symptoms return. On the other hand, if he has no real idea that he's ill, or that he takes medicine to stop his condition getting worse, then the prospects of him achieving any real independence are bleak, to say the least."

"I see," It made good sense to Pete, but he knew what he saw, day after day and sought more information to confirm his own observations. "OK, but even if he does know he's ill, he's still all over the place."

Ian sighed. "Well, you're right. Sort of. He takes things in OK, but he can't really integrate it into what other things he's holding in his mind, so it just stays as separate bits of facts."

"Sorry, you lost me!" Pete was genuinely muddled by the psychologists explanation.

"I'm not surprised. I'm not making myself very clear, am I?" Ian paused for a second and started again. "He was told, for instance, by someone or other when he was at school, that he was very good at mathematics and could go on to be a maths teacher if that's what he wanted. OK?"

"We've all heard him say it," Pete confirmed the observation. "Go on."

"He left school before he could do any A Levels, he didn't go to University or teacher training. He's been hospitalized since God knows when and he's suffering from a serious mental illness, as far as we can tell, since just after his O Levels. All these individual facts he'll be able to tell you, if you're persistent enough to get the information. Am I right? You know him better than I do."

Pete nodded in confirmation.

"But he can't put all the bits together to give him the overall picture. "I'm going to be a maths teacher" was what he said, as though the past few years just haven't happened and yet all the reports I've heard would indicate that he can tell you a lot of things, as I've said, that would prevent him from doing what he was told he could do all those years ago, namely to go on to be a maths teacher."

"Surely that's just him being unrealistic, wouldn't you say?"

"Well, just about all of us are unrealistic from time to time, but no, I wouldn't say that in his case. Reports indicate that he's an intelligent lad and although it's easy to forget that sometimes, we shouldn't be treating him as though his illness has made him stupid!"

Pete looked slightly affronted by the last statement, so Ian felt that he needed to substantiate his views some more. "When someone's thoughts are as fragmented as his and conversations are as difficult to establish and maintain as I know they certainly are, it's easy to just not bother, or to come to the conclusion that he doesn't and probably never will, understand anything. If we carry on doing that, we'll just make him worse. He does understand things and God knows, at least we seem to have had some success in making him less paranoid and deluded!"

Pete, still affronted, saw this as a challenge to established tried and trusted practice and just couldn't let it go. "You're not making sense, Ian. You're telling me that because we don't sit down and hold his hand every minute that we're making him worse. Is that it?"

Now it was Ian's turn to feel annoyed, although he tried his best not to show it. "No, I think you know what I mean. I know that you, for instance are always on the ward chatting to the patients, I'm simply saying that when you sit with him you need to be doing a bit more than just passing the time of day with him, or telling him that his dinner's ready!"

"OK, so what exactly are we trying to achieve?"

Ian realised that he'd blundered in with both feet and knew that Pete's resentment meant that the conversation was going nowhere. Time to tell a couple of white lies. "Tell you what, Pete, let's just drop the defences for a minute. What you do is valuable and you do a good job when you keep the patient's safe and assess their mental state."

Pete correctly predicted the next part of Ian's dialogue. "But?"

"But don't you think it would be a good idea to try and engage him a bit more, rather than to just assume that he won't be able to respond in the way you want him to do?"

Pete calmed down a little. "Ian, I've known this guy for a long time. You know and I know, that he's got as well as he's going to get. We've tried everything with him apart from ECT and that wouldn't do anything for him anyway. So I still can't see what you're getting at!"

Ian gave a deep sigh as though he was in the midst of expounding a theory that he'd little or no chance of substantiating. "Well, let me put it like this, the longer he goes without using his brain the less likely it is that he ever will and sitting out there staring into thin air and waiting for the next fag or mealtime is just going to make things worse!"

Pete felt as though the psychologist had overstepped the mark. He'd crossed the boundary into what was simply not his domain, but for the sake of interdisciplinary harmony he managed an unconvincing reply. "I'll bear that in mind." Almost as an afterthought to give him the last word on the subject, he added "In any case, schizophrenia is incurable… ask anyone, or perhaps you know better!"

Ian was aware, not for the last time, that he'd just wasted his breath.

October 19th 1978; 11:10 hrs

Thoughts of Mum. Sadness always came with the thought. Missing her. Seeing her sitting with Nan at the dining table. Gone. The thought didn't stay for long, or rather the feel of it stayed, but the detail changed, as it usually did after a little while, flitting from one thing to another and sometimes to very little.

Not mad. Not insane, just unable to follow the thought to where it should go, or the memory to where it should have been. Thinking things through? What things? Dipping in and out of a book of short stories, usually just enough to get the gist of each one, but moving on before too much detail emerged.

It was raining outside. The place seemed different when it rained. Not the drizzle type of rain, but the really heavy stuff that made the windows misty from the inside when anyone came from outside into the warm of the dayroom. It was even better when rivers of water cascaded down the outside of the windows making everything on the outside look blurry and distorted.

It was Monday, not that it made any difference. Every day was almost identical to the one before and the one after. But today it was raining and raining hard. That was different.

Different, yes, but Eric still moved everything. And then moved them back again, even though it still rained.

Grandpa. He used to come and visit, but one day he didn't come to visit as he'd promised. Loss. Not the depression of loss but more of disbelief. Not really denial that something had happened, because he wasn't there and that couldn't be denied. The thought wouldn't go any further, just to nothing.

Rodney shuffled by, chatting away to himself, sometimes smiling and laughing and sometimes not. He stopped in front of Danny and for half a minute he muttered as Danny sobbed. Then he moved on.

Sitting in the chair, the chair that gives familiarity, grounding, reassurance. The urge to move. Move to do what? Just move. Just get up. Need a cigarette. Need to smoke. Hungry? The queues mean that all will be there, when there's a queue. No need to ask, but cigarettes are different. Walking around without a thought, or perhaps there is one, or was one, but the chairs always there. Always there to go back to.

Move the ashtray, move the chairs around the table, shift the book on the chair. Return to the chair. No intent, no guiding thought, but thoughts nevertheless.

Dr Trafford had been in today. He was still standing at the office door. Said he was ill but doing very well. But why was he ill? Outside it was raining. Was that why Dr Trafford said he was ill? Surely not. He hadn't said it last week; it wasn't raining last week when Nan came. She didn't say much, but she brought the chocolate.

Mentally ill, that's what he'd said. Mentally ill. That's the reason for being here, but "here" doesn't matter if "there" doesn't exist. Home. A memory that doesn't seem to want to become real. Nan's house. Just a memory that won't quite form. A need for warmth, human warmth, affection. The image of home was difficult to form, the thought of the physical comfort and surroundings, but the emotion was still real. Still made him sad.

Sadness made the restlessness worse, but it wasn't the cause. Out of the chair again. Need a cigarette. For a moment it seemed as though Grandpa would reappear through the door, but he didn't. But he could, couldn't he?

Craving for the warmth of being close, of having people he loved, but nearly impossible to put it into words. It didn't matter. The smell of dinner, the reassuring queue. All was well, but was it?

Grandpa hadn't come through the door.

Tears, but only just and only briefly and then the queue. The comfort, the reassurance. Pick up the plate and move towards the Nurse who was dishing up, and everything was fine as far as everything went, but the rain wasn't important any more.

February 20th 1980; 07:45 hrs

Curtains in the ward drawn back and the noise of the staff waking everyone in the dormitory. Straight out of bed, grab the clothes and towel on his locker and off to the toilet before joining the queue for the bathroom for a wash. Toothbrush lost, doesn't matter. Don't know when it went. No bath today. It's not bath day today. Wrong day. Bath tomorrow.

Get dressed. No choices. No point, just wear what's been left out. Hospital clothes, carelessly ironed in the hospital laundry, baggy or tight, buttons or not, it didn't matter. It wasn't noticed.

Down the stairs to the day room and wait for the cigarette and the sweet tea. Into the chair and back out again. Tea drank quickly as it always was. No sedate slurping whilst pondering life. No thoughtless and laid back smoking before facing the rigors of the day. Five gulps of the tea and seven drags of the cigarette and both were finished.

Legs crossed with the top one impatiently moving up and down as though it was resting on a nerve. Both hands on the arms of the chair as if preparing for the urgent propulsion from which intention should have been a part. But it wasn't.

August 19th 1980; 08:10 hrs

The medicine trolley was rolled out and opened. Its emergence from the office and into the dayroom was enough for a queue to form. No instructions. No orders or requests, or arguments as to who should be first or last, just a silent shuffling to get the medication and the drink of water to wash it down. Every now and again, a comment or greeting from the nurse giving out the medicines and every now and again, a coherent response, usually from the same people every morning.

November 12th 1981; 08:15 hrs

One queue to another. This one for breakfast. No-one asks what the queue is for, or whether they should join it. No need to ask what to do or where to sit, but sitting was almost momentary before jumping up again and taking the empty dish and placing it into the plastic washing up bowel on the table where the breakfast had been served from just a few minutes earlier.

March 3rd 1982; 08:25 hrs

Dish disposed of and into another queue for a cigarette. The nurse gives them out from a packet to seven or eight at a time before providing a light in bulk to the eager group of nicotine addicts. Back to the chairs for some and back to wandering for others. For some others, it was a mixture of both, but peaceful repose and reflection for no-one.

August 6th 1982; 10:20 hrs

Wandering and sitting. The odd interaction, but only for a purpose, rarely for the sake of just talking to someone. "Have you been to the toilet, Rodney?", "Have you swallowed your tablets, William?", "For Christ's sake, give it a rest, Danny!" Now just sitting and watching. Waiting for the next cigarette. Radio One in the background, but it doesn't make any difference as no-one ever seems to listen to it. It's just there. Switched on every morning and switched off in exchange for the television at five o'clock.

November 30th 1982; 11:55 hrs

Plates being put on the table by the office door and the smell of food. The same time every day. The same pile of plates with the same plastic basin at the other end of the table for the dirty plates and cutlery, but no-one starts to queue. Not yet.

February 8th 1983; 12:05 hrs

Medicine trolley queue. Waiting in line once again, but the repetition was reassuring. The repetition just happened. No-one complained. No-one questioned what they were taking, or why they were taking it. Everyone conformed without question.

May 26th 1983; 12:20 hrs

Plate in hand at the head of the queue as always. Dinner dished up by the nurse standing at the dinner trolley. Return to the table and gulp it down, then back to the meal trolley for afters, or to be more precise, something with custard, in a small plastic bowl. Meal over. Plate and bowl into the blue plastic bowel and cutlery in a separate one.

September 18th 1983; 12:35 hrs

Dinner over. Queue for the fag and the sweet tea, before going back to the chair. Watching without really seeing the things that were there every day. Wandering and sitting without purpose. The radio carried on, regardless of whether anyone was actually listening to it.

November 16th 1983; 14:05 hrs

Wednesday afternoon. Wednesday's chocolate day. Wait outside the office and one of the nurses will open the door leading out into the hospital grounds. The hospital shop was past Elm Villa, past the bench under the tree, then past Maple Villa and through the green door in the main building. Straight there and straight back. They used to walk over with him. For a long time they came all the way with him, stayed with him whilst he bought his chocolate and then took him back to the ward.

But they didn't come with him anymore. Dr Trafford had said that if he was good and didn't do anything silly, then he'd be allowed to go to the shop on his own, as long as he came straight back to the ward. Eileen, the lady in the shop, always seemed to know he was coming and was always nice and smiled and always asked how he was. Eileen was a nice lady and if she wasn't serving, he'd wait until she'd finished what she was doing before buying his chocolate.

Straight there, buy the chocolate and sit on the bench under the tree for a couple of minutes on the way back. Just because it felt good. People spoke to him when he sat on the bench.

At least one person at any rate. She always spoke. She talked to him today. Told him about her day, about her Dad coming to visit.

Time to go back to the ward. He got up reluctantly and hesitated, as he always did, when it was time to go. Waiting for the words that he needed to hear, and always they came without asking. "See you tomorrow, William!" And the parting was bearable.

February 15th 1984; 14:35 hrs

Standing outside the ward door and ringing the doorbell to be let in. The sound of the key turning, the door opening and the short walk back into the dayroom and to the chair with half a packet of chocolate still in his hand. Up and walking, but more of a shuffle now. Queue for the cigarettes, then back to the chair. Rodney sits down, talking himself and nobody else and seems to take some comfort, no matter how little, in having someone else nearby if only for a few seconds.

May 16th 1984; 14:45 hrs

Chairs in a circle. Dr Trafford sitting with Dave, waiting for the nurses to gather everyone up and deposit them. Rodney rocks and talks to himself, giving sideway glances but never looking up. Danny sits down again and Eric starts to move the chairs around until one of the male nurses, Craig, stops him and guides him back to his chair, but it doesn't last for very long before he's up again. Danny jumps up every few seconds, but goes back to his chair when he's told to and Mike just sits and stares, his hands on his knees, knuckles whitening with the effort. Anthony, the new staff nurse, joins the group, apparently for little reason other than to be a shepherd, but with rather less understanding and patience than if his charges had been stray sheep.

"Good afternoon everyone," Trafford evidently considered that he didn't want to wait any longer, and ploughed on regardless. "Now who wants to start us off this afternoon?"

No-one spoke.

"Shall I just choose someone to start us?"

Still no-one spoke, and Trafford took charge accordingly. "Mike, how are you feeling today? You said you felt very lonely last week. Have you made any friends yet?"

Mike just shook his head in reply, but otherwise didn't move.

"Do you still feel sad, Mike?"

Mike nodded this time.

"Would you like to tell us what makes you feel happy and sad, Mike?"

"I feel happy when we have spotted dick and custard." Eric filled the void left by Mike's silence.

"Thank you, Eric, but we were trying to find out what Mike thinks," Trafford was anxious not to be distracted.

"I want to go home. I don't like it here, I want to go home." Mike stated the obvious.

"I know, Mike, but do you think that some things make you more unhappy than other things?"

Mike pulled the shutters down, avoided the stare of the psychiatrist and said no more.

"Does anyone else want to say anything today?" Trafford decided to try another approach, or to be more precise, the same approach with slightly different words. "What about you, William? What have you been doing today?"

"I went to the hospital shop and bought my chocolate."

"Ah yes. You enjoy your visits to the shop, don't you William? I hear that you stop and have a chat with someone every day when you go for your walk. Do you want to tell us all about your new friend?"

William looked sheepish, gave a shy grin and looked away. After a few seconds, the pressure of the silence precipitated a response. "Sandy... she's called Sandy." A couple of nervous, almost adolescent laughs came from the group.

"Is that right?" Trafford's question required no answer and more for the purpose of informing William that he knew exactly what was going on, he added, "That's Sandy who's a patient on Fern Villa, isn't it?"

William nodded.

"Well I'm very glad that you've made a friend at last, William. And have

262

you been able to talk to you Mother about going home for a visit, Danny?"

Danny showed little interest in answering the question that had been directed at him, if indeed he'd even heard it, mainly because the subject of William's new acquaintance was far more absorbing. "William's got a girlfriend, William's got a girlfriend!"

Scattered giggles around the group as everyone's attention is drawn towards William.

"Now come on, gentlemen, let's leave William alone now and carry on with our meeting." Trafford realized the distraction he'd unwittingly caused and was attempting to regain some sort of order, but his attempts were not destined to succeed, with the meeting eventually recommencing its short lived disjointed journey until its inevitable gravitation to the next cigarette queue.

August 29th 1984; 17:10 hrs

The smell of food and the clatter of cutlery. The nurses drain their cups and put out their fags in preparation of the imminent spurt of activity that meal, medicine and cigarette times always precipitated. Into the queue. No debate, no argument, just queuing. No change, nothing different, no choices that could be made, no activity that could be focused upon. The food, the sweet milky tea, the medicine and the fags. All over in a few minutes and then it was back to the chair.

Plates and cutlery collected.

Everything cleared away.

Radio off and television on.

Nurses resumed their position at the table next to the office with refilled mugs.

Rodney carried on talking to himself.

Martin carried on rocking and crying.

Adam carried on walking around, wringing his hands and asking questions about train and bus timetables.

Danny carried on darting excitedly from place to place.

Eric carried on shifting things from one place to another.

William carried on sitting in his chair, jumping up every few minutes and flitting from thought to thought even more often.

Night staff emerging from the office and the medicine trolley being wheeled out with them. Everyone gravitates towards it and forms an orderly queue. Medicine, cigarette and the last drink before bed. Television off at 10.30pm and the lights turned of lest any stragglers should not be under any illusion that it was time to go upstairs to the dormitories and go to bed. No queues, no ceremonies such as teeth cleaning or washing, just putting on the hospital pyjamas (usually with the buttons missing) and into bed.

April 16th 1985; 14:20 hrs

Spring. The flower beds erupting with daffodils, but now with one missing and that one was being clasped most attentively by a young chubby, dark haired lady sitting on the bench. Next to her, although not clasping anything, was an equally attentive and even chubbier, William Phillips. There wasn't a lot of conversation going on, but that was usually the way it was.

What did matter, was that now they could meet every afternoon. William had developed the habit of going to have a wash straight after his lunch, in preparation for his daily time in the hospital grounds. Sandy had got her Aunt to bring her in some Yardley's perfume which she applied liberally at about the same time that William was having his wash.

When they did talk, they understood each other. It didn't matter that one or both of them could go off at a complete tangent, although, in fact, that didn't happen very often. It didn't matter that one or the other might suddenly get up and seemingly wander off, apparently aimlessly, before returning to the bench a couple of minutes later.

It wasn't important at all.

Much of their time together was spent without words and when they did speak it was usually in short sentences that didn't require prolonged concentration on either part. They were instinctively sensitive to each other's attention spans and were accepting of the occasional breakdown in the continuity in their conversations.

It was the feelings of safety, comfort, acceptance and companionship that were more important than anything and it didn't matter what anyone chose to call it.

Love? Certainly in one form or another, but that wasn't the point. That certainly evaded the relevance of their relationship, because any importance that it may have had, came a poor second to the trust and empathy they had for each other.

In a funny sort of way, the meetings on the bench by the flower bed, just a few yards from the main block, were almost as institutionalized as the rest of William's behaviour, except that no one had made him do it and no one insisted that he continued doing it. Sitting with Sandy had become the focus of each day, but the rest of the day carried on as it always had. Today, though, was not the same as other days. As she sat close to William, the social worker's words repeated time and time again. "I'm so sorry, William, but your sister has just rang us to say that your Nan died in her sleep last night… I'm so sorry… I know you were close to her."

He couldn't remember anything else about the conversation. Didn't need to. The words kept on coming, but his feelings and thoughts were not as reliable and not so uniform as to make mourning inevitable.

Only sadness. The sadness that comes from the memories of things long past. Her visits had been infrequent and awkward, but at least she'd come. Both for the time she took to visit and the memories from happier times, he loved her and missed her already. For the person she was whilst he had been at Greenbeck and for being the survivor of the double act that had been his grandparents, he couldn't grieve. But the memories made the tears sting and his mind confused as he plucked first one and then another to revisit. As the sadness became almost unbearable, he made no attempt to stop disjointed but cherished memories from forming the documentary in his mind that had been his early life with his grandparents.

Sandy was holding his hand now, but not speaking. She could feel the pain, if only because it hurt her to see him upset.

It could have been and indeed it should have been possible for William to have sat there with Sandy long into the afternoon, but the routine and habits of ten years or more wouldn't allow it. Not even at a time like this. Not even bereavement could break through the institutionalization. To follow the same old pattern wasn't done with resentment, let alone any thought. It was just done because it had always been done.

That was the way of things.

"So where do they think they're going to put this lot?" Dave was as cynical as ever. He'd read the memo about the closure of Greenbeck a dozen times or more and now had Reg Knight, the senior union steward, sat in his office.

"They're all going to be assessed and moved to other units," Reg repeated for the third time in as many minutes, but this time decided to prevent further repetitions by holding his hand up and adding to his well-worn sentence. "And before you go any further, we can't fight it or stop. You must know that this is part of the Department of Health's programme of closures for these old Victorian mental hospitals?"

"So you've said... several times! So what happens to us?" Dave was anxious to get down to the real question on his mind.

Reg clearly felt that he was on safer territory talking about jobs. "All the staff will be offered posts within the Health Authority, or given early retirement if they haven't got much longer to go" then adding, as though to justify his presence, "We've negotiated a generous compensation package. No-one will miss out."

"So I could stop work and they'd give me a load of cash? Sounds good to me" Dave had entirely missed the point.

Reg tried again. "Sorry, Dave. I don't think that you quite understood me. The Health Authority will offer all staff, employed at Greenbeck, alternative employment which, under most circumstances, they'd be expected to accept. And I'm afraid that you're too young to qualify for early retirement... before you ask!"

Dave wasn't happy. "My contract is for me to work at this hospital. I'll fight it!"

"Fight what? The place is closing down. You don't have a choice in this." Reg decided to put something else on the table. "They are offering extra training in some circumstances. Have you ever thought about taking a position as a Community Psychiatric Nurse, or perhaps you could go into nurse education and teach." Reg managed a hopeful expression, but his mind had already predicted the response.

"Oh fuck off, Reg. Is that the best you can come up with? You're saying that I should go and bang on doors just to see if they're still as big a fucking loony as they were when they were in hospital? Make sure they're taking their medicine? Listening to a bunch of fucking relatives droning on and on? Do me a favour!" Dave stood up with the express purpose of letting Reg know that the discussion was at an end. Reg took the hint and followed the charge nurse's lead, quietly relieved to have done what he had come to do. As he reached the office door he turned to give Dave the final, parting shot. "Don't forget that someone from Personnel will be in touch over the next few weeks, so try to think about what I've said." Reg didn't wait for a reply, mainly because it wouldn't have been worth hearing. Instead, as he made his way towards the ward door, he felt a sense of dread at someone as arrogant and ignorant as Charge Nurse Hicks teaching the next generation of psychiatric nurses.

November 28th 1985; 15:00 hrs

The hospital boardroom was a stark contrast from the wards, with its dark wood panelling, highly polished floor and its enormous solid oak table. Any onlookers could have been forgiven for thinking they'd been transported, as if by magic, into an entirely different world, whereas in reality, only a corridor and two or three strategically placed locked doors separated them from the patients, whose future was about to be debated.

Seated around the table were the Senior Nursing Officer, Harry Adams, the Hospital Administrator, Graham Curtis and Greenbeck's five Consultant Psychiatrists. The meeting had been called to give an update on the closure of the hospital, or to be more precise how they were going to deal with the problem of where to put eight hundred patients.

Max Arbury, appointed following Trafford's retirement, was pouring himself some coffee and was responding to the various laments regarding the closure. "Well, it's about bloody time that someone closed it. This place is no more than a looney bin out of the Dark Ages."

"They didn't have looney bins in the dark ages," Graham Curtis fancied himself as something of a historian and couldn't help himself, but his remarks only had the effect of attracting a disapproving look from Alan Wallace. "History lessons aside, Mr Curtis, you were, I believe, about to update us regarding the strategy for mental health service provision within the Authority." Wallace had little enough time for managers and even less when they were as irritating as well.

"Ah, yes, well if we are all ready," Curtis made the remark mainly for

Arbury's benefit, who was now busily engaged in conversation with one of the other psychiatrists.

Curtis continued. "As I'm sure you'll all remember and indeed glean from the minutes of our previous meeting, a facility is being built on the Connaught Street site, which consists of twenty eight Villa type buildings, each one of which will take fifteen patients. As you will also recall, ten of these villas have been designated for learning disabilities, with the remaining eighteen for mental health."

Arbury had been jotting down the figures and was quick to express the opinion of everyone present. "So we're still no further down the line of solving the problem of how to put over eight hundred patients into the available beds?"

"Well actually, I can inform you of some developments on that front," Shifting in the seats as the anticipation grew that the hospital manager might have something positive to say. "As you know, the main block of Greenbeck Hospital in which we are sitting, currently houses ten wards, kitchens, administration, sewing rooms and the like. This will be used as the new Health Authority Headquarters and the plans to convert it to its new function have now been approved."

"So, no beds, just administrators and managers?" Dr Andrew Conway appeared to temporarily emerge from his semi slumber to add his comments, much to everyone's surprise.

"If you will allow me to continue?" Curtis was clearly trying to say something that would detract from the news of the Health Authority's new accommodation.

"It has been decided to retain four of the wards, namely Rose, Larch, Beech and Elm Villas and these will be used to house one hundred and forty patients who are either detained under the Mental Health Act, or who have particular difficulties with coping in the community and hence would be unsuitable for Connaught Street. Additionally, part of Larch Villa will be used for acute admissions."

Harry Adams looked even more uncertain than anyone else around the table. "I don't think that another hundred and forty places would do it! What are you going to do with the remaining patients?" He immediately wished that he'd kept his mouth shut, as Wallace jumped in to put him firmly in his place.

"The senior medical staff of the Hospital," He paused briefly and respectfully looked around at his fellow psychiatrists "have already carried out a series of reviews on all the patients and with respect, the decision of where to place them will have little to do with the nursing staff, unless of course, they have any useful comments to make on the subject!" Wallace, like Arbury, had little time for Adams or indeed, for most of his nursing staff. He clearly felt that they created more problems than they ever solved, although, of course it wouldn't have occurred to him that he was being as bigoted and stereotypical as the very people he held in such low esteem.

Curtis gave a nervous cough and tried to fill the embarrassing silence. "I can quite see how the situation is confusing. The review that Dr Wallace refers to has been carried out over the last few months and has revealed that amongst the patient population at Greenbeck, there are a considerable amount who, to put it bluntly, shouldn't be here." Adams looked more confused than ever, so Curtis continued. "To take Dr Arbury's point, although the physical numbers involved do not equate terribly well with the places being made available, the amount of beds available for those with a clinical need is roughly adequate."

"So, how much progress has been made?" Terrence Young, the consultant with responsibility for many of the long stay patients, was clearly anxious for the discussion to address the needs of the remaining population of Greenbeck.

"Quite a lot. I'm pleased to say. We have identified a number of nursing home and hostel beds within the area, and we are currently looking at placements further afield." Curtis was quite obviously pleased with himself. "And don't forget that many of these patients were not mentally ill when they were admitted many years ago and had merely done something that someone didn't approve of. Now, I know very little of clinical matters but according to the reviews I have read, the major problem that they share is that they are highly institutionalized and hence incapable of independent living."

Arbury clearly had something on his mind. "Yes, that's true, and that's good news about the nursing homes and hostels, Graham, but surely the fact that there is now a decision to keep more of the wards open will affect the plans for the site?"

"Thankfully not," At this point, Curtis handed out copies of the building plans to the assembled medical staff. "As you can see, the new District General Hospital will not be affected by the retention of the wards, and in fact, if I can refer you to Appendix A, you will see that the cluster of wards that are being retained are located on the site scheduled for the second phase of the development."

"Which is what?" Arbury was still none the wiser.

"Conveniently, the second phase is the building of a new acute psychiatric unit, but this is not due to be started until 1989… always assuming that the rest goes to plan."

Wallace was quick to see the long term implications of what Curtis had just revealed. "And presumably, that will be the only psychiatric service on this site?"

Curtis nodded.

"At which point, we're going to have to go through this all over again!"

But no-one around the table seemed particularly concerned about events that may, or, for that matter, may not happen in the future.

December 24th 1985; 14:30 hrs

"Julie came to see me today!" William was anxious to tell Sandy his news.

"I've run out of my shampoo. I'm always running out of my shampoo." Sandy touched her hair as if to emphasize her point. "My Aunt's coming today. Who's Julie?"

"She's my sister. She's never been to see me before. Nan said she wasn't allowed to." William was looking down at the ground, as though he was having to say something he was ashamed of, but if he was, it was lost on Sandy who had other things on her mind.

"It's Christmas tomorrow. Are you having a party in your ward?"

"Frank kept hitting Rodney yesterday and they had to sit on him and give him an injection." William hadn't intentionally avoided the subject of Christmas parties. He was quite literally verbalizing the things that appeared in his mind rather than working out responses to points of conversation. It was like that sometimes.

"My Auntie May say's that I've got a lot of smelly things for Christmas." Sandy extended her wrist to just under William's nose. "This one's "Youth Dew". I got it for my birthday."

William gave a sniff. "That's a nice one. Julie bought me a book for Christmas. It's "The Time Machine" by H.G. Wells. It's a science fiction book." From the hand that wasn't holding on to Sandy's, he produced the book for her to look at, but she didn't take it from him.

"I don't like science fiction," Sandy was dismissive, but William still held it in front of her for another few seconds, as if expecting her to change her mind.

"Why was Frank being naughty?" She couldn't understand violence, regardless of who the perpetrator was and William's comment about Frank was obviously bothering her.

"Dave said he looked like a fucking poof in the shirt his mother had bought him and everyone laughed at him, but Rodney wouldn't stop laughing and calling him a poof... so he hit him."

"Dave doesn't like Julie." Another thought that needed to come out.

"Why did he say that?"

"He didn't really say that. Not really." Again the gaze diverted towards the ground.

"I like parties and music. Do you, William?"

William nodded and shuffled awkwardly "He said to Pete that if she cared so much about seeing me, she would have come to see me earlier. He said she was dressed like a tart and they both laughed. He doesn't like her, I know he doesn't."

Sandy squeezed his hand and reached behind her and produced a large envelope with his name on it. Eagerly, he opened it and read her message as though he was absorbing and relishing every letter.

To William
Love you loads and loads
Sandy xxxxxxxxxxxxxxxxxxxxxx

Carefully, he put it back into its envelope and squeezed her hand as a thank you, before they both fell into a comfortable silence for a few seconds. It was a cloudy, dismal day, and the light was beginning to fail.

"I don't like it when it gets dark and you're not there." Sandy's comment appeared to come out of nowhere, and she put her head onto William's shoulder in order to emphasise her feelings.

The moment of closeness wasn't lost on William, but he just didn't know how to respond, but that was OK with Sandy. As long as he was there.

It was beginning to get dark and on the day before Christmas William felt excited, not because of anything other than the fact that he'd bought

Sandy a present and had managed not to give it to her until now. As the daylight faded, the time had arrived.

"I've got you a present," The words were suddenly blurted out without any preamble or ceremony.

"I've got you one, too!"

William produced two packages from underneath his jumper. They were carefully wrapped in Christmas paper and he was obviously proud of his handiwork. Bashfully, he handed them over before jumping up and walking quickly round the flower beds and returning to his seat next to her a few seconds later.

"I bought you two presents," He added unnecessarily, as Sandy had already extricated the bath salts and soap from their festive wrappings. William looked on anxiously as she held each package to her nose in turn.

"Do you like them?" Then rather obviously. "I bought them in the hospital shop."

They were cheap and unspectacular, but to Sandy, they were priceless. "That's just what I wanted, William!" She leant over and kissed him on the cheek. "Are you going to open yours?" Sandy pulled out a parcel that she'd been concealing behind her and held it out to him. Eagerly he accepted the large square package and ripped off the Christmas paper to reveal a tin of chocolate biscuits with a picture of a kitten on the lid. Sandy had clearly bought the biscuits (and, more especially, the picture) that she liked most of all and couldn't contain herself any longer. "Can I have one?" but William was busily engaged bashfully returning the kiss.

"I like Diana Ross and the Supremes… is that the music that you like? I don't think that they should have said those things to Frank. I like Frank, he's my friend."

Silence as William and Sandy helped themselves to the biscuits.

"I've got to go back now," William got up suddenly and hopped from one foot to the other and looking down at the floor, as he always did when he wanted to say something. Sandy got up as well and hesitantly moved towards him.

"Happy Christmas, Sandy!" William stole another kiss before quickly turning away and starting the short walk back to the ward, but he didn't get very far before he turned and scurried back to where Sandy was still standing. Carefully he took the tin from under his arm, opened it and gave Sandy half of the remaining biscuits.

"I love you!" Followed by another kiss on the cheek before he turned on his heel and scampered back to the ward. Pausing only briefly to turn and wave as he heard Sandy's reply. "Love you lots!"

December 24th 1986; 17:30 hrs

Bill Coleman hobbled into to sitting room with a tray of tea and biscuits and proceeded to place them on the small coffee table, next to which sat his distraught great niece. Almost as though she'd only just remembered just how unsteady on his feet he really was, she jumped up and took the tray in order to help it on the final few inches of its journey to the coffee table.

With the tea and biscuit arrangements dealt with, Bill sat down heavily in his chair next to the gas fire. Behind him, on a small table in the corner of the room, was a rather sad looking artificial white Christmas tree, complete with a flashing set of fairy lights. He hadn't seen her since she'd left for University some months earlier and her visit now didn't appear to be getting off to a joyful start. Julie blew her nose, and took a deep breath. "I'm sorry, Uncle Bill, but I just didn't know who else I could talk to." She instantly felt as though she shouldn't have said it and began sobbing again. "I mean, I know you said I could come and see you at any time, but I only seem to come and see you when I need something, or I'm upset, or I don't know what to do, or I can't… "

Bill held one hand up to stop her speaking and produced a replacement tissue with the other. "My dear… you're babbling!" Julie gave a nervous giggle as she blew her nose once again.

"So, you went to the hospital to visit William, yes?"

Julie nodded.

"And it upset you to see him in there?"

"Well, yes… no, not really, well sort of… Oh Uncle Bill, it was horrible. I never thought it would be that bad. Nan always said that it would upset me, that's why she'd never let me go."

For a few moments, it could have been Jean, Julie's mother, sat in front of him. Except for the obvious age difference, the similarities were stunning; the same height, same build, the waist length dark brown hair and of course, those green eyes that Jean had always used to such good effect to get precisely what she wanted! Bill gave himself a mental shake and returned to the matter in hand.

"Yes, I know. Whenever your Grandpa went to visit, it put years on him. I know that he felt that William wasn't being looked after properly, but whenever he saw the Consultant, he said it was like talking to a brick wall. I only went a couple of times to see him, mainly because he didn't seem to recognize me, but I must admit, it shocked me. Anyway, tell me what happened."

Julie composed herself and sat on the edge of her seat with her hands between her knees as though she was being interviewed. "Well, I got there at about one o'clock because the bus was early, and I went to the reception office like you said I should do."

"Were they OK to you?"

"Oh yes, they were no problem. The woman in reception asked me to take a seat for a moment while she rang the ward to ask them to send someone to take me there."

"And, did they keep you waiting for long?"

"No, as I said, they were no problem at all, and the male nurse came and got me after a few minutes and took me to the ward. He seemed a nice enough guy, could only have been a bit older than me. He was a student nurse."

Bill was anxious to make sure he was keeping up. "So, they weren't rude to you, and they didn't make you feel unwelcome in any way?"

"No, not really. I mean the woman in reception asked me a couple of times if I was expected, but that was all. Anyway, we got to the ward and the nurse took me to the office to see the Charge Nurse. David Hickson, or Hicks or something. Anyway, I was shown into his office and I sat down."

"Was he alright to you?" Bill had met Hicks a couple of years earlier and had been seriously unimpressed at the time.

"Well… " Julie hesitated. "Sort of. What I mean is, there was nothing I could put my finger on. I just got the impression that he didn't particularly want me to be there, that was all."

"OK, so what happened then?"

"Well, I introduced myself, and told him that I'd come to visit my brother."

"And what did he say?"

"Not much, at first. He just told me that I could find him in the dayroom by the window and when I didn't get up he asked if there was anything

274

else he could do for me, but he sounded as though he really couldn't be bothered."

"Did he say anything else?"

"Only when I asked how William was."

"And what did he say?"

"He said that there was no change and that William was the same as he always was and then he said he was sorry that he'd forgotten that I hadn't ever come to see him, so I didn't have any idea what he was like anyway. But he wasn't serious. He hadn't forgotten, and he wasn't sorry at all. He was just being horrible."

Bill could just imagine Hicks being like it, so he wasn't in the least bit surprised.

"I didn't think that I'd get much sense out of him... no, that's not really true... he'd upset me, but I wasn't going to let him see that, so I asked him to show me where William was sitting. He couldn't even be bothered to do that. He called one of the other nurses to "take Miss Phillips to see her brother" even though he wasn't doing anything himself."

"But, of course, you can't complain, because he might have insincerely apologised saying he was too busy". Bill sympathized, "I remember your Grandpa talking about that bugger. He used to be a staff nurse on the ward where they first took William. He used to work for that Charge Nurse that William was so afraid of... what was his name? Richard something or other." Bill pulled himself back to the subject in hand. "Anyway, then you went to see William?"

Julie nodded and started sobbing again. "I didn't recognize him, I just didn't know him. The male nurse showed me where he was sitting and I walked straight past him!"

"Your Nan was quite upset the last few times she went. That's why she didn't go much in the year before she died. It used to upset her so much." Bill was trying his best to be reassuring.

"Why didn't she ever tell me what he was like? He's my brother. She should have told me, warned me... Anything." Julie's sobbing was louder than ever.

Bill sighed. He knew it would come to this one day. He'd tried to tell his sister in law on numerous occasions, to no avail and now he found himself trying to defend her. "She was just trying to protect you, honey; you can't blame her for that. She used to say that Greenbeck was no place to take a child visiting. I think she had a point. Don't you?"

Julie nodded and blew her nose again. "I know, I know, but he's still my brother. She should have told me something other than "he's just the same" or "there's no change!" What bloody use was that?"

"Slow down, Julie. Your Nan went through agonies over you and William. I think that she was entitled to make the odd mistake here and there!"

"I know… I'm sorry… I just don't know what to think anymore."

Bill put a reassuring hand on her knee. "That's understandable. Look, why don't you just carry on telling me what happened when you got to the dayroom?"

"Yes… yes, sorry. Anyway, the nurse pointed towards one of the windows and said that William was in the chair next to it, but when I looked I couldn't see him, so I asked the nurse again, so this time he pointed towards this guy and when I didn't move, he took me over to where he was sitting, and… oh, Uncle Bill, you should have seen him. He looked terrible!"

"Tell me," Bill genuinely wanted to know, even though he knew how painful it would be.

"He'd put on about two or three stone since I saw him last and he was wearing tatty old hospital clothes and his hair. His hair was greasy and uncombed and horrible. And you should have seen his fingers… they were almost black with the stains from his cigarettes and his fingernails needed cutting and they were dirty and…"

"I get the picture. But did he recognize you?"

"Not immediately, no, but when I said who I was he seemed pleased to see me, although he didn't try to make much conversation and I was so shocked, all I could manage was "how are you?" and he didn't seem to be able to say much to that!"

Julie looked over at the Christmas tree and the tears started again. "I just can't stand seeing him like that. Not at Christmas. Not ever! It just isn't fair. He's never hurt anyone, or done anything wrong, but he's been locked up in that place for all these years."

Once again, Bill reached over to comfort his great niece and he pondered for a few seconds over what she had just said and whether his response would just make things worse. But he decided to say it anyway.

"Actually, honey, he's not locked up in the true sense. I mean, he isn't sectioned anymore and hasn't been for some time" Bill paused and by the blank expression in her face, correctly assumed that Julie didn't understand what he was talking about. "He's what is known as an "informal patient," that is, he is not being detained against his will, not anymore at least."

"So they could let him out?" Julie stopped sobbing and a puzzled, yet hopeful look came over her face, but Bill had anticipated the confusion that his statement had created and held his hand up in order to stop her in her tracks.

"Well, not really. You see, all it means is that he is in hospital on a voluntary basis."

Still she looked puzzled, so Bill decided to spell it out.

"Look. Medicines for William's condition have improved a lot over the years since he first went into hospital, but unfortunately, in William's case, they haven't controlled his symptoms enough for him to be able to look after himself. He's still a poorly young man and he probably always will be."

"But they must have thought he was getting better, otherwise they would still have… how did you put it, "detained" him. Isn't that right?" Another hopeful look.

"It's not as straightforward as that, I'm afraid. You see, it's not like having an operation or having an ulcer, or anything like that, when they come round to your bed and inform you that you're cured and that you can go home. At least, not in William's case. Listen, a few months before your Nan died, I went with her to see her GP, mainly because your Grandpa had always told her how impossible it was to get any sense from William's psychiatrist. She trusted Dr Allen, and so we went to have a chat with him."

"About William?" Julie was struggling to keep up.

"Well, about a lot of things, really, most of which were to do with William."

"But Dr Allen wouldn't be able to tell you as much as the consultant. Surely?"

"True, but the purpose of the visit was to have someone explain what was happening in plain language we could understand and what he told us was helpful."

"Go on," Julie didn't seem convinced.

"Well, what he told us was that the law, the Mental Health Act I think he said it was, stated that someone should only be kept in hospital against their will if two doctors agreed that the person was… "Bill paused as if he was trying to remember the words the GP had used. "A danger to themselves, or others, or both. Yes that was it."

"So the hospital is now saying that he's no longer dangerous to anyone or himself, so he must have got better. Isn't that right?" Julie hadn't quite got the point.

"Well, I suppose if you put it like that, his condition must have changed, but that doesn't mean that he is capable of looking after himself. Now I haven't been to see William for some time, but I'm pretty certain that when you saw him today, he didn't strike you as someone who could live independently, or anything like it. Am I right?"

"Uncle Bill, he was in a hell of a state. He couldn't even keep still for more than a couple of minutes without jumping up and it wasn't as though he was jumping up to do anything in particular. He just got up, walked around a lot, tried to get cigarettes from the nurse and then came and sat down again. He kept asking me for a cigarette, but he didn't seem to remember that I'd already told that I didn't smoke. I had to keep saying it time and time again." Now she'd started again, she couldn't stop. "And his teeth, they were brown with tar stains and old food stuck in them. God knows when he'd cleaned them last." She paused and thought briefly. "And you should have seen his shirt, he had most of his dinner down the front of it. Doesn't anyone in there make sure that people are looked after?"

Bill sat and listened and her look of realization wasn't lost on him. "You've answered your own question, haven't you?"

Julie nodded. She understood, but to tell the truth, she'd understood the minute she saw her brother that afternoon. "But they can't keep him against his will, can they? I mean, he could come home. Couldn't he?"

Bill's sad smile gave a prediction of what was to come. "Well, that was the other reason why we wanted to see Dr Allen. It was something that had to be discussed and after the last time that William came home, we needed to get things sorted out."

"I'm not sure that I know what you mean." Julie was genuinely puzzled.

"You were only a girl at the time, so you wouldn't have been aware of how William came to be sent home from Greenbeck." Bill, silently and gently remonstrated with his deceased sister in law for not explaining all of this to Julie earlier.

"Your Grandpa always said that he'd been put in an impossible position with William, because he was told that William was well enough to come

278

home and was made to feel as though he had no choice in the matter, even though he believed that William was still too ill to be discharged."

"That wasn't like Grandpa. If he believed that something was wrong, he'd say it. You know that. You must have got it wrong." Julie was getting clearly upset by the conversation.

"Darling, can I ask you whether the visit upset you today?"

"You need to ask?" Julie couldn't believe her ears.

Bill smiled to reassure her that his question wasn't meant to doubt what she'd seen at Greenbeck earlier. "Exactly, so how do you think your Grandpa felt, eh? How do you think he felt every time he walked into that place? Every time he saw him in that state? How do you think he felt? Bill was aware that he was allowing his emotions to get the better of him and by the look on Julie's face, he'd managed to upset her all over again. He reached out to hold her hand. "I'm sorry, darling; I didn't mean to upset you. You were so young when all this started and I know that he tried so hard to make sure that you and for that matter, your Nan, didn't see the side of him that I saw."

Julie looked questioningly at him, so he felt that he couldn't avoid saying more. "Your Grandpa always blamed himself for what happened to your Mum." Then in reply to Julie's puzzled look. "When she was alive, he always tried not to interfere with her life. He couldn't tolerate your Dad, but he would never say anything to your Mum because he felt that it wasn't anything to do with him." Bill reflected and smiled. "I remember him sitting in his chair and reading his newspaper as your Nan had a go at him for saying nothing. "It's her life" he used to say. "It's not up to us to interfere" and he'd carry on reading his paper. Of course, when she died…"

Julie had never heard this before and it was obvious to her that there was more to come.

"Of course, he always adored you and William and quite apart from all the tragedy and upset. I think he saw you both as a chance to try and put things right, silly though it may sound."

"But William was already ill when Mum died. There wasn't anything he could do about that, surely?"

"Not in his eyes. You see, William and your Dad didn't get on at all, particularly when William started to get ill, although, of course, we didn't know he was ill at the time. Anyway, I think your Grandpa tried to make up for all the attention that William couldn't get from your Dad, so they became quite close and when he ended up in Greenbeck, your Grandpa felt somehow responsible."

"But it wasn't his fault. It didn't have anything to do with him. It was an illness; he must have known that he couldn't have done anything."

"He knew that, even said as much on countless occasions, but that didn't stop him feeling the way he did. Every time he visited William, he'd get himself into a hell of a state, so he'd call in here on the way back home so that by the time your Nan saw him, he'd composed himself."

Bill was aware that Julie was hearing these things for the first time and deliberately paused between each new revelation, but in the absence of any comment from her, he carried on.

"Not only did he feel guilty, but, the way he saw things, your Nan wouldn't have been able to cope with seeing him being unable to cope. As it was, your Nan couldn't face going to visit William and she only visited once with your Grandpa and that was just after your Mum died. Come to think of it, I seem to remember that your Grandpa told me that she waited in the corridor on that visit, so she never did see William in hospital until after your Grandpa died."

"I never knew he felt like that… I mean, I knew how much he loved both of us, but I never knew that he was doing anything but taking it in his stride." Julie, unreasonably, felt that she should have noticed something, but Bill pre-empted any protests. "That's just what he wanted you to think. He wanted to protect you both, probably more so because he blamed himself for everything."

It took a few seconds to take everything in, and for that time, nothing was said, but it didn't take long for the questions to start flowing. "So, is that why Grandpa let William come home, because he felt guilty?"

"Well, to be honest with you, he felt that he wasn't being cared for properly at Greenbeck. He said to me, on more than one occasion, that he thought that they were being cruel to William and that he'd complained to the consultant who just glossed over everything and told him that all that could be done was being done, but that he'd made a note of his comments and would look into them. Needless to say, nothing happened."

"What sort of things was he complaining about?"

Bill thought carefully, as if composing a list. "Never had any clothes that fitted him and they wouldn't let him wear his own, always looked filthy and usually hadn't shaved, teeth were brown from the fag habit he'd picked up in hospital, couldn't hold a conversation, shuffled around aimlessly and couldn't, and still can't, pay attention to anything, and oh yes, your Grandpa believed, probably with good reason, that he was being tormented and abused by the staff. Apart from that… "

"Apart from that?" Julie couldn't imagine that there could be any more, but Bill hadn't quite finished. "And apart from that, he's so bloody institutionalized now that he would probably never be able to survive outside the damned hospital, even if he wanted to." Bill was becoming agitated and Julie realized the strength of feeling and frustration that her brother's continuing hospitalization had aroused. "And that's before you even consider that he's still and always probably will be ill, despite the medication."

"So, although he's free to leave, he can't because he couldn't cope, is that right?" Julie was, at last, grasping the predicament her brother was in, but Bill drove it home a bit more anyway.

"Absolutely. Plus the fact, of course that he's got nowhere to go. All in all, if he left the hospital, he'd be back in Greenbeck within days."

Julie blew her nose and gave a rueful smile. "And I bought him a book for Christmas. How bloody stupid am?" The question was rhetorical, so she didn't wait for an answer. "I just remember all his books that he had in his bedroom at Nan and Grandpa's. Science fiction, the whole lot! I thought it would be nice to buy him one for Christmas. I just didn't think. I didn't know and I should have done!"

Bill acted as sternly as he could. "Now listen, young lady, it wasn't your fault. Your Nan would never allow you to see him in hospital. She used to say that it was no place to take a child and whenever you asked questions, neither of them ever went into detail, because they didn't want to upset you."

Julie nodded, almost relieved that Bill had taken some of her self- imposed responsibility away from her. Assured that he'd made her listen for her own good, he turned his well-intentioned severity down a few notches.

"And besides that, you should have told me that you were going to see him and I would have come with you."

"I know, I know, but you haven't been well and I thought that I could handle it and I didn't want to bother you and… " Bill held his hand up to stop her in midstream. "And you wanted to prove you could do it on your own, is that it?"

Julie nodded and gave a relieved laugh, reassured in the knowledge that someone was still looking out for her.

"And are you going to tell me that you can do Christmas dinner on your own, as well?" Bill looked hopeful, and Julie knew that there wouldn't be too many Christmas' where she would be as needed and wanted as much as she was now. "Turkey?" She enquired.

"Chicken!" Bill corrected her, and she knew that this was one invitation that she wouldn't turn down for the world.

July 27th 1987; 14:30 hrs

It was a hot day, made worse by the dust and noise caused by the diggers in the hospital grounds. William and Sandy were sitting on their usual bench and the construction work didn't appear to have any effect on either of them. The demolition and the digging had been going on for some weeks that had started with the demolition of the old gatehouse at the front of the hospital.

Then, it had seemed interesting. But not anymore.

"Charlotte came to see me this morning," Sandy's remarks came after a sizable silence and a couple of William's short, quick walks around the flower beds, now packed with red and yellow tulips and blue lobelia.

William had met Charlotte a few times. She was the Occupational Therapist who went around seeing what people could do and what she could help them with whether it was cooking, shopping, working out your money, or doing some washing. William enjoyed going over to the kitchen, but he'd always want to go back to the ward after a couple of minutes and never managed to make anything.

"She took me to Boots in the High Street so I could buy some talcum powder," She paused as she rolled a cigarette and lit it. "I've already got some talcum powder, but Charlotte said that I had enough money to buy some more."

William sat on his hands and rocked for a few seconds before reaching for his own tobacco and papers.

"I made some fairy cakes this morning," He announced proudly. In fact, he'd put the flour, butter and sugar in a bowl and then asked if he could return to the ward for a cigarette. "Did you get me any chocolates when you went out with Charlotte?"

282

"No. Charlotte said that we needed to see how good I was with looking after my money when I went shopping, so I didn't really go out to buy anything. Not really."

The two sat in silence for a couple of minutes, before William got up and walked round the large flower bed in front of them, before returning to the seat and taking hold of Sandy's hand.

"Rodney and Eric went to their new places this morning. They were very excited." William, as usual was just verbalizing things as they came into his head.

"Charlotte said that I was doing very well. She said that we could open a bank account next week. I've never had a proper bank account before." Sandy was apparently quite absorbed in the whole Charlotte thing.

"I used to go to the bank with my Grandpa." The memory was still a cherished one.

"Do you still love me?" William was in need of reassurance, but Sandy was still in full flow.

"Does my new talcum powder smell nice?" She leant towards him so he could give an approving sniff.

"Yes, it's nice. I like that."

"Yes, of course I still love you!" Sandy's answer, disjointed by the time lapse, was, nevertheless welcome.

"Dave said that I'd probably go onto one of the new wards here, when they're done up." William was recalling a conversation he'd had with the Charge Nurse a day earlier when he'd asked him if he would be going to Connaught Street.

They both sat in silence for a few minutes, before Sandy returned to the subject of Charlotte's visits to her. "Charlotte said that I could do lots of things if I had the right support in the community."

William felt pride at someone being so approving of Sandy and didn't make any further connection between what the occupational therapist had said and any future plans for Sandy's care. It would have been obvious to just about anyone. But not to William.

"Julie said that if she got a flat, I could go and see her, but I can't at the moment because she hasn't got one yet." William sat on his hands and started rocking again. "I've got some money that Dave gave me. I want to get some chocolates." He got up and made his way to the hospital shop, leaving Sandy sitting on the bench. By the time he returned, he saw Sandy walking back to her ward with Charlotte.

"Bye, Sandy." He called out to her but she didn't hear him. "See you tomorrow!" But she didn't hear that either. William sat down on the bench and rolled another cigarette before he started on the bar of chocolate, saving two pieces for Sandy, as he always did, for when he saw her the next day.

Tea time approached and William made his way back to the ward, completely unaware that by the following day, the workmen would have removed the bench, Sandy would be in Connaught Street and he would have seen her for the last time.

October 18th 1988; 15:20 hrs

"Can we move on, if that's OK with everyone?" Max Arbury was getting impatient with the speed of the patient reviews. The dining area had been temporarily turned into a meeting room, with an assortment staff, including nurses, psychologists, the social worker and occupational therapist, all of whom started to shuffle papers at Arbury's prompt.

"We, or to be more precise, I, need to be a little more dynamic with the process of finding appropriate placements for the patient's on this ward. I don't need to remind you that the building work on the new District General Hospital is now nearing completion, which means, of course, that these remaining wards from the old Greenbeck Hospital will be scheduled for demolition, probably within the next six to nine months, to make way for the acute psychiatric facility." Arbury looked around, and saw that his colleagues just didn't get the point, so in order to inject some urgency; he employed his fingers to count off the problems to date.

"One: We lost nearly a quarter of the available beds at Connaught Street to learning disabilities at the last minute. Two: St Joseph's Hospital, which could have been our standby, is also scheduled for closure in the next eighteen months or so. Three: We are still seriously understaffed as far as Community Psychiatric Nurses are concerned and finally, we have a further twenty one long stay patient's to fit into seven available beds." Arbury's gaze rested on the social worker, Glenda Sharpe, who had more contact with funding authorities than anyone in the room.

"Well, we've identified a number of placements in the community which range from hostels to nursing homes," Glenda looked around expectantly and when no response was forthcoming, Arbury voiced the concerns that many of them were harbouring.

"And are these hostels and nursing homes geared up to deal with mental illness?"

"Well, of course, each establishment will be carefully assessed to ascertain the facilities and expertise that they can offer," Glenda clearly thought that she'd done as much as could be asked of her and no one at the meeting could argue with that. That wasn't to say, however, that such solutions were to anyone's liking, but Charge Nurse Kevin Meed, managed to ease a few consciences.

"Well, I know that these placements aren't exactly perfect, but it's not like we're doing much for them here, is it?" A few nods around the room, but Arbury felt as though he needed to state the obvious. "But at least they're safe here, get their medication, get fed, get looked after. Can we guarantee as much for these hostels and nursing homes?"

Glenda felt pressured to remind everyone of her statement of a few minutes earlier. "As I said, they'll be carefully assessed before we use any of the places."

Arbury had tried to move the meeting along, but had merely succeeded in slowing it down. It was time to try again.

"So if we can move on? William Phillips? Charlotte; shall we kick off with you this time?"

Charlotte sorted out her papers. "Yes, right. William Phillips: Well. No changes really. His attention span remains very poor and as a result, he's difficult to engage for any length of time. As far as life skills are concerned, he can carry out his personal care, but needs prompting with things like brushing his teeth, combing his hair and so on. He hasn't shown any enthusiasm for cooking and loses interest after a few minutes and just wants to leave. As far as shopping is concerned, again, it seems to be a concentration issue. He usually knows what he wants to buy, and can find the right shop that sells it, but he does have considerable problems with budgeting, even with something as simple as being realistic about the things he can buy with the money he has in his hand. Problems, therefore with looking after his money." She looked up from her notes to see Arbury's response and was rewarded with an acknowledging nod from the consultant.

"Kevin?" Arbury looked at the charge nurse.

"About the same really. William finds it difficult to take part in anything, although he did enjoy going to the hospital shop before it closed down. He can engage in conversation, although he tends to jump from one thing to another. Having said that, he does remember things he's been told, although if he doesn't get the answers he wants, he'll keep on asking the same question over and over again, particularly when the subject has anything to do with cigarettes!" Some smiles around the room, and Arbury took it as a sign to add his contribution.

"From my point of view, I have to say that he's probably as well as he's going to get. He's still on his Amitryptilline for his depression, and he's been on that for… " Arbury rifled through the notes on his lap. "about fifteen months now." The psychiatrist made a note on the notepad by his side. "I must review that again. Depot injection would appear to be working well for him."

Arbury glanced over at the occupational therapist. "Charlotte, I feel as though we need to redouble our efforts with this young man."

Charlotte nodded and made a note.

"Glenda. Any contact from his family?" Arbury redirected his attention to the social worker.

"Since his grandparents died, he gets visits from his sister." Glenda looked down at her notes "Julie, I believe her name is. She's currently away at University on the south coast, and visits during the holidays."

"And how does William react to her?"

Kevin responded to the expectant gazes from the consultant and social worker. "Good. Yes, he's always pleased to see her and if he knows that she's coming, he'll go on and on about it until she arrives."

"And does he have any friendships in the hospital?" Arbury was at least making an attempt at trying to ensure a comfortable transition to wherever it was going to be.

Kevin Meed thought for a moment. "No. No I don't think he has anyone in the ward that he's particularly close to."

"I seem to remember Dr Trafford and David Hicks, before he left, mentioning that he was friendly with a female patient from one of the other wards. Can't remember her name."

"Ah, that was Sandy Mitchell. She moved to Connaught Street last year." Charlotte remembered her well.

"And were there any visits? Any more contact between them?" Arbury was interested in anything that would give him some hope that William could show some signs of independence, but his hopes were short lived.

"Well, we did try to arrange a visit, because he went on about her for ages!" The charge nurse did his best to oblige.

"And?" Arbury was clearly irritated by what he was hearing.

"Well, by the time we sorted things out, she'd gone to live with her Aunt in, eh… Northumberland, or Cumbria, I believe it was?"

Charlotte nodded in response to the question.

Arbury wouldn't let it go "When exactly did you try to, "sort things out", as you put it?"

Charlotte came to the assistance of the charge nurse. "We did contact Connaught Street in August because William had been talking about her so much."

"She left last July and you decide to wait until August? Could someone explain why, exactly?"

The embarrassing silence said it all, with no-one daring to ask the consultant for his excuses for either being ignorant of a relationship that his predecessor had obviously documented, or for not doing something earlier himself.

"Well, there's clearly nothing that can be done now!" Arbury opened the medical note in front of him as everyone else gave a quiet sigh of relief that the subject of William's long lost relationship appeared to be closed.

"He's still on depot medication I prescribed some months ago and there's no problem with that?"

"No, none, except that he gets a bit more distracted for a couple of days before his injection is due, but nothing apart from that." Mead was anxious to show that he's got something right.

Arbury looked at the prescription sheet. "I can't increase the dose by much, he's virtually on the maximum dose anyway, and he's notoriously difficult to stabilize so I'm reluctant to try him on anything else at the moment. When I saw him last week, there were no obvious signs of hallucinations or any ideations that would indicate any changes in his condition. Charlotte?"

The occupational therapist knew what was coming, and she was ready for it. "It's difficult to see how William could live more independently given his inability to concentrate and his unwillingness to engage in any life skill development sessions that are arranged for him."

287

Arbury was similarly ready, and having heard the account of William's abortive attempts at cookery some minutes earlier, asked the question that he already knew the answer to. "And how often do you see William?"

Charlotte, quite unnecessarily, rummaged through her diary in order to gain more time, but it was a fruitless exercise. "I have an appointment slot for him on Monday afternoons."

"I see." Arbury was clearly displeased, but that didn't stop Charlotte digging the hole she was in, a bit deeper.

"There is a large workload, and I do have a considerable amount..." but Arbury didn't want to hear any more excuses. "So, that's settled. I'm sure that you'll be more than anxious to fit Mr Phillips into your busy schedule for another two sessions a week and then perhaps, at the next review in a few weeks' time, you'll be in more of a position to give us your informed opinion!" Arbury's glare told the entire meeting that his statement was not for debate. Mead was relieved that Arbury's impatience had been diverted away from him, but the relief was short lived as Arbury held up the nursing notes as though he'd just retrieved them from the toilet.

"And I'm sure, Kevin, that you will be as enthusiastic as I am to see a more descriptive set of nursing records reflecting a more energetic proactive approach."

Mead made the mistake of looking mystified and was rewarded with the detail. "According to the records in front of me, William invariably has had a "good day", "quiet day", has "no changes" or "slept well"! Perhaps some reflection, in the notes of the expert care that your team provides, wouldn't be too much to ask for?"

Mead nodded dumbly and wished that the ground would open and dispose of Arbury.

January 10h 1989; 11:05 hrs

"Miss Phillips?" The manager extended his hand to greet his visitor. "I'm Rob Jarvis. Shall we go to my office?"

Jarvis seemed genuinely pleased to see his visitor and by the way he bustled around to find a spare seat and to make Julie feel welcome, he was anxious to create a good impression. "I presume that you've never been here Connaught Street before. Am I right?"

"Yes. Yes, that's right." Julie gave the polite smile and tried to disguise her discomfort at visiting, what she fully expected to be, a smaller version of Greenbeck.

"I'll show you around in a moment. Would you like some tea or coffee?" Jarvis was fussing around his office and having seated his visitor, he now stood expectantly at the office door, ready to get someone to fetch whatever drinks were needed.

"No. I'm fine. Thank you." Julie was still trying to work out what to make of the young manager. Certainly, she wasn't expecting to find someone who was barely ten years her senior dressed casually in shirt and jeans. Even less was she expecting anyone as personable and welcoming.

Jarvis finally sat down and reached for his notebook. "So, you've come to have a look around before William gets here next week. Am I right?"

Julie nodded, so Jarvis continued. "How do you feel about William being transferred to us?"

"I don't really know, to be honest with you. I mean, I'm just glad he's leaving that place at last."

"Greenbeck?"

"Yes. I dread going there. It's horrible, and nobody ever tells you anything unless you make them speak to you. It's just a foul place." She shivered as if to underline her horror. "Anyway," she continued. "Yes I've come to have a look around to make sure he'll be comfortable and looked after."

"I trained at Greenbeck." Jarvis was in danger of losing a dozen or so credit points with Julie and had to jump in quickly to retrieve them. "So I know exactly what you mean."

"Well. OK, this place, as you've already gathered is one of several on this development and it provides a facility for 14 adults with enduring mental illness," Jarvis' introduction was innocuous enough, but Julie felt as though there just had to be a snag around every corner.

"Does that mean that there are male and female dormitories?" Julie thought she detected shades of Greenbeck.

"No, no, not at all. Everyone here has their own bedrooms, although we've only got two bathrooms." Jarvis seemed almost proud that he could dispel at least one of Julie's fears so easily. "We encourage everyone to make their rooms as personal as they like, with posters, music. You'll see as we go round."

"I don't think that my brother has got anything to put in a room. He's been in Greenbeck for so many years now that anything he did have is now long gone and forgotten."

Jarvis winched at the all too familiar story that Julie was relating, but there was nothing he could do except offer snippets of hope for the future. "We'll soon get his benefits sorted out when he gets here, and I understand that Greenbeck has a little money that it holds on your brother's behalf, so he'll be able to get himself a few bits and pieces, once they've transferred it to us."

Julie nodded, but was clearly in need of some time to take in all the differences. Jarvis decided that the best way to reassure her was to show her around the building, so without any further delay, he suggested the grand tour, and ushered her through the office door, down a corridor and upstairs to the sleeping quarters.

"I'll show you this bedroom. I know Martin wouldn't mind." Jarvis opened the door for his visitor, and she poked her head in. "As you can see, we encourage the residents to have their bedrooms the way they want them to be."

"So they can have their own stereos and things?" Julie was still wrestling with the contrast to Greenbeck.

"Of course they can!" Jarvis closed the door and led his guest downstairs to view the kitchen and dining area. As they entered the lounge, Julie was, for some unknown reason, surprised to see some of the residents. Two or three were sitting and a few were just wandering around, seemingly without any purpose. She smiled at all of them and gave them all a "good morning" to share amongst them and got one or two fleeting smiles in return.

On the way back to the office, Jarvis noticed that his guest had become quieter, and after they settled themselves down again, he tried to find the reason. Julie sat and thought for a moment. "They're all obviously well looked after, I mean they look clean and have decent clothes, but… Christ, just listen to me… I sound like I'm talking about animals in a bloody zoo! God, I must sound so bloody insulting and I don't mean to, it's just that they don't seem to have any purpose or any meaning to what they do. They just wander around or sit and stare just like the patients did in Greenbeck!"

Jarvis did his best not to become defensive towards his visitor. "Well, actually, four or five of our residents attend a day centre where they have a range of activities and of course, others will spend their time going out and doing a bit of shopping, going to the library or just having a mooch around the town."

Julie must have looked as surprised as she felt, as Jarvis jumped in to answer the question before she asked it. "Of course, we'll be going out with your brother at first to make sure he's OK."

Still, Julie looked dazed by the turn in the conversation, so Jarvis continued. "This isn't like Greenbeck, where they have loads of detained patients. This isn't a hospital. We are in the community and our residents have more choices as to what they do or don't do."

"So will William be attending this Day Centre, or whatever you call it?" Julie at last, managed to muster a question.

"Well, not straight away I'm afraid. There's a bit of a waiting list, and when he does get a place, it will only be for a couple of mornings a week at first." Jarvis was all too aware that the answer he had given would simply give rise to more questions and he was right.

"I'm a bit confused." Julie was only too aware of her understatement, but Jarvis had obviously thought that he'd made everything very clear, and now it was his turn to look puzzled.

"Look, I'm sure that you make this place as homely as possible, and it's very nice and all that, but I don't quite see how William will benefit from being here… I mean, it's a lot better than Greenbeck, but then, just about anywhere would be!"

A lot of misconceptions and even more explaining to put them right. Jarvis made a start, uncertain of how successful he was going to be. "I really do think that you are getting a little bit confused here, Miss Phillips. Just about all of our residents are really as well and stabilised as they'll ever be. Our job is to improve their quality of life and to help them to have some sort of access and independence in the community, although that will vary tremendously from person to person."

"So he won't really get any better when he comes here? Is that what you're saying?" Julie revealed the full extent of her misunderstanding.

"I wouldn't put it quite like that because all of our residents have far more independence than they would be able to have in hospital, so their quality of life is improved as a result."

"OK, so what happens if he gets worse again, as he did a few years ago when he came home?" Julie was anxious to cover every angle, and Jarvis was obviously warming to his task.

"We do have our own psychiatric team in the community, so we'll keep

291

an eye on his condition, and if his medication needs adjusting, then our psychiatrist will see to it. If necessary, we can always have him admitted to hospital for a time until his condition settles down again, so don't worry about that."

"And you'll make sure that he's safe if he goes out? I'm really not sure about that bit, I mean, anything could happen if he went out on his own, couldn't it?"

Jarvis went back a few steps. "This is going to be home for your brother, Miss Phillips. We are in the community here and there are risks. Of course there are! What I will tell you, though, is that he has been assessed by the occupational therapist at Greenbeck as being suitable for Connaught Street and we won't let him just wander around without having spent some time with him, in the community, to make sure he's OK." Jarvis looked for a hopeful response, but, by the look on Julie's face, it simply wasn't going to happen.

"I do understand what you're saying, but look at it from my point of view, Mr… "

"Please… call me Rob!"

"Right, Rob. Anyway, Rob, you've got to remember that I've been accustomed to seeing my brother in that place, so you telling me that this will be William's "home" is a bit too much of a leap to take in all at once!"

"Yes. Absolutely understandable, but… "

Julie cut him short, as she clearly became less composed. "Not to mention the fact that he's leaving Greenbeck with more problems than he went in with! So I'm sure that, although you're probably doing a great job here, you'll forgive me if I feel that all this… " She gestured with her eyes and hands to indicate that she was referring to the whole building. " This is too little, too late for my brother." Julie rose from her chair and walked towards the door.

Jarvis felt as though he knew what was coming next, but under the circumstances was relieved that there was at least the traces of recognition as Julie turned around to deliver her parting shot.

"It's a pity that it took this long for someone to care."

March 20th 1991; 13:15 hrs

"Want one of my roll-ups?" Toby had already made the roll-up and had it in the palm of his hand ready for William to take it. They were sitting on the bench in the High Street bus shelter. William usually went there and sat alone, every day, after lunch, but today he had a companion.

William took the cigarette and Toby provided a light. William wasn't accustomed to having company on his walks into town, but it didn't really bother him unduly. Toby had come to Connaught Street a few weeks earlier and occupied the bedroom next to William's. They usually had their meals together at the same table, but they hadn't really got to know each other.

William inhaled the smoke from the cigarette and was taken off guard by its strong and uncharacteristic taste. He took another drag, and another, before Toby surprised him by taking if from between his fingers, taking two drags from it before handing it back to William who was still acting a little perplexed at having the cigarette taken in such a way and even more so at being offered it back again.

"Be back by three thirty. Dr McKenna's coming this afternoon. Have you got your watch?" William nodded and waited for Rob to give him his £5 daily allowance to spend if he wanted to. "You may see Toby in town. He's gone out to get some shaving stuff."

And, sure enough, he did see Toby. He was sat on William's bench in the bus shelter and he was with another man, who, upon seeing William approaching, quickly gave something to Toby and walked away before William had got close enough to speak.

That was fifteen minutes earlier. William was feeling quite content with life. He didn't usually feel like this. Often, he didn't feel anything in particular, except agitated if things didn't happen the way he thought they should happen. But for now, he felt content. More than content. In fact, to me more precise, nauseous and content.

Toby took a last drag of the cigarette, extinguished it and put the dog-end back into his tobacco tin, and as he closed the lid, leant over to William, and in a low voice. "They can't see us now!" By his knowing wink and nod, obviously took it for granted that William knew exactly what he was talking about. William had difficulty in understanding Toby's comments, but at the same time, he felt as though he was safe. He felt as though no-one was going to hurt him and that was enough for him to find some superficially common ground with his companion's words.

From their vantage point in the bus shelter, they could see all the traffic, the people, all their movements, and William felt as though he could have sat there all day, just for the sheer enjoyment of being there, the happiness of watching people, the security of knowing that he was safe and protected. Across the street, a lady who had been struggling with bags of shopping, tripped over, sending groceries flying everywhere.

It was, without doubt, the funniest thing he'd ever seen, and he started to giggle, but it was only a few seconds until the giggle grew into uncontrollable and completely engulfing laughter. Toby was laughing too, but not nearly so much. Every time William looked at the woman, now struggling to pick up her shopping, his laughter became charged with a new vigor, until just about everything set him off into further bursts.

"I'm going to the shop to buy some more cigarette papers. I'll be back soon." Toby got up and disappeared in the direction of the tobacconist and by the time he returned about forty minutes later, William was still giggling, but his raucous laughter had abated.

As they sat in silence for a few minutes, William was aware of two small children approaching the bench on which they were sitting. William had always been fond of children and didn't hesitate in smiling at them as they approached. "Hello! What's your name?" He greeted the little girl who reached the bench slightly ahead of her brother, but before she could answer, her mother had arrived on the scene. "Mandy! Come away from there!" She grabbed her daughter roughly by the coat to pull her away.

"She's alright!" William tried to reassure the distraught mother, but all he managed to achieve was to spark a verbal onslaught. "Don't think that I don't know what you are, you're from that place in Connaught Street where they keep fuckin' nutters. You should all be fuckin' locked away. It's disgusting letting people like you out. Come on Mandy. David, come on." She dragged both children up the street, giving them what she obviously considered to be good advice and completely ignoring their small legs that struggled to keep up with her.

William didn't show it. He never did show it, but he felt hurt, no matter how many times people hurled insults at him and that was nearly every day, he felt hurt. Every time he went into town. Every time he sat on the bench in the bus shelter, there'd be someone there to tell him exactly what they thought of him. He was used to it, but it didn't make it any better.

Toby broke the silence that had followed the departure of the children and their outspoken mother. "Rob said we had to be back by half past three. We'd better get going!" Toby tugged at William's sleeve, pulled him

294

to his feet and together they made their way back to Connaught Street.

March 20 1991; 15:45 hrs

Dr Ruth Mckenna took over any room she entered and Rob Jarvis's office was no exception. As she sat in his chair with her glasses perched on the end of her nose, browsing through medical records, Jarvis felt as though he was about to be given the third degree by a stern headmistress.

"William Phillips, how's he doing?" McKenna's question was distractingly simple, considering the amount of detail she required of the manager.

"He's doing fine. He needs less prompting with his personal care than he used to, and we've spent a long time with him concentrating on budgeting skills and checking his road safety awareness, so now he goes out on his own, as you suggested he should be doing at his review last year."

"And has he had any problems with his community access?"

"Nothing really. His timekeeping wasn't very good at first, but we managed to talk him into buying himself a watch and since then, there doesn't seem to have been a problem in that direction." First hurdle cleared! Jarvis gave an inward sigh of relief.

McKenna looked down at the notes. "According to the notes from Greenbeck, he didn't have a problem with getting back to the ward on time when he was on leave in the grounds."

Jarvis remembered Greenbeck only too well and was able to provide the community psychiatrist with the explanation. "Well, quite apart from the clock that was on top of the main building, patients used to know when to go back to the wards when they heard the heavy meal trolleys being moved from the kitchens in the main block."

McKenna thought for a minute, as if trying to picture the scene that Jarvis had described. "Yes. Yes of course. But you say that there are no real problems now?"

"No. No problems."

"What about his time at the day centre? Have you had their report sent to you?" McKenna's next question required much more thought on Jarvis's part.

"Right. Yes we've had the report." Jarvis reached over the desk to find and hand the report to Dr McKenna. As she began to read it, Jarvis gave her an edited version.

295

"As you'll no doubt remember, William had to wait for over a year until a place became available for him and he now attends for four mornings a week. They report that he's compliant, and does enjoy music sessions, but has trouble, as predicted, with any activities that require concentration for any length of time, and that includes art and crafts which he needs considerable encouragement with."

"According to the report, they've managed to get him to do some basic cooking? That's a surprise!" McKenna was obviously keen to see any signs of progress and now, clearly thought she had found some.

"Yes, that's a plus, but he'll only do things that he can see the results for very quickly, such as sandwiches, putting toppings on a pizza, that sort of thing. When we have cooking nights here, William always likes to do the pizza's, but if he has to wait while someone else gets something done in the kitchen, then he'll just walk away."

McKenna made some entries into the wad of medical notes in front of her. "You say that you've been helping William with his budgeting skills. How's he doing exactly?"

"Well, he has quite a lot of control over his money, although we still limit him to £5 whenever he goes out, unless, of course, he wants to get himself anything specific, and then he has to come and discuss it with either myself, or my deputy before we release the funds."

"So, presumably, he buys things like his toiletries and the like?" McKenna seemed happy with the arrangement, but it wasn't all positive as far as the psychiatrist was concerned. "And he buys his own tobacco?"

"Yes, of course."

"And is he still smoking as much, or has he cut down, by any chance?"

"Not a hope!" Jarvis couldn't help sounding surprised that McKenna had even asked the question, but, undaunted, the psychiatrist persisted. "I daresay that you've read the letter from the GP following William's episode of bronchitis in January?" She didn't wait for a reply "It's not exactly an account of a man in good physical health!" She read the salient comments from the letter. "I quote: "morbidly obese", "heavy smoker", "indications of chronic bronchitis", "longstanding dyskinesis" and all before the age of forty!"

McKenna, fearsome as she could be, held Rob Jarvis in high regard, and was aware that the manager would, quite unjustifiably be taking the blame for William's ill-health, and she backtracked before his guilt deepened. "I can't help feeling, though, that if Greenbeck had done its job properly, that William's condition would be a good deal better than it is. Is he back from his walk yet?"

"Yes, well I think I heard him come in. I'll get him in." Jarvis opened the office door. "William. Will you come and see the doctor for a minute?"

William was making his way towards the kitchen and it took him a few seconds and a further summon from Jarvis to make him look up and change direction.

"Hello William! Come in!" McKenna had a different persona for her patients. A less intense, less formal, chattier persona that put her patient's at their ease.

"Hello Dr McKenna. I was just going to get a cup of tea. Do you want a cup of tea?"

"No thank you, William. I'm sorry to have disturbed you, but we won't take long and then you can make your tea. Is that alright?"

William nodded.

"So, how have you been?"

William thought for a couple of seconds. "I had a cold. Last week I had a cold, didn't I Rob? Rob said I had to stay indoors in case it went to my chest."

"Bit of a sniffle. Nothing much really." Jarvis filled in the details for the benefit of the consultant who used her own powers of observation to continue. "But you're better now?"

William nodded and gave an uncontrolled giggle at the same time. McKenna followed his lead and smiled. "Is there something funny that happened, William?"

A shake of the head, this time, followed by a few seconds of silence whilst William composed himself.

"So, what have you been up to today?"

"Went to the shops."

"Did you? And did you buy anything?" McKenna was still smiling in an attempt to encourage a response.

"No... Yes... I bought my tobacco."

"Anything else?"

"No."

Jarvis stepped in. "Didn't you say that you wanted to buy some shower gel and deodorant, William?"

"I forgot."

"Oh well never mind. You can get them tomorrow, can't you?" Mckenna couldn't see much point on lingering on irrelevancies and wanted to press on.

"Did you go to the day centre today?"

William nodded. "We did a load of painting, because Brenda was there, and she always lets us do painting."

Again, the divisive enthusiasm. "Really! And what did you paint?"

"I can't remember." William's answer, based on past performances, came as little surprise.

"Do you do anything else at the day centre?"

"We do cooking. On Tuesdays, we do cooking."

"And do you enjoy that, William?"

"Sometimes."

The topic of the day centre was yielding very little with regard to useful information, so Mckenna decided to change the subject in the hope of stimulating some more revealing answers from her patient.

"Has your sister been to see you lately?"

"She comes to see me every month, on a Saturday."

"Well that's good. What do you do when she visits? Do you go out?" Mckenna already knew perfectly well where they went, but she was attempting to assess William's memory and grasp of reality.

"We go and have lunch at Wimpy's in the High Street."

McKenna noted the correct answer and proceeded.

"And what do you have to eat when you go to Wimpy's?"

"Burger and chips. And Coke." William was smiling, apparently at the thought of his favourite food.

"Is that how you got to have a big tummy?" Mckenna smiled as she pointed to his stomach.

William reflected the smile, and patted his stomach. "I like burgers and chips. I could eat it all the time!"

"Yes, I bet you could! Can you remember how long ago it was that you last went out with your sister? Can you remember when she came last?"

William thought for a moment and began to fidget. "She comes every month, on a Saturday."

"Yes, William, but can you tell me how many days it's been since her last visit?"

298

"Five days!" William's answer sounded as though it was a panic answer, but regardless of whether it was or not, it was wildly inaccurate.

McKenna didn't pursue the point, but moved on. "Do you do anything special when you go to the High Street, or do you just do your shopping and come straight back?"

"Come straight back." His response precipitated an intervention from Jarvis, who had been following the conversation.

"Don't you like sitting on the bench by the bus stop before you come back, William?"

William nodded, looking embarrassed at his omission, or even from a misplaced sense of guilt at sitting where he did every afternoon.

McKenna wasn't blind to his reaction, and jumped in quickly to stem his unexplained anxiety.

"You like watching the people go by, and all the shoppers?"

William nodded and smiled, but said nothing.

"Does anyone ever come and have a chat to you while you're having a sit down?"

"Toby was in the bus shelter today, and he gave me a roll up. I'm going to get a drink?"

McKenna's experience could distinguish between impatience and a poor attention span, and she carried on accordingly.

"So, what did you do when you saw Toby? Did you have a bit of a chat?"

"No, he gave me a cigarette, but he took it back because he'd run out of tobacco... " William had thought it strange at the time and had jumped to the only conclusion that his limited experience would extend to, whilst McKenna and Jarvis completely missed the only relevant thing that he'd said all afternoon and looked no deeper than the explanation that William had invented. William's mind, in the meantime, was characteristically going from one thing to another.

"Julie bought me a new jumper," He grabbed a handful of the woolen garment from around his middle in order to show it off. "What's for tea, Rob?"

McKenna knew the interview had a very limited lifespan remaining once William's thoughts began to go to other things, but, nevertheless carried on, more in hope than anything else.

"Do you feel safe here, William? I know that sometimes you feel that people are trying to hurt you. Do you feel like that at all at the moment?"

299

William was still fingering his jumper and shook his head, almost absently, in response to the question, as though other thoughts had taken over.

"Do you hear voices sometimes, William?"

Again a shake of the head, but this time it was accompanied by a "No," as he got up from his chair and without any further ceremony, announced it was teatime and walked out of the office.

Rob made a motion to say something to bring him back, but McKenna put her hand on his arm and shook her head. "Don't bother, Rob. We weren't going to get much more from him today. What's your opinion?"

Rob thought for a moment and it really didn't take any longer than that for him to consider what he was going to say in reply to the psychiatrist.

"Well, he seems happy here, and he doesn't appear to have any problems. His attention span is probably as good as it will ever be, but at least he doesn't seem to be experiences any distressing ideations or hallucinations. Of course, he's so institutionalized, we can't stop him queuing up for everything from meals to tablets, but we'll just have to live with that."

McKenna nodded in agreement. "Would more hours at the Day Centre help, do you think?"

"Possibly, but they're hard pushed to supply us with the amount of hours that they currently do, so it's unlikely that we'll get any more out of them in the foreseeable future." Jarvis clearly felt as though such matters were totally out of his control.

McKenna picked up her pen and began to write in William's notes, pausing only for a moment to look up to ask Jarvis a question: "has William got anyone here that he's friendly with?"

Jarvis thought for a moment. "If you'd have asked me a couple of weeks ago, I would have said that there really wasn't anyone he was friendly with at all, but he seems to have struck up a bit of a friendship with our new chap, Toby."

McKenna nodded and went back to her notes. "Well, that can only be for the good! Who are we seeing next?"

March 24th 1991; 14:10 hrs

Sitting on the bench in the High Street with Toby. "I'm working undercover," Toby's whispered announcement took a while to sink in, but even when it did, there wasn't much of a reaction on William.

"You don't work." The reply.

"No, it doesn't look as if I work, but really I do work... undercover."

"I've got to go and buy some toothpaste," William's dialogue continued to be everything that Toby didn't really want it to be, but he didn't give up.

"I'm really a millionaire. I'm only in that place so no-one can find me." A knowing wink, which was also lost on William. "I have to remain hidden until I get orders to go back to HQ."

A group of teenagers passed the bench, sniggering and pointing towards William and Toby.

Toby nodded in the direction of the youths. "I'd normally take that lot on, but I don't want to blow my cover."

William was still having trouble in keeping up. "Rob says that I've got to go on a diet. He said that I was too fat."

Toby carried on without William.

"I have to stay hidden, because I've got information to pass on, and I'm just waiting for HQ to make contact."

"What HQ?" William had picked up the initials on the second time of asking.

"HQ is where we work from. It's where I get my orders." Toby's voice was lower than ever.

William didn't respond immediately and when he did, he didn't seem to have grasped the concept of "undercover". "Does Rob know that your undercover, Toby?"

"No-one there knows who I really am, except you!"

The two men sat in silence for a few seconds, until Toby broke the silence.

"I have to trust someone, and I chose you. Normally I take special stuff that makes other people see what I want them to see. Special issue from HQ."

"What? Like an ointment?"

Toby shook his head but said nothing as two women walked close by. Satisfied that they were out of earshot, he continued.

"Not ointment, no." But William had lost interest by this point and left the bench to go to the supermarket opposite, returning some minutes later, clutching his newly acquired tube of toothpaste. Toby was smoking, as William resumed his place next to him on the bench and taking his tobacco pouch out of his pocket, rolled a cigarette of his own.

The two men sat in silence for a couple of minutes, both noticing a group of teenagers approaching the bus shelter from the left.

"Been talking to the fuckin' fairies, have we?" The opening gambit from one of the boys attracted guffaws from the rest of the group, and they obviously weren't going to let an opportunity like this, go begging. "Can't remember where you fuckin' live? That why you sit there all day?"

Neither William nor Toby responded, and that elicited a spate of face pulling and spitting. The youth who started the insults hadn't finished.

"Can't find any kids to play with? Men like them fuck babies! Don't you? You filthy fuckers!"

One of the girls in the group had an expression on her face as though someone had just put rotten eggs under her nose. "Do they really mess around with kids?"

The ringleader was well into his stride now and went up to Toby and slapped him around the face a few times. "Course they do... like little boys, don't you, you fuckin' nutter?" A few more slaps. "Don't you, fuckin' retard?"

Toby didn't respond and the youths, having hurled a few more insults and saliva in his and William's direction, departed to find some entertainment elsewhere.

William was quite shaken by the experience, despite being used to people insulting him, but Toby seemed quite buoyed up by the encounter. "See how complete my cover actually is, William? They can't see through it. They can't tell what I really am!" Toby was getting quite excited about what he was saying. "See what I mean? I told you, didn't I?"

"Your ointment?" William was lagging some distance behind the discussion.

"No, William. I said it wasn't ointment. Remember?" William nodded, although he really didn't remember. Toby, on the other hand, really didn't need agreement or anything else in order to continue. "Whenever I take it, I'm safe from their agents. They can't find me. Clever, isn't it?"

William didn't nod this time, instead he just rolled another cigarette, but Toby was determined to finish his bout of self-congratulations. That's what they think. That's what they're supposed to think!" Toby reached into his pocket for his own tobacco and rummaged around in the bin next to where he was sitting and found a discarded cigarette packet. Carefully tearing a thin strip of the packet, Toby set about making himself a joint, taking special care with the black resin that he had wrapped in foil at the bottom of his tobacco pouch. He took even more special care to make sure that no one was watching what he was doing.

"What's that?" William genuinely didn't know what he was looking at.

"It's the stuff I was telling you about. The stuff that keeps me hidden. I gave you some the other day. Remember?" The joint was nearly complete, but that didn't stop Toby shooting glances in every direction, just to make sure.

"It tastes horrible… I didn't like the taste at all." William was remembering his experience of a couple of days earlier and couldn't help noticing the apparent reverence with which Toby was making and handling the joint. "Why do your cigarettes taste funny?"

"It's not a cigarette," Toby corrected him. "It's a joint." Further comment was cut short as he lit and deeply inhaled on the carefully constructed object as William watched.

"You shouldn't be taking drugs. Joints are drugs." William was shaking his head and being quite sincere in his disapproval.

"Nah! It's not a drug. That's what they tell you. They tell you that it's bad for you, so you don't try it. They don't want you to be able to hide from them, so they tell you that it's a drug and you shouldn't use it. Don't you see? They're trying to trick you. All the time, just trying to trick you."

William still wasn't convinced, and was still shaking his head. Toby decided to tackle the argument from a different front. "You had some the other day. Did it do you any harm?"

William had stopped shaking his head, so Toby persisted. "Well, did it?" Toby still couldn't get an answer, so he carried on a bit more. "You were giggling when you had some!" As if to underline his comments, Toby started to chuckle. "You couldn't stop, could you?"

William smiled at the memory of his uncontrolled laughter of a couple of days earlier, but his resistance hadn't quite gone. "It tasted horrible. I didn't like it. It made me feel sick."

"Medicine doesn't often taste nice, does it?" Toby wasn't going to give up easily.

"You didn't say it was medicine. Did the doctor give it to you?" William's naivety was making it much easier for him to be convinced of what he was being told.

"No, the doctor doesn't give it to me. Doctors don't know anything.

They don't know about the special powers this stuff has. It stops the enemy from recognizing me. They try and stop people from taking this stuff because they think that if people take it, then they won't get ill and they wouldn't need doctors any more. Anyway, a lot of the doctors work for the enemy. You can't trust them." Toby was becoming more emphatic as the conversation progressed.

"I like Dr McKenna, she's always very nice to me. I don't think she's an enemy agent."

Toby shook his head and smiled ruefully at William's comment. "Of course you don't think she is. She's probably one of their top people. She knows how to weed people out. You really don't know anything, I'm worried about you. You just make it too easy for them." Toby's last comment being followed by a long drag on the joint.

William got up and went for a walk, but was back, a few minutes later to join his companion who, by that time had finished smoking.

"I can leave any time I choose. I can just walk out and go back to my villa in Portugal. I think that's what I'll do when this assignment's over. I need a break from special ops for a while." Toby's delusions were as active as ever, but were strangely plausible, in a funny, implausible yet compelling way. William was a captive audience, although he couldn't handle the amount of information being hurled in his direction.

"Does Rob know that you're going to Portugal?"

"I'm undercover! Of course he doesn't know, I… " Toby stopped in mid-sentence as someone walked by, before resuming, this time in a whisper. "I can't let anyone know, in case I'm caught."

William nodded, although he still wasn't quite sure what he was nodding in response to. The two men sat in silence for a few minutes. William was looking at nothing in particular and Toby was staring at everyone that passed, as though they were about to threaten his very existence. When he was satisfied that no-one was approaching, he reached into his coat pocket for his tobacco pouch and once again began the ceremony of rolling another joint, having first extracted the remnants of the previous one that he'd kept from earlier and adding it to the mix. William watched and went for another wander, returning a couple of minutes later as Toby was packing his joint making materials into his pouch, and then back into his pocket.

William was still watching as Toby took his first deep drag.

"Want some?" Toby was holding the joint under William's nose and without thinking he took it and started smoking. Two drags later and Toby was holding out his hand to take it back.

"It tastes funny. Why do you want it back?"

Toby looked cautiously around once more before answering. "I have to buy this stuff because HQ can't get any supplies to me, besides, it's strong stuff. Gotta be careful with it." Two more drags and he handed it back to William again.

Within seconds, William's head began to swim, within minutes, the whole world was hilarious and within days, William was handing Toby chunks of his allowance to buy some more.

October 25th 1991; 08:00 hrs

"Are you getting up today or are you planning to spend the rest of your life in bed?" Rob Jarvis was doing his daily "get up and round up" bit. Effective as Jarvis could be, it was William's full bladder that was the determining factor that eventually tipped him out of bed and sent him shuffling down the corridor to the toilet.

"Come on you lot, let's get breakfast over and done with!" Always so chirpy.

William dragged on his clothes and began to go downstairs to the dining room, but was sent back before he could make it past three steps. "I didn't hear any water running in the bathroom, William!" Back he went for a wash and to clean his teeth, before making another attempt on the stairs.

"Now, you don't have to stand there, do you William, we're not at Greenbeck now." Pauline had been working at Connaught Street since William was transferred there and still had to prompt him every morning in order that he would help himself to breakfast cereal and not just stand there, trying to form a queue.

"Are you alright, William?" He looked up from his cornflakes to see Rob standing over him. "You look a bit peaky, mate." William nodded and carried on with his breakfast and Jarvis went back over to where Pauline was standing.

"I see what you mean, but I got Ruth to see him a couple of days ago after I'd told her that he seemed sluggish compared to what he normally is and she said that she couldn't find anything wrong." He shrugged his shoulders and glanced over as William was tipping his usual four teaspoons of sugar into his tea.

William wasn't holding his thoughts in one place for as long as he usually could, but the change was subtle, and he didn't notice.

December 8th 1991; 08:50 hrs

On the transport to go to the day centre. Window seat behind the driver. Always the window seat and always behind the driver. Cooking today, but is it today? What day is it? Engine started, Pauline driving. Stopping now at the traffic lights at the end of the road. Looking down at the blue Rover in the next lane and its driver looking straight ahead. Looking ahead at the traffic lights, is that it? Or perhaps he's avoiding eye contact. That's it. Scared that he'll be recognised for what he really is.

March 17th 1992; 09:20 hrs

Cooking biscuits today. So they say. Standing in the kitchen at the day centre with a plastic bowl in front of him. Daphne, the lady running the cookery session, standing behind him getting impatient: "Now, William, where's the flour? It's not doing much in the bag is it? Come on now, six tablespoons of flour into the bowl!" and she moved on to the next candidate, who was evidently doing much better than William. Daphne moved across to Michael who'd just spilt his bowl over the floor and William took the opportunity during the chaos, to switch his bag of flour and packet of margarine with Daniel, who was too busy laughing at the mess caused by Michael's mishap, to take any notice.

William hadn't seen Daphne put anything into his bag of flour and packet of margarine, but he knew that she'd put poison in them. Her little plan wouldn't work now.

August 17th 1992; 11:10 hrs

Sitting and having coffee at the Day Centre as he always did at this time of the morning. Feeling very isolated, alone, but that's the way he wanted it to be. Apprehension. People keep looking... staring for no reason.

"Where are you going, William?" The centre manager, Jeff happened to be coming out of his office door and saw William edging towards the exit which lead to the street.

"I want to go back to Connaught Street." William knew what he wanted, but he allowed himself to be led back to the lounge area and accepted a second cup of coffee that Jeff offered him.

"You sure you're alright, mate?" Jeff was concerned, and made a mental note, later forgotten, to mention the attempted absconsion to whoever came to pick up the Connaught Street residents. William started spooning sugar into his coffee.

"I'm fine... I'm OK."

January 6th 1993; 12:30 hrs

Sausages and chips for lunch. Watching as the packet of sausages and oven chips were taken from the Sainsbury's carrier bag that Pauline had just brought in from the bus. Watching as the food was cooked. Watching as it was served. No movement was unnoticed. No additions made to the food on its way to the table. Don't want the tomato ketchup. Only use stuff out of a bottle if it's never been opened before.

May 19th 1993; 13:45 hrs

Toby went to the High Street first, because he said that his cover would be blown if they were seen together. Rob said that he should remember to get some razors, but the Co-Op in the High Street probably couldn't be trusted.

September 11th 1993; 14:10 hrs

Sitting on the bench with Toby. Two packets of tobacco in payment and Toby shares his joint. Feeling good, but so many thoughts. Fast thinking, but without detail, flitting from one thing to another as though scanning different headlines in a newspaper. Careful, always so careful because everyone's watching.

December 7th 1993; 15:30 hrs

"I met him when I was at University, so we've been friends for a long time now." Sitting in the café with Julie who was talking about the new love in her life. "His name's Mark and he's an engineer." Julie wasn't one of them; she's immune because she took on Uncle Bill's protection when he died. "So it seemed natural that we'd get together. He was there for me when Uncle Bill died. William, are you OK? You look as though you're frightened of something."

A shake of the head and a smile and Julie carried on. "So we just got married on the spur of the moment, really and we've moved into a flat in Plymouth." she paused as she stared again and then continued. "I'll bring him up to meet you soon!"

February 17th 1994; 16:40 hrs

Dr Mckenna had her arms crossed. "Now Rob has been telling me that he's a bit worried about you, William and I've spoken to your sister, Julie, who's also very concerned." Julie can't be trusted! She's talking to them. That's such a stupid thing to do. McKenna continued. "So we'll increase your depot injection, but if that doesn't work, we'll have to try another medication because we've gone as far as we can with this one." McKenna left a pause, but she was really talking to herself and not really expecting an answer. "Having said that, I'm not sure why the medication isn't being as effective anymore, but of course, that can happen. OK, William, go and get your tea!"

June 16th 1994; 17:10 hrs

Pick at the food on the plate. Didn't see it prepared. Don't trust it. The only other person at the table is Michael and he's getting up to get his pudding. Grab the pie from the plate and run to the bedroom with it. Put it in front of the stereo speakers for three minutes with the music turned on to get any poison out of it and take it back downstairs again before anyone notices. Rob looks at him as he sits back down at the table. He's not to be trusted. None of them are to be trusted.

308

October 17th 1994; 18:50 hrs

The television is blaring out in the corner of the lounge. So many messages that no-one was aware of, or, at least if they were aware of them, they weren't showing it. Can't hear the hidden words, but they're there just the same. They wouldn't be there if this was near the sea, but it isn't. It can't be, not anymore, but there again, not all of the music can be trusted whether this is by the sea or not, so care is needed. Sweating now with the strain of resisting the messages, but the effort is worth it.

January 3rd 1995; 19:30 hrs

The sanctuary that is the bedroom with the door closed. Safety is paramount and achievable. Control of the area is all important. Control of the sounds is even more important. The sounds are solid, touchable, if they're good sounds. Can't quite do that yet, but it'll come. Bad sounds just penetrate and invade. Cross the floor to the stereo … walk in straight lines only, no diagonals. They can get through if the angles are wrong.

March 2nd 1995; 21:00 hrs

Looking out of the window at the street below. Empty now, but not for long. The television downstairs continues with its messages. The music on the stereo goes on but it is necessary that all words of the songs are known, predictable, familiar. Another familiarity in the background, but not a song this time. Straining to hear but it keeps going away.

May 3rd 1995; 23:05 hrs

"William… William!" The voice was there. It was real and familiar. More than familiar. "William… don't trust the doors. The doors don't lock and you're not safe!" Jack was insistent and compelling. And he was there. Thoughts in and out of range, forever flitting and changing, but Jack was there.

Confusion, but confusion that now had a direction. Barricade the door. Everything piled up against it. It's the only way.

Sheila Green wasn't a psychiatrist. She wasn't a nurse either. Indeed her attendance at William Phillip's Mental Health Tribunal was precisely because she was because she'd been appointed to act as the "lay member" of the group. She was in fact, a retired social worker, but that really wasn't terribly relevant to anything apart from the fact that she was very good at asking the right questions and looking at things that her professional companions, now seated around the table in the ward meeting room at Greenbeck, may have missed. For the moment, however, she was busily occupied transporting four cups of freshly poured coffee from the trolley by the door over to her two colleagues and William's solicitor, Anthony Barnes, who were pouring over a mound of papers spread out in front of them.

"So Mr Phillips was admitted her to Birch Unit in May of last year under Section 5, all the renewal papers are in order, following a marked deterioration in his condition, identified on his papers as paranoid schizophrenia." Judge Grant was summing up what he'd just read, for no one's benefit apart from his own. Sheila and the other Tribunal member, Dr Khan had, as a matter of routine, been sent copies of exactly the same papers that the Judge had in front of him now. But Grant was in full flow. "… apparently culminating in destruction of property and other behaviours which were deemed as being a danger to both himself and others." He flicked through a few more papers. "His psychosis is still giving cause for concern. You've seen this gentleman already this morning, Dr Khan?"

"I have, Judge," Khan referred to his notes, looking up briefly to see the immaculately dressed lay member of the Tribunal finally take her seat after safely depositing three cups of coffee. Having assured himself that he had the attention of both his colleagues, he continued. "Mr Phillips was first admitted to what was the old Greenbeck Hospital in June 1974 when he was just 19 years old with a diagnosis of schizophrenia and was detained under Section 25 and subsequently Section 26 of the old Mental Health Act and proved very difficult to manage for a considerable time, although he was discharged into the community under the care of his grandparents in March 1975. In a short space of time he relapsed and was re-admitted, although it's probable, according to his notes, that his symptoms hadn't

310

been particularly well controlled."

Khan temporarily removed his glasses to add a comment to his account. "This wasn't particularly unusual at the time, given the limited variety of antipsychotic medication available, then."

"Presumably, his psychiatrist must have deemed it as appropriate to discharge him at the time?" Judge Grant was trying to follow the extensive history, both by listening to Khan's summary, and by reading the wad of notes in front of him.

"I would have thought so, Judge." Khan replaced his glasses and carried on with his summary and findings. "Eventually, with the substantial closure of most of the wards here, Mr Phillips was transferred to Connaught Street where, initially, he seemed to settle well, and even develop a little independence, until he suffered another apparent relapse, as you've just read, Judge, and was admitted here, initially under Section Two, and later under Section Three of the Mental Health Act."

The Judge nodded as he looked at the Section administration papers. "Everything seems to be in order from the administration side of things and I see that we're here because Mr Phillips' solicitor, Anthony Barnes, has lodged an appeal at his behalf and at his request."

Both of the other Tribunal members nodded and the ensuing silence prompted Dr Khan to continue with his findings. "When I interviewed Mr Phillips earlier today, he was apprehensive and quite markedly paranoid. His behavior was highly indicative of someone who is experiencing auditory hallucinations. As far as his cognitive abilities were concerned, these were difficult to assess, but appeared to be seriously impaired, as was his attention span. In short, Mr Phillips' appeared to be markedly psychotic."

"Thank you Dr Khan. I think it would be appropriate for us to call Dr Arbury at this stage." Mrs Green got up and opened the door to summon Max Arbury who had been waiting outside.

The Judge introduced his colleagues to the Consultant. "You've been Mr Phillip's Consultant Psychiatrist since he was admitted to Birch Unit under Section 2 and subsequently under section 3 of the Mental Health Act. I am sure you are aware that the purpose of this Tribunal is to determine, following a full discussion with relevant parties and examination of relevant reports, whether the detention should continue or not. As you are also aware, we are, on this occasion, hearing witnesses in Mr Phillips' absence due to his attention difficulties."

Arbury nodded to indicate his understanding, and the judge continued. "Could you begin by giving us a summary of his overall condition as you see it, Dr Arbury?"

Arbury reiterated the remarks made by Khan, who proceeded to ask the consultant his opinion of William's prognosis. "I am able to confirm that Mr Phillips continues to be resistant to anti- psychotic medication and therefore continues to be a risk because of his inability to maintain any form of independence, as I indicated in my written report that was sent to the Mental Health Tribunal Office." Again, the shuffling of papers as the all four scrutinizers searched for the relevant bits. After a few seconds, the Judge looked up.

"Thank you Dr Arbury. Do you have any questions Mr Barnes?"

"Do we have any indication as to why Mr Phillips' condition should suddenly have deteriorated when he was in Connaught Street and hence any indication that his condition may or may not improve?" Barnes had got right to the crux of the matter, but even he was surprised when an answer was forthcoming.

"According to a report by the Community Psychiatrist, Dr Ruth McKenna, who was responsible for Mr Phillips' care in Connaught Street, a number of smoked joint dog ends were found hidden in his room when they went to clean it just after he was admitted here."

The Judge was distinctly interested to know more. "Are you saying, Dr Arbury, that this could account for his condition? Surely any such effects would have worn off by now?"

"The possibility of a substance induced psychosis is, at the very least a very plausible explanation." Arbury was anxious not to commit himself, but all the facts seemed to point in this direction. "It could certainly make treating psychotic illness almost impossibly problematic and I have to say, that we have only noted a marginal improvement in his condition since he was admitted. I have no reason to be hopeful that any further improvements will be seen in the foreseeable future, although, of course, that is only my opinion."

"I see… thank you Dr Arbury. I'm sure you're aware that it is not the job of this tribunal to review the circumstances of his admission; rather we are here to decide whether the detention should continue. Your comments on the prognosis are most hopeful and I believe coincide with Dr Khan's opinion?" He looked over towards the medical member of the tribunal and was rewarded with a nod. Is there anything else that you may feel we haven't covered, Mrs Green?"

"You say that he is not capable of any form of independence, Dr Arbury. Is this the grounds for keeping him in hospital?"

"Not on its own, no. I believe that Mr Phillips, because of his poor attention span, inability identify or take steps to fulfill his basic needs, not to mention the apparently persistent presence of auditory hallucinations, that he is a serious risk to himself." Mrs Green made a note.

"Thank you, Dr Arbury"

"We'll call you again if we have any further points to raise. Thank you, Dr Arbury. Could you possibly ask the Unit Charge Nurse...?" He looked down at his notes again: "Mr Owen, if you'd be so kind."

John Owen took his turn in the chair and his account, peppered with incidents of bizarre behaviours, impossibly irrational discussions, seemingly directionless behavior and the ever present paranoia and inability to concentrate on anything for more than a couple of minutes, backed up the emerging picture of a man with a serious and apparently treatment resistant psychosis.

"Does he have any next of kin?" Mrs Green asked the question and Owen obliged by giving a potted history of William's circumstances. "And is his sister here today?"

"She doesn't get up to see William more than about once a month as she lives in the west country, so, in answer to your question, I'm afraid she's not here today." Owen supplied the answer and the small team returned to their perusal of the copious paperwork in front of them.

10:50 hrs

William's large frame virtually filled the tiny interview room inside the Birch Unit and he made matters even more congested by being so restless. His solicitor, who had just extricated himself from the tribunal room, did his best to bring some calm to his client by encouraging him to sit down, opposite him, at the small table in the centre of the room and to drink the tea that one of the nurses had just delivered.

"Now, William, do you feel OK? Don't feel nervous at all? There's nothing to worry about." No one could deny that Barnes was a good solicitor, but as far as his abilities with regard to empathetically interacting with his mental health clients was concerned, he was never better than "hit and miss". On this occasion, he was entirely missing the fact that his client wasn't worried or anxious or nervous, at least, not of the Tribunal.

"You've seen Dr Khan today, haven't you?"

William took a gulp of his tea. "Was that the Indian man I saw this morning?"

"Yes, that's right. How did you get on?"

William slowly reached into his jacket pocket and took out his packet of tobacco and proceeded to make a roll up, leaving Barnes' to look on, his question still unanswered. Slowly and deliberately he made the cigarette, looking like someone who had drunk a little too much and was having trouble in keeping anything in focus. Barnes repeated the question, and this time was rewarded with a response. "Alright ... can I go now?"

"No, William, not yet. Don't you remember what we talked about? Do you remember that I told you that we were going to see some people today who want to see if all your treatment is the best thing for you? Do you remember that?

William nodded unconvincingly and brought his cigarette to his mouth and lit it.

"You're going to have to put that out when they call us," Barnes wasn't trying to tell his client what to do, so much as trying to cover up his own frustration at not being able to get any other useful communication going.

"Do you remember that I told you that these people would want to ask you some questions? Do you remember that?"

Another nod, this time followed by William getting up to leave and Barnes, once again, having to remind him why he couldn't.

11:05 hrs

"Do come and sit down, Mr Phillips," Judge Grant waited for William and his solicitor to make themselves comfortable before he introduced himself and his two colleagues.

"I think that Mr Barnes would have explained to you about this Tribunal, Mr Phillips?"

William didn't respond, but instead appeared distracted and to be paying attention to something else.

"Mr Phillips!" The Judge made an attempt to ensure that he had William's attention. "Are you alright?"

This time a nod, so the Judge decided to carry on. "As you are no doubt aware, Mr Phillips, you are currently detained under Section 3 of the Mental Health Act 1983 and apart from regular Hospital Manager reviews," A brief pause while he checked his notes. "Which I believe you attended a few months ago, there is a statutory obligation for your detention to be reviewed by a Tribunal. Since you have not requested this, your solicitor has asked for this Tribunal on your behalf. Do you understand?"

"I think so," William's answer came slowly and unconvincingly and he was clearly unhappy about having to sit still any longer, as his fidgeting demonstrated.

"You've been seen by Dr Khan here," He gestured to the psychiatrist sat on his right. "And we've had a chance to have a chat with Dr Arbury and Mr Owen. Can you tell us why you think you're in hospital, Mr Phillips?"

Slowly he pondered the question, and for all the world looked as though he was listening to someone. "They killed my Mum. She can't come because they killed her." Barnes knew the history and jumped in to help with a coherent answer. "Do you know why you are in Birch Unit at the moment, William?"

"Hiding! Can I go now?"

Mrs Green decided to pick up the thread. "Hiding from whom, William?"

"Can I have another cigarette?" William hadn't even registered the question, so Barnes repeated it, and got an answer slightly more relevant.

"The people who want to take my thoughts away. Can I go now?" This time he didn't wait for an answer, but instead, he got up out of his chair and walked out. Barnes looked at the Judge, who indicated that further questions directed at William would be unlikely and a cursory glance into the corridor confirmed that his client wasn't going to hang around for further interrogation.

14:30 hrs

Arbury stood in the Unit Office and stared out of the window at the snow falling. Sat at the desk was John Owen, leafing through the Tribunals findings. "Not a bad outcome, then?"

Arbury didn't really have to think about it. "No, not bad at all. They couldn't do anything else apart from recommending that his detention continues, although they have recommended that we find a more suitable placement for him. Can't argue with that, I suppose. God alone knows how we'll achieve that miracle, and if we do manage it, how long will it take before we can move him?"

The question didn't need answer, as they both knew that their acquaintance with William Phillips wasn't going to come to an end in a hurry.

June 3rd 1997; 09:20 hrs

Raining outside, so at least that was good for a start. To everyone else it was a nuisance, but it stopped the messages, so it was good.

"Hello William, I'm Trisha." Nice smile, but Jack didn't like her. Jack didn't trust her.

"She's changed form, she's the same one! Remember him... Morgan. That's him... Clever!"

"I've been asked to come to find out... "

"He's just trying to trick you. Wants to make you talk so he can get into your head!"

"If you'd be suitable... "

"Move away, don't look him in the eyes!"

"To move to a hospital where... "

Got to move, but he's still there.

"William, as I was saying I have been asked to come and assess you to see if you would be suitable for..."

"It's a trap, William!"

"A placement in another..."

So much rain, but it can't always make things better, although it might make Julie come. Julie likes the rain, because she's special. Because she's immune. Answer the questions. Always questions. Jack says not to answer, but Morgan won't go away without answers.

The Trisha body of Morgan goes at last and the rain stops, but Julie hasn't come. Hasn't come for ages.

September 9th 1997; 11:45 hrs

A group of them now, round a table and all smiling and talking slowly at him… said they were Hospital Managers and all with loads of papers they were looking through.

"We are here to make sure that you're getting the right care." The bald headed man with the glasses perched on the end of his nose was smiling as he spoke, but that fooled no one.

"Here to make sure they've still got hold of you!"

"… need to make sure that the hospital… "

"Keeping up the pretence… always the pretence… They don't know what to do next!"

"… want to know how you're feeling… "

"Bet they do!"

"Now, I understand that your sister wanted to be here today, but, unfortunately, she couldn't get the time off work at the last minute."

"And you're glad she's not here! She's not afraid of you… she knows who you are!"

"Have you read the reports, William?"
CPA Meeting
Mr William Phillips

Tuesday, 9th September 1997

The headings were clear, but didn't mean anything: "medical report… readmitted… substance induced psychosis… ideations continue… difficult to engage… "

Jack wouldn't allow any reading that said those things.

"Yes."

"Who the fuck do they think they're fooling with their made up bits of typing?"

"Do you agree with what all the reports say, William?"

A cup of tea put in front of him, so in go four sugars before starting on the plate of biscuits in the middle of the table.

"William, Mr Phillips. Do you agree with what Dr Arbury and his colleagues have written about you?" Again the man with the glasses. Turn the page over to keep him happy. "Remain on Section 3… catatonic type movements observed… life skill difficult to… "

Still doesn't know what they're talking about. "Yes."

"That's good, William, keep them quiet!"

317

Too, many people, too much to take in and when Julie comes, they'll have to disperse because she'll be too strong for them. The equations shouldn't match them, but they do.

"William? Is there something wrong, William?"

"Don't let them follow your thoughts, William!"

"Is there anything that you want us to do, or to ask the hospital to do for you?"

"Tell 'em to let you leave!"

"Can you tell them to let me go home?"

The man with the glasses gives a sympathetic smile.

"No, I'm afraid we can't do that, William."

Time to go, although everyone tries to make him stay, but Jack is insistent that he leaves.

February 17th 1998; 14:05 hrs

"Let me listen to your chest, please, William."

Dr Mansfield, he said his name was. The cold stethoscope confirmed that he was a doctor.

"Take a deep breath in for me. That's it."

"Doctors made sure the soldiers were fit during the war before they executed them!"

"And again."

Writing and touching and listening. Dr Mansfield does the lot. "I'm going to change your medication, William and if you'll take my advice, give up smoking, your chest's in a terrible state."

"Why do they always say to give up smoking?"

"You've got to lose at least four and a half stone, William. Do you understand? You have diabetes and you need to keep off all the chocolate and other sweet things."

Silence. Who's he talking about?

"He's just trying to scare you... to take control!"

"I'm being absolutely serious, William. I'm going to have a word with the Charge Nurse about your weight and diet and see if we can do anything to help you. In the meantime, I've prescribed some tablets to help keep your blood sugar under control. Dr Arbury's doing his ward round this afternoon, so I'll have a chat with him when he's finished, because he needs to know about the diabetes and bronchitis."

"Don't know who he's talking about!"

"Can I go?"

Dr Marshall nodded in a resigned sort of manner. "Yes William. You can go."

14:45 hrs

"William, I'm stopping your current anti-psychotic medication and then in a few days, I'll prescribe a new one. Do you understand? It's quite a new drug and it may be that it'll be better for you than the medicine we've been giving you, because it's supposed to be more effective with patients such as you, who have been difficult to treat."

"Does Dr Arbury think you're stupid? Of course you understand what he's doing, even when he tries to lie to you!"

"I can't guarantee anything, of course, but I'd like to take you off section as soon as we can get some of these symptoms under a bit more control. That would be good, wouldn't it?"

"Good if you do exactly as he says... Good, if you take the muck he gives to you... Good, if you don't make a fuss!"

"So you're OK with that. Yes?"

Nodding this time, but only to keep Arbury quiet.

November 4th 1998; 15:20 hrs

Allowed out with Julie on leave. "Section 17" leave John called it. Two hours leave when they could go to town. Julie had her husband with her today. His name was Mark. She said that she'd told him about getting married, but he could only vaguely remember her saying anything about it.

"How are you feeling now, William? Julie says you've been having a bit of a rough time."

"I'm OK, thank you." This was said with a polite smile, but not altogether sure what he meant by "rough time". Nice man, Mark, but sharing Julie wasn't easy.

"Shall we go to the café and have some tea and something to eat, William?" Julie was always bouncy and cheerful.

"Yes. I like eating out." The invitation was certainly appealing and the feeling of being with Julie and doing something together that wasn't just a hospital visit, produced feelings that he'd forgotten about long ago.

Parking the car in the market place near the bench at the bus stop. Familiarity, but the memories were fuzzy, unclear and unimportant. What was important was being with Julie and Mark.

People looking as they walked across the market square. Uncomfortable being watched, but they won't do any harm to him. Can't do any harm to him. Julie and Mark will make sure nothing happens.

In the café now, with a cup of tea and two sausage rolls in front of him. "What have you been doing today?" They both look interested to hear about his blood test in the morning. Thoughts coming and going. Thoughts of Nan especially and Grandpa's chocolate.

"Are you alright, William? You look as though you're somewhere else?" Julie was smiling at him.

"I was thinking of Nan. She always used to buy me a sausage roll when we went shopping."

"Do you think of your Nan and Grandpa a lot, William?" Mark this time.

A mouthful of sausage roll and a nod, followed by a pause as he swallowed.

"I wrote a letter to Sandy, but they said she'd moved away."

"Who's Sandy, William? Was that the young lady that you used to know in hospital?"

Another nod, and a rare smile. "I love Sandy." Julie suddenly excuses herself and runs to the toilet, blowing her nose on the way.

"Uncle Bill's got a chalet in Lowestoft." Mark looks puzzled, but smiling at the same time. Julie returns a couple of minutes later, looking as though she's got a cold, but still smiling.

"Everything OK with you boys?" She sat back down at the table.

"I like it when you come." Bits of flaky pastry from the mouthful of sausage roll, but Julie and Mark carried on smiling. "John said I can buy myself a radio if I've got enough money."

Julie looked puzzled. "Do you like the radio now?"

"Sometimes… Sometimes it makes me worried."

Julie and Mark sat around a table with Max Arbury, John Owen and the social worker, Yvette Goldman. Care Planning meeting, they called it. William was sitting at the table with everyone else, although after only ten minutes or so, he was showing signs that he wanted to leave. Written reports from just about everyone from the Consultant to the Occupational Therapist and Arbury was making sure that Julie and her husband had any points clarified. For her part, Julie was encouraging her brother to read his copies of the reports, but his attention span simply wouldn't allow it.

"Of course we're delighted that William's come off his Section, but is there really any different to what he was like when he was a sectioned patient?"

Arbury welcomed the chance to explain the difference. "Well, you have a good point. I'm sure that you're refers to his fragmented thoughts, Am I right?"

"And his lack of concentration and getting up to wander around every few minutes?"

Arbury held his hand up and smiled. "Point taken, but the essential difference between William's condition now compared to when he first came back to us is that we've managed reduce his paranoia and abnormal ideations and more especially, his auditory hallucinations. Having said that, however, he does have some days that are worse than others."

Julie was still concentrating on getting William to read the relevant passage in the report which came under the heading 'Current Mental State'. "I'm sorry, Dr Arbury, could you explain that a bit more please?"

"Of course. William used to believe that everyone around him, apart from a few people, had been somehow altered by some form of aliens. He believed that these aliens were trying to get into his head to steal his thoughts. He also believed he was receiving messages from the television and radio and that he could hear a voice that was telling him what to do."

Julie thought for a moment. "Does that mean that William buying himself a radio was a positive step?"

Arbury was pleased that his description was clear enough for conclusions to be drawn. "Absolutely and combined with the mood stabilizers that I put him on, mean that he can interact a little more normally as well as being rather happier in himself."

"Why do I hear a "but" coming on?" Julie had learned not to be optimistic where William's prospects were concerned.

"No "buts", well, not on that score anyway. As always, though, the doses that I've had to prescribe are high, so there's always going to be side effect, particularly with his shaking which I'm sure you've noticed. Oh and of course, I'm sure you will have read quite a pessimistic report from the Occupational Therapist who has noted only a marginal improvement in his ability to consistently engage in any life skills activities."

"So quite a few "buts" then?" Julie knew the score by now.

Arbury smiled, as though he'd been found out and clearly thought that now was the time to mention something else that had been concerning him. "I should also bring to your attention, Dr Marshall's report on William's physical condition, which is giving some cause for concern."

More shuffling of papers, as everyone around the table tried to find the appropriate section. When it looked as though everyone had found it, Arbury continued. "Dr Marshall points out that William has type 2 diabetes which is poorly controlled, even with medication, because of William's unwillingness or inability to control his diet in any way. He further goes on to mention that, for a man who is only in his mid-forties, William has a disproportionate amount of chest infections, the last couple of episodes requiring courses of steroids."

"Smoking?" Mark asked the obvious question.

"Smoking and weight, yes."

Arbury added the correction, but was saying nothing that wasn't already known. After a bit more rifling through the reports to make sure they hadn't missed anything, Julie returned to her original point. "So, to get back to my earlier question about coming off his section of the Mental Health Act?"

Arbury thought for a moment. "Ah, yes. Well, William has made no attempt leave here and he does seem to have, at least some, insight into his condition. I believe that given the right environment and care, that he no longer merits being detained."

"So he's now a voluntary patient?" Julie had to search her mind for that one.

"The term's a little old fashioned, but yes, he is." Arbury was clearly pleased to give some good news for a change.

"Does that me that he can come to visit us when we move house in a couple of months?"

"If you're happy with that, then of course he can!" Arbury thought he could see a glimmer of light at the end of the tunnel.

"What now, then?" Julie was anxious to make the most of anything positive that went in William's direction. "You're not going to keep him here, surely?"

Yvette Golding became suddenly animated. "May I, Dr Arbury?" The Consultant gestured for her to continue. "I'm trying hard to find an alternative placement for William. Somewhere that will be a lot more homely than a hospital." She clearly thought that her news would be welcomed, but was met with caution rather than relief.

"The last time someone found him somewhere "homely", my brother ended up taking cannabis and ending up back here!"

Arbury jumped in straight away. "I'm sure you'll be pleased to hear that Connaught Street has now closed, and that none of us would entertain any placements that weren't going to maintain a close watch on William."

Julie still looked skeptical. William had left the room, and the social worker had started rustling through her papers before finding what she was looking for. "William was visited by Trisha Martin who is the Manager of the Clover Unit near Brighton about eighteen months ago and she said in her report, that although your brother was too ill at that time, she would be delighted to consider him for transfer if his condition improved. That's a lot nearer to you, I believe?"

Hopeful, but defiant. "OK, but he's not going anywhere that Mark and I haven't approved of."

Everyone around the table suddenly became animated in an attempt to reassure her, with a variety of "of course not's" which only ceased when Julie held her hand up and announced that she would await their call to say that something had been arranged, but then asked the question to which definite answers were not as forthcoming.

"When is this likely to be?" Mark asked the question that was on his wife's lips, but it obviously wasn't the question to ask in the midst of so much positivity. Julie could feel the meeting deflate, but Yvette at least, tried to remain buoyant.

"As soon as Trisha's been back to assess him and of course, as soon as they have a bed available."

Julie just smiled and nodded. She knew that the "but" would be somewhere. And now she'd found it. "How long will that be?" The hesitations in answering her questions told her that it could be months away.

March 17th 2000; 21:35 hrs

It wasn't an unfamiliar sound, but the hissing from the oxygen and the bubbling of liquid in the nebulizer somehow made the place even more foreign and detached, but William knew from past experience that it would bring some relief from his breathlessness.

Everyone was so busy and from where he was lying on the hospital trolley, William could see white coated doctors and uniformed nurses busying themselves doing things that looked important, although he couldn't see what they were doing.

"Are you feeling any better yet, William?" Trisha Martin had come with him in the ambulance after the GP had said he had a chest infection and would probably need some oxygen to help him. William nodded in response, but he really didn't feel much better than when he'd come into the A&E Department.

The two of them sat in silence for a while until a flustered looking houseman arrived on the scene, pulled the curtains round the trolley and announced that he was going to "put a drip up" so he could give some antibiotics. Trisha looked on, not knowing how her patient would react to having a cannula stuck into his vein, but he'd had so many blood tests over the previous couple of years that it really didn't bother him anymore.

Cannula in and secured and a bag of something or other on the drip stand attached to the trolley and Trisha and her charge resumed their awkward silence for a few more minutes.

"Mr Phillips?" A young nurse with a clipboard appeared round the curtains. "Dr Airdale would like to admit you for a couple of days, just to make sure everything's OK." Trisha stirred out of his hospital waiting room slumber.

"Hi, I'm the manager of The Clover Unit. How long did you say William's going to be admitted for? Roughly?"

"Oh, sorry, yes. Forgot you were there. Yes, about a couple of days, because the antibiotics will be more effective if we give them intravenously... Sorry, you already know that don't you? Yes a couple of days and that should be that! OK?" She didn't need an answer, in fact, she spoke as though there wasn't anyone there at all and in any case, she didn't hang around long enough for any sort of answers or response.

William was making a noise over the noise of the nebulizer and Trisha had to remove it in order to hear what he was saying. "Going to see Julie and Mark tomorrow!" William managed speak in between wheezing and coughing.

"I don't think so, William. I'll give Julie a ring and see what we can do about you going to visit one day next week, but you never know, she'll probably nip up and see you before then, especially when I tell her you've landed yourself in hospital again! Anyway, has she told you anything about their new house?" Again a noise from behind the mask and, again, Trisha had to remove it to hear what he was saying.

"Mark decorated a room for me, so I could stay overnight." The words were a struggle and took three or four breaths to complete. Trisha replaced the nebulizer mask.

"That's great. You've been waiting so long to go and see them, haven't you?"

William nodded and smiled from behind the mask, before settling into a silence as he watched the comings and goings of the doctors and nurses.

23.20 hrs

The hiss of the oxygen as it entered the mask, muffled all the other sounds around and was strangely hypnotic, so despite all the noise and still being breathless, William had managed to doze off, only to be woken by the sound of someone releasing the brakes of the trolley on which he was lying.

"Let's get you to the ward, Mr Phillips." A nurse he hadn't seen before had made her way to the head of the trolley. "Do you want to come with him, Mrs...?"

"Martin." Trisha supplied the missing name. "Yes, if I could. Thank you." She picked up the plastic bag of William's toiletries that she'd hurriedly put together in preparation for the anticipated stay.

Nobody took any particular notice as the trolley trundled its way through the A&E Department and down a variety of deserted corridors, until the sound of opening swing doors and the slowing of pace announced their arrival on the ward the nurse found her voice again, having been silent for the duration of the short journey. "If you'd just like to wait here for a moment, until we get him settled." The comments were directed at Trisha who took a seat just inside the ward entrance, leaving William to take his chances as the trolley entered the dimly lit ward.

"Hello Mr Phillips. Will you be OK hopping over onto the bed for me?" The words from the young staff nurse were muffled by the hiss of oxygen through the mask. William edged himself over. "You're still very breathless, aren't you?" William nodded as the nurse covered him with a sheet and blanket. "I'll just go and get your friend."

Two minutes later, Trisha came into the ward, complete with the bag of toiletries which she proceeded to deposit in the bedside locker. "Now, I rang Julie and told her you were in hospital and she said for you not to worry and she'd drive over tomorrow to see you. Have you got everything you need?"

William, who had been watching the locker filling activity nodded to indicate that he did indeed have everything he needed.

"Right then, I'll be off! Don't forget, you've got a drip up, so you'll need to ask the nurse if you want to go to the toilet. And I've had a word with the staff nurse about you wanting to have a bit of a wander, so she's going to keep an eye on you. Try to get some sleep now. I'll send Kieran in to sit with you tomorrow, so you'll be OK. Hope you feel better; I'll pop in and see you tomorrow." All of which was being said in a loud whisper, as she picked up her shoulder bag and made her way towards the ward entrance. One final wave and she was gone.

The bed lamp was directed toward the drip and its light seemed to make the rest of the ward darker and somehow, unreal. His breathing was slightly easier now, but it was still an uncomfortable process to get the air in and out of his lungs. William had little option other than to stay in bed, despite Trisha's fear to the contrary and from where he was laying he could see two or three staff sat at the nurse's station, all of them busy writing and re-arranging clipboards and charts. The nurse who'd helped him into the bed collected a few papers she'd been working on, and made her way towards him.

"OK, Mr Phillips, I'm going to do a few observations on you, in fact, I'll be doing them about every half an hour."

William just nodded, now feeling quite exhausted by the effort of breathing and trying to cough up phlegm. His head was swimming and his chest was aching and he somehow felt so much safer now that the staff nurse had returned. "Now, I'm Jenny, and I'm one of the night staff nurses. What would you like me to call you?"

William muttered something through the mask, but Jenny had to reach over to take the mask off for a couple of seconds to understand what he was saying.

"Call me Billy"

March 18th 2000; 16:20 hrs

"I came as soon as I could after Trisha called me, but I thought it would be silly to have come to see you last night. It would have been about three o'clock in the morning before I could have got here and I thought, well, I thought that I might as well come a bit later since the hospital said you were comfortable when I rang."

William didn't say anything.

"Mark said he wanted to come in, but I told him that I wanted to come and see my big brother first, so he's waiting outside." Julie opened her handbag for a tissue. "Trisha's such a nice lady. She thinks the world of you. She said I could go there anytime, so I went there on my way here. She said that you always took this with you wherever you went and that she'd meant to bring it in with her today." Julie reached down to the floor to the biscuit tin she'd brought with her and put it on her lap.

"Grandpa always used to say that you were the rascal of the family. Always cheeky when you were younger. That's what Trisha said this morning. She said you always had a twinkle in your eye and loved it when people were having a joke with you." Julie sighed and fell silent for a few seconds as she opened the tin on her lap. Gently, she sifted through the contents, and lifted out a birthday card and read it out loud.

Dear William
Hope you have a Happy Birthday.
Get better soon. We all love and miss you. We'll be in to see you soon
Love from
Nan, Grandpa, and Julie xxxxxx

She looked at her own writing and smiled as the tears began to fill her eyes. "I must have only been about six when I wrote that. Do you know, I used to ask where you and Mum were every night? Poor Nan and Grandpa, it must have upset them so much, but I just wanted to know why my best friends weren't there anymore, I didn't understand. Christ, I still don't! I just missed you so much and just hoped you'd suddenly come home and make it all OK again."

She reached for another tissue and mopped another batch of tears as she looked over at her brother. "Would you mind if I looked at what other treasures you've got in your tin?" She didn't wait for a reply before she gently extracted more cards, mainly from Nan, Grandpa and herself and a few from Uncle Bill.

"Do you remember the last time we went to stay at Uncle Bill's chalet in Lowestoft, when you kept hiding that Minnie Mouse toy I had and kept telling me she'd gone home on the train?" Julie gave a sad smile. "That was the last time we ever went on holiday as a family. It seems so long ago." She reflected for a couple of seconds before resuming her exploration of the box, talking all the time.

"Poor old Nan. You know she could never bring herself to say that you had a Mental Illness. She'd only ever say you'd had a "breakdown" after Mum had died. She loved you to bits, but she just couldn't cope very well after Grandpa died. She so wanted to have you home. She always said she'd ring Greenbeck so you could come home, but she never did."

Moving the birthday and Christmas cards aside, she revealed a book, "The Time Machine" and as she lifted it out, she felt a combination of stupidity at how naive she'd been for thinking that he'd be able to concentrate for long enough to read it and pride that he'd kept it as one of his treasures.

"Nan would never let me come and see you. She said that Greenbeck was no place for a child to visit." She smiled at the memory of the score or more times her grandmother had said it to her. "You must admit, she had a point!" Julie fell into silence as the memory of her first visit to Greenbeck came flooding back.

"God, how the hell did you survive that dump? How could anyone?" She bit her bottom lip and winced at the memory of her first meeting with Dave Hicks. "I used to hear Grandpa telling Nan about that bastard of a charge nurse. He was sure he'd been cruel to you. Him and that other one, but he couldn't get anyone to believe him." She looked over at William and held his hand. "I didn't even recognise you when I saw you, didn't even recognise my own big brother for Christ's sake!"

Again, she mopped the tears and smiled as though she was trying to disguise her crying. "At least you've had a shave today!" and then she realised how stupid her comment had been and fell silent for a few more seconds, as she looked in the biscuit tin again, and took out another card, and read it.

To William
Love you loads and loads
Sandy xxxxxxxxxxxxxxxxxxxxxx

"Was Sandy the young lady form Greenbeck that you fancied?" She immediately felt as though she was trivialising something that had obviously meant a lot to him. "Whatever happened to her? You never talked about her. I'd love to have met her. If you loved her, she must have been someone very special!" She felt something of what she imagined his turmoil must have been to have lost her and the tears started all over again, as she put the card carefully back into the tin, dismissing as nothing significant the two ancient squares of mouldy chocolate.

"I'm going to have to go soon, William, but I just don't want to leave you. Not like this. Not ever." At last, the sobs gave way to uncontrollable crying as she held his hand close to her cheek and wanted so much to be able to tell him of how she felt about his pain, about his life, about how he'd been treated, about how much she missed him. "I love you." Repeated, time and time again through the tears. "I love you."

She felt gentle hands on her shoulder. Mark was there, comforting her, gently easing her away from William's body, but as they turned to leave the Chapel of Rest, she broke free and gathered up the biscuit tin that she'd left beside her seat, hesitating only to search for the lid. Satisfied that she hadn't forgotten anything, she tucked the biscuit tin with the kitten picture under her arm, but made no attempt to leave.

Mark was on the brink of returning to her side, when Julie put her handbag on the seat and opened it. Taking out two small and well-worn dolls, she laid them on William's lap, before kissing him on the forehead.

"Look after them for me."

Lightning Source UK Ltd.
Milton Keynes UK
UKOW03f2022120913

217111UK00017B/1331/P